DUNRAVEN HOUSE

Dunraven House

A Novel

John McMahon

Sincerely John McMahon

SHAMROCK PUBLICATIONS
SALTSPRING ISLAND, BC CANADA
2002

National Library of Canada Cataloguing in Publication Data

McMahon, John, 1921-
Dunraven House

ISBN 0-9731509-0-4

I. Title.
PS8575.M246D86 2002   C813'.6   C2002-911030-0
PR9199.4.M22D86 2002

Cover image: "Irish Jaunting Car" postcard *circa* 1900
Cover design by Aquarius Design

This book is a work of fiction. Names, characters, and incidents are from the author's imagination, and any resemblance to persons, establishments or events is coincidental.

Available from
Shamrock Publications
P.O. Box 615
Saltspring Island, BC
Canada V8K 2W2
shamrock@saltspring.com

and from
John McMahon
P.O. Box 615
Saltspring Island, BC
Canada V8K 2W2
shamrock@saltspring.com

Printed in Canada

For my friend Sally

My thanks to Jeanne Hilman who many years ago helped to launch Dunraven House into unknown waters. To Edith Campbell my sincere thanks for her assistance and undaunted enthusiasm to ensure that Dunraven House characters would at least get into type. And a multitude of thanks to Ursula Vaira for her support and friendship and for her many patient hours at the keyboard.

Sincerely,
John McMahon

Part One

1

Patrick and Sally

In the year 1871, on the second day of the second month, Patrick was born to Mary and Michael McGuinness.

Patrick's mother and father were in general terms "well off" and lived in a very respectable area of Dublin. On one of the big double gates at the entrance to their home was a brass nameplate, which read "ERINDALE."

Michael McGuinness was a coal merchant who had developed a large delivery business serving households and commercial establishments. Emblazoned on each rear panel of his five horse-drawn four-wheeled delivery wagons was the painted picture of a happy family. They were being warmed by the McGuinness coal that burned in their fireplace. Above each panel was bold gold lettering that read, "To keep warm, only the best comes from McGuinness and Son." The addition of "and Son" was made on the day after Patrick's eighteenth birthday, when his father took him into the business and entrusted him with one of the delivery wagons and a route of his own.

Patrick's father was a tall, rugged-looking man with a crop of curly black hair. His weathered leathery features made him appear much older than his forty years. Looking down at his son, Michael McGuinness's dark blue eyes held a thoughtful expression. With one hand on Patrick's shoulder, his words were spoken softly: "Some day, Patrick you will own this business, but now you are starting at the bottom as the new coal salesman. I hope you will learn and also understand what it is like to be low man on the pole and I hope you will always remember the experience. I am certain it will help you in future decision-making when you take over from me."

Patrick was a strong, healthy young man entering a world that entailed working full days of loading and unloading heavy coarse bags filled with coal. Through time, this built for him a muscular body that was to be the foundation for his future survival in a life far removed from the middle-class security he enjoyed with his parents.

Working with coal and coal dust was a dirty job, but Patrick was very particular about his appearance. It was his ritual, each evening, to scrub clean and change. As years passed, he proved to be a great asset to McGuinness & Son. Business boomed, and his father was proud and happy.

Patrick's good looks brought many interested glances from the opposite sex. His fierce-looking steel grey eyes belied his soft and compassionate nature. Perhaps it was the wild, unruly fair hair coupled with those eyes that caused strangers to sometimes avoid him.

It was dark-haired Sally Elizabeth O'Hagan who had no fear of his stern looks. She knew the real, wonderful Patrick. Her soft hazel eyes often followed his movements, because she had loved him for years. Time passed too quickly for Sally and Patrick. They spent many wonderful hours together. Patrick would rush home from work, do the ritual scrub and clean. His mother called it "The Sally Clean-up." After a quick meal, he'd be off to see his Sally.

Sally's father frowned on his daughter's friendship with Patrick. "Not a good match," he would say to his wife, and he often reiterated those thoughts by warning Sally, "At seventeen, young lady, to have continual personal contact, and to go walking with a young man is not advisable without a chaperon." His favourite saying was, "Young lady, when your twenty-first birthday is celebrated it will be time enough to think of dating young men of breeding and social status, not the son of a coal delivery merchant. Your mother and I may very well decide to refuse our permission for you to be alone with this young man."

Sally had anger towards her mother for supporting her father's views. She knew Maureen O'Hagan was afraid of her husband and always sided with him.

One snowy evening in early December 1889, her father was admonishing Sally for being with Patrick and returning home fifteen minutes after her curfew time. Sally angrily responded. "Father, you're hiding behind family laws you make for us. According to you, I'm too young to know what I want in life. You have assumed the role of my authoritative keeper, so I must obey your commands. Yes, you are my Father, but I am Sally O'Hagan. Me! A Person! One week after Christmas, I'll be eighteen. I love Patrick, and I will marry him, in spite of you. You married Mother on her eighteenth birthday and ever since, except during childbirth and recuperating, she has worked, 'not for you but under you!' in the grocery store. She is afraid to disagree with you, because you have always taken it upon yourself to make your laws regarding this family, and we are supposed to obey them without question. I will move out of this house if you demand I stop seeing Patrick. I am a woman, Father, not a child!" Then Sally turned away.

Ignoring her father's angry request to "Come back here, young lady and listen to me," Sally stomped up the stairs to her room and locked the door.

Next morning at breakfast, no one spoke about Sally's fiery outburst. Father and mother were pleasant, her brothers quiet, and she feared there could be a conspiracy. From that morning, her father refrained from making derogatory statements regarding her association with Patrick, and he never broached the subject of their altercation again. She felt a thrill of accomplishment at having stood up for her rights and won, yet was a little apprehensive regarding her father's true thoughts.

Christmas came and Sally was delighted when her parents agreed to invite Patrick for dinner. They did not argue against her accepting a dinner invitation to Patrick's home on New Year's Eve or participating in the chapel service, welcoming in the New Year of 1890, when they hoped so many of their plans would come to fruition.

For Sally and Patrick, the winter of 1890 was wonderful. They spent most of their leisure time together. Patrick bought Sally a friendship ring for her birthday. They had a joyous time choosing this gift. Again, Sally's parents acknowledged their togetherness, and she was very happy. At times a little doubt would arise in her thoughts: "This is too good to be true. Father never wavers in his demands that everyone in his household obey the plans he has woven for them—no objections permitted."

Sally could not fathom why he had capitulated to her demands for freedom, to have her own plans regarding Patrick and herself. It was foreign to all experience with her father's often ruthless administration of what he thought best for his family.

At times, her Irish intuition would emerge from the sea of wonderment that she and Patrick were sailing in. It would say, "Sally, glean all the love and happiness of this time. Clear a big storage area in your memory, where you can gather all the beauty and fulfilment of your togetherness, because somewhere there are dark undercurrents almost at flood level. They are fast flowing beneath this happiness Patrick and you have attained, and could carry both of you away in opposite directions."

Sally would push these intuitive thoughts aside and replace them with the memory of her victory the night she faced her father and spilled her thoughts. "Yes, you are my father, but I am Sally O'Hagan! Me! A person! I love Patrick, and I will marry him in spite of you!"

Since then, Sally had presumed by her father's silence that he exuded in his own way understanding and respect for her outburst of thoughts.

Sally's parents invited Patrick to their home for her eighteenth birthday. What a joyous turn of events for Patrick and Sally to realise that now her father must have recognised their love for each other and had now accepted Patrick.

One evening, Sally's father relaxed in his big chair by the fireside. Sally stood behind him, put her arms around his neck, and thanked him for that understanding. She received only silence in return; that hurt, and it concerned her.

As the River Liffey threads its way through the great Irish city of Dublin, its murky waters rush under O'Connell Bridge. Often from this bridge viewpoint residents and visitors peer down into its dark depths.

Sally liked to walk hand in hand with Patrick along the riverbank. She felt safe with her tall, handsome young man. Her shapely five-foot-three of beautiful Irish colleen came only to Patrick's shoulder height.

With dancing mischievous eyes, Sally would sometimes look up at him, and say. "I think I love you Patrick McGuinness," Then let go of his hand, and run off along the riverbank, with Patrick in pursuit.

Purposely he always permitted her to get away a fair distance, knowing she'd stop suddenly, whirl around, then stand with outstretched arms waiting for him to pick her up and enfold her in a bear hug and say, "Sally O'Hagan, I know I love you; someday I will marry you."

On evenings out together they enjoyed the walk home, always stopping on O'Connell Bridge to look down at the flowing waters that on dark evenings reflected light from the gas street lamps. They played a game of deciphering imaginary messages from the numerous reflected images on the water's surface. Sally could always find their own reflected initials on the dark waters. One evening she cried out "Look, Patrick, out there in midstream. Do you see it? A replica of the house we'd like to buy someday in Kingstown. I can see the lighted windows and big double doors. Don't you see it? Look it's coming closer, Patrick you must see it."

Patrick was unable to see Sally's vision, although on his own mental screen, he could see the Kingstown house she'd fallen in love with. So he said, "Yes I do," as Sally's House turned into a fair-sized piece of wood flotsam that rushed to disappear in a swirl of water under the bridge.

Sometimes on a cold night they stood until their feet felt frozen. They were content just to be standing close, two young people in a world of their own. Sally wanted to fill that beautiful Kingstown house with half a dozen or more wonderful children. Every year for them would be a wonderful dream unfolding each day with their very own plans for the happiest of futures.

With his arm around her, Patrick pulled Sally close and whispered, "I don't think the owners who are selling your house will keep it until we have enough money to buy it, Sally." With a wistful look, Sally turned to him. "Patrick, can't we just pretend!" He took her in his arms and kissed her. "Sure! Sure!" he replied. "We will move in tomorrow." Holding hands, they walked home the longest way possible.

One beautiful spring day in April, they boarded the steam tram going to Lucan and got off at Dublin's city limits. They wanted to see, capture and remember the glorious eruption of colour against the deep green lush grasslands. Multitudes of yellow primroses fought for space on each side, making the country roads appear as lighted pathways, then yellow gorse hedgerows tried to outdo the diminutive primroses in their race for golden beauty. Daffodils bowed their heads to a soft

Irish wind, tulips said, "I'm next to bloom," then a host of spring flowers looked up in praise and gave thanks to a blue Irish sky and the sun's golden light.

Sally and Patrick walked hand in hand across a pastureland of green, where sheep grazed contentedly.

With Sally in front, they crossed a narrow stream using a log that had been put there to span the clear spring water. With arms outstretched for balance and with much laughter, they carefully negotiated the simple bridge. Finding a narrow trail through a forest glade, they emerged close to a crossroads where on one side a tea shop snuggled close to a giant laurel hedge. They spent two hours over tea, talking, planning, and exchanging thoughts. Time didn't matter; it was Saturday afternoon, and Patrick had rushed to finish early his morning coal deliveries so he and Sally could enjoy this glorious afternoon together. They explored the area and saw a sign at the end of a lane leading to a farm house. It read "Fresh Eggs."

"Let's buy a dozen," suggested Sally.

The farmer's wife was delighted to talk. She introduced herself as Kate Devenny and of course would not hear tell of them leaving without a cup of tea and home-baked soda bread covered with freshly churned butter and strawberry jam.

When she heard of the distance they had walked, Mrs. Devenny insisted her husband Peter pull the jaunting car out of the shed and harness up old Charlie. Old Charlie was the only horse they owned, so his jobs varied from pulling their wagon, ploughing a straight furrow or, between the shafts of the jaunting car, taking them off to chapel every Sunday. He earned his keep in many ways.

It was dusk when Peter Devenny at their request dropped Sally and Patrick off on O'Connell Bridge. They thanked him and stayed a short time playing their game of deciphering messages from the reflected images on the water's surface, then ran all the way home without breaking an egg.

The weeks passed and spring turned into summer. Patrick and Sally were two happy young people very much in love. Sally bought a new wicker picnic basket, as she and Patrick had planned a whole day in the country. It was close to the middle of June, and the weather was glorious. She had finished writing out a list of wonderful picnic items to buy for their happy day together. On the way out, she passed her mother and father's bedroom and saw a large new steamer trunk on the floor. It was open and packed almost full with her mother's best clothes. Running down the stairs, Sally accosted the only person at home, her oldest brother.

"What is happening?" she asked, and before he could answer, Sally continued, "Where is mother going? Is father taking her on a holiday? Why have I not been told?"

"Take it easy, Sally," he answered with a knowing smile. "I'll be in trouble for telling you. Father didn't want you to know until late today, in case you ran away."

Anger flared in Sally's eyes. "What do you mean, I might run away? I knew a long time ago there was a conspiracy in this house, everyone has been too nice. Has father been doing something underhanded to get back at me for telling him the truth about himself? He has been nice to Patrick and me for months. Many times I've had intuitions that he was planning something awful. Tell me what you know, Shawn, all you know, and now before someone returns. Are they going on a holiday, and if so, who will be looking after the store?" Then she listened in shocked silence.

"Yes, Sally, you could say it's a holiday, and a long one. We are all going away and not coming back to Ireland. We are emigrating to America on the sixteenth, and this is the fifteenth, so tomorrow this family will be on a ship heading for New York. Father has it all arranged. He sold the grocery store months ago to Peter McQuire. His family will take over the store and our house and contents this weekend. It was all worked out in a deal before Christmas, over six months ago."

Sally was dumbfounded, unable to comprehend the situation. Eventually she found speech and very quietly said, "I am not going."

"Oh, yes, you are," retorted her brother. "Already you have passed the emigration medical, and father has tickets for all of us."

"I don't care," she exclaimed. "You knew about this scheme to emigrate months ago, didn't you?"

"Yes I did, but father swore us to secrecy. You were not to be told until it was too late to do anything."

Then Sally asked, "What emigration medical?"

"You remember father said that TB was a disease killing hundreds of people and he wanted all of us to have a medical examination? It

15

was a long time later I discovered it was an emigration medical and father had warned the doctor not to tell us. He's been nice to you and Patrick for months because he had these secret plans. Father never forgave you for the things you said to him. Your steamer trunk is at Peter McQuire's house and ours are in the freight room at the store. You will have a strict curfew imposed for the rest of today and tomorrow morning until we leave. Mother said she'd pack your clothes. Father gave her money to buy you lots of new stuff."

"I don't care Shawn, I'm not going. I'm leaving this house now!" Turning she faced her father entering the doorway.

"You are going nowhere young lady." He was blocking her exit and his harsh words were like a death sentence. Her thoughts flashed to the plans and wonderful dreams of a house at Kingston to be filled with happiness and many children. She knew how wonderful their future could be. Now this man had his own plans to destroy their dreams.

"You can't make me go! Father. I will not go! I will marry Patrick because I love him."

"Child, you are not leaving this house until tomorrow when this family embarks on the most thrilling journey of our lives. America is the land of the future. In New York I will invest in a new store. To my sons and to you daughter, I'm offering opportunities beyond your wildest dreams. My sons know of them. You, Sally, will thank me someday for taking you away from that coal-dust-covered boy. I will give you ample opportunities to rub shoulders with young men of class."

"I hate you! I hate you! I'm not going to New York with you. I will marry Patrick and I'm going to him now." Sally tried to pass her father but was restrained by him.

"You are still a minor and therefore under my care and jurisdiction. I have already alerted Sergeant Murphy to watch this house in case you try something stupid. You will stay in your room until I give you permission to leave it. Now your mother will be home soon, she will help you get things together. This evening your steamer trunk will be here; Mr. McQuire is bringing it over. Already by your mother's and my generosity it is half full of new clothing for you. When we arrive in New York you can dress like a modern young woman, not as a wild and homeless person like you do now."

With heart-rending sobs, and tears streaming down her cheeks, Sally flung herself at her father. Taking him by surprise, she pummelled his face, bloodying his nose and closing one of his eyes before he got a grip of her wrists.

"I hate you," she screamed. "I disown you as my father. I will return to Ireland when I am twenty-one and you will not stop me. If I can save enough money before that time, I will disappear and you will never see me again."

Sally was locked in her room all day. It was seven-thirty that evening when Patrick arrived. He had heard rumours the O'Hagans were emigrating to America. In disbelief he had come to investigate. Her father answered Patrick's knock and refused to let him have time with her. "She is busy packing all her beautiful new clothes for her life in America." With a sly look he said. "I asked my family, for business reasons, to keep the sale of my grocery store a secret until Mr. McQuire takes over. With plans to emigrate, I'm surprised Sally didn't tell you months ago. I was concerned she might, but of course she is very loyal and wouldn't break a promise. She is looking forward to her new life in America. Now I have lots to do in preparation for tomorrow's departure and Sally is busy. Oh! She did request, if you called, to give you her good wishes for the future.

"By the way, Mr. and Mrs. McQuire have two daughters close to your age and your class standards. My plans are for my daughter to marry a gentleman of means from an aristocratic family. Now go about your business and don't come back to bother my daughter again, or I'll have you forcibly removed!"

Sally's father had the door halfway closed when Patrick heard Sally cry out from somewhere in the house. "Patrick, I love you! I don't want to go to America! He is holding me prisoner."

Patrick immediately put his shoulder to the door. The force sent Sally's father staggering backwards. The door opened inwards and slammed noisily against the wall. Patrick was at the bottom of the staircase leading to Sally's room when he was stopped and held in a vicelike grip by two men, Sally's father and Sergeant Murphy, who had just arrived.

"Do you want to lay charges, Mr. O'Hagan?" the officer asked.

"No! No! Sergeant, we will be gone tomorrow, just take him out of here and watch he doesn't return till my family has vacated this house."

The Sergeant looked uncomfortable as he listened to Sally calling out to Patrick she was being held captive and did not wish to leave Dublin.

As the two men forced him towards the door, Patrick shouted back to Sally, "I will follow you and I will find you, Sally!"

"Not if I can help it," Her father interrupted.

Sally's last loud message from her locked bedroom was, "Patrick, we leave on the boat train for Queenstown in the morning at ten o'clock. Please do something."

Then she turned her anger on Police Sergeant Murphy. "As for you Mr. Murphy, I bet my father is paying you for this dastardly action. If I am forced to go to New York, I will write to your supervisors and tell them you took a bribe to keep me prisoner, 'cause I know father gives money to gain his wishes. I will come back someday and you will be sorry."

Patrick was at the station when Sally and her family arrived. She broke away and rushed to him. June 16, 1890, was a beautiful summer morning but the saddest one of their lives for the two young lovers. Sally's father did not interfere. He knew that in forty minutes all the O'Hagan family with luggage that included three large steamer trunks would be on the southbound train to Queenstown harbour, to embark on the Steamship SS Cumberland.

Sally and Patrick stood a fair distance from her family, vowing to love one another forever. Sally promised to write every week. Patrick planned to work at two jobs to save enough money and follow her to New York in a year. The O'Hagan luggage was soon stowed in a freight coach already almost full of personal luggage, all with the big green tags that were clearly stencilled in black capital letters SS *CUMBERLAND*, DESTINATION NEW YORK. Whistles sounded, railroad employees hustled here and there assuring the rail coach doors were closed and baggage properly stowed. When she heard the "All Passengers aboard!" call, Sally clung to Patrick. "Please follow me," she whispered.

"I will Sally, I will," was all he could say as he looked into her beautiful hazel eyes, flooded with tears that hesitated for a moment before spilling over her long lashes to rush down already wet cheeks.

"Come dear, the train is leaving now." It was Mr. O'Hagan who gently but firmly released her from Patrick's arms.

Without a handshake he said, "Good luck to you Patrick." Then he guided Sally away to where her family was already seated in their rail coach.

As the train moved slowly past where Patrick stood, there was no Sally at the open window. She was sitting between her brothers with her face buried in her hands.

Patrick was nineteen when he lost his Sally. His world disintegrated; and he felt lost, bewildered, heartbroken, and trapped in his father's coal business. Patrick did take a second job in the evenings in a restaurant on O'Connell Street. It was an easy job, but a very tight schedule after his own day's work. He was always eating on the run and rushing to clean himself before the evening job. His father and mother were kind but had their own thoughts and reasons for Patrick not to think of going to New York.

During the first six months he received many letters from Sally urging him to fulfil their plans of one year when they'd be reunited in New York with its wonderful opportunities. By the time that first year ended he had not earned the steamship company's price for a New York ticket. Sally's letters became less frequent and ceased eighteen months after her departure.

For two weeks he wrote a letter each day but to no avail. There was no return correspondence. Once, he wrote to her mother and father and gained no reply.

Disheartened and sad, he asked his father and mother to help him pay for a ticket to New York. They refused and chastised him for being so glum and upset over a girl who was thousands of miles away and by now probably going out with some rich American.

1895

Five years passed and Patrick never fully recovered from his heartbreak. He treated the opposite sex with respect but never filled Sally's place with a permanent girlfriend.

There was trouble in his father's business. Competition appeared in the form of a new company, Harper's Coal Delivery Service. With Harper's new colourful delivery wagons and a price cut to all customers, McGuinness & Son were very soon losing business.

Patrick tried to convince his stubborn father to meet the competition price, but got an adamant refusal.

Harper's continued their price cut and eventually McGuinness & Son lost two of their drivers and most of the customers on those routes.

Patrick's anger showed and he threatened to leave home and the business. "I'll travel elsewhere and find a good clean job with better pay. Then I'll find Sally," he boasted. His father capitulated but too late. The winter of 1894–95 became a fight for business that continued into spring, and Harper's came out on top.

Unknown to them a greater tragedy was about to take place. Patrick's mother became ill with typhoid fever in the late summer of '95. One day in October, as fall touched winter, a gusty wind from the Irish sea stripped brown leaves from the trees that stood guard at Erindale Gates. Leaves rushed here and there in the wind, chasing each other in their descent to the well-kept lawns and gardens. Then suddenly the gusty wind ceased, the last fluttering leaves fell to earth, and Mary McGuinness, Patrick's mother and husband Michael's dear wife, passed on to the other side of life. This new tragedy was to have repercussions that would change Patrick's life for always.

After the death of his wife, Michael McGuinness's attitude towards business changed. It seemed he didn't care any more so the responsibility was thrown on Patrick's shoulders. Now in his twenty-fourth year Patrick was quite capable but concerned that his father was drinking too much and disappearing for days, offering no explanation. Patrick hired another wagon driver to maintain delivery schedules because his father was not dependable. Patrick's own free time was now being curtailed so it was long working days completely taken up with business, staff problems, and his father's gambling and drinking binges.

Years passed and Michael McGuinness would remain sober for a couple of months, relapse, then be gone for weeks. Books were not balancing and money set aside as petty cash was missing on numerous occasions. It was the gambling that disturbed Patrick most.

Things were not good in 1901 and Patrick feared it was going to be a tough year for McGuinness & Son. Then Michael James McGuinness collapsed and died of a heart attack in Murphy's Pub half a block from home. It was an odd thing that England's Queen Victoria also died that day, the 22nd of January, 1901. Her sixty-three-year reign was the longest in the history of England. Patrick smiled at his own thoughts: "If those two souls meet on their way to the other side, there will be no pleasantries from the old rebel Michael James McGuinness."

The big shock came in the form of Patrick's first visitor after the funeral, Walter Mulligan, the bank manager, who in ordinary times was not a man to break bad news gently. Without an invitation he walked in and sat at the kitchen table. Opening his briefcase he fumbled with a number of papers that looked very official. He spread them out very carefully on the table before declaring that Patrick's father was indebted to the bank for a very large amount of money, namely ten thousand pounds, a large fortune. Looking very pompous he said, "I now give you notice Michael McGuinness, that my bank has already put in motion the legal necessities to take control of McGuinness & Sons Coal Delivery Service, as the business' total assets and family home plus land will in all probability not cover the total debt when sold."

"What do you mean sold?" shouted Patrick, cutting in on Mulligan's little speech.

"Young man," retorted Mulligan, "don't raise your voice to me. Have you lost respect for those with authority? Your father gambled away a prosperous business and I'm afraid there will not be a penny left for you when this is over. My man will be here in a few minutes to affix notices on prominent places indicating to the public that all properties Michael McGuinness & Son owned are now in my hands to arrange a time for the auction of the business, plus house and household effects.

"I'm afraid, young man, you will be destitute. You are strong and will probably eke out a living working for someone, I hope, who has Christian ethics where drink and gambling have no place. After meeting with bank elders tomorrow, I will inform you when and what time we wish you to leave this house. Being Christian gentlemen they will give you a few hours to get some clothing bundled up, and someone will be here at all times to ensure you do not abscond with valuables."

At that, Patrick exploded, "You pompous little bastard!" and gathered Walter Mulligan's neat papers into a crumpled heap before stuffing them into the briefcase. He grabbed the obnoxious little man by the collar of his costly dark suit and hauled him to his feet before throwing him and the briefcase out into the wet and miserable day.

"His man" arrived as Mulligan was picking himself up from the muddy wet path. He could have passed for Mulligan's twin: same suit, same thick glasses, same air of importance. After a quick consultation they both left together.

Patrick looked around the sparsely furnished dirty-smelling cell. It was anger and frustration that kept him from crying. It had taken four policemen to arrest him.

It had been a very short appearance before old squint-eyed Judge Henry Murphy. "Young man," he said, "you came from good God-fearing parents and I cannot understand what evil has been bestowed upon you by the devil. I am here to pass judgement on those who believe in civil disobedience. It's my job to uphold law and order and to protect our enforcement officers from hooligans like you. I'm certain that Dublin streets will be safer with the likes of you in prison. For obstructing an officer of the bank doing his duties and causing him bodily harm, resisting arrest, and assaulting a police officer, under the power given to me by this court, I sentence you to three years and six months of hard labour."

For Patrick this turn of events was unbelievable. He had no money for his defence and no one he could send a message to for help. He'd lost his mother and father, the McGuinness coal business, everything, including his Sally. Now he would have a criminal record; it was a bleak outlook for his future.

1904

On a bright sunny morning in July, 1904, the gates of Dublin Prison opened for the release of another prisoner who now had a criminal record. A dishevelled white-faced Patrick McGuinness, age thirty-three, was free having served his sentence.

It was a bitter and disillusioned Patrick who shaded his eyes from the sunlight when, after a long walk to the old house he once called home, he stood outside the gate with the plaque "Erindale" still attached. The house looked the same except that someone had painted the doors white and that the drapes were also white. Mother had loved those pale green ones that she had made herself. His thoughts travelled back through the years. He had been so proud when his father gave him that coal delivery route of his own. At the end of a day's work when he did his "Sally Clean Ups," Mother would call him for his favourite Irish stew served with home-baked soda bread and fresh country butter on the side.

He had a great urge to walk up and knock on the front door and pray for a miracle that his mother would open it and say, "Why did you knock? You're already late for stew!"

He was very hungry and turned over in his pocket the two-shilling piece that had been returned to him on release from prison. He thought, "Where can I get the best meal, if I were to spend sixpence on it?" His thoughts were interrupted by a command; "Move along! Don't loiter here or you'll finish up inside again." Two of Dublin's police force on their foot beat were looking aggressively at him. "We were asked by the owner of this house, Mr. Harper, of Harper's Coal Deliveries, to patrol here. He heard you were being released today. I guess you know him very well being at one time business competitors." It was the taller of the two who spoke, an older man. "Best you move along son, better for everyone. We don't want trouble but we will be watching you."

"There is no justice," was all Patrick could think of saying before moving off. He made his way to O'Connell Street, where he spent a penny on a big plate of Irish stew, plus bread and butter. Not like his mother's, but it tasted great after the swill he had been served in prison.

That night, he lingered a long time on O'Connell Bridge, peering into the waters and trying to visualise Sally's house in the reflected shadows. He spent sixpence for bed and breakfast in a house beside the river and dreamed of Sally. They were standing close on O'Connell Street Bridge looking down at the Liffey's murky waters. The night was cold so he opened his overcoat and wrapped it around her saying, "There is room for both of us." She snuggled into the warmth of both the coat and Patrick as he held her close.

Morning came but there was no Sally, just a knock on the door and a request, "Would you like bacon and eggs, Master Patrick?" He was surprised at the "Master Patrick," but answered, "Yes please!"

A wonderful breakfast of bacon, eggs, soda bread, and potato farls, plus a great mug of strong tea was set before him, and the old lady who owned the house sat facing him with her own mug of steaming tea. "I was one of your father's first customers," she told Patrick. "A fine man was he and I remember you as a young boy helping with coal deliveries on Saturdays and school holiday times. You know Patrick, it was a disgrace how that man Walter Mulligan got rid of you by laying charges and making sure it was that old fool Judge Henry Murphy who sentenced you. He was in debt to Mulligan's bank, so old Walter used him to make things happen his way.

"The day you were sentenced to prison, I put an Irish curse on that wee rotten man." Her old blue eyes seemed to light up with mischief as she leaned closer across the table. "Do you know Patrick, it took a year before my curse worked. You probably didn't hear, being in prison and all, but old Mulligan is dead, gored to death by a bull." Then she leaned closer across the table and spoke in almost a whisper, "Wish I could have watched it happen!"

At that she stood up and asked, "Another mug of tea Patrick?" Without waiting for a reply she filled his mug almost to overflowing from the massive brown teapot.

"How did it happen?" Patrick asked.

"Well he was out in the country serving papers to a farmer and his wife because they were overdue on payments. It was a bad year for everyone and Walter was happy. It gave him and his bank the opportunity to steal property from defenceless people. When Walter Mulligan got up to leave he wasn't sure how to get back to the road where 'his man' waited. There were two narrow trails getting up to the farm cottage and he was confused as to which one to take.

"It's been said around here that the farmer deliberately gave Mulligan directions for a shortcut to the road. The shortcut was through a field where a bad-tempered bull was kept, and it gored old Mulligan to death."

"Did the farmer purposely give those directions?" asked Patrick.

"Well young fellow, there was a big inquiry and the farmer was questioned. Then his wife was questioned separately. They both told the inquiry people that Mr. Mulligan was told not to cut through the bottom field because of the dangerous bull grazing there, and they couldn't understand why he did! So that was the end of it but he got a grand funeral, and a big crowd of moneyed people attended his wake."

Patrick thanked the old lady and left two extra pennies as a tip. It was sort of security against the chance of an Irish curse on him. With her blessing and wishes for good luck he said goodbye to Dublin.

For Patrick, the Dublin he was leaving behind seemed robbed of happy memories. Circumstances had changed the smiling carefree young man in love with the most beautiful girl in Dublin. The girl who had planned with him their wonderful future to be. The loss of Sally, the deaths of his mother and father, and the confrontation with the unscrupulous Mr. Mulligan that resulted in his three-and-a-half-year jail sentence all left him with a bitterness foreign to his happy and generous disposition.

"Why did this happen to me?" he asked himself. "What did I do to deserve the devastation of all my dreams? Why silence from the girl I'll always love?"

Patrick knew that to permit all of this fermenting in his thoughts would end in mental problems with no chance of a future. He reassured himself that work in the country areas away from the city would heal his broken heart. Perhaps a farm job, caring for animals and working the good earth would earn him a few shillings and a roof over his head.

It was a difficult decision-making time for Patrick. Stay in Dublin and hope to find work or start on a journey to somewhere unknown with only one shilling and a few pennies in his pocket. His decision and resolution was to leave Dublin far behind.

Patrick had walked many miles with only intermittent short rides on a variety of horse-drawn vehicles. On reaching the summit of a long hill, he was tired, hungry and disillusioned, when a large blue-and-white wagon drawn by two magnificent Clydesdales stopped. Its grey-haired cherub-faced driver shouted, "And where might you be going young fellow?"

"Anywhere in the country where I might get work," Patrick replied.

"Well on this route, I'll be able to drop you off somewhere in the country, so I guess for you that would be anywhere. Now work, that's another kettle of fish, but if you want a ride to that anywhere on my route jump up beside me. I like company."

Patrick didn't hesitate. He was glad to settle on the seat beside this jovial plump little man. Patrick answered many questions from the inquisitive driver. Eventually he had spilled out his life's history, yet all he knew about his benefactor was that his name was Shawn O'Grady and that he had worked sixteen years for McCormick's Delivery Service.

The wagon driver made frequent stops, first in a large village then at a farm where he delivered a few small packages. At each stop, Patrick assisted with the unloading of the assortment of parcels (the new plough, a heavy crate, and numerous miscellaneous items).

It was close to seven o'clock when they drove into the little town of Ballyshea. Patrick was still very hungry although Shawn O'Grady had shared his lunch when they'd stopped beside a small lake at noon.

"If you drop me off anywhere here, I'll be okay," said Patrick with an air of confidence he did not feel.

"So anywhere here will do, will it?" Shawn smiled. "And where might you be thinking of staying, may I ask?"

"Oh, I'll find a place, there must be a hotel in town."

"Sure, sure," replied Shawn. "And 'tis a grand one my lad, the best this side of Dublin. Now Patrick, if my memory is not deceiving me I think it would be correct to say you have one shilling and two pennies as your monetary worth. If that be the truth I'd like to invite you to dinner at my humble cottage. I live here and in consideration for your assistance in unloading and your wonderful company today, I think for tonight my family will find a corner for you to sleep. Now think about it Patrick, but if you wish to check at the hotel and ask what they have available for one shilling and two pennies, I'll drop you off at the main entrance."

Patrick was welcomed by Shawn's wife, Molly, and their two teenage boys. He enjoyed a hearty meal and spent the night in their comfortable little cottage. Next day was Saturday and Shawn suggested Patrick go with him to a farm house just a short distance from the village. Shawn knew the farmer was looking for good help.

This turned out to be a wonderful opportunity for Patrick to get a new start. He was hired with the bonus of room and board.

Patrick tried to blank out the degrading and horrible three-and-one-half years in jail. It was an injustice he felt could never be reversed or completely forgotten. By force of his own strong will he was able to lock out most of those horrible memories. His objective was to sink them so deep that time would lose them altogether.

Being in the coal business with his father seemed like a dream. There he was the person responsible for hiring staff, keeping the flow of business smooth and profitable, while paying employees reasonable wages, and treating them in a respectful manner. Also in that dream was his lost Sally, the beautiful dark-haired girl with hazel eyes. She was still very much in his thoughts.

Now he was depending on someone else for employment and his livelihood.

It was a cruel to wonder if this was his future. A lost wanderer eking out a living anywhere he could find it. Certainly a drastic change from life at his parent's home with its manicured lawns, flower beds, rose gardens, and its double entrance gates with the polished brass plate that read ERINDALE.

Patrick's employer was Ben Murphy, a little sharp-featured man in his late fifties. His sallow complexion and bad yellow teeth didn't complement the pale blue eyes or the once black bushy eyebrows now mixed with grey. Those eyebrows had never been trimmed and Patrick thought perhaps Ben hoped they'd make up for the baldness above.

Maureen, Ben's wife, was short and skinny and wore her grey hair shoulder length. Patrick never could decide if her eyes were blue or grey because in areas of different lighting they seemed to change colours. Maureen was in poor health and had never had children. Almost immediately a friendship grew with Patrick and before many months passed she treated him as if he were the son she couldn't have.

Patrick and Ben worked well together and soon became good friends. Ben had a bad limp caused by an accident when he was a boy. Despite his handicap he maintained full farm days of hard work.

It was really two families who 'adopted' Patrick, Ben and Maureen Murphy, plus the family of truck driver Shawn O'Grady. Often Shawn invited Patrick to a Saturday night out at the Iron Plough. At other times it was Sunday dinner at Shawn and Molly's home.

Patrick integrated into village life and became a popular resident. Of course it was certain to happen that a number of eligible young women in the area had eyes for the good-looking man who had come from the big city of Dublin to live at Murphy's farm. Behind the scenes, the villagers asked questions. "What brought him to this village and why?" "Does he have a family in Dublin?" "Is he running away from someone or something? He never leaves the area." "Is he hiding from the law?"

The Murphys and O'Gradys didn't answer questions. But they had a secret story they wouldn't tell. When little Ben Murphy was asked direct questions, he always answered as his father had taught him: "I speak no evil, I hear no evil, I see no evil. He's a fine young man, a good worker and if I don't ask questions, I won't hear any lies."

Patrick had confided in Ben and Maureen. They knew his sad story and so did truck driver Shawn O'Grady. Not a squeak of Patrick's past life was ever discussed with villagers.

Patrick evaded getting into a serious relationship with the opposite sex, with one exception, the pub owner's daughter, Irene. She was a tall slim girl in her late twenties who seemed to glide through standing bar crowds or around crowded tables. Her tray of full glasses and mugs was always held perfectly in balance as she served and willingly bantered with customers.

Irene's features were not beautiful but her facial skin devoid of blemishes glowed with health. The dark brown eyes set well apart held an impish expression. Her white and even teeth showed when she smiled or laughed at a customer's jibe or joke.

Irene was good at returning her own brand of jibes before she'd be off with a tray of empties. Numerous male eyes watched her willowy figure glide swiftly through the throng of boisterous young men seated at the bar. Her long black silk-like hair glinted reflections from the glow of her father's pub lanterns.

Irene was Patrick's partner at many village dances, and he accepted numerous invitations to her home for dinner.

When Patrick realised his feelings for Irene were progressing towards more than friendship, he decided to back off. Deep inside his visual memory something held him back. It was Sally's face that day so long ago on Dublin's railroad platform. Through the tears her pleading request was, "Please follow me," and his reply had been, "I will Sally, I will."

Patrick tried to rationalise why he was still in love with someone he felt certain was gone out of his life and whom he'd never see nor hear from again. "What foolishness," he scolded himself, "Irene is here, a vibrant wonderful young woman. Not a memory of someone who is thousands of miles away." But he still had thoughts of someday earning enough money for a ticket to New York where he'd find Sally.

Patrick had told Maureen and Ben about the tragedy of losing his mother, his father and the coal business, all culminating in his jail sentence. Then he spilled out his loss of Sally.

"Probably married and now with her own children," Maureen said, and Ben added, "You should marry Irene; it would be a great opportunity for both of you. Paddy McQuire will, I'm certain, leave the pub to both of you when he goes. You're not thinking straight Patrick."

Patrick's only answer, "You both sound like my mother and father." Then he added with a smile, "And I like that."

Many months turned into many years and Patrick had long ago become the third family member of Ben and Maureen. He learned much about farm life from the fierce-looking little Ben.

A great worker was Ben, but often he'd say to Patrick, "Fate sent you to me because the work load was becoming too much for one man. Maureen's health is deteriorating and many house chores are being added to my outdoor work. So, you see Patrick, it's working out great for all three of us. I don't know what I'd do if Maureen died. Haven't you noticed she's going downhill quickly? I do what I can for her and I have seen you Patrick, do a lot of things for her that she can't. It'll break my heart if she dies. 'Tis a good woman, she is."

Patrick put his arm around the shoulder of his little friend. "I won't leave you alone Ben, and Maureen's not going to die."

It had been many years since Ben and Maureen Murphy had opened their home and hearts to the young stranger from Dublin who was looking for work.

On a dark wintry Irish morning at ten-thirty on the thirtieth of November, 1914, Maureen Murphy died of pneumonia. A great blow for Ben, and for Patrick it was like losing his mother again. Maureen had continued to treat Patrick like her own son. He had told her many times that her Irish stew was equal to and maybe just a little better than his mother's.

Then she'd laugh and say, "Patrick, you're full of blarney and taking a rise out of this old woman."

Patrick would then give her a hug and say, "Ach! Sure Maureen, you know I wouldna' tell you even a white lie."

It was a sad funeral, and after the service and burial at the village cemetery, Ben decided he would like to walk home and asked Patrick to walk with him. "It's not far," he said, "and the guests can wait for us."

They walked in silence for a while before Ben spoke. "Patrick, people think better when walking and I'm sure it's the exercise that sends more blood to the brain, don't you agree?"

"I guess so," was Patrick's only comment.

Ben was again silent. They walked until the little man continued, "Patrick, now that I've lost my Maureen, God bless her soul, it's decision-making time. I'm going to sell and get out of this farming business. You have many friends in the village and I'm sure you will be okay. Now the start of this war with Germany will boost farm prices so I'm hoping to take advantage. Maybe I'll keep a corner of the farm where I can build a small house and have enough land for a vegetable garden."

Patrick was about to answer when Ben spoke again.

"Marry Irene and move in above the pub. If you don't I'm sure you'll regret it. Think more about that Patrick, she's a fine-looking girl. What do you say, my lad?"

Patrick's thoughts were racing, as he hadn't bargained for this. He had become part of the village and its people and their honest-to-goodness friendly way of life. He'd become an adopted family member of the Murphys and loved those two wonderful people.

Now Maureen was gone, what was he to do?

Ten years of work, ten years of putting down roots. This house of the Murphys had become his home and now Ben was selling it. Again those cruel thoughts emerged from hiding. Could it again be that in his future life he was to be a lost wanderer eking out a living anywhere he could find it?

"You haven't answered me." It was Ben breaking into Patrick's disturbing thoughts.

"If you sell Ben I'll go on the road again."

"If that's your decision Patrick, I won't say what I think because I wish to keep your friendship. You know I love you like you were my own son. It will grieve me to see you leave the village and your friends. It is now your home and has been for many years. You are a stubborn foolish man to give up Irene and all this area can offer you. How can you allow some pipe dream about finding a Dublin girl who about twenty-five years ago sailed away to New York? I was sure you had more sense, Patrick. I think perhaps you've gone a little bit soft in the head.

"Now I've said what I think. We are almost home and the house will be full of people, so let's go in and celebrate Maureen's wake. But one thing more, I won't be selling until next spring 'cause winter's a bad time to sell farmland. That gives me at least five months to talk sense into your head and see you and Irene married."

Ben and Patrick worked hard during the winter months getting house and lands prepared for best showing when spring came. In the end, Ben was unable to convince Patrick to stay.

The first week of May of 1915 saw Patrick on the road again. It caused many sad farewells, especially with Irene, who pleaded with him to stay, but his own strong impulses to move on were pushing him to his destiny somewhere in the future. Fate had turned over a card.

During the months that followed, Patrick covered a considerable distance by various means of transport, including his own strong legs. He met and travelled with a varied group of interesting companions. This road would take him far away from Dublin and the sorrows he left there, but for now, farmland was a necessity for survival.

He worked anywhere and at anything for his food and lodgings. Sometimes it was a few days or a number of weeks, and once he was hired for six months as a farm labourer. He had learned much under little Ben's guidance.

Patrick's gypsy life style continued for a number of years. One night he lay awake with adverse thoughts regarding his decision to leave Shawn, Ben, Irene and the village folk. It was a long trail to go back to that friendly place, and this sparked thoughts of how curious it was that those good people who had travelled the roads with him were all going northwest. He hadn't given it much thought before but now his Irish intuition was in action. That inner something, a driving force he was unable to dispel, like a compass heading he had subconsciously set for himself as the direction to his unknown destiny, always northwest.

Six years had passed since his big decision to travel the roads again. It had brought him to a farm close to the town of Rathmelton in Donegal, the most north-western county in the Republic of Ireland. He worked there for eighteen months before it, too, was sold.

The new owner family had three strong sons, and Patrick's services were no longer required. He was faced with the knowledge that this time he was being forced to move on. There was no Ben or Irene to plead that he should stay.

Early on a crisp October morning in 1920, he continued to walk, where else but northwest. He walked to the banks of Lough Swilly and the village of Rathmullan where he asked around regarding work.

The postmistress there suggested he should try a few miles up the road at Dunraven House on the O'Conor Estate. Patrick thanked her, then with a "Sure an' I will," he was off at a brisk walk.

Sixteen years ago, Dublin's jail gates had opened to give back freedom of movement to Patrick McGuinness, and he had travelled many roads since then. Patrick was forty-nine when in midsummer of 1920 James O'Conor hired him as the Dunraven House estate handyman. The job included meals and a corner of the milk house as sleeping accommodation. In a short time Patrick proved to be an industrious and competent addition to Dunraven House's work force. James O'Conor moved him to the comfortable two rooms attached to the main storage shed. There he had a bedroom, a living room that also served as a kitchen, and a fireplace as a bonus.

It was the beginning of a friendship between master and servant that was to involve Patrick in a turbulent journey on a road that brought a kaleidoscope of events, but fate never shows all its cards quickly. For some people, whether it is to bring tragedy or happiness, it turns the cards over very slowly, and so it was in the life of Patrick McGuinness.

In October 1920, the same year Patrick was hired at Dunraven House, a prominent player in Patrick's turbulent journey was born to James and Cora O'Conor, a son to be named George David.

James O'Conor was proud to have a son but had always wanted a daughter. Whenever he approached the subject, Cora's reply was always negative.

"I've given you a son as you hoped for, so I did my duty."

Cora didn't want to have more children and she insisted one was enough. Her favourite rebuke to James was, "I don't want to go through that degrading of my figure and the terrible long nine months. I did it for you once and I'm not doing it again." She was thoughtful for a moment before saying, "If Father Cullen asks you why we are not having more children, you can tell him what I just said!"

It was a short time after little George's fourth birthday that James noticed many of his young son's toys were broken. The little cars were crushed and other toys were flattened. It looked as if they'd been stomped on.

The day after receiving a gift box of toy soldiers Cora had bought for her son, James discovered the little boy had deliberately broken all the foot soldiers. The head of each soldier had been torn off and the bodies were missing arms and legs. Only the horsemen survived and were lined up, all ten of them in file.

George looked at his Dad and said. "I'm going fox hunting. My horses are ready."

"Why did you destroy the soldiers and take off their heads, arms, and legs?" asked James.

"I wanted to hear them cry," was George's reply.

"Did they?" asked his father, dismayed at his small son's actions and reply.

"No," replied George defiantly. "So I stomped on them to make sure they were dead."

"That was a very bad thing you did George."

"No! Daddy, they were bad soldiers," came the reply. "They didn't cry. I wish they had cried."

James was shocked at the little boy's callousness. Taking George by the arm, he tightened his grip until the boy cried out in pain. "Would you like me to twist your arm off?"

"No!" cried the child. "That hurts."

"Yes," replied James, "because you're alive. The soldiers were only toys but now you know just a tiny, tiny bit of what it would be like if they were alive and you did that to them."

"Then I would hear them cry," was the four-year-old boy's shocking reply.

James made the boy get a small cardboard box then lay the broken soldiers in it. He took George into the garden and made him dig a small grave and have a short burial service, but little George David O'Conor refused to say he was sorry.

After dinner that evening James told Cora about the episode, but she brushed it aside. "He's only a child James, boys get rambunctious sometimes."

"That's not the point Cora; the boy wished those soldiers were able to feel pain so he could hear them cry. That is not normal for a little child of his age."

Cora was angry at James. "What are you trying to say James, that my child is a demon of some sort?"

"He's our child," broke in James, "and I don't like it. He has broken and stomped on a number of toys and next time I will punish him where it hurts."

"You will not thrash our child, James O'Conor. I will talk to him. You men don't know how to handle children. You think beating them makes you good parents."

"Cora, if a child likes to dish out horrible punishment to toy soldiers and other toys, it is a warning sign. If his aggressiveness continues, he could have a troublesome life ahead."

Cora was impatient. "Go about your business James. Let me handle the child."

"I'll be watching him," replied James, "and I will take him with me more often around the estate."

Cora O'Leary was the youngest child born into a family of three brothers and one sister. Her mother had been a fragile, quiet little woman. With five pregnancies over a period of eight years, her life had become days of almost twenty-four-hour service to her husband and family.

Neal O'Leary, Cora's father, had risen to the rank of Sergeant in the area's Guarda (police force). He was a large rough coarse-spoken man who gave little thought to his family or his wife's welfare. From his wife Evelyn, he demanded absolute involvement in looking after the family, but he often said, "As I'm the breadwinner, my requirements come first." Neal O'Leary organised his home life as he did his police detachment; in a military fashion, and he was in sole charge.

Household chores, the demands of her husband and family, the five pregnancies in eight years eroded her resistance to colds, influenza and other viruses. Evelyn O'Leary died from pneumonia when her little daughter Cora was only four years old.

It was Jessie, the older sister, who had to take over the household duties. Cora was sent off to her mother's unmarried sister Sarah, a Letterkenny school teacher.

Sarah liked the little girl and gave her a good education. Cora was a quick learner and an industrious student. Although short in stature, she turned out to be a good-looking, well-educated young woman with an attractive figure.

Cora had a quick wit; she was sharp with answers and had no fear of mixing with intellectual company. She would laugh at their jokes and fend for herself with quick returns. So Cora O'Leary was a popular young lady who maintained she would not marry for love nor money.

But all that changed when her aunt casually introduced her to James O'Conor at a pre-Christmas school celebration to which Cora and a few other ex-pupils had been invited. Later Sarah whispered to Cora that James O'Conor had recently inherited Dunraven House and the great expanse of arable land with many cattle and other livestock plus control of the numerous employees who worked and lived on his large estate.

Cora moved among the little groups of regular and ex-students, finding old friends and teachers to reminisce with. They talked about the almost forgotten pranks and a host of reborn stories about people and things.

Soon it was time to find their places at the decorated dinner tables. The seat next to Cora was still unoccupied, so she casually leaned over to see whose name was on the card. Suddenly a deep voice from behind her said, "Yes, Cora O'Leary, that's me, James O'Conor."

Embarrassed, Cora froze in the position she had taken to read the name. James, with a smile, continued, "Cora, we met about an hour ago, and if you can first introduce me to your friend and then move slightly, I can take my seat and hope to have a wonderful conversation over dinner."

Across at the next table Cora's aunt Sarah was smiling as she picked up her glass of red wine and made a slight gesture before putting it to her lips. Cora got the message. Her aunt had placed James O'Conor's seating card next to hers. Her smile said, "It's up to you now."

Cora played her cards well and snared this wonderful prize. One year later she married him and became mistress of Dunraven House.

The honeymoon period lasted many months, and James was content with this talented, intelligent, good-looking wife. From those first wonderful times there remained a host of happy memories, but things were to change.

James wanted a son and heir. Cora was not happy with the thought of carrying a child; she became belligerent.

From deep down inside there emerged a part of her that had remained dormant all through the years of school, courtship and the life of luxury with James O'Conor.

James was very angry when she told him she didn't want children. His answer was a definite, "It will have to be, Cora, because I want an heir to this domain."

The memory of her mother's death was now prevalent in Cora's thoughts, a memory made all the more horrible since aunt Sarah had explained that the death was the result of too many pregnancies forced by an abusive Neil O'Leary. Now James O'Conor indicted he would force her to be pregnant so he could have a son and heir.

James had taken charge of everything pertaining to staff and expenditures since his father died. Eventually he gave Cora her wish: complete control of all household day-to-day business, and staff would answer to Cora O'Conor and take orders from her alone. So officially Cora became mistress of Dunraven House, and George David was born. James was happy to have a healthy youngster whose legacy would be master of the estate.

When possible, James took George with him on business trips to other towns in the area. He talked to the little boy about things they came across on their journeys. He told him the names of the birds and animals then explained how they survived. Little George liked to pretend he was a hawk swooping down on little birds and eating them up.

At times, he would become sullen, refusing to talk or answer questions. James tried to be careful in his conversations, hoping to get close to his little son who seemed to have more aggressiveness in his personality than a normal child should. Suddenly he would change and become a delightful happy little boy asking dozens of questions like any normal child of his age. George's fifth birthday passed and business demands kept James away. There were many times when he could not take his little son with him.

Without saying anything about his suspicions of a dark side to the young boy, James asked Patrick to take the boy under his wing and teach him how to do some of the easy everyday tasks that had to be accomplished.

Patrick loved horses and had been thrilled when he was put in charge of the O'Conor horse and carriage. It became his hobby to maintain in top shape the carriage and Black Beauty, as Cora O'Connor had named the black Friesian horse they kept to pull the carriage.

On good summer Sundays in the early nineteen-twenties Cora loved being driven to chapel in the estate carriage. She liked to show off and even dressed Patrick in a coachman's uniform so he would tie in with their grandeur and the sleek black horse he cared for.

This magnificent Friesian gave Cora great delight, especially when at times Patrick permitted Back Beauty to go into a speedy high-stepping trot. The sight of that head into the wind, those powerful shoulders, the arched neck with its flowing black mane, and Patrick in his coachman's uniform was nothing short of elegant.

Weather permitting she'd squeal with delight when Patrick came to the mansion's front doors with horse and open carriage. Cora O'Conor of Dunraven House, her young son George, and her husband James would ride majestically out of the estate grounds to Rathmullan Village and be received by Father Cullen at the chapel door. Then came the grand entrance to their own velvet-cushioned pew, second row from the front. Cora did not like feeling exposed during the service so the front pew was her shield of privacy, and no parishioners were permitted to use it. Patrick of course stayed with the horse and always had the carriage waiting when chapel service ended. Again Father Cullen would shake hands at the door and make small talk as a little crowd of parishioners obediently waited until the great lady with her little boy and husband departed. Father Cullen condoned this procedure knowing the collection plate would be minus a substantial amount if he did not gracefully show outward respect. His own thoughts regarding the three O'Conors he kept to himself. On other Sundays in winter or on inclement summer days the new Daimler limousine was used while Patrick did chores back at the estate. The young child George was often left in Patrick's care.

Patrick liked the O'Conor child and they were almost inseparable pals. As a little boy of five, George would follow Patrick everywhere possible and there seemed to be a bond of true friendship. By the time little George turned eight, Patrick had taught him many things, like how to set rabbit traps, and where the best fishing holes were. Also included was the quickest way to harness Black Beauty to the carriage, how to handle a shotgun, sharpen a scythe blade, and cut a neat clean swath of wheat or grass. Patrick had said, "With all this new machinery George, you must still know how to sharpen and use the scythe so when the reaping machine breaks down you can cut the harvest." Young George gleaned much learning from this soft spoken man's store of knowledge.

As the years passed Patrick was dismayed to find a cruel streak in George's personality. He watched him kick a sleeping dog for no apparent reason, and once George picked up a farmyard cat by the tail, swung it above his head a few times then threw it high in the air. When the poor creature landed on a rock and broke its neck, he showed no remorse as he poked at the dead animal with a stick. When Patrick lectured him on the inhumanity of such a deed George got angry. Now a big boy of twelve, he put his fist close to Patrick's face in a threatening manner. "I wanted to see if the cat would land on its four feet. Anyway, it's none of your business Patrick, and if you tell my father or mother, I'll get you in trouble somehow." At that he pushed Patrick out of the way and ordered, "You bury the stupid cat and forget what you saw."

Four years later, George was sixteen and Patrick had watched this handsome-looking young man become a bully and a cheat who at times had a strange, dark and almost sinister look in his eyes. One day Patrick was on his way for a midday break when he saw George at the horse's water trough. He was having a wonderful time drowning kittens that were a number of weeks old. Always numerous cats were permitted on the estate to keep it free from rats. Some kittens were drowned at birth but that was too humane for George. This was more fun as these were older, and the poor little things twisted and turned in his hands under water. He would dunk a kitten in the trough and count a number of seconds; then he'd pull it out and allow it a breath before submerging it again. Patrick lost his temper and grabbed the sadistic boy by the arm then slapped him across the face so hard George fell to the ground. Patrick's hand was in the water taking out the kitten when George came at him with both fists flailing. Patrick ducked the left but George's right fist got him in the face. The force of it made him stumble off balance and into the water trough.

Patrick knew he could still thrash this young man to within an inch of his life, but that would get him in trouble with George's parents, so he smothered the great desire to do so. George stood scowling as his old friend got out of the water then before walking away, he pointed his finger at Patrick. "Don't you ever touch me again Patrick

McGuinness or next time I'll drown you in the water trough instead of stupid cats."

Shortly after this incident George was sent off to a school in Dublin. During the next three years Patrick saw little of George O'Conor. His short periods of vacation from school were spent mostly with classmates he brought home.

2

Timothy O'Neill and Kathleen O'Brien, 1939

Timothy O'Neill, at nineteen, was a fine-looking young man, tall and bronzed, whose still very boyish complexion complemented his blue eyes. They always had a sparkle in them even when he was serious. His dark head of wavy hair was always well groomed, and had its own natural brilliancy.

Timothy lived with his family in a small cottage close to the village of Rathmullan in County Donegal, short in distance but very different from the grandeur of Dunraven House. He had an older sister and three younger brothers, so there was much activity in their crowded living conditions. Seven in a family and only two tiny bedrooms was not uncommon in these parts. His sister slept in a corner of father and mother's room. Timothy and his two brothers slept in the other bedroom. Little Kevin, the four-year-old, had a hole-in-the-wall cot in the one and only communal room that served as family room, kitchen, dining room or whatever. A big percentage of the cottage area was this room, and taking up most of one wall was a great fireplace wherein burnt a peat fire that seldom went out. It was banked up at night and spread out each morning. As the red glow spread over the great hearth it was renewed with more peat to start off another day's cooking. The big black pots, pans and griddle were never at rest. The family was poor but always had enough food. Rabbit stew was often on the menu. "Champ" was a favourite back-up whether things were tough or not.

Champ was a big pot of potatoes cooked to perfection with a mixture of green onions. It was mashed together, salted to taste and served as a plateful with big blobs of fresh country butter in the middle. Timothy's father had no land of his own but found work helping other farmers. For the young men there was little work of any kind. Sometimes Timothy earned a few shillings digging peat and stacking it to dry then helping cart it to storage sheds. The money earned went to assist with the necessities at home. From the front door of the family cottage, Timothy looked across Lough Swilly and promised himself that one day he'd leave this place to find his fortune elsewhere. Once he had been to visit his aunt just across the border in the city of Derry in the British part of Ireland. Timothy thought he'd like to see the big city of Belfast, capital of Northern Ireland. From there he would go a hundred miles south to that great and famous city of Dublin, the capital of his own land, the Republic of Ireland. He would take beautiful Kathleen O'Brien with him.

"It's just a day dream," he would say. "How could I afford the price of a bus or train ticket?" He scolded himself for even thinking of such a wonderful journey. It was an impossible dream. He hadn't even had a shilling for tickets to take Kathleen to the big dance at the chapel hall last Saturday night, so her escort had been George O'Conor, the rich land owner's son. Timothy had strong feelings for Kathleen. She had allowed him to kiss her once when they were up in the heather-covered hills above Lough Swilly. Now George O'Conor would probably be taking her to everything.

It was August, and there was much harvest work that should earn a few shillings and maybe a little surplus. Timothy worked hard. By the middle of August he had earned money to augment home necessities plus a few shillings for himself. He had a wonderful time with Kathleen at the Saturday night dance as George O'Conor glared from the sidelines. Kathleen and Timothy were holding hands, laughing and singing, as they danced the long road home together. Kathleen was one of those beautiful Irish colleens endowed with a wonderful shapely figure. She had tresses of auburn hair like burnished gold that reflected 'stars' borrowed momentarily from the sun's own light. They instantly returned as she shook her head or ran across heathered slopes or just stood still to let the wind blow her golden 'threads' into tangled knots.

Kathleen and her almost fifteen-year-old sister Eileen enjoyed sitting on the stone bridge that spanned the outlet of the little river that had splashed its way to the sea.

Sometimes on hot summer days, with dresses held high, they liked to wade across, barefooted in its cool mountain waters. Soft breezes carried their happy laughter out to sea or up and away to fade among the heathered slopes above. Their bronzed legs pushed against the current as their bare feet sought out the flat rocks they knew as stepping stones to the other bank.

They would come across multitudes of little fishes named Sprickly Backs. So many that the little silver darts on their swift journey to the sea would continuously bounce off their legs.

Father Cullen on his visitation rounds sometimes took the short-cut path beside the stream on his way to the big O'Conor house at Dunraven Estate. He liked to visit often, as the O'Conor donations were the cornerstone asset in his balancing of the chapel budget. One day, Kathleen and Eileen were wading across the stream with dresses pulled up so not to get them wet. Eileen said with a mischievous look in her eyes, "Kathy, Father Cullen is on the other side watching us, let's pull up our dresses as high as we can. I bet you two pennies he will admonish us."

"You brazen young lady," laughed Kathleen, but they both hitched their dresses up as high as they dared.

When they neared the other river bank where the priest stood, it was Eileen who shouted, "Good afternoon Father, sure and 'tis a grand warm day. Have you ever crossed here in your bare feet?"

Father Cullen was taken by surprise. His intentions had been to speak first and take control of any conversation. "Not since I was a boy," was his reply. It was almost lost in the soft wind and noise of the stream and reached the girls as a whisper.

Kathleen looked surprised and said to Eileen, "I saw him cross last summer one late afternoon."

The priest stood on the grassy bank watching the girls making their sure-footed steps towards him. Their faces were the picture of innocence. They stood at the river's edge with their dresses held up higher than necessary. Their shapely bare sun-tanned legs were embraced by the little whirlpools of clear rushing water close to the bank. Father Cullen stood silently waiting until they scrambled out, then in a stern admonishing voice, he said, "Good afternoon young ladies. Yes! A very nice day. Now I don't wish to lecture you, but I have seen you once before cross the stream barefooted with your clothing pulled up almost to your thighs. It's very unladylike and totally unnecessary as the water is not deep here."

It was Eileen who answered still holding that innocent expression, "Father, it is in some places. The stream is higher now than many years ago when you were a boy. Are you sure it's that long ago? My sister is certain she saw you crossing here late one evening last summer?"

Her question startled the good Father. He did remember one evening that he had visited old Tom McCarthy the bachelor who lived upstream a little way. During the visit Tom had poured a few glasses of good Navy Rum. It had been a warm thirsty sort of day and he'd stayed longer than expected. Rather than meet some of his parishioners on the road home, he had taken the shortcut across the stream. With his boots tied together around his neck and pants rolled up, he reckoned on the cool water to help him make sober steps as he crossed on the flat rocks. After a few stumbles and two good dunkings, he decided that was not the case. He had praised the Lord when he reached the rear entrance to his quarters at the chapel without meeting anyone.

Looking very stern he answered Eileen's query. "My child, I said to you, Not since I was a boy!" but his words didn't ring true. He continued, "Now in future act like genteel young ladies and I hope to see both of you in chapel for early mass on Sunday morning." With that he was off and they were certain they heard their laughter. Then Eileen voiced her thoughts, "I bet when he's around this way on his visits he looks for us crossing and hides in the bushes to watch. I think he lied!"

Kathleen put her hand on Eileen's shoulder. "He's a smart and good old priest and it sounded like a lie but remember he just repeated himself plus the four words, 'I said to you'. If he had added 'and that's the truth' then it might have been a big lie. I guess priests are allowed little white lies just like you and me.

"Last summer I did see him one evening walking downstream on the path from old McCarthy's cottage, and the Father was not very steady on his feet. I cut off on the old trail because I didn't want him to lecture me for missing two Sunday masses. When I got to where the paths joined again I looked back and he was struggling up the opposite bank and looked soaked. I think he must have missed a stepping stone or two, and fallen in. He's a good old soul, Eileen. If you ever have troubles he's so kind and understanding."

"Thanks," was Eileen's reply. She thought of asking her sister how she knew, but changed her mind. Instead she said, "Race you home," then barefoot the two beautiful young Irish sisters ran through lush green pastures, and the sound of their laughter was carried by the wind away upwards to be captured somewhere on that heather-covered hill.

It was September, 1939. Britain and France had declared war on Germany because Hitler had defied the ultimatum to stop his army's assault on Poland. The Irish Republic did not follow Britain's and France's war declaration. Although war had been declared and expectations were that Britain's capital city of London would be bombed by the Luftwaffe, nothing happened, just a great lull with visions of horrible times to come. Timothy often visited friends in the village to hear war news on their radio because his parents couldn't afford one. Young men from other towns had already gone to Derry and Belfast to join the British Forces. It was rumoured that before leaving, some had been told that if they joined to fight for England their families would disown them. These thoughts were in Timothy's mind as he mused over the idea of joining British forces. He would see Belfast and cross the Irish Sea to England, where he'd probably have an opportunity to visit the great metropolis of London and a host of other sights.

If he did join what would his parents say? Would they accept him home on leave? They might have to disown him against their will because some of the land owners were anti-British. If Timothy's father condoned his son's decision to join British forces he might lose jobs and that would be financial disaster for the family.

One evening, high up on the heather-covered slopes above Lough Swilly, Timothy sat on a big rock looking at the seemingly endless sandy beach of the Strand. Its vast emptiness and beauty captured in the sun's setting rays turned sea and sand into the most wonderful hues of red and gold that blended with low cloud into one great carpet of breathtaking beauty. There, Timothy made his decision. He thought, Someday I will follow that setting sun and meet its sunrise in New Zealand or Australia. Now, I will get to Derry or Belfast and join one of Britain's forces.

The very next week, he was able to arrange a ride to Derry with a truck driver. His father was angry when he learned of his son's intentions, but when the time came for Timothy to leave he relented, and before going off to work in the fields said, "You do what you have to do but take care of yourself young man." His mother cried and hugged her eldest son until he had to tear himself from her arms. Quickly he bid goodbye to his sister and brothers then ran to the waiting truck. "Tough leaving, my boy, isn't it?" remarked the old driver as he engaged the gear lever. Timothy couldn't answer as there was a great lump in his throat. He waved to the little group of five who were huddled together at the garden gate. Kevin in his mother's arms, brothers and sister waving frantically. It was a farewell to everything he'd known in all his nineteen years. Timothy smiled, remembering little Kevin saying, "Maybe Timmy you'll go a hundred miles into the big world out there." "Maybe little Kevin, I'll go farther perhaps to the end of the world and I will come back to tell you all about it." "Promise?" was little Kevin's request as Timothy rushed to the truck.

Kathleen O'Brien had snubbed him in the village that morning by crossing the road and turning her head away when he approached. She must have known he wished to say goodbye. George O'Conor passed at a gallop in his father's horse and buggy and shouted, "Traitor!"

The old trucker broke into Timothy's thoughts, "The British now have troops in France and the Royal Air Force is there too." He wanted to talk about the war. He had been in the first world war and he told Timothy stories about many things Timothy didn't understand, especially about girls.

With a 'good luck' farewell, his truck driver friend dropped him off at Derry's recruiting office, where Timothy joined the Royal Air Force as an airframe mechanic. He stayed with his buxom good-looking Aunt Molly, his mother's sister, who had strong political leanings towards a United Ireland. He reported as requested at the Padgate RAF Induction Centre in Lancashire, England, and for Timothy O'Neill all transport costs were paid. He arrived at his destination a bewildered young Irishman whose only previous travel experience was to the fair-sized town of Derry. Now part of his dream had come true. He had been to Belfast and had sailed in a ship across the Irish Sea. Timothy thought the multitude of people he had seen rushing here and there must have made up half the population of Great Britain. It seemed they were all in the same place at the same time.

Timothy found the Air Force did not waste time. In a few hours Timothy O'Neill became Aircraftsman O'Neill. They gave him a seven-digit number that he must not forget as it was his identification. To his new-found buddies he was "Tim O'Neill" just another Paddy from Ireland. Timothy liked the shortened version of his name. His mother had always maintained it was Timothy, never Tim. On numerous occasions she had become angry when people called him Tim. The parish priest one day called him Timmy. His mother very quickly but firmly said, "Father, his name is Timothy and you christened him." With a wry smile and a wink at Timothy, Father Cullen apologised. Only one person in the family was permitted to call his big brother Timmy and that was little Kevin.

The influx of recruits, both conscripted and volunteers, had strained the training facilities to over the maximum, so Timmy's lucky contingent of recruits was sent home on leave for two weeks.

Tim couldn't go home in uniform, his Ireland not being at war. Any uniformed combatants found in neutral territory would under convention rules be interned for the duration of hostilities. He asked spinster Aunt Molly to keep his uniform and other equipment safe in Derry while he spent time with his family. She hesitated but complied and hid his uniform behind her clothes in the bedroom closet. His kit bag she folded neatly and put under linens in the bottom drawer of her dresser. Out of her hat box came the blue hat with the ostrich feathers that she wore to chapel every Sunday. It was replaced by Tim's steel helmet. Tim apologised for all the trouble but Aunt Molly just nodded her head and said, "It's best that some people around here don't know I'm looking after your British uniform." Tim knew that Aunt Molly and his mother had never been close friends, and like a few of the farmers his father worked for, she and other family relatives living in Derry were very anti-British.

"Aunt Molly, the town is full with British sailors and other armed forces personnel. The River Foyle is overflowing with British Navy ships everywhere."

"I know Timothy, I know, it's not that. It's other family members around here. I don't want them to think I condoned and helped you join the English Air Force. You can stay here one night on the way

46

back but that's all. Now, I've made stew. Would you like some?" That was Tim's reception on his first stop home bound.

He borrowed Aunt Molly's old battered suitcase and packed into it things needed from his emptied kit bag. Next morning early he was on the bus to Rathmelton. After crossing the border into the Irish Republic, he remembered something, and chuckled. Where would Aunt Molly hide his air force boots and the other paraphernalia he had left in the kitchen? Tim felt at a loss out of uniform. His civilian pants were worn and baggy. The shoes hurt his feet, but he was going home for two whole weeks. Kathleen O'Brien would be there and he would have much time to talk to her.

The late September sun had a warm smile for Tim's mother as she ran to meet him with welcome-home tears. One would think he'd been away for years. Then there was little Kevin shouting, "Timmy, Timmy, where is your uniform?" "Hush dear," mother said and ushered them both inside.

It was two weeks of welcome, of disdainful looks, of hesitant handshakes, of numerous snubs, and many questions. Friends rushed away after chapel on Sunday not waiting to talk as they usually did. Timothy expected a few people might ignore him but not so many. Kathleen O'Brien was not at chapel. He asked a friend did he know why? The answer disturbed Timothy, "George O'Conor's parents invited her to accompany them and George on a holiday to Dublin. Isn't that something?" "Yes, isn't it," was all Timothy could think of saying. Then he asked, "When are they coming back?" The answer was another blow to Timothy. Kathleen would return four days before he had to go back to England. Timothy was disillusioned. He wanted so very much to talk and walk with her as they had done so many times in the past.

Being home was grand and his mother fussed over him every day, but he was counting the hours till Kathleen would arrive home. With four days left of his leave, the O'Conors and Kathleen arrived on schedule. Next day Timothy visited Kathleen's home. Her mother told him, "There's a party this evening at the big house for George O'Conor's nineteenth birthday and Kathy has gone to help with the decorations. Lots of young men are invited, but I guess you're not Timothy, or you would have known before now. That's too bad, but I'll tell Kathy you called." Timothy thanked Mrs. O'Brien and requested she tell Kathleen that he would call again before he had to go back. While inside the cottage he had realised Kathleen's parents must be a lot poorer than his own. It seemed they didn't have the bare necessities, although Kathleen at chapel was always dressed in clean and attractive clothes.

A few of Timothy's friends asked did he get an invitation to the big house for George's party. Timothy tried to appear unconcerned when he replied, "No."

"Old Patrick," as the family now called him was on the threshold of seventy and still a bachelor. During that time he had become an important personage to the estate's workers. He was a good organiser and was elected by those he worked with to delegate necessary daily jobs.

In all the years since Sally's letters had stopped, Patrick had heard nothing of her in New York. Sometimes he would purposely not light his oil lamp at night and would sit in the darkness of his quarters trying to visualise Sally now, almost five decades since he lost her.

He knew her hazel eyes would still have that glow of warmth and depth of sincerity, but he wondered what New York had done in fifty years to her beautiful fresh and clear Irish complexion. Had she married? Would her face show happiness, or would it be lined with sorrow? Was she still living? That last question tore at his heartstrings because he had no way of ever finding the answer.

Even with short notice Cora O'Conor put on an elegant and colourful nineteenth birthday party attended by many youthful guests. Son George basked in the limelight and danced with young and older female guests but kept close watch on Kathleen and showed her great respect, always the gentleman. Even when dancing he held her gently and at a respectful distance. "A very proper boy," was what one older lady was heard to say.

As he was a mature young gentleman of nineteen years, his father bestowed on him the title Overseer of Outside Staff, his duties to begin immediately. The outside staff included all farm workers. They were the staff who cleaned the stables, outhouses, cattle biers and all milking processes, also a variety of menial tasks. It was a shock to those involved, as Patrick, without awards or fanfare, did this job according to the needs of the day. For years everything had been working smoothly and without friction or big problems. Patrick's word was respected and he was trusted. Now young O'Conor at nineteen would be their boss and that frightened them.

George did not take long to show he was in charge. The morning after his birthday he called a meeting of all outside staff, and proud of this new power thrust upon him, he made no bones about who was now calling the shots. Without introductory niceties he stated, "I want you people to know that as of today you take instructions regarding the running of all Dunraven Estate jobs outside the house from one person only, me! I know old Patrick has been fumbling along for years acting as self-appointed supervisor. That is no more. No one, remember, no one is to go to him for advice, instruction, or whatever. He is forbidden to act in any manner that could be interpreted as supervising. If he tries to break, overrule or amend any instructions I lay down, he will suffer. Do all of you understand?" The workers mumbled a yes. That didn't satisfy George. "I want to hear a 'yes' in unison, and a loud one, okay?" They could not do otherwise but comply.

Not satisfied George asked Patrick to step forward. "Now Patrick McGuinness, I want you to repeat after me: I Patrick McGuinness, will respect and obey all orders that Mr. George O'Conor issues and will carry them out to the letter." Patrick looked at the faces of his fellow workers who were already nodding their heads as a signal to Patrick. It was, "Forget your pride for now, do as George demands." Patrick repeated the request slowly and distinctly knowing this dangerous young man had him for now in a corner.

George was delighted to hear Patrick's capitulation. "Thought you might disobey, Patrick, and that would have been curtains for you. I'd have you terminated immediately and thrown off the estate." Patrick had to quell a great urge to smash his fist into that cynical smile.

George allocated jobs for the day and then told the workers he was adding one hour to each work day starting right away and there would be no extra pay. You can blame old Patrick McGuinness as under his mismanagement it will take some time to get the agriculture and general duty staff working to maximum benefit for Dunraven Estate. Then he urged the staff to hurry about their duties and so dismissed them. George grabbed the sleeve of Patrick's jacket as he passed and his words held a threat. "If anything goes wrong old Patrick, I'll hold you responsible and I will be the one to discipline you, not my father."

Patrick looked him in the eye, and although his words were spoken softly they carried to a number of his friends who had stopped to hear what threats George was making at Patrick. "I feel very sorry for you

George O'Conor. You are a young man who could have a wonderful future. I loved you as a child, now there is a monster inside you. I'm afraid it will destroy many people before it destroys you." Then leaning forward, his weather-beaten face almost touching George's youthful countenance, Patrick continued, "Someday George it will destroy you and I hope to God it's soon." With that he jerked his sleeve from George's grasp and walked away. George was furious and shouted after him, "Old Patrick, you will pay for those words and pay dearly. How dare you speak to me like that." Patrick was striding away out of earshot with his head held high.

With his father's permission Timothy took the 'jaunting car', harnessed with old Kate the mare, and started on his way to the village. Kate hadn't been in the shafts for a long time. She seemed delighted and set off at a good trot. Timothy could hardly believe his eyes when he saw Kathleen walking towards the village. "Take it easy Kate," he said. "We are stopping here." He reined Kate to a stop, and looking down at the beautiful upturned solemn face, his heart seemed to beat a hundred times faster than normal.

"Would you like a ride Kathleen O'Brien? That is if you're going to the village."

She hesitated for a moment and Timothy was certain she would say no. Kathleen looked at the narrow dusty ribbon of road ahead of her. "Yes I will Timothy O'Neill, but that's all. Just a ride to the village."

Timothy was so eager he almost fell off instead of jumping down. He helped her up while she complained. "I can get up myself. I don't need your help."

"I know," murmured Timothy, thinking maybe he should have permitted her to do that. Kathleen sat on the left side seat away from him. Only with sideways glances could he see her. He thought, "I could sit beside her and still handle the reins. Old Kate knows the road to the village anyway without guidance, but then Kathleen might get angry if I tried that." Timothy was in a quandary so he had to be content with turning occasionally to make conversation. Kathleen had been silent since she'd climbed up. As the old mare trotted along with her head into a fair breeze, Timothy turned once to say, "How was the birthday party last night at the O'Conors?" but he was tongue-tied as he looked at her beautiful face and figure. The wind playing with her dress was helping to show her shapely brown legs dangling over the side.

Thinking they'd be in the village too soon at this rate, Timothy reined Kate in just a little. Then on a second try he asked, "You were in Dublin. Heard it is a grand city."

"That it is, beautiful."

"Did you have a good time?"

"Sure an' I did, was with great people."

"The O'Conors?"

"Yes."

"You like George O'Conor?"

"Yes."

"His parents are big land owners and rich."

"That's not why I like him."

"Oh! Really," Timothy's tone was sarcastic and he realised Kathleen was putting up a guard against his questions. There was a minute of silence with only the gusty wind singing its own song and old Kate's clippity clop as she brought the village nearer. Right now Timothy wished it was miles away to give him time to break down Kathleen's resistance.

On impulse he reined in to an unscheduled full stop and moved quickly beside Kathleen. He gently took hold of her arm while old Kate started munching on the lush roadside grass.

"Kathleen I've only one more full day then I have to report to my base in England."

"Why did you join the English?"

"It's not just the English Kathleen, it's everyone who cares. New Zealanders, Canadians, Australians, South Africans, even already some Americans and others. They are joining from all over the world."

"You joined the English Air Force when our country decided to be neutral."

"If my country was at war and I joined the Irish Army or Air Force would you be proud of me?"

"But you didn't Timothy O'Neill. You didn't and we are not at war."

"Do you think George O'Conor would risk his neck and join up if we were in the war?"

"I'm sure he would be one of the first to fight for Ireland and I don't think it is any of your business, Timothy O'Neill."

Timothy caught a doubt in her voice and he knew that O'Conor senior with all his money and power would make sure his son would not have to go to war. He was angry, and his grip tightened on her arm, but she did not flinch. "It is Kathleen. It is my business," he sounded fierce. "It's my business with thousands of others to help keep my family safe, and yours, and all the thousands of families in many countries. You just don't understand."

Old Kate had been moving continuously towards the village, looking for more and better lush grass. Timothy knew his time was running out, so putting a hand on Kathleen's shoulder, he turned her towards him. Looking into those blue Irish eyes he said, "Kathleen O'Brien, I'll be gone very soon. Will you go with me to the hotel? I'd like to buy you dinner then we can talk. I may not be home again for a long, long time. Rumour is we are going to France. Might be that we will never see each other again."

Maybe it was the last pathetic sentence that made Kathleen say yes. Who knows? Yes it was, and Timothy had to curtail the impulse to give old Kate a little smart with the whip so they would gallop into the village.

"Then I'll call for you at six o'clock tomorrow evening."

Kathleen jumped down unassisted. Timothy asked, "Do you need a ride home?"

"No I've got one thanks," she countered.

George O'Conor I suppose, thought Timothy, but he didn't say.

"Thanks, Timothy, see you tomorrow."

He watched her sprint across the road, auburn hair flying in the wind and he cursed George O'Conor. With a strong pull on the reins he turned old Kate towards home. She trotted all the way at a good speed while he sang, "I'll take you home again Kathleen." Tomorrow he'd be sitting in the village hotel dining room with the most beautiful girl in all Ireland.

They had a wonderful dinner together and Timothy knew he would remember it for the rest of his life. Kathleen looked fetching in a light blue dress and royal blue jacket. To Timothy's surprise she wore around her neck a small locket and chain he had bought for her at Rathmelton Fair when they were very young. It was a cheap gift but worth a million pounds, for it sent a message their friendship was not dead. They talked about times they went fishing together, the Saturday night dances, the hikes up in the heather-covered hills, the walks through Glenalla Woods. They laughed often and agreed there were so many wonderful moments to remember.

It was while drinking tea after dessert that Kathleen was very quiet and seemed uneasy. She finished her second cup then slowly placed the china cup on its saucer and raised her eyes to meet his. For seconds there was silence as he tried to find answers to his thoughts in their blue depths. Kathleen lowered them and when she looked up at him again it was with eyes pleading for understanding.

"Timothy my dearest friend I have to tell you. I must tell you and hope you understand. When we were in Dublin, George O'Conor asked me to marry him."

Timothy's rose-coloured world suddenly shattered as he looked into unwavering blue. "And what did you say Kathleen O'Brien?"

"Timothy, I said yes."

"Do you love him?"

"In a way, yes. But please understand his family are big land owners and his father has promised to build us a house with three bedrooms and a nursery, and to give my family an estate house with guaranteed employment for my father."

Timothy composed himself. "I wish you good luck Kathleen. Hope you will be happy, and if Ireland stays neutral, maybe you will be able to keep your George safe and sound at home." It was a chippy answer but it just slipped out.

Kathleen looked away and said, "I hope so." Timothy knew he had hurt her feelings. Thinking he would never again have the chance to dine with this beautiful girl, he reluctantly rose from the table and paid the cashier. With his arm around Kathleen's shoulder he led her into the evening darkness. Young Alfie McCracken, the grocer's son was stroking Kate's neck and talking to her. Timothy gave Alfie the shilling he'd promised him to sit in the buggy while they had dinner.

Timothy had changed the jaunting car for this more cosy means of transport, the Sunday-use trap, a two-wheeled buggy. It was very old but in fair condition. He had borrowed a sheepskin blanket as it was cold this early October evening. On the way home he wrapped the sheepskin over their knees and Kathleen sat close to him. He could feel the warmth of her body. His thoughts were scattered. Kathleen's parents were so poor; he was sure they would have pushed her to accept marriage into a rich family. He decided it wasn't her decision only.

Timothy wanted to say, "Kathleen O'Brien, I love you. I've always loved you. Please don't do this," but he was going away off to England and probably Europe and didn't know when or if he'd ever return. He moved a little closer and his leg touched hers. She did not move. It was a wonderful feeling. Old Kate plodded along the dark road and the chill of this October night made their closeness more inviting. Timothy pulled Kate to a stop under the archways made from the branches of the three great oak trees at the entrance to Kathleen's lane, then he turned, took her in his arms and kissed her. She didn't resist.

"I love you Kathleen," he whispered. "Wait for me. Tell him you have changed your mind."

"I can't. I can't. Oh! Dear Timothy, I can't. Arrangements were made in Dublin and my parents are so happy."

"What about you Kathleen, are you happy?"

"Timothy, George's father is going to move my parents and my brother and sister into one of his estate houses. I must be happy."

It was apparent Kathleen was trying to convince herself this would be so. For a long time they held each other like two frightened children and cried in each other's arms. After a long kiss Timothy let her go and urged old Kate to continue up the lane to the corner shadows of the cottage. Kathleen took both of his hands in hers. In Donegal Irish brogue, her softly spoken words would remain with Timothy for his lifetime. "Timothy O'Neill, I will never know another man as good as you. I do love you very much. I think I always have since we were children playing together, but this is best for all of us. I'll be praying for your safety. Please think of me as a very close friend. Isn't that also what love is?" She kissed him full on the mouth then turned swiftly away, but not before Timothy saw the flood of tears. Kathleen jumped out and ran to the cottage. He watched her beautiful silhouette caused by the light of the lantern hanging at the door. She turned, waved goodbye and went inside. Stemming the urge to run to the cottage, Timothy sat for a few moments considering facing her parents and saying, "I love this girl and she loves me. Don't force her to do this." What had he to offer Kathleen or her brother, sister and parents? Nothing! He had no security for anyone, or for Kathleen. They would all be comfortable on the O'Conor estate.

He pulled on the reins and as old Kate turned away he saw the light from an oil lamp shed a glow in the room he knew was Kathleen's bedroom. It was with turbulent thoughts that he looked away, knowing that soon George O'Conor and Kathleen would be sharing another bedroom in their new house. He spoke quietly to Kate, "Come on girl." He gave her a gentle slap and she took off at a canter. Timothy felt both sad and angry as he unhitched Kate, undid the halter around her neck and followed her into the stable where he gave her extra feed. In the darkness he put his face close to her head and whispered, "Kate, she did say she loved me." The old mare seemed to understand this grown-up boy who used to ride her bare-back out to the fields, when she was also young. She nuzzled him and snorted. Timothy patted her neck, put his cheek again close to her head and said, "Good night my dear old friend."

Soon it was time for goodbyes to his family. This time it was a more serious farewell. Timothy was going on active service, probably to France. His brother Michael, who was now seventeen years old, took him to the village where the bus stopped. Timothy gave his brother a quick hug, jumped down, stroked Kate's neck and said, "Look after Kate, Michael. She's a wonderful animal." "I will! I will!" Michael replied, then he was gone. The bus arrived and Timothy was stepping aboard when he heard someone call his name. It was Kathleen's sister, Eileen. She was out of breath. "I almost missed you Timothy, this is for you," and she gave him a small package. "It's from Kathleen. She's at home crying. She was coming here to see you off but changed her mind saying it would only make things worse. She loves you Timothy and is only marrying George to help us all. I'll be fifteen in a month, Timothy O'Neill, and I will wait for you till the war is over if you want me to."

Timothy looked at Eileen with her golden hair, blue eyes, and fresh young face, and knew that in a few years there would be another beautiful O'Brien lady. "Thank you Eileen, I appreciate your wonderful offer but please don't wait for me because I have the world to see when the war is over." Timothy kissed Eileen's cheek. He thanked her again for delivering the package and for her offer to wait, then climbed aboard. As the old bus groaned its way out of the village Timothy walked to the back seat. It felt like the most private place. He held tight to the package but did not want to open it yet. Timothy wanted to just hold it as Kathleen had held it a short time ago. It was wrapped in light blue paper similar to the colour of the silk dress she had worn at dinner, and it was tied with a deep blue ribbon. Neatly inscribed on the left corner of the package were the words, "To Timothy." Slowly he untied the ribbon and unwrapped the gift. There were two gifts. One a small beautifully framed picture of Kathleen. It had been coloured by an expert. His work had highlighted the beauty of her face and the tantalising magic of those blue eyes and auburn hair. The other gift was a silver bracelet with his name engraved on the tiny portion where the clasp locked. On the reverse side was another inscription so small he had difficulty reading it. There were three words "I love you," and her initials K.O'B. A neatly written note was tucked in the wrappings.

> My Dearest Timothy,
> Of me, this is all I can give you. Please remember us as we were in each other's arms last night. Wear the bracelet for luck and may it and the good Lord bring you safely home.
> My love and prayers go with you,
> Kathleen

Her signature and the last two lines were blotched with tear stains. Why Kathleen? Why? was all he could whisper to himself. Later he thought she could not have bought the bracelet and had the engraving done since dinner last night. She must have done it when he went off to "join the English" as she had put it.

3

The Wedding, 1939

Kathleen O'Brien's father worked occasionally for a farmer whose acreage bordered the O'Conor estate lands. Shawn O'Brien did not know Patrick McGuinness, but had heard about his honesty and integrity. He found Patrick cleaning out the stables and told him what had occurred in the last few weeks. The wealthy young O'Conor boy George had come several times to their cottage in his new Bentley sports car, and had taken his daughter Kathleen to dinner at the big hotel and sometimes to dances. He appeared to be a very pleasant young gentleman with good manners; good-looking and a good physique. Kathleen had said how George always treated her with care and respect when in company or alone. He hadn't even tried to kiss her. Shawn continued by saying that Kathleen and George had known each other for years. It was only very recently he'd been courting her and already he was asking her hand in marriage. The O'Conor family had taken her as their guest to Dublin on a holiday.

Putting a hand on Patrick's arm, Shawn said, "I'm concerned Patrick, and I would like your opinion. My wife Maureen is so happy that Kathleen would be marrying into a wealthy family, but I have a feeling that the young man is hiding something."

Patrick thought for a moment before answering.

"Shawn, I do not talk about the family I work for because I am obligated to them for my daily bread, but I will tell you what I would do if in your shoes. I have seen your beautiful daughter in the village, and in these parts. I say this to you. If she were my daughter, I'd lock her up in chains before giving my blessing to marry George O'Conor, and she would be better off. He is a dangerous young man. You do as you wish Shawn but in all probability your daughter will or already has made up her own mind and decided for you. It happens that way."

Kathleen's father thanked Patrick, shook his hand, and continued home to try and convince his wife Maureen that Patrick McGuinness, a fine and honest man who worked for the O'Conors, had similar thoughts as himself regarding young George.

"Maureen," he said, "my intuitions were right. Patrick McGuinness indicated there is something sinister about young George that is covered up by his polished manner and his good looks."

"Ach! You men," retorted Maureen. "I think both of you are jealous of this wonderful young man just because he has very rich parents and will fall into a fortune when they pass on. Look at the beautiful flowers he brings me when he calls for Kathy, and he brought that nice gift for my birthday. Come have your supper, and, by the way, Kathy told me that George's father has promised to do lots of things to help. Like moving us into one of his estate houses. Wouldn't that be wonderful? So come on Shawn, you're looking for trouble that isn't there."

"OK Maureen but remember I warned you and I'll warn Kathy. Wish she had taken up with her own kind like young Timothy O'Neill."

"Now why would she do a thing like that Shawn? Aren't you ashamed of yourself for even suggesting it? He went off to fight for England. Where is your Irish pride?"

Shawn gave in but ate his supper with Patrick's warning uppermost in his thoughts.

The October sunlight shone through the great stained-glass window to the right of the altar. It created colourful rays that turned the white marble baptismal font into rainbow hues that spread across the altar floor where Kathleen stood in the shimmering white wedding dress ordered by George's mother from an exclusive bridal store in Dublin's Grafton Street. She had insisted it be one of her gifts to the bride.

Kathleen had hoped to wear her mother's wedding dress, a gift long ago from a brother in America. The dress had been preserved carefully for two decades so that one day Eileen or Kathleen would wear it. Mrs. O'Conor immediately squashed that idea. "My son and his bride are going to have the most elegant wedding that ever took place in this whole area. It will be talked about for many months." Kathleen had not told Timothy of George's insistence for a quick wedding so that her family could be settled in a comfortable home before winter.

The grand house, as the village people often called the Dunraven House mansion, had been a hive of activity since the Dublin vacation. Mrs. O'Conor had the servants scrub and clean every corner before starting the decorating. The long guest list included the gentry and their ladies of the area. As far afield as Derry, Belfast and Erin's capital, Dublin, had come many affluent and prominent couples.

Following her attendants, Kathleen glided down the aisle on her father's arm, feeling the roughness of his only tweed suit, the same one he had worn at his own wedding. She stole a quick glance at her mother, sister and brother, and the few relatives that were able to attend. They seemed a poor-looking group in comparison to the grandeur of O'Conor guests. Her bridesmaids were picked by George's mother. Kathleen had shyly suggested she would like her sister as a bridesmaid but that request was overruled with, "I know what is best my dear."

George stood like a statue beside his best man, and as Kathleen reached his side he looked down at her with a smile that showed no warmth or love, just, "I've won this prize."

Kathleen had to steel herself to go through the vows, but it was security for her family and she had to think of that first.

She repeated her vows in a dream, pretending it was Timothy she was vowing her love and obedience to. Then the ring was put on her finger and Father Cullen pronounced her the wife of George O'Conor, to "love, honour and obey till death do us part." George kissed her and she was frightened. The only man she had ever kissed with passion was Timothy O'Neill. In a trance she walked on George's arm down the aisle to the organ strains of the Wedding March.

As they arrived into the late fall's pale sunlight, there were crowds throwing confetti and wishing them happiness. Although it was late October the day was clear. The morning wedding gave ample daylight for Cora O'Conor to put on her display. As a backup the O'Conor limousine was decorated and prepared in case of inclement weather. Cora's dream was now to be fulfilled and the Dunraven House open carriage was to be used so that her son and his bride could ride in their horse-drawn carriage like the King and Queen of England. This would be the "Royal O'Conor Parade." Her instructions were that all loyal O'Conor estate staff not on duty and their families would line the parade route to wish the young "Royal O'Conors" every happiness. She hoped that the villagers would augment the well-wishers lining the route.

Old Patrick, looking wonderful in his coachman's attire, stood solemnly by the carriage. As the young couple made their way through the great throng of well-wishers and clouds of confetti, Patrick's look was thoughtful. Kathleen stepped up into the carriage with help from one of her bridesmaids. She looked startled as Patrick said, "May God bless you, my dear," and George scowled at him.

The sleek all-black horse, with harness decorated, sensed this was a special occasion and with its reins held loosely in Patrick's hands, it trotted majestically to the village photographers. The rest of the wedding party had gone in the O'Conor limousine. They would be waiting for the bride and groom all posed in correct positions according to Cora's instructions. To ensure the photographer and his equipment would return to the reception before the bride and groom, a Rolls Royce waited with its white uniformed chauffeur.

After the wedding group pictures were taken, the best man and the bridesmaids returned to the reception. While the excited photographer, assisted by the white uniformed chauffeur, hastily gathered his equipment, they were off to Dunraven House leaving the bride and groom with their horse carriage, and Patrick waiting outside.

As Kathleen turned to leave the room, George grabbed her by the arm and pulled her to him in a tight embrace, then putting his hand under her chin, he made her look up at him before pressing his lips to hers in a kiss that left her breathless. Before she could take another full breath he repeated his long passionate kiss. She was afraid and appalled at his actions. When she tried to pull away he looked down at the upturned beautiful but frightened face and said, "We must give the photographer time to get things set up for our big entrance. And remember Kathleen you are now mine to love and obey."

Outside, Patrick had waited patiently beside the horse and carriage. Finally Old Patrick appeared at the door. "Sure and I think we should be going Mister O'Conor."

With an expression of anger George replied, "You're right, Patrick."

Old Patrick was thrilled at being permitted to drive the carriage but his thoughts were sad that a beautiful and innocent young lady had fallen under the power of this handsome but strange and sadistic young man.

People on the road shouted good-luck greetings. Outside each cottage, women and children stood and waved as the bride and the son of the great and powerful O'Conors passed by. At the large gravel area relegated to parking, the scene was like a car show. There was a score of new and late- model automobiles from brightly coloured Bentley and Lagonda sport cars to elegant black Daimlers and Rolls Royces. A crowd of George's male friends with drinks in their hands waited outside the grand entrance. Again it was showers of confetti and the old photographer tried to get his pictures while being jostled by the already inebriated mob of young men. From some of them came remarks like, "Lucky old George always gets what he wants."

Kathleen cringed when George put his arm around her waist and pulled her close. He gave his taunting male friends a smile of victory and said, "Eat your hearts out, she is mine."

At the great bar in the lower lounge, Protestants, Catholics, and many people of other denominations drank in harmony. Cora O'Conor had no qualms regarding religion; if they were rich they were welcome. For certain, Cora expected lavish wedding gifts in return for the invitation. Cora's thin red lips were curled into a fixed smile and her facial expression was almost pensive. Her cold calculating eyes surveyed the guests in a condescending manner. She could perceive the majority on this occasion were obligated to stay. In her way of thinking they were her prisoners and she could manipulate them to her own advantage. In her pink silk dress with the big sash and wide brimmed multicoloured hat, she paraded through the throng of guests like a little sergeant major inspecting a platoon. With her matching pink high-heeled shoes, Cora Sarah O'Conor was elevated to no more than five foot two. To all the grand ladies present and to their escorts she evoked the necessity of being treated as queen of her domain.

George guided Kathleen through a throng of guests, displaying her like a treasure. She almost welcomed her mother-in-law's request, "Come dear, I want you to meet a number of good friends." In a dream Kathleen acknowledged their good wishes, and she continued conversation in a detached manner.

Tables in the grand and spacious dining room were set for two hundred guests. Wine and hard liquor flowed freely. The abundant assortment of food included pheasant, turkey, ham, roast beef, salmon, caviar, a great variety of vegetables and what seemed like an endless choice of desserts. The five-tier wedding cake was a magnificent display of culinary art. Kathleen's hand shook as George placed his over hers and together they cut the cake.

Kathleen listened to the speeches that went on for hours praising George the wonderful son of James and Cora O'Conor. He was now following in his father's footsteps by taking a beautiful bride as his father had many years ago. Hopefully they may have many healthy children to keep the great O'Conor name alive and respected in this area and afar. As liquor flowed it freed more tongues whose owners struggled to their feet to make drunken spiels.

When George had made his speech some time before, he had thanked Kathleen's parents for his wonderful and beautiful bride. George finished amid laughter by saying, "I will love her as long as she obeys all and I mean all of my demands!" This made Kathleen tremble and almost cry out, Oh! Timothy, Timothy. She now knew it was not a joke but a threat.

The hired musicians played until well after midnight and Kathleen had to dance with all of George's friends. As the evening wore on, they became more intoxicated. George sat on the sidelines and grinned as each of his drunken friends took turns stumbling around the dance floor with his wife. They made her want to rush out of the room to cry aloud, No! No! This is a mistake. I'm not married to George O'Conor. I love Timothy O'Neill and I made my marriage vows to him in chapel today. She knew it was too late. She was the wife of this young man with a cruel look in his eyes. The church said there was no escape.

It was James O'Conor, George's father, who waded in among the throng of youthful drunks to take her hand and say, "Can I have the honour of another dance before it's too late?" George and Kathleen had led off when the music first started. For minutes he had whirled her around the dance floor to applause from the guests. His father and mother joined them and there was great applause.

When they exchanged partners Kathleen found herself dancing with the charming James O'Conor. He was a marvellous dancer and light on his feet for a man of his size. Over six feet tall, barrel-chested and built like an athlete, James was in his early fifties with just a little grey showing in his mop of unruly red hair. His weather-beaten face still held good looks, and the charming smile complemented his dark blue eyes.

This for Kathleen was a pleasant interlude of escape to be dancing with someone who did not "paw." James kept a respectable distance, yet held her firmly and never missed a step. It was so easy for her to follow him. As they danced, his conversation was light but his blue eyes seemed to pierce her thoughts. "I hope you will be happy my dear with us. I'm thrilled that my son picked an intelligent and also beautiful bride. I will start building your new home as soon as possible and you have my assurances that your family will be taken care of." The music stopped and he gently took her hand and led her across the floor to where George was waiting with friends. "I'm bringing back your bride to the shelter and safety I hope of her husband. Take good care of her my boy." At that he kissed Kathleen on the cheek and said, "Good night beautiful lady and welcome again to my family." Kathleen felt she had just made a friend, someone she might need in the future. George danced again with her, then it was the last waltz.

The musicians packed away their instruments and guests started to say their goodnights. A majority of the guests were registered at the village hotel. Many others were going to their homes. The remainder were being put up in the mansion's many bedrooms.

Kathleen felt George's hand on her arm as she said good night to her family. He had had a fair amount to drink, but being built like his father, strong and athletic, he showed little sign of the alcohol he'd consumed. His brown eyes, like his mother's, now seemed to bore into her very soul. Standing almost alone with this man, she was afraid. Taking her hand in a vice-like grip he said in almost a whisper, "I've waited a long time for this moment. In our bedroom we will have complete privacy."

She wanted to flee from this awful nightmare. Where was her so tender and kind Timothy? It was a night of terror for Kathleen. George O'Conor almost dragged his prize along corridors towards the great master bedroom.

It had not been used for years, as George's parents had separate bedrooms in the living quarters at the south end of the mansion. George had requested it be reopened until his new house was built. His mother complied and had it completely refurbished. Decorated to his requests with heavy drapes and silk bed linens, everything was in keeping with the beautiful new furniture he had chosen.

George stopped at a wide panelled door where he picked Kathleen up in his arms and said, "Must carry my bride over the threshold." They entered a bedroom bigger in area than her parent's whole cottage. A massive bed took up the centre of the room.

George pushed the door closed with his foot. He stood her against the door and locked it then kissed her repeatedly until she gasped for breath. "No Patrick to intercept us here Kathleen, my wife." Then he carried her to the great bed and ignored her pleading until finally he fell asleep.

Kathleen sobbed quietly as she sat at the big window with the drapes partly drawn back. She watched the full moon's waning light touch the lush green fields. She prayed for strength to maintain the appearance of a new and happy bride. A pale moonbeam crawled like a paralysed searchlight slowly liberating from shadow landmarks and places she loved, then it passed on to leave them again in shadow. For some time the moon's light was lost in a clouding sky. Kathleen sat like a statue at the big window, her thoughts for the future dark and foreboding. Then she slipped into the immense bed and slept as far away as possible from the snoring form of her new husband.

Kathleen had not redrawn the small portion of window drapes. She awoke to a new morning spreading a sliver of light into the bedroom, making it the beginning of the first full day of her married life.

It was eight-thirty when she quickly washed in the white tiled bathroom with its royal blue porcelain sink and gold plated faucets. She slipped into a mauve dress and matching slippers and brushed her auburn hair. She unlocked the door. It opened and closed silently with little guidance. Quickly descending to the corridors she made her way to where overnight guests were already having breakfast. Greeting her warmly they were overjoyed that the new bride would sit and have breakfast with them. Kathleen chatted with the guests as she partook of her own meal. A congenial twenty minutes had passed when James and Cora entered. James smiled with a warm greeting,

"Good morning Kathleen, my wonderful new daughter." He placed his hand on her shoulder in a friendly manner as he moved to take his own place beside Cora. Kathleen now realised there was a very special table reserved for the two Mr. and Mrs. O'Conors.

Some guests also realised the new bride had made a big error in O'Conor etiquette. They looked at her with smiles indicating, "Sorry, young lady you've goofed already." Others indulged in audible conversation, "Where is the groom?" "Maybe they had a misunderstanding?" "Wonder, did they or was she too tired?" This last remark caused subdued laughter. Kathleen glanced over to the other table and saw Cora O'Conor's furious look. Her brown eyes were half closed and aflame with anger. Casually Kathleen stood up told the guests it was a pleasure having breakfast with them and excused herself. With a china cup of hot tea in her hand she moved to the reserved table and sat next to her father-in-law.

"Where is George?" was Cora's blunt request. There was no "Good morning Kathleen."

"Asleep," was the only answer that Kathleen could give. "At least when I left," she added.

"Why didn't you wake him?"

"Should I?"

"My poor boy! You should have waited. He will be disturbed. Imagine James if I had left our wedding bed while you slept. Anyone with breeding would never have done such an inexcusable thing." Cora was being vicious in her remarks. It was James who came to Kathleen's rescue.

"Now Cora," he said, "I think Kathleen made our guests very happy by breaking bread with them and by her presence until we arrived. You, Cora overslept just like George is doing, otherwise we would have been here to greet our guests prior to breakfast. Now let's enjoy this first breakfast with our new daughter and I, for one, am not waiting for George." Then with a glint in his unwavering blue eyes and a quizzical smile he asked Kathleen, "Did you keep poor George awake all night and now he is drained of energy?" Kathleen blushed and those guests who overheard the question half turned in their seats to hear her answer. She was saved from that embarrassment by the entrance of her husband.

George looked handsome in his Irish white wool sweater and navy blazer with the O'Conor crest embroidered on the top pocket. He had made a grand entrance and moved now from guest to guest shaking hands with those he'd missed the previous day. He kissed the cheeks of some ladies and held the hands of others. George spoke of the great pleasure and honour it was for both he and his most precious beautiful bride that so many wonderful friends turned up to wish them happiness. That was his own very dear wish and plan for Kathleen and himself. Then with a charming smile he excused himself, "Must sit with my bride, I have already this morning lost one precious hour without her."

George moved his chair close to Kathleen and through clenched teeth he hissed, "Don't you ever leave my bed again without my permission! You will pay for this; you have made me look like a fool in front of my guests." His mother's wicked smile seemed to say she endorsed her son's remarks. James O'Conor pretended not to hear but Kathleen met his eyes and thought there was a message in them that she didn't understand.

After the last wedding guests made their exit, the big wrought-iron gates of Dunraven Estate closed. Patrick watched as the convoy of aristocrats in their grandeur sped towards the village and their separate destinations. He was glad to see them go. All the drinking and revelry to celebrate this wedding was to him deceitful and a mockery of how it should be with two young people in love. It disturbed Patrick that Shawn O'Brien did not follow his advice and his own intuitions regarding the devil in disguise.

Patrick had felt so helpless when he drove the young couple from chapel to the photographers. He saw the look of triumph on George's face. His heart went out in sympathy to the beautiful young Kathleen who had no idea she had just married a good-looking monster. It was not by chance Patrick interrupted George's immediate advances as soon as he had Kathleen alone in the photographer's room. As he closed and locked the massive gates he felt sad. Patrick told himself there was no time to ponder what should not have happened. Kathleen must have made up her mind for whatever reason to marry George.

Cora O'Conor decided she needed a rest now that her guests were gone. "I have had such a strenuous time," she told James. "It will take a few days for me to renew my energy." With instructions to Mrs. Kernaghan, the cook, regarding menus for the evening meal, she asked not to be disturbed until the pre-dinner cocktail hour.

Kathleen had spent most of the morning entertaining guests and now that they were gone she felt the wall of defence against being alone again with George had been torn down. James O'Conor retired to his study and Cora to her room. George now said, "Kathleen, my dear wife, let's you and I retire to our bedroom and rest awhile before dinner." She had no option but to obey and submit to hours of another cruel sexual orgy.

Four hours later they were seated at the massive mahogany table with James and Cora. It was set with a great variety of silverware and a bountiful supply of wines. The Sheffield silverware, crystal glasses, fine china, and goblets of red and white wines sparkled in the light from two huge silver candelabras. Kathleen sat spellbound at the grandeur to serve four people.

"Your glass, my dear." George was doing the honours. With his hand squeezing her shoulder he poured a glass three-quarters full of red wine. When the four glasses contained what he reckoned was sufficient for a first drink, it was his father who rose to make a toast. "To Kathleen, my beautiful daughter-in-law, I have the great pleasure in welcoming you to our family table. We wish you much happiness and a long life of doing wonderful things as you walk life's path at the side of your loving husband, our son."

Kathleen had not tasted wine until her wedding day and now she wondered if this was the usual procedure each night at dinner. "Drink Kathleen." It was more a command than a request from George. Kathleen permitted Cora's favourite red wine to just touch her lips. That was the only toast she'd give to her life with George.

The main dish was chicken breasts stuffed with mushrooms. The servants moved quietly and efficiently serving a variety of additional wonders that Kathleen had never seen before. The food was delicious and she was surprised to find her wine glass was almost empty. George quickly replenished it and topped it up as the meal progressed. Liqueurs followed, resulting in more toasts from both George and James. Cora ate her dinner and drank in silence but her eyes seldom wavered from Kathleen. She then called for Irish coffees. Cora was drinking her second 'Irish' when she decided to make a toast. "To the bride and mother-to-be, that there will be many healthy sons to carry on the great and respected name O'Conor."

"We will drink to that Kathleen won't we?" George's slurred words and leering look made her want to rush out of there. To run where the three great oak trees stood guarding the entrance to the lane where Timothy and she had stopped one night in another lifetime before she waved goodbye from under the lantern outside her parent's cottage door.

Perceiving that before her was another nightmare in the grand bedroom, she downed two quick drinks hoping it would dull the pain and degradation.

For hours George refused her sleep and then in desperation she cried out, "Old Patrick was right when he told my father to stop me from marrying you. I wish I had listened." Immediately he released her, sat up in bed and with a wild look on his face asked, "When did old Patrick say that?" Kathleen knew she'd made a great mistake. "I don't know, I don't know, I think it was a dream I had."

"It was no damned dream. I will make him pay dearly for such a statement." George got out of bed and poured another drink from a bottle he had brought up from the liquor cabinet. He paced the floor swearing profusely and making threats of skinning old Patrick alive or whipping him off the estate. Kathleen was very scared and upset that the drink had loosened her tongue. She had got old Patrick into serious trouble. She also knew as a bride of only two nights that the warning Patrick had given her father was proving to be the truth.

It was almost seven-thirty the next morning. The workers had already prepared themselves for another day of chores on the estate. Patrick, with two pails three-quarters full of frothy fresh milk, was leaving the cow barn on his way to the churn room. He was accosted by the bleary eyed unshaven George. With a pail of milk in each hand Patrick was a helpless target as George without warning downed him with two fierce blows from his fists. Patrick was sprawled in the muck close to the midden. The quarts of good fresh milk made a river of white that almost immediately disappeared into the foul-smelling pig midden. As Patrick started to get up, George took a riding whip from where he had pushed it in his belt and lashed out at him. The first lash caught him across the face and the second curled around his neck. With it

George was pulling Patrick towards him. "You good-for-nothing in-terfering bastard, McGuinness. I should skin you alive right now. How dare you try to interfere in my marriage, telling Kathleen's father she should not marry me. I knew you would cause me trouble. If I was in full control here I'd whip you off the estate."

Patrick's face was lacerated and the whip had caught the corner of one eye and he knew one tooth was broken. As he was pulled strug-gling out of the mud and manure, the whip uncoiled from around his neck. He made straight for George, trying to dodge the whip's lash as the demon of a young man continued to punish him. Patrick received stinging cuts before reaching the swearing out-of-control George. As the whip came down again, Patrick wrenched it from George's grip. Right there before most of the estate workers who had surrounded them, he could have given George the thrashing of his life. Instead Patrick, blood streaming down his face and neck from severe cuts, walked steadily to the front door of the mansion. He was followed by most of the outside workers who refused to obey George's command to get on with their work, and by using force they made him follow Patrick.

James O'Conor was already standing at the door having been alerted by one of the servants that an altercation was taking place between Patrick and George. James looked horrified when he saw Patrick's bloody face. Quickly thrusting the whip into James' hand Patrick said, "Mister James O'Conor, I've worked for you and with you to help build and take care of this estate for twenty years. I have faithfully served you, done my job and then some. Your son may be your pride and joy but he has a bad streak in him. I'd love to make him feel a whip's lash but I am not his father, so I give the whip to you hoping you might try to chase the devil out of him yourself, before he destroys what you, with my help have built."

After a few seconds of silence James looked at his bleary-eyed son, then at the bleeding Patrick. There he saw a strong man now almost seventy with guts and a hold on life's experiences. He had learned compassion for fellow workers, had proven respect for his employer and already proven by his deeds to be an employee who respected fair play and justice. James O'Conor hesitated for only a few seconds more. Outdoor staff stood in silence waiting for his move. George started to speak, "Father, Patrick tried to stop . . ." The crack of the riding whip across his shoulders stopped him. James lashed his only son, avoiding searing his face but staining the white shirt George wore with blood. George just stood there, no protest, no trying to evade the whipping.

It was Patrick who said, "James, enough is enough." James replied, "I am the master of Dunraven House and its estate, Patrick, I will decide." Ten more lashes and George was whimpering like a child. Only then did his father stop. Looking at his dishevelled son he said, "Always remember George, I built this estate without ever laying a finger on any one of my workers. I gave you a little responsibility, but you couldn't handle it. I will give you a second chance and if there is a repeat of what I've witnessed today against any one of my employees, you may never be master of Dunraven. My will can easily be changed. Now go clean yourself up and don't go crying to your dear mother. Be a man!"

He asked the servants to go about their designated duties, leaving him alone with Patrick McGuinness. Even at this early morning hour James was immaculately dressed. The bleeding Patrick stood beside him clothes filthy and stinking from sprawling in the manure midden. Both of them had much in common: honesty, integrity and fairness in dealing with disciplinary actions. Their decisions on even the most infinitesimal problems brought respect from everyone.

"Why the ruckus?" James asked. Patrick told him that Shawn O'Brien had asked questions regarding George before the wedding and that he had given him an honest answer.

"And may I ask you Patrick, what was your honest answer?"

Without hesitation Patrick informed James of the changes he had seen in the child he once loved who had become the man he despised. James gave no sign of anger or surprise. He thanked Patrick for his frankness then invited him to use his bathroom to clean up and get antiseptics for the deep gashes. Patrick accepted. Both men were approximately the same build so Patrick went back to work wearing some of James' clothing as gifts.

Kathleen was having breakfast alone as eight o'clock as it was too early for Cora. George's father had not turned up for breakfast and she had no idea where George was. Still unaware of general procedures, she decided to have her own morning meal. Kathleen needed more boiling water for her tea. Not wishing to ask the servants, she went off to the kitchen herself. From the kitchen window she was surprised to see James and Patrick passing by. Kathleen was shocked when she saw Patrick's face and his dirty torn clothing. He was closest to the window and the terrible-looking bloody gashes still trickling blood made her gasp. Oh no! She knew it must have been George who inflicted those wounds. Realising someone was behind her, she turned swiftly to face soft blue angry eyes, round rosy cheeks, and a very firm strong mouth.

"Mrs. Kernaghan, I didn't know you were here, I need boiling water for my teapot."

Ignoring Kathleen's request and blocking the exit, Mary Jane Kernaghan, cook for the O'Conor family, faced the new Mrs. George O'Conor. "Your man did that and I'm telling you now Kathleen O'Conor, look out for yourself 'cause your husband is rotten and wicked. Some day he will come to a bad end. He is just like his mother. James is the only decent one of the three. Now you can tell Cora I said that, I don't care. I can cook anywhere in Ireland. There's always work for good and honest people."

Kathleen met Mary Jane Kernaghan's angry look with a calmness that showed. "Mary Jane," she said. "I came here for boiling water but thank you for being concerned. I've already discovered my mistake in marrying George and I don't tell tales especially to Cora O'Conor."

Mary Jane's eyes widened in surprise. Here was a young woman with spirit. Hastily she filled Kathleen's request and insisted on taking the hot teapot to the breakfast table. Before retreating to her kitchen she whispered, "You can count on me my dear, anytime you need help."

Kathleen thanked her then poured herself a cup of tea. She was trying to piece together in her thoughts the tragic disappointment of her marriage when Cora O'Conor took her usual seat at the table.

"Good morning," Kathleen opened the conversation. "I had whole wheat scones with marmalade. They were delicious."

Cora looked at her as if she were a stranger. "What do you know about the altercation between George and Patrick? I have a feeling you must be involved somehow."

"I don't like the insinuation, Cora. Perhaps you should ask your husband. I saw him with Patrick passing the kitchen window a short time ago. I'm sure Mr. O'Conor will tell you what happened. George was not in our room when I awoke this morning and that was around seven."

Kathleen was surprised by her own cool response and was certain cook Mary Jane had listened from the kitchen door. Mary Jane now stood beside Cora with a smug smile and asked, "What would Madam like to order this morning?"

"Just tea and scones, Mary Jane."

"Right Madam!" and off she went.

Kathleen never knew if Cora found out the truth about George, Patrick and James. Cora was told only that Patrick had fallen into some dirty place and had cut his face quite badly and that James had had to lend him clothing.

George abided by his father's warning and refrained from telling his mother. It took weeks for his and Patrick's wounds to heal. During that time George kept his mother at a distance and complained he had pulled a back muscle. Cora, in her spiteful mood quipped, "Maybe your dear wife will rub it with liniment."

George sulked for days following his father's punishment. Kathleen had a respite from his attentions. She was surprised that a large number of workers had witnessed the thrashing yet none had been browbeaten by Cora's insistent questioning to give her the details. Their loyalty was to Patrick and James O'Conor.

One morning in Mary Jane Kernaghan's kitchen domain, Kathleen was making tea. Mary Jane spoke quietly. "Got something to tell you Kathleen. I heard Patrick tried to convince your family to decline their permission for you to marry George O'Conor. Pity he hadn't succeeded, but anyway somehow George found out and that was the reason for going after Patrick with the whip. So our Patrick knew the rotten character George is and tried to save you."

Kathleen pretended to be surprised and did not volunteer the information on how George found out. She knew George was brooding over the mortification of being whipped by his father in public and that promised problems for old Patrick and herself. George never talked about it nor did he ask questions. It was as if it never happened. But knowing his wicked temper and mean disposition, she was scared for Patrick's safety.

Kathleen decided that someday soon when George was away on business she'd find Patrick and tell him that under stress and too much wine she had blurted out the words that had caused George to go berserk. She hoped he would understand and accept her apology.

In early December, James O'Conor kept his word by moving Kathleen's parents into a newly renovated house on the estate, where they had more space than their wildest dreams ever envisioned. The original house had only one large bedroom and a den but an addition had been attached to the house by an enclosed breezeway. It had a private entrance. The addition contained a good-sized bedroom plus a small sitting room with a fireplace. It was really private from the main house. Kathleen's sister Eileen was thrilled with having this part all to herself. She had her own key and said it was, "To lock out the world, if I so desire."

Her brother Brian thought he should have had a choice, he being the eldest, but mother decided that a young lady should have her own bedroom and privacy.

Brian had the comfortable little den that doubled as a bedroom. "Better for a young man," was his mother's comment. Maureen O'Brien had much praise for the O'Conors, but Shawn said he'd reserve his decision for a few months.

George had a meeting with his father regarding the new house promised for Kathleen and himself. A decision was made by his father to put it on hold. Although the Irish Republic was not at war, costs of building materials had already escalated tremendously. To compensate, part of the north end of Dunraven House would be refurbished. It would be upgraded in keeping with the luxurious bedroom restoration. This would start immediately.

Now let us leave Dunraven House and the tragedy of Kathleen's marriage. She loved Timothy but made the decision to marry George with genuine thoughts of helping her family out of poverty and with no idea the good-looking young George O'Conor had set out to deceive her and won. Her Timothy was gone and she was married to a monster.

Now our question is: How is Timothy O'Neill adjusting to the loss of Kathleen and life on the Royal Air Force? Let's travel to England and find out what we can.

4

Timothy and Sharon, 1939/40

Timothy O'Neill finished his training course and was posted to a squadron where he was immediately put to work with the ground crews. Two of his buddies from the training course were there and Timothy felt good being with people he knew, so he again became "Tim." They were working on a "Fairey Battle" aircraft already war damaged and flown back to its English base for repairs. Rumours were strong that the whole squadron including ground crews would be going to a secret French air base.

It was his mother who wrote telling him that soon after he left there was a wonderful wedding at the big O'Conor house, and beautiful young Kathleen O'Conor was the radiant and happy bride. Tim had not told his mother of the love he had for Kathleen. She had thought he borrowed the horse and buggy to go and visit friends in the village because it was his last evening before going back to England. It was Charlie Ward the little redheaded kid from Yorkshire who shouted from across the barrack room, "Tim, Tim are you okay? You've been staring at that letter for a long time and I wasn't sure if you were still breathing. Looked like you were struck dead. Bad news Tim?"

"You could call it that, Charlie."

"Anything I can help with?"

"No, just a real good-looking old girlfriend of mine went and got married. I still have a crush on her and I was sitting here thinking that the guy she married is a real creep."

"Oh! Is that all Tim? Why don't you come out with us tonight? We are going to Lincoln. Boy! Tim, you should see the 'pieces of fluff' at the dances. Singles galore and the married ones whose husbands are overseas: Wow! Do they know a thing or two. Boy, oh boy! A good-looking Irish man like you will be smothered in females the first ten minutes. Come with us. It will get you ready for all those French girls when we eventually move over there."

"Sorry Charlie I'm a bit short of cash. Remember I was on fourteen days leave some weeks back, and I spent a lot of money on many women so I haven't caught up yet." Tim surprised himself. When he lied so well, it sounded truthful.

"Look Tim." Charlie put his hand in his pocket and produced two bills. "Here's two quid. We'll hitchhike in and I bet there will be a squadron truck around Lincoln somewhere that will bring us back before midnight. Pay me back when you can afford it."

Reluctantly Tim accepted the loan and promised Charlie he'd be ready at five and would meet him at the checkout gate. They were through the Air Force Service Police check at one minute to five and in the Black Swan pub twenty minutes later.

"Do all Irishmen drink Guinness?" It was Peter Mahaffy, Charlie's friend balancing six pints of beer on a tray. Two pints of Guinness were set in front of Tim who did not drink. Drinking age in Ireland was twenty-one and here he was at nineteen in British Air Force uniform in England with two pints of Guinness in front of him. His friends were already drinking big gulps of the famous Dublin thirst quencher.

"What will we drink to?" asked Charlie.

"Let's see. Oh yes, to the girls we've known, and to the ones we are going to know tonight." Tim raised his glass and drank his first Guinness. Charlie spoke up again, "Tim, let's drink to the one that ditched you and hope the creep she married keeps her pregnant every year until she has ten kids. She ought to have waited for a good Irishman like you, Tim O'Neill."

Tim was certain his anger must have shown on his face, but how were Charlie or Peter to know he was still desperately in love with Kathleen, now a married woman? He raised his glass but did not drink to that toast. Then he downed all of his first Guinness.

"You drink like a seasoned Irishman. Join us anytime, Tim," said Peter.

They had cheese sandwiches and more beer. Tim was feeling much better. By the time they entered the big dance hall Kathleen O'Brien and George O'Conor were not foremost in his thoughts. His thoughts were a little fuzzy.

Charlie introduced him to a dark-haired girl. "This is Tim, straight from Ireland, Sharon, so take good care of him."

Sharon had a good figure. Tim felt shy when she took his hand then led him to the dance floor. In the dimly lighted hall she pressed close to him as they moved among the throng of servicemen and their partners.

During the evening Tim danced with a number of girls. He couldn't remember how many beers he had. Shortly after nine, Sharon took his arm and guided him to the crowded dance floor, where they danced a slow waltz. Tim liked the feel of her long dark hair and the silky material of her dress in his hands.

"Are you having a good time?"

"Sure I am, thanks to you," he replied.

"I live just around the corner. Would you like a cup of tea or another drink before you go back? We have an hour before you're due to be in camp. I have a car and petrol, so I can give you a ride to the air base."

Tim hesitated, "But I came with Charlie so I should go back with him." Her green eyes widened in surprise. With a whimsical smile, she said, "Tim, my friend, I have never met a shy Irish lad like you before. Don't you know Charlie and Peter will not be here to go with you? They left with Margaret Murphy and Betty Graham an hour ago so it's just you and me." Then she kissed him. They finished the dance and Sharon guided Tim to the door, where she picked up her coat at the check counter. With a smile and a mischievous light in her eyes she looked up at the big handsome boy, put her arm through his and said, "It's this way."

In a few minutes she turned the key to a small but tidy and warm living room. Sharon threw her coat over a chair and invited Tim to make himself at home. He took off his tunic and sank into the soft cushioned chesterfield. Sharon returned with two glasses of brandy. "Just a wee drop of good brandy, Tim to warm our innards and to properly introduce ourselves. My name is Sharon Marshal and all I know is you are Tim the shy good-looking boy from the Emerald Isle. A three-letter name sure as hell doesn't do justice to what I see."

Tim looked up into questioning green eyes as she stood with the two glasses in her hands. She handed him one as he spoke. "My name is Timothy O'Neill from County Donegal in the Republic of Ireland, where I'm called Timothy. Here my friends call me Tim." Sharon sat beside him then clinked her glass with his. "To us, dear Timothy O'Neill from County Donegal in the Republic of Ireland. Now tell me about yourself. Have you a girlfriend or girlfriends? Bet you were in great demand and there must be many Irish colleens mourning their loss." Tim didn't wish to say he had only kissed one girl in his life and that she was now married. "Sharon, you're right. I'll have to find a half dozen or more to make up for the ones I left behind in Ireland."

With a questioning look Sharon said, "Sure Tim, I kinda thought it would be that way." Tim told her about his family, especially his little brother, Kevin. He talked about the harvests and peat cutting and the few shillings he earned to help with home necessities. He purposely omitted Kathleen O'Brien. Another brandy, and it was time to return to the air base.

Tim was getting out of Sharon's car when Charlie and Peter alighted from a crowded Air Force truck. "Did you make out?" Charlie asked with a grin as they joined the line-up at the main entrance to the air base.

Not quite sure what Charlie meant by the question, Tim answered, "Sure I did."

"Wow! Good for you Tim, my boy. First night!. You're a fast worker, Timothy O'Neill."

Tim evaded an answer and showed his pass to the Service Police at the gate and was soon tucked into his single bed thinking about a beautiful girl with mischievous green eyes, and listening to the chatter of those who had been out for the evening recounting their escapades.

On several occasions during the next two weeks Tim joined Charlie and Peter at the Black Swan pub. Each time Sharon turned up, and by listening to tidbits of the conversation he was sure that Charlie had arranged for Sharon to be present. Once Charlie cut in with, "Hi Irishman, don't corner all the beauty!" Soon after that Sharon suggested that Tim pop around to her place for a snack. "I want to learn more about Ireland and Tim O'Neill in quieter surroundings. We have almost three hours till midnight. I'll drive you back to the base."

Along the wartime darkened street, close together under Sharon's umbrella, they ran the gauntlet of pouring rain to Sharon's little cosy flat just around the corner from Elm Street. With that mischievous light in her eyes she asked, "Tea or brandy?"

"Brandy please!"

Sharon held up the bottle, "Enough for two good drinks each." She brought two glasses and poured a drink.

Tim told her about the golden sands, the heather-covered hills, the beautiful glens and the poor living conditions, and of his ambition to see the world, even the other side of the world, New Zealand and Australia. He would do all that and more when the war ended.

Sharon sat very close to him and listened intently to his every word. Twice, she leaned close to interrupt him with a kiss full on his lips. She felt his hesitation and smiled, remembering his comment about all the Irish Colleens he had left behind. She thought, Timothy O'Neill from County Donegal in the Republic of Ireland, you have so much to learn.

She poured two more drinks. "Just sip your brandy, Tim and I'll be back in a minute."

Tim relaxed in the cushions and relished his drink and thought this was better than being at his air base.

Sharon returned, picked up her glass and sat beside him. She'd changed into a flimsy negligee, and when she crossed her legs it fell open showing the whiteness of her naked thighs. Tim sucked in his breath. He'd never been close to a woman wearing almost nothing.

Casually Sharon took his glass and put it on the coffee table. She undid his tie and unbuttoned his shirt. Tim felt powerless as she slowly undressed him. When she took his hand and placed it firmly on her breast he could feel the blood rushing through his veins and his heart battering his ribs. Sharon kissed him full on the lips, gently at first then more demandingly. Tim responded in kind, then he was borne away into the ecstasy and wonderment of his first sexual intimacy.

A long time passed before they spoke and when they did, both of their stories poured out. She told him about her husband who had been in the Air Force before the war. He was a pilot instructor killed a year before in a plane crash. Tim poured out his story of Kathleen, their love for each other and why he had lost her. It was the beginning of a new warmth, a union between two people who were searching for something, perhaps a mysterious and wonderful ending to a sadness in their hearts. Each had lost a loved one.

Sharon drove Tim to the air base, promising they'd meet again soon. They kissed goodnight. Tim turned and waved to her then passed through the checkpoint with a minute to spare before the midnight deadline.

"My Irish luck is holding so far," Tim thought but he knew his days in England would be numbered. He had to take advantage of being close to where Sharon lived. Two days later they had another date. After that Sharon was there each day or evening he was free.

There were many episodes and escapades during Tim's first winter months that storytellers would love to expound upon. It never ceased to amaze Tim how quickly loopholes and opportunities were pounced upon by some quick thinking servicemen. Not only to obtain extra leave time but anything that was in short supply, like chocolate, cigarettes, gasoline, and any other items that could be traded. Always there were those enterprising individuals who could come up with what you required, at a price, of course.

Charlie Ward was in that enterprising category. He didn't like paying black market prices for what he needed so he depended a lot on his own resourceful capabilities. One day after visiting an old aunt who lived near Lincoln, he trundled into base in a little Morris Minor car. Charlie claimed he had bought it from his aunt, but it was believed he had coerced the old dear into loaning it to him. Regular gasoline ration coupons would not come up with sufficient fuel to make many trips to Lincoln and the Black Swan Pub, but Charlie said he had a brain wave.

Gasoline in wartime was dyed different colours to distinguish aircraft fuel from commercial and that used by regular citizens. The dyes used were red and green. The civilian fuel had no dye added. Spot checks were made, especially by Air Force Service Police, to ensure that the good and honest young men of the Air Force were not tempted to acquire gasoline for cars when filling up the aircraft they worked on. One Sunday morning Charlie Ward had the back seat out of his aunt's car. He had been working industriously cutting bottle shaped recesses like a wine rack in the wood framework below the seat. He had placed there five soda pop bottles with the spring loaded caps that ensured a no-leak fit.

"What's in the bottles?" asked Peter Mahaffy.

"It's not Dublin Guinness," retorted Charlie.

"Doesn't smell like it," was Peter's reply.

Al Stewart, the little cockney engine mechanic who worked with Charlie looked worried as he asked his question. "Are we supposed to sit on top of those?"

"You can stay here on the base if you'd prefer that," grinned Charlie.

To Al's next question, no one replied for a moment. "What happens if someone rear ends us?"

Charlie stopped what he was doing, looked up at Al and spoke in his most serious tone, "Al, my friend, if you're scared maybe you'd prefer to ride the bus to Lincoln. That's okay with me but remember there's no late bus from the Black Swan Pub and the air-base trucks always leave early. Now this little old vehicle powered with aviation fuel will have us back here in a flash and before the bewitching hour of one minute to midnight."

Al's worried look remained when he replied, "Yeah, Charlie, I know. A great big flash; that hundred-octane fuel is dangerous stuff."

Peter broke in with a question before the discussion mushroomed. "Why do you need two different types of gasoline?" Charlie had four bottles filled with aircraft hundred-octane gasoline and one with clear ordinary civilian ration product.

With a knowing air he said, "Look, guys, I know it would be too much for any one of you to figure out . . . probably overload your brain to think up this simple equation, so I'll explain. In the gas tank of this little buggy there is enough regular civilian gasoline which this law-abiding serviceman needs to motor off the base. Then my friends, down the road at a nice quiet spot the tank will run dry. Now that will be no problem 'cause with you three good men and true to stand around and hide from prying eyes, operation fill-up will begin from these bottles of wonderful hundred-octane gasoline, a gift from Air Ministry."

"Where did you steal the hundred octane?" Ignoring Tim's query, Charlie continued to lecture like a stern school teacher trying to make backward children understand how to solve a mathematical problem.

"I've worked it out that on four bottles this little buggy will take us to the Black Swan and back to that quiet spot not far from this here air base. Now if you Tim O'Neill will put your Irish brain in gear and if Al Stewart can wake up his London cockney grey matter surely between both of you, I can get an answer. What should my next move be after we've used those four bottles and we are parked with an empty tank in that quiet area on the way back?"

Quickly Tim retorted, "Use the other bottle of regular gasoline."

"See, Al, this Irishman thinks quicker than you."

"Ach! That was only a lucky guess," replied little Al. "Irishmen's brains are so slow they can't get past the turf carrying donkey and creel age."

"Better having a slow brain than none at all," bantered Tim.

Charlie continued, knowing he had started something that could escalate into trouble. "Now," he explained, "at all times when this little car sits minding its own business on the air-base parking lot the Service police snoops checking gas tanks will always find regular gas in her tank. Don't you guys think I'm smart?" All agreed but still voiced their opinion that two people would always be sitting for most of the journey on a gasoline bottle bomb.

Charlie's borrowed little car made many trips to Lincoln and back that early winter of 1939, and the bottle gasoline racket worked like a charm. Other Air Force personnel would ask, "How many miles to the gallon do you get, Charlie, because you seem to go a long way on your ration." Always he replied with the same answer, "I've got a secret carburettor, so a thimbleful takes my little car that long way you just mentioned." Charlie always dropped Tim off at Sharon's apartment, and Sharon would drive him back to the air base before the one minute to midnight deadline.

Close to their air base was a small community, and at the end of the village street stood a stone house painted white. It blocked passage to anyone who tried to continue in a straight line. At that point the road turned a sharp forty-five degrees to the left. There was no garden, no sidewalk, or any other barrier to protect this house from those who for some reason forgot to turn. Only its white painted stone walls stood as a warning to weary or intoxicated travellers that if they turned left they had traversed safely to within a few miles of the air base. If they didn't turn there would be a few additional marks on the white stone walls, and a story for each.

One night in early December, because of unexpected bad weather Charlie and his buddies picked up Tim at Sharon's place and were returning to the base in a snowstorm. It was the night Charlie went snow blind, at least that was his excuse. Peter who had too many drinks of Guinness was sound asleep in the rear seat and snoring happily and right now unconcerned that he was sitting on a gasoline-bottle bomb. He had bet little Al that he could down more Guinness than any London Cockney. Little Al won the bet but Charlie maintained Peter was the real winner, because he was drunk and broke, so little Al had to pay. Under protest of course.

Tim was in the front passenger seat and for miles the little car had slithered all over the road. Charlie was wearing his glasses and had his nose pressed almost against the windshield. He kept saying, "Can't slow down. Got to keep this little girl moving or we'll be stuck all night in the snow." Then he kept repeating, "Sure as hell is difficult to see where we're going."

Little Al's slurred reply was, "You're an ass Charlie. You're so close to the windshield your drunken breath has fogged it and your glasses too. Why don't you stop and let me drive?"

Back came the reply, "All you London cockneys know how to drive is a two-wheeled hand cart. Tim O'Neill here is sober like myself and I wouldn't let him drive. Why don't you go to sleep like your drunken friend?" And that's what Al did. So coming into the village there were two sleeping drunks in the rear seat as Charlie gunned the little Morris down what was now a one-lane roadway. The car's headlights with wartime restrictive blackout covers gave a minimum of light reaching only a few yards. In this almost whiteout condition Charlie was driving by memory of where and how the road turned and twisted. The snow was falling in large flakes as they approached the white stone house at a fair speed. Too late Tim realised that Charlie had no intention of slowing and there it was, the white house, a few yards ahead. Tim grabbed at the steering wheel and yanked it towards himself. The car did two or three crazy doughnuts in the snow, ending up with a crash as its left side and the white house made contact.

"Holy Mother of God!" came an exclamation from the now wide awake Al. "I told you, Charlie. You were fogging up the windows. Are you trying to blow us up?"

"I went snow blind, I tell you. I went snow blind!" cried Charlie. He was gripping the steering wheel as if he was certain it would disappear if he let go. Peter was still in a drunken sleep and Al was trying to push him back to an upright position after the sudden crazy stop. Charlie, gripping tightly to the steering wheel, made no comment. The motor had died, so quietly Tim said, "Might be a good idea to get going if we can start the motor."

Charlie turned the key in the ignition and presto it started. With snow flying everywhere he reversed and pointed the car in the right direction.

There was an exchange of verbal abuse from Peter when he was turfed out into a snow bank so they could get at the bottle of regular gasoline under the rear seat. Charlie wanted to leave him there but saner minds prevailed. Eventually they arrived back at the air base.

At breakfast Peter complained. "Our contact with the stone house could have resulted in a gasoline bottle bomb explosion and four less airmen to feed this morning." It was the last time the car was used. Charlie's story was he sold it back to his aunt, but others believed his aunt decided he had the loan of it long enough. Only Charlie knows what trouble he got into when she saw the damaged left side. The unanswered question was, What would her reaction be if she ever took out the back seat and found a nest neatly cut to hold five large pop bottles? Had Charlie taken out the empties before returning it?

Christmas 1939 was in its last two weeks, and hopes for better news were on many lips. Tim had no chance of getting home because he had had that unexpected leave when he took Kathleen to dinner and learned she was marrying George O'Conor mainly for her family's betterment.

Tim and Sharon spent a wonderful Christmas together. He invited her to the air-base Christmas party. Her mom and dad came down from Coventry to spend Boxing Day with them at Sharon's apartment. Tim and Sharon had spent happy laughter-filled hours decorating it for the occasion.

Months passed and what was called 'the phoney war' on the Western Front continued into 1940. Hitler, although expected to, had not attacked Britain. It was reported in London that the 300,000 children evacuated in case of air attacks had returned home.

During this time Tim and Sharon took advantage of every hour they could be together. Spring was in the air and soon it would be the merry month of May. Fate had given them time to know each other and realise there was more than friendship in their relationship. War-time has a habit of rushing or ending decision making. When Sharon drove him to the air base each night, they clung to each other knowing their next date may never come. (Unknown to each of them their time together was running out fast.)

It was a Friday and Sharon picked Tim up at the air base. In his pocket he had a weekend pass good until that deadline of one minute to midnight on the Sunday night. Then it would be off to somewhere in France. Tim did not tell Sharon right away as it felt so good just sitting beside this wonderful person. He wanted to cherish and hold on to these precious moments as long as possible.

Much later, after another of Sharon's home-cooked meals, he said, "There is something I have to tell you."

"And what might that be, secretive Irishman?"

When he explained what was happening, her green eyes, like beautiful jade, took on a sombre look.

"Timothy O'Neill, my man from the land of shamrocks, I love you, and will wait for you no matter how many months or years."

He took her in his arms and she whispered, "We have forty-eight wonderful hours and if it is our wish we don't have to sleep away even one little minute unless you and I agree to it."

They laughed a lot, made love, and spent most of the long week-end listening to radio music or dancing to the tunes of Tommy Dorsey's Big Band Orchestra on Sharon's record player. They sat on the floor eating fish and chips and drinking too much. Then falling into bed to wake up in each other's arms and talk for hours. It was a wonderful time for two people with their own separate tragedies. Sharon and Tim vowed that no matter what happened, no matter how long the war lasted, or what lay ahead, they would somehow keep contact, no matter where Tim was sent to. It was a tearful farewell at the air base. They waited until the one minute to midnight deadline before part-ing.

Tim lay awake for a long time, listening to the snores of some and the heavy breathing of others. His fellow comrades had divorced them-selves from the scary thoughts of their wartime future. His own thoughts were scattered. Tim hoped that George was taking good care of Kathleen, but he had strange intuitions that everything was not right and that disturbed him. Sharon was foremost in his thoughts. He had learned so very much in a short time with this wonderful lady. So with thoughts of two women Tim drifted off to sleep.

6:00 a.m. came swiftly with the cry to "rise and shine," and after the usual morning rush it was a shock to learn that he and thirty other men were being shipped out within the next four hours. They were to report at the adjutant's office immediately. Permission to leave the air base was denied.

During the hours that preceded their departure Tim tried without success to get a message to Sharon. It was a frustrated Timothy O'Neill who journeyed to the Port of Dover in Southern England where his contingent boarded an old camouflaged pleasure ship conscripted for war service. Tim's dream journeys weren't unfolding the way he had planned when he sat on Irish soil not so long ago. They crossed the rough waters of the English Channel to land at Calais. An air force truck and driver waited to whisk them off to an old French air base a few miles inland.

Before leaving England, Tim had written to Sharon and to his mother. In case the censor held up his letter, he had written a second one and Charlie had promised faithfully to find Sharon and deliver Tim's farewell.

At the French air base they were soon working at a furious tempo repairing damaged aircraft. Some aircraft returning to England would often take a passenger with them. It was still the early days, but there were rumours that the phoney war was over and that the real thing would soon engulf them. Divisions of the British expeditionary force commanded by General Lord Gort had been in France for some time, along with squadrons of Royal Air Force planes.

The Germans had invaded Norway in early April, and by the first day of May thousands of Norwegian troops had surrendered. If all the rumours were true, German armour would soon be launched against France, Belgium and Holland now that Norway and Denmark were under the Nazi heel. Tim and his buddies felt they had been sent into a very scary situation.

A few days later, May the tenth around 5:30 a.m., German airborne troops landed on bridges at Rotterdam and at Dordrecht and

Moerdijk in Holland. The phoney war on the western front certainly was over. Tim and his fellow ground crew got little sleep. They worked around the clock trying to keep the aircraft flying, but the old Fairey Battles were no match for Hitler's up-to-date superior aircraft. News on the 11th of May was that the Port of Calais had fallen the previous night to the German 10th Armoured Division. That would have been one of the Allies' evacuation ports.

A big percentage of base personnel had already gone to evacuation areas. Numerous non-combatant airforce personnel were hitching rides in aircraft flying back to England. A complete evacuation order was announced: "Ground personnel to report at vehicle transport area immediately."

Rumours were that the evacuation would be from Dunkirk on the coast as main ports were already in German hands. All serviceable aircraft were ordered to fly to England so they could participate from English bases in a massive air cover to protect those forces trying to embark at evacuation areas.

Tim did not like the idea of climbing into trucks and driving on roads with enemy tanks everywhere and the Luftwaffe's aircraft expected overhead. He volunteered with two engine mechanics, little Al Stewart and his buddy, Fred Armstrong, to stay with three volunteer pilots and their aircraft, which needed to be repaired. Their reward would be a flight back to home base, a very short skip across the channel. For Tim that would mean home to Sharon. He and the other two volunteers quickly went about the task of repairing the minor problems that kept the aircraft grounded. While they worked hurriedly to complete the job, they listened to sounds of battle coming from the coastal area where the evacuation was taking place. They could see German aircraft dive bombing and although it was miles away they realised it was their own and allied troops who were on the receiving end of those bombs. When the aircraft were ready for flight, the men drew lots as to rotation for takeoff. Wait until dusk was the plan. Take off at five-minute intervals skirting Dunkirk, then low over the channel to home.

The pilot and Fred the mechanic of 'A for apple' drew first off. Tim and Simon Beckett, the sandy-haired young pilot from 'B' flight would be number three. At sunset 'A for apple' was airborne, and it disappeared flying low over the trees that skirted the air base with Fred #2 mechanic as passenger. 'C for Charlie' was next. Squeezed in behind the pilot was little Al Stewart, the top notch #1 cockney mechanic who had worked so hard to get the aircraft serviceable. Tim operated the booster trolley to assist engine start-up. He watched as the single propeller moved slowly, hesitated and then sprang to life. Quickly disconnecting the power plug, he moved the trolley away. With a thumbs up sign Tim waved farewell as the aircraft moved slowly from its dispersal stand. Little Al gave him a return gesture with both thumbs up. He had promised to have a beer waiting for Tim at the air base in England.

Pulling the booster trolley towards the last aircraft, Tim listened. He could hear C for Charlie's engine and it sounded smooth. Dragging the heavy trolley, he thought, Now there are only two of us on this whole damned air base and that won't be for long. He could visualise himself sitting in the Black Swan with Sharon, a glass of brandy for her, and a big pint of Guinness for himself. He had been in France such a short time and already here was this chance to fly back to his Lincolnshire base and Sharon. "Just my good Irish luck," he thought.

Hearing the Merlin engine revving to full throttle, he watched the second aircraft as it headed into the wind scurrying across the grass.

Back to the task at hand, he didn't look up again but listened to the sound of "C for Charlie" diminish in the distance. He knew it was at the end of the takeoff run and lifting off for home. Tim could visualise little Al, scared because he had never flown before. Tim was excited now as he plugged in the booster trolley to this last winged escape chariot. Simon gave him the thumbs-up signal. Tim was about to press the button, hoping there was enough juice left to turn the prop, when he heard a sharp staccato sound and the scream of a Merlin engine. Moving slightly away from the trolley, Tim looked up as the number two aircraft came hurtling back across the air base in a vain attempt to get away from a German M.E. 109 whose cannon shells were ripping it to pieces. Al and the pilot must have been airborne less than a minute when the Messerschmidt jumped them. Tim stood in horror and utter disbelief when the crippled aircraft swept past in flames almost at ground level. Its wing tip was not more than a hundred feet from him. It was almost completely enveloped in flames. For a split second, by the light of the flames, Tim glimpsed the face of little Al behind the pilot. Then "C for Charlie" plunged into the ground and cartwheeled its way in a great ball of fire across the airfield then exploded. The ghostlike silhouette of the M.E. 109 disappeared in the dusk.

Al's first flight had ended.

Stunned for the moment, Tim was immobile. Suddenly he catapulted into action, yelling at Simon and gesturing that he should get out quickly. Tim dashed for the cover of a slit trench some distance away and dove in head first. From experience he knew the German fighter pilot would be back. After a few moments he thought, Where the hell is Simon? He knew where the slit trench was. God knows they had all used it two days earlier when another German aircraft had strafed the air base. It was May 29th and Tim could have bet by what he had seen in the western sky today that all German aircraft would be concentrating on Dunkirk area. This M.E. must have been a stray, probably going back to base for more fuel. Hope he's almost dry and won't chance another circuit. Damn that Simon anyway! He always was a slowpoke. All he had to do was jump down and follow me. His canopy was open and he wasn't strapped. Tim took a deep breath and peered over the top of the slit trench just as the M.E. 109 came roaring out of the dusk. Its cannon shells were ripping the ground open in a straight furrow to their last hope of freedom. Simon was out of the cockpit looking skyward making no attempt to move. Dusk was turning to darkness but there was light flickering across the air base from the burning pyre of "C for Charlie." Simon seemed oblivious to danger. He stood with one arm reaching out so his hand could rest on a blade of the stilled propeller as if he were posing for a picture. Simon seemed to be frozen there and was still looking to the heavens when the cannon shells reached his aircraft. With a great whoosh Simon and the plane disappeared in one massive explosive sheet of flame that turned the dusk to a bloody daylight.

Huddled well down into the slit trench, his whole body trembling, Tim realised he was crying, not from fear but sheer frustration. "Why, Simon? Why didn't you run? Why did you just stand there? That was committing suicide!"

The enemy aircraft made two more low passes then soared away into the darkening sky. Knowing the Germans must be very near Tim pulled himself together. He heaved his unwilling body out of the protective trench. Taking one look at the two burning wrecks, he walked away from the scene. It seemed strange to him that no French inhabitants of the nearby village had come to investigate. Fifteen minutes later he walked down the one main street and realised it was deserted. A sign that the Germans must be close by. A little panic-stricken and still in shock at recent events, Tim started to run and soon reached the open countryside. He knew which direction to go to reach Dunkirk where the British and French armies were evacuating. He would make a super effort to get there.

Looking westwards he could see great flashes of light in the sky. On this soft late spring night air came the rumble of heavy gunfire. He knew that many hundreds of servicemen were dying over there while thousands of others, he hoped, were being rescued. Tim was becoming very enthusiastic about being one of them.

The country road twisted its way westward. He knew that and was familiar with its poor surface and crazy curves. He decided to get off the narrow road and make his way as straight west as possible. His plan was to walk through fields but parallel to this snakelike ribbon probably now being used by German armour. Anyway he reckoned by taking to the open country he'd cut off all those twists and turns. The distance to the coast would be much shorter.

Putting his plan into action, Tim trudged for an hour through grasslands and across ditches. Once skirting a farmhouse he was discovered by a barking but friendly dog and he had to chase it away several times before it finally got the message.

He stopped to listen at ten-minute intervals. This time instead of only the country night sounds, he distinctly heard the clank of tanks. At that point he was very close to the road where it turned forty-five degrees to the right, then straight for about a mile before taking another forty-five-degree turn left continuing westward. He knew this stretch of road, as a few days ago Tim and little Al were detailed to ride in a transport truck to pick up supplies at a small town.

Tim lay down in the grass close to the first bend and waited. Almost immediately the clatter of heavy armour was close by and out of the dark came the first tank. It slithered around the forty-five-degree turn too fast. He thought it was going to slip sideways across the deep ditch on the opposite side of the road. It regained forward momentum and straightened out then passed so close. He could see the head and shoulders of the tank commander in the open hatch. For a long time Tim lay there and counted fourteen tanks as they passed.

Following the tanks were numerous armoured personnel carriers and an assortment of other military equipment. Tim waited for almost twenty minutes after the last vehicle had gone by before crossing the road to the open countryside. Sometimes he ran till he was out of breath. Sure a confident bunch of bastards, he thought. A long ribbon of armour on a country road and they must have been cocksure no British aircraft would be harassing them!

It was on one of Tim's scary dashes across fields and streams that he goofed. He had decided to widen the gap and stay farther away from the road, putting a greater distance between himself and other German armour. He walked for another half hour then started jogging. He felt good although he stumbled many times over unseen obstacles, none big enough to cause him injury. Once he rolled to the bottom of a grassy slope and got up swearing all the Irish oaths he could remember and all the ones he'd learned since leaving that lush green land.

With a feeling of elation at not being discovered, he plodded his way westward. This feeling of security may have led him to forget caution. He did not stop to listen periodically as he had been doing.

Jogging along in the dark he fell three times in the space of a few minutes. He was losing that confident feeling and didn't realise a tiny bit of panic was creeping into his actions. He came to a small stream too wide to cross by jumping from a standing position. First he knelt down and tasted the water. It seemed clear and pure so he quenched his thirst. Tim peered across the darkness. He was attempting to judge the distance as best he could. He stepped backwards a few paces then took a run at it. He flew through the air and made a perfect two-point landing on the opposite soft bank only to find himself face to face with a German patrol who were as surprised as he was. There was a moment of inaction before he was grabbed by two burly soldiers. Tim wasn't sure if it was fear, shock, or just plain consternation that he felt. The Germans seemed equally astounded at this unarmed British airman jumping into their midst.

The patrol leader spoke English and questioned Tim. "Who else was out there? Where was he going? Where was he from?" The leader tried to explain that Tim was lucky not to have been shot. Apparently the patrol itself had become lost and had stopped to read the map. If Tim had been cautious he might have noticed the glow from their small map-reading light. If the patrol had been spread out it was highly probable that a figure jumping towards them would have immediately drawn their fire.

Now Tim was a prisoner of war and, with his Irish luck, still alive.

Charlie Ward found Sharon Marshal in her cosy rented apartment a few minutes from the dance hall where she and Tim had met. He gave her Tim's farewell letter. She had not received the original he had mailed.

"Censor hold up," suggested Charlie. "They always do that just to feel important."

He accepted tea and cookies, and on leaving promised to keep her informed if he got information on Tim. Sharon thanked Charlie and assured him she would probably be the first to get a letter and that proved to be right. It had been written just two days after his arrival at the French air base. She kept his written words in their envelope under her pillow. As days passed, she memorised every word but still read it each night before going to sleep.

On the tenth of May, Sharon heard a BBC news broadcast that German army forces had reached Holland, then Belgium, then France. During the last days of May, tens of thousands of Allied troops were being evacuated from a French beach named Dunkirk. She listened to every radio broadcast hoping and praying that one of those many thousands saved would be her Tim.

Charlie and his friend Peter Mahaffy came often to help boost her morale and maintained Tim would be one of those evacuated. "He will just walk in some of these days and say, 'Hi, I'm home.'"

Weeks passed and then came the 22nd of June when France capitulated and her leaders signed an armistice with Germany. There was no word of Tim. Sharon's morale was shattered. It had been eighteen months since her husband was killed. Could it be that now her Irish Tim O'Neill was also dead? The next two months she lived in despair. Each day and each hour she waited for someone to come and tell her, "Tim is dead" or "Tim is alive." She didn't have his home address in Ireland nor had Charlie or his friend Peter. At her request they contacted their air base adjutant and as weeks passed the information was the same. Aircraftsman Timothy O'Neill was missing in action and that was all.

Sharon was watering the geraniums in her window box at sunset one beautiful evening in July when Charlie brought her the news. "Tim is a prisoner of war in Germany." With a whoop of joy Sharon hugged him, then she and Charlie danced up and down the sidewalk with Sharon laughing and crying at the same time. Suddenly she stopped and said, "Lets drink a toast Charlie, to Timothy O'Neill of Rathmullan, County of Donegal in the Republic of Ireland who will someday come home to me." Then she looked inquiringly at Charlie. "How did you find out he was a prisoner?"

Charlie smiled, "One of our Service Police came to my barrack room then escorted me to the Adjutant's Office. All he said was, 'The adjutant wants to see you.' Thought I was in trouble until the Service Police was dismissed. Tim's family received the Air Ministry telegram informing them that he was now a prisoner of war in Germany. His mother wrote to the air base Commanding Officer asking that a Charlie Ward be told his friend Tim was alive and a prisoner. Tim must have written home sometime telling his mother what good buddies we were. I've got his home address for you, and I'm told if you write to his mother she will send you information on how to mail letters and parcels to Tim. He must have told her about you too."

Sharon's green eyes were full of light and hope. She drove Charlie back to the air base and on returning home immediately wrote to Tim's mother.

She received a very short letter in return. Just a few words of a mother rejoicing that her son was alive, but no words of comfort for Sharon except for what she needed most: the address of his prison camp and his prisoner number. It was a line of communication to her Timothy O'Neill.

The late summer days passed quickly then it was fall, and the dark winter evenings were just around the corner. Sharon wrote to Tim every week and sent him a number of parcels containing clothing and cigarettes. It was well known that cigarettes were currency in prison camp. She hoped some of her letters and parcels would reach him. The war news was not good and predictions were it might last for years.

5

Dunraven House, Ireland, 1940

Mary Jane found Kathleen making tea in the kitchen. With a sparkle in her blue eyes and a big smile that spread her rosy cheeks almost from ear to ear she exclaimed, "I have good news for you my dear. As courier for one Michael O'Neill I deliver to you this note, and Michael said he was sure you would appreciate the information. With tears in her eyes, Kathleen absorbed the message.

Timothy was being held prisoner in Germany and was OK. The note gave his prison camp number and mailing instructions, and also his personal prisoner-of-war number. It was the beginning of a secret mailing system.

When Kathleen decided to write, she wondered whom she could trust to mail the letters. Mary Jane was the only one, but Kathleen would be putting her in an awkward position if something went wrong and George or Cora found out.

Mary Jane kept the address as Kathleen was afraid to have it. Mary Jane then took the letters home and addressed them. She travelled to Rathmelton, Letterkenny, and sometimes to Strabane in the British part of Ireland to post them on her day off. It was too risky mailing the letters at the village post office close to Dunraven House. Some employees might talk about letters going to Timothy O'Neill in prison camp with cook Mary Jane Kernaghan as the sender.

Kathleen always repaid Mary Jane for her bus fares and paid her handsomely for the trouble. The correspondence became Kathleen's oasis in the terrible marriage into which she had sold herself for what she thought was security and happiness for herself and her family.

It was a warm Irish Sunday morning in August and bright sunshine glinted on Kathleen O'Conor's auburn hair as she waited at the grand double-door entrance to Dunraven House. Kathleen was crooning softly to the baby in her arms. Her little girl had been born three weeks previous on July 27th.

Kathleen was immaculately dressed in an Irish green tailored suit and white blouse. Her child was wrapped in the whitest and most expensive shawl that Cora O'Conor could buy. Kathleen's beauty was unchanged except for the darkness under her eyes, the telltale sign of her unhappiness and the terrible pressure she lived with as George O'Conor's wife.

It was christening day for little Evelyn Cora O'Conor, and James stopped the great black Daimler limousine close to his daughter-in-law and her baby. He was thrilled at having a little girl as a grandchild, and fussed over making them both comfortable before George and Cora's arrival. Cora had insisted on both of the child's names, Evelyn, after Cora's mother and of course her own to be carried on for posterity. There was no consideration for Kathleen or her parents. The others sat in silence during the short drive to chapel. Cora prattled on in her high voice, laying out all her plans for the christening dinner to be held later in the day.

To Kathleen's relief the baby slept throughout the service and stirred only a little when Father Cullen sprinkled the holy water on her forehead.

Shawn and Maureen O'Brien, although ignored by Cora, were at the service with daughter Eileen and their son Brian. Now outside chapel they gathered with other parishioners congratulating the new parents. James O'Conor made a point of seeking out Kathleen's father and mother to shake their hands and to congratulate them on becoming grandparents.

For a long time they talked in a congenial manner then continued to converse with the circle of well-wishers including Father Cullen, who was admiring the baby. Cora O'Conor stood apart by herself, frustrated and angry that her intention to whisk the child back to

Dunraven House immediately after the service and so away from Kathleen's parents and friends was being thwarted.

Later that day a large group of invited guests was being entertained in the mansion's lounge before dinner. At Kathleen's insistence her family and friends were among those invited. Cora had been flitting around like a butterfly from one group to another trying not to miss any of her high-society friends.

It was close to dinner call when Cora made a quick and furtive exit to the dining room where she opened a package of gold trimmed cards. On each one was printed a guest's name and Cora placed the cards where she had decided each guest would sit. The cards for Kathleen's parents and other family members and also those of their guests were placed far away from the head table and Kathleen's new little daughter. With a satisfied smile Cora stood back and surveyed her handiwork.

Cook Mary Jane Kernaghan was working industriously in her kitchen preparing the grand menu for dinner when Cora entered to verify everything was in order.

There was one person who saw Cora's furtive exit from the lounge to the dining room, and Kathleen's intuitions were to investigate. On the pretence of checking with the cook, she asked her mother to hold the baby. From a screened advantage area in Mary Jane's kitchen, Kathleen watched Cora place the cards and realised what she was doing. She whispered to Mary Jane, "I'll be back." Mary Jane's eyes twinkled with delight. She didn't know Kathleen's intentions but if they were to upset Cora, she was all for it.

Quickly Kathleen returned to her mother, took the baby, and mingled with the guests until Cora returned. With a casual air she approached Cora who was already holding the attention of a number of her friends by telling stories about wonderful George when he was very young. "Excuse me Cora. Little Evelyn never cries when in your arms. I've got to visit the ladies room. Would you please take her for a short while?"

Father Cullen on his way to the men's room was both thirsty and hungry so he took a peek into the dining room to see if there were signs of food to be served soon. He was surprised to see the new baby's beautiful mother changing place-sitting cards. With a chuckle he hastily retreated without being observed.

Cook Mary Jane opened the French doors leading to the dining room. It was the prearranged signal dinner would be served in approximately fifteen minutes. Cora took her cue and made the announcement.

"Ladies and gentlemen please make your way to the dining room. If you haven't finished your drinks feel free to take them with you. To make seating arrangements more compatible to everyone, small gold-trimmed cards have been placed at each dinner setting. Just find your name and claim your seat. Isn't that simple? You have approximately ten to fifteen minutes before the first course. The dining-room bar will be open so those guests without drinks can replenish, relax, find your name and seat. If you have not met the person sitting next to you, introduce yourself. I know you will find them interesting." Cora excused herself to check with kitchen staff and insure their culinary efforts were up to Dunraven House standards. By asking unnecessary questions, Mary Jane kept conversation with Cora longer than usual on this kitchen inspection.

When Cora returned to the dining room almost all the guests were seated but something was drastically wrong. At the head table were Kathleen's mother and father. Cora was livid with rage. Someone had changed the cards. Who could it be? James wouldn't dare meddle in her dinner plans. That was her domain and no one knew of the gold-trimmed cards. Secretly she had had them printed and delivered only to herself.

Her face darkened for suddenly she remembered. Kathleen had asked her to hold the little one until she returned from the ladies' room. That was it and Mary Jane Kernaghan must have been a conspirator. They would both pay for this. At the head table immediately to the right of Cora's seat was her son George, then her husband James and Kathleen's father, Shawn O'Brien, who were in deep conversation. Next, Kathleen's brother, Michael, now eighteen years old, and his beautiful young cousin, Mary Kennedy, were conversing and laughing happily.

Cora couldn't make a scene in front of this gathering. She had to control herself, but the O'Briens had seated themselves where she had placed cards for Judge Henry Moffat and his wife, and Sean O'Hara, lawyer and prosecutor from Belfast, with his second wife, Clara. Cora took her own place and realised the seat to her left was vacant and the card was gone. George was supposed to be seated there next to his wife and child.

Kathleen smiled happily. Her mother and sister Eileen occupied the chairs to her left so her family had their rightful place at the head table. The best seats at the guest table were occupied by Kathleen's relatives and friends.

Cora had trouble containing her anger and frustration. She was already planning a showdown with Kathleen, and if Mary Jane was involved she would be fired. George asked, "Why Mother, did you separate me from my wife and child? Did you make a mistake putting out your cards?" "No," hissed Cora. "Someone changed them and they will pay a high price." Then she almost spluttered in exasperation when Father Cullen, a glass of rum and Coke in one hand and his gold-trimmed card in the other, sat beside her. "It is a great honour Cora to sit at your left hand." Then holding up his card for her to see, he exclaimed, "I took it with me to the bar to ensure no one would change my seating."

The good Father had already had a little too much to drink. James, realising someone had upset Cora's seating plans, did not calm matters by saying, "I like this arrangement. Cora, you and Father Cullen at the centre of this very important gathering of two united families. You have males to your right Cora, and to your left Father Cullen has beautiful ladies. You did a good job." The good Father leaned over the exasperated Cora towards James, raised his rum and Coke and said, "I'll drink to that, James O'Conor."

Cora was still shaking with anger when Mary Jane's staff started serving the first course. Father Cullen nudged Cora, "Would you like me to say grace?" All she could muster was an almost inaudible, "Yes." Shakily his Reverence stood up and steadied himself with a hand on Cora's shoulder then raised both hands for silence. He prayed for blessing on the food about to be served, then for a blessing on the new little 'soul' sleeping so peacefully. "She is born into these two wonderful families where a union of those with abundance of worldly goods and those less advantaged have blended. As we can all see at this head table, they have a happy and understanding togetherness. We give thanks for this gathering to celebrate the beginning of a new life — little Evelyn Cora O'Conor. We pray for our host and hostess, James and Cora O'Conor, for George and Kathleen, the happy parents of this wonderful new baby. May the families continue to enjoy love, understanding and peace that shows and shines its light from the faces of these fine people. In your name Lord, we give thanks. Amen."

Father Cullen's whisper to Cora was audible for all to hear. "How was that Cora? I need another rum. Do you think someone could bring me one?" James O'Conor was enjoying his wife's discomfort, and on hearing the Father's request he called one of the servants to comply with the good man's needs.

For Kathleen the christening was a success. Her parents had obtained their rightful place at the head table, but she knew there would be some confrontation with Cora. When that confrontation came, Kathleen stood her ground and felt she came out a winner. She believed she had convinced Cora that she alone had changed the gold-trimmed cards and that Mary Jane had not been involved.

With fire in her eyes, Kathleen informed Cora, "When the north wing changes are completed, it will be my domain and you Cora, will not meddle in any matters concerning little Evelyn. It is going to be my home. I will not bar you from visiting but if you step out of line Cora, with your dirty tricks, you will not have time with them. This mansion is big enough to create what could be called sealed borders. With my new kitchen and dining room I will be cooking most of my family's meals. My guests will sit beside their friends and not where Cora O'Conor would have put them. I'm sorry it has turned out this way but that's how it is going to be. I will protect my children and myself from you. I want to show and teach them how ordinary people live. There are many wonderful honest, trustworthy, loving and God-fearing families in this world who are very poor but equal or better in character than we are. I feel sorry for you Cora. You will probably die an unhappy and lonely old lady."

Cora for the first time in her life was speechless. When she recovered and gathered the words to rebuff her daughter-in-law, Kathleen was gone. Afterwards Cora had been very evasive, and during household communications Kathleen was surprised that she refrained from mentioning the one-sided battle of words. It just wasn't Cora's nature not to retaliate in some manner.

Even though Kathleen came out the winner with Cora, with George it was a different story. She knew one night a few weeks later when he stumbled drunk into their bedroom that he was in one of his brutal moods, but Kathleen did not expect and was not prepared for the beating she got. His closed fists pummelled her for minutes and only when she fell to the floor almost unconscious did he stop. She heard his drunken slurred words. "Don't you ever talk to my mother again without showing respect. You destroyed the christening banquet for my daughter and made fools out of Mother and me by changing the table sittings she had arranged. Your family and friends are tramps. I dragged you into a society where you don't belong. You don't understand or appreciate what I've done for you but my children will and never will you bar my mother from visiting Evelyn or any of our children to be born in the future. It will always be an open door for her. Do you understand, you O'Brien tramp?"

George opened another bottle from his own private bedroom stock. In a short time he drank enough for him to sleep where he was, in the chair close to the big window where Kathleen had sat ages ago with the drapes partly drawn. Where she had watched the full moon's waning light touch lush green fields and had prayed for strength to maintain the appearance of a happy bride. Kathleen's lip was split, two teeth were loose, blood was dribbling from her mouth, one eye was closed and she felt sure a rib was broken or cracked. Struggling to the bathroom she applied cold wet cloths to stop the bleeding. Bruises and ribs would take their own time to heal.

Next morning George warned Kathleen to say she fell down stairs after drinking wine. It was George's father who surprised them when Kathleen was feeding Evelyn her breakfast bottle. "George that damned fox has been in the hen house again and we have lost . . ." Then he saw Kathleen's face. "My God child, what happened to you?" George got two words out, "She fell . . ." and it was there Kathleen cut him off. "Your son, proud and brave O'Conor that he is, was drunk again last night and he beat me because it was me who changed the seating cards at our daughter's christening dinner, and I don't apologise for that. My family are as important to me as Cora's friends are to her, and I told Cora that. So your big hero son and heir decided to beat me for being honest. I am afraid for my child and any other children we may have. Now that I have told you I will probably get beaten again for doing so. I am also pregnant with my second child, and I don't wish to lose it. Do you James O'Conor?" James stood in horrified silence as he listened to this beautiful proud young mother and child. He looked at her battered face, her black eye and her swollen lips and then at his six-foot strong son. In three strides he crossed the space between them, but George's fist made first contact and knocked his father to the floor. James O'Conor in shocked surprise rose slowly and wiped blood from his mouth, and while taking off his jacket said, "George, you shouldn't have done that. The whipping has taught you nothing regarding respect for other human beings whether they be Dunraven workers or your own wife. You don't have one shred of normal decency but seem to enjoy dishing out pain and suffering. I'm going to show you and make you feel what pain and suffering is like."

The two men fought ferociously for ten minutes and Kathleen thought her father-in-law was going to kill his son. James beat George until he was pleading for mercy, but none was shown until a final blow knocked George unconscious. James dragged his son's limp body outside where he poured pails of cold water on the still form until he saw conscious movement. His father stood over him and a few workers watched from a distance. "If you ever lay a finger against Kathleen again or her child or my future grandchildren, I will kill you. Do you understand?" George nodded.

His father grabbed him by the shirt front and pulled him to a sitting position and held him there. "I asked you do you understand?"

"Yes, yes!" replied the frightened George.

In disgust James O'Conor let go and left his son to crawl, stumble, or walk if he could, to find help. When James O'Conor returned, Kathleen was holding baby Evelyn to her breast and sobbing. James' face was bloodied and his knuckles were skinned. His voice trembled with emotion. "Kathleen, my dear, I'm deeply sorry is all I can say, but it is from the heart. I love you and I will try to protect you and the child from George and also from Cora." He put out his hand, touched her auburn hair, then turned and left the room.

Work on the restoration and refurbishing of the north wing was completed before Christmas. Little Evelyn at five months was the wonderful bright star in Kathleen's troubled life.

In her own kitchen Kathleen prepared the festive Christmas dinner and served it in her own dining room to a happy and delighted group, her father, mother, and sister Eileen. Also brother Michael, who had one week before followed Timothy's footsteps and joined the Royal Air Force and volunteered for aircrew.

Kathleen was surprised that George volunteered to help with the dinner preparations. He was a wonderful host, and reminded her of the charming, kind, gentle young man she thought she knew in those days before their marriage. But Kathleen noticed that George was paying much attention to her younger sister Eileen, who was blossoming into a very beautiful young lady now in her seventeenth year.

The new year and spring of 1941 were busy and interesting times for Kathleen. With Mary Jane's help she had put her own final touches to the refurbishing of her own domain. They had had a wonderful time arranging and rearranging furniture, picking colours for drapes, bed covers, and so on. That resulted in necessary and unnecessary trips to make purchases. Everywhere she went Kathleen took little Evelyn with her. Numerous times James O'Conor was happy to volunteer his services as chauffeur. A number of times Cora was invited, but she declined.

It was springtime and the end of May on one of their final excursions to the big town of Letterkenny. The purchase to be was china for the beautiful cabinet James O'Conor had bought for Kathleen. He insisted on going along to look after little Evelyn, now almost ten months old. Leaving James in charge of the child. Mary Jane and Kathleen happily went about their purchases. The assistant was wrapping each piece of china very carefully in soft tissue paper, when there was an eruption of voices outside and the sound of hand clapping. Checking to see what was of great interest, Mary Jane, Kathleen, and the store clerk were surprised to see the Master of Dunraven House surrounded by numerous residents, but the main attraction was little Evelyn. James would place her standing in the centre of the circle, back up a few paces, and hold out his arms while Evelyn tottered her hesitant footsteps to him. He was so thrilled at seeing Kathleen, he shouted, "She's walking, she's walking, she's walking, Kathleen, to me. Look, watch, isn't it great?"

One would think this was the only child ever to take its first faltering steps, but James showed no embarrassment as he picked up Evelyn and turned to those who watched and said, "Isn't she great? She is my granddaughter, my first one but there will be more."

Kathleen's eyes had tears in them as her father-in-law with the unruly mop of red hair showed his emotions so openly to strangers. His genuine love for this little girl, and she knew also for herself, made her feel more secure when she thought of future years. Inwardly she prayed that James O'Conor would be around for a long, long time. On the way home he interrupted a number of conversations to say, "Imagine she took her first steps in this world to me. Isn't that great?" Of course, Mary Jane and Kathleen agreed it was very wonderful.

It had been ten months since Evelyn's christening, Kathleen's altercation with Cora, and the awful beating James O'Conor had given his son. George had become sullen and in one way satisfied his frustration by driving the outside staff to work even longer hours, calling for more and more production but giving nothing in return for their efforts. He was losing staff and did not replace them, just increased the load on others.

Very soon Kathleen's father was showing signs of overwork and she was concerned. Old Patrick seemed to thrive on the extra load. He was like a boxer in training, his bronzed body and rippling muscles could be envied by men much younger. On different occasions Kathleen had noticed bruises and cuts on Patrick's face. Once when he was working outside without his shirt, she saw an ugly recently healed scar on his back.

"What happened to your back, Patrick?" she asked.

He looked surprised at her question then with a quizzical expression and strange answer he replied, "I will take more care next time, Madam Kathleen." Then he stopped work, turned to her, leaned on his shovel and with questioning eyes continued, "I hope you are taking care of yourself, young lady."

Without hesitation she replied, "I am, Patrick, I am."

"Good," was his only retort as he continued with his chores.

Next day Kathleen asked her father about Patrick's bruises and healing wounds. She had seen them on several occasions over the past few months. His reply was in two words, "Your George." He then refused further explanation. Kathleen realised George was still settling old scores trying to work her father to death and beating up on Patrick. She had considered telling James as her father's welfare was at stake, but James seemed to have given his son more leeway since their fistfight. Perhaps George had convinced his father that he'd learned a lesson and had changed his outlook. Financial reports of areas under George's domination showed increased profit and output. Kathleen, Patrick and her father, plus the hard-pressed men and women forced to work long

hours knew how George obtained the good reports. George was becoming the most hated employer in the area.

James enjoyed his horses. He loved riding and was often away full
days with other gentry.

Cora and James went for an extended vacation, leaving George in
full control. There were numerous nights George did not return from
what were supposed to be day business trips. One morning George
told Kathleen he would be away for a few days on business. "Where
can I find you if there is an emergency?" she asked. "This is my business trip. Any emergency can wait until I return. I don't have to tell
you where my business dealings take me. I am master of Dunraven
House when my parents are absent and best for you to remember. I am
also your master."

Kathleen knew not to further the conversation. When George had
gone, she picked up little Evelyn and was off to find Mary Jane. As
usual she was working in her kitchen and in the process of packing a
lunch basket. "Who is this lunch for?" Kathleen asked. Before answering Mary Jane carefully set a large piece of fruit cake on top of sandwiches already in the basket. She had reserved a corner space beside
the sandwiches and cake for two large apples. Turning to Kathleen she
said, "That will keep things from moving. This is Patrick's lunch. He is
fixing a leak at the pump house for #2 well. It's the best water of our
four wells and we sure don't want it to go dry."

"Could I take his lunch to him?" Kathleen's question surprised Mary
Jane. With a solemn look she said, "Certainly Miss Kathleen, certainly!"
Carrying Evelyn and the lunch basket, Kathleen set out for #2 well.
Patrick was cleaning his hands on an old piece of cloth when she approached. His was a quizzical expression when he asked, "And what on
earth have I done to deserve this honour? Kathleen O'Conor bringing
my lunch?"

"It's a pleasure Patrick, and I volunteered because it is the opportunity I've waited for. James, Cora, and George are away so I felt the
time was right to visit with you."

"I don't have a chair out here. I wasn't expecting royal company."
Patrick reached out his hand and touched little Evelyn's hair. "Your
daughter is a sweet child, Madam Kathleen." He then picked up the
basket, looked serious and said, "That was a long way for you to carry
Evelyn and this. I don't know what Mary Jane has in here. It's usually

much more than I need. Let's put it on the old bench and the three of us can investigate."

Kathleen accepted a sandwich and a small piece of cake for Evelyn. Looking steadfastly she said, "Patrick, I wish to explain why I took this opportunity to visit with you. Very soon after our marriage I discovered George had a dark side and at times he was cruel. The evening prior to the time he whipped you it was at George's insistence I consume more than sufficient wine. In our bedroom that night it was horrible and under great mental pressure I exclaimed, 'Old Patrick was right, I should not have married you.' I am to blame that you suffered for my stupidity. It is the first clear chance I have had to tell you how very sorry I am that I caused you so much pain. Please accept my apologies. I know George is still settling, when he can, his own twisted thoughts on what he believes are old scores between both of you."

Patrick looked at this wonderful young woman and child. He was thinking what a waste it was that such a beautiful human being was married to George O'Conor, a monster in sheep's clothing. Patrick spoke quietly, "Kathleen, thank you for telling me, I had presumed something like that had happened. Certainly I except your apology but I don't blame you. The problems and fears I have are not only for you but for many of the workers, and rest solely on the shoulders of George O'Conor. I told him once there was a monster inside of him and I hoped it would destroy him before it destroyed too many people. So you see he has other scores to settle with me not just what you said to him. If you need help anytime in any way please ask. I appreciate this conversation and I will always be here for you if you need me."

Kathleen with tears in her eyes was about to pick up the basket to return the remnants of lunch but Patrick restrained her. "You have the child to carry my dear, I will return this to Mary Jane." Looking at the man who had known the dark side of George O'Conor's character and had through conversation with her father sent a warning to her family, Kathleen felt a warmth towards Patrick and held out her hand to him. As he grasped it she leaned forward and kissed his cheek. "Thank you Patrick McGuinness, you are a great gentleman." Then she turned and picked up little Evelyn. With her arms tight around her child, she took a shortcut through the fields to home. Five days later George returned home and immediately made the rounds checking on his employees.

Everything was in top shape, as Patrick had rallied the work crews to make sure George could find little fault in their work. Of course George did find fault with everything and then demanded extra hours of work, insinuating they had not been working to his expectations so now they would have to make for 'their little holiday.' Patrick was furious but could do nothing but control his anger.

6

Kathleen's second child was born on July 18, 1941. It was a healthy boy, and George was ecstatic. This time she insisted it was her turn to name the child. She won that right and introduced to the world Sean James O'Conor, male heir to Dunraven House. James O'Conor and Kathleen's father were delighted the boy had both their names. Cora made no comment. Another very important person also thrilled with the new baby was Evelyn, almost a year old, now walking and talking her own language. At first she was mesmerised by the little doll who could move and cry. Evelyn became her mother's very industrious little helper.

Kathleen's days were devoid of free time until the two children were asleep. She often lay on her bed watching them, thrilled at the wonderment of motherhood. Her great sadness was that she had no understanding and loving partner to join her in this rejoicing.

Her thoughts would go to Timothy and the terrible mistake she made that last night before he went away, when under the branched archways of the great oak trees, he told her of his love and asked if she would wait for him. If only she had investigated Patrick's warning, Perhaps her school friends and the crowd of boisterous young men at their marriage banquet could have told her George's dark secrets. To those who did not know his dark side, the wolf in sheep's clothing was the charming, handsome, well-spoken twenty-two-year-old heir to

Dunraven House and its estate. Many older ladies had been heard to say, "Wish I were twenty again! What a wonderful young man!"

Christmas 1941 was a pleasant one. Kathleen had her parents and sister for Christmas dinner with James and Cora, who was seriously ill. It was the first time James and George had been together with Kathleen's family since she had switched the seating arrangements at the christening. James O'Conor was stretched out in the old rocking chair grasping a tall drink. "We could have invited that old hypocrite Father Cullen," he suggested.

"Your wish Sir, will happen," laughed Kathleen. "He will be here soon to visit. Cora and I invited him for dinner."

Cora looked like a small child sitting in her own extra large deep-cushioned chair that had been brought from the main living room.

Her emaciated body was enveloped in plush cushions and wrapped in a soft red blanket. This stern mistress of Dunraven House, who had for many years ruled her staff with strict discipline and at times with vicious uncalled-for demands, was depending for her needs on those around her.

Perhaps she knew it would be her last Christmas. For this family occasion somewhere deep inside she searched, found and liberated the hidden captive. The part of her locked away for so many decades.

It was most likely what James had seen and known when they were very young and he'd fallen in love with her so many years ago.

In her weak state Cora made a brave effort to participate in the happy conversation even to tell a few comical stories of her own. She held out a white shaky hand to clasp that of Kathleen who sat beside her. Perhaps it was an unspoken message indicating that she was not capitulating but was sorry for her years of antagonism. Perhaps she was asking for forgiveness.

It was a happy time with much laughter. Father Cullen told endless stories about many old happenings, and James recounted both recent and long-past stories of his own. George was on his best behaviour and was very quiet but again he paid much attention to Kathleen's sister, Eileen.

Cora had been diagnosed as having cirrhosis of the liver. She died on the 15th of February, 1942, and was buried two days later in the private O'Conor plot in the northwest corner of the village graveyard. During the chapel service Father Cullen went overboard in his praise for the great and honourable lady who would be sadly missed by her loving husband and family, the congregation, and the community. He continued lamenting about the great loss to the chapel, but saying he felt sure James O'Conor, his wonderful son George and wife Kathleen would remain loyal to the needs of this ministry and chapel programs.

George seemed unmoved by his mother's death, and James looked solemn but showed no appearance of grief. Perhaps it was relief that his wife passed on quietly. For many months before her death Cora's sustenance had been largely alcohol.

Kathleen's scattered thoughts stopped at one possibility. Would James remarry and bring another lady to be Mistress of Dunraven House? This concerned her, as James had been a good father-in-law and close friend. Now would this New Year of 1942 bring with it more problems for her and her children?

She knew George would not improve and now that Cora was gone, James might feel free to travel more by himself and leave George in complete control. With fear in her heart she tried to visualise another year as George's wife.

Kathleen and Mary Jane became the counterparts of James O'Conor and Patrick. There was the unspoken bond between master and his trusted employee, Patrick. So it was with Kathleen and Mary Jane. Their friendship became a strong bond.

As the New Year became older it slipped into spring. Dunraven House outdoor staff changed as employees found other work and gladly gave notice of their intent to leave the tyranny of George's management. Others didn't turn up for morning instructions on the day after receiving their pay. Having previously packed their meagre possessions, they quietly left the estate to avoid contact with George, leaving him to throw another morning temper fit and swear he would make sure no one within miles would give them employment. Jobs they did get, as George's notoriety had spread far.

Things were not good with Dunraven House's outdoor staff. It had become more difficult to find employees to work for George. So he was pushed to hire transients. Change in the family character of the staff he had inherited from Patrick backfired. Production declined and there was antagonism between old employees and the new. Fights broke out over food and accommodation. The transients moved on but often stole from others before leaving.

James O'Conor questioned George regarding the numerous new faces on the work crews and the failure to meet even minimum projected targets. George immediately tried to blame Patrick's men for not pulling their weight.

James was not enthusiastic with that explanation. He informed George that he was considering reversing management of outdoor staff back to Patrick. To be fair he would make his own investigations why things had gone so very wrong. Only then would he decide what course to take. James looked at his son with disdain. "You haven't learned how to handle people. I tried to guide you but I'm afraid old Patrick was right when he told me there's a devil in you. I'm sorry but after watching you drive your staff and punish people by making them work extra hours without pay to make up for your inefficiency in supervising, I have no confidence in you and God help Dunraven House if you are ever in full control.

"Now go about your business. I will give you my decision in a couple of days. In the meantime the fox is still getting into the hen house and I'm arranging a fox hunt! See if you can behave yourself and remain sober."

Without softening the impact of his words, James O'Conor turned and strode away, leaving his son to contemplate his future.

It was the spring holiday in May. James had organised the fox hunt with his horse-riding friends to include dinner at Dunraven House later. He asked Kathleen to help Mary Jane with the banquet to be served in the great dining room. "You will take Cora's place my dear, in making it a wonderful evening so I'm leaving it in your capable hands."

Around 10:00 a.m., Saturday, May 14th, the assembly began. Beautiful horses and red-coated men arrived in trucks and powerful cars pulling elegant horse trailers.

On this glorious morning the women riders were wearing the most up-to-date riding-habits and looked so elegant on horseback.

Kathleen took the children with her to welcome and talk to the group. She had little Sean in her arms and Evelyn, two years and nine months, holding onto her mother's skirt. Evelyn was not sure about all this activity, especially the big horses. James O'Conor made a big fuss of Evelyn, showing her off to his lawyer friend Sean O'Hara. He loved this little girl. James picked her up and placed her on the saddle of his horse. It was a remarkable chestnut-coloured stallion, sixteen hands high.

The hounds were ready to go, and it was Patrick dressed in his best work clothes who took Evelyn from James, held her in his arms, and stood beside Kathleen. James turned to his daughter-in-law. "You have the most beautiful children, so much like you." He kissed Kathleen's cheek then mounted his horse. She thought how handsome and strong he looked sitting there in the saddle of his magnificent animal.

"Tally Ho! Now for the fox!" he shouted. Horns blew, dogs were away and the hunt was on.

Kathleen hadn't seen George in the hunt group but she knew he was participating in the ride. The next few hours were busy preparing for their return. Kathleen helped Mary Jane and the staff set up for the splendid feast that was being prepared. She felt proud that James had asked her to be the Dunraven House mistress to receive and entertain his guests. He had given Kathleen a card with a scribbled diagram and instructions. "I'd like these four O'Conors and close friends placed at my table in this manner. Little Evelyn to my immediate right, then you, with baby Sean, your sister Eileen, then my good friend Sean O'Hara and his wife, Mary. To my left, put your father and mother, Judge Henry Moffat and his wife Harriet, then George. I think Harriet can keep George from getting out of hand." There was a P.S. "If you so desire my dear, change the seating to suit yourself," and he had drawn a little smiling face beside the last line.

When the big grandfather clock in the foyer chimed five, Mary Jane had a strange look on her face. She knew the hunt should have been over a couple of hours before and her intuitive Irish spirit was troubled. A lone horseman arrived. It was Sean O'Hara, the lawyer from Letterkenny, and James's best friend. He had ridden out beside James at noon. Without Kathleen asking her to, Mary Jane hurried to meet him. Kathleen watched from a distance. By their motions and Mary Jane's turning to look her way so often, Kathleen realised something serious was wrong. She ran to them. Mary Jane was crying and the lawyer looked distraught. His riding breeches and coat were covered in mud. He was speechless as he looked into the questioning eyes of this beautiful lady.

"Tell me! Tell me, please!" was all Kathleen could say.

He stammered out the awful news. "James is dead. His horse failed to make a high gate and threw James over it. He broke his neck."

Kathleen stood in shock for a moment, then with a loud cry of "Where is he? Where is he?" she ran out to the courtyard where the rest of the hunt group had returned. Some were standing in a daze by their horses, while others sat still on their mounts with unseeing eyes staring into space.

It was Mary Jane who ran after Kathleen and gathered her into her arms where she cried out her grief in great gasping sobs. "Mary Jane, Mary Jane," Kathleen sobbed. "What will I do? What will I do?" Then she asked, "Where is George?"

Sean O'Hara told her George and two other friends had taken James' body to Rathmelton to prepare for burial. Father Cullen was with them.

The guests who were able to drive home dispersed. Others accepted the offer of accommodation at Dunraven House. Mary Jane took control of that and served a meal to all who were staying overnight. Afterwards she went to Kathleen and her children, staying with them until George came home very late. His sullen manner and apparent lack of grief did nothing to ease the awful pain of the unexpected tragedy for Kathleen. Her world was engulfed in the darkest of clouds. Now more than ever she feared so much for her own future and that of her children.

George refused to answer questions or discuss the accident. Instead he proceeded to get drunk. Mary Jane refused to leave when he tried to dismiss her. She slept in the single bed in the room where both of Kathleen's children had been born.

Mary Jane and her kitchen staff prepared breakfast in the morning for the overnight guests. She served Kathleen and her children in their private apartment.

George was still asleep.

Next day, without telling George, Kathleen asked Patrick to go with her to Rathmelton Funeral Home. He accepted, so the lady of Dunraven House drove the big limousine to Rathmelton, accompanied by her outside staff handyman and friend Patrick McGuinness. Mary Jane looked after the children, and when George asked where Kathleen had gone her only answer was, "To mourn her great loss as

111

you should be doing." Apparently George had not missed Patrick or the limousine.

Kathleen requested time by herself in the room where James' body lay in the solid oak casket. She put her hand on his brow, touched his cheeks, and was shocked at the coldness and rigidity of rigor mortis. She smoothed his hair and tried to clasp his hand in her warm one. Kathleen spent an hour there talking to what a few hours before had been a vibrant, handsome wonderful man, asking him and God, "Why? Why did he have to leave this world right now?" He was the only one who could have protected her and the children from George.

When Kathleen had emptied herself of grief she kissed the cold brow, and fixed a few hairs that had been ruffled. Then dry-eyed and determined to win her own battles and her children's, she left to permit Patrick his time paying respects to the man who had been the Master of Dunraven House and also his friend.

Kathleen stood in the sunshine on this bright spring day. Her father-in-law James O'Conor, a solid 'corner stone' in her life was gone. She remembered once at confession telling Father Cullen that often she wished her husband dead. "I'm surprised that a beautiful young mother like you should have such sinful thoughts," had been his admonishment. Kathleen remembered thinking there was no anger in the priest's voice and the rebuff did not sound genuine. Perhaps there had been a time when Father Cullen himself confessed to someone his own sinful thoughts. His own hopes that George O'Conor's punishment for his dastardly deeds would be a demise from this world.

Could it have been that Father Cullen, when listening to his own parishioners and others in his confession booth, had learned much about George O'Conor's behaviour?

Patrick left the room and outside he put his arm around the still proud figure that stood dejectedly beside the car. "Come Kathleen, my dear, James O'Conor is not here anymore. Let's go home."

This May day of 1942 had turned into a beautiful afternoon. Kathleen was silent and drove slowly. New life was everywhere. New grass, tender leaves on trees, and spring flowers were in abundance and the hedgerows were alive with birds singing their songs. Kathleen stopped the car outside a little tea shop where tables had fresh chequered tablecloths and brightly coloured umbrellas. On this day, with so much grief and pain still to come, here was an oasis, for a small portion of time. "Patrick, would you join me for tea and scones? I've been here before and they are wonderful."

It seemed she had crossed a bridge from grief to determination. She had changed. It had happened during the hour beside her father-in-law's coffin or as she drove slowly in this land filled with new spring life.

They spent a long time in the warm sunshine. The scones were finished and Kathleen poured another cup of tea for Patrick and herself. With questioning eyes she looked at this rugged man who from her wedding day it seemed had always been there watching out for her safety.

With teacup grasped in both her hands Kathleen's blue eyes met Patrick's steel grey ones and she leaned closer. "Why did you not marry, Patrick? Were you never in love? You're a good-looking man today, surely when you were young there must have been someone. Did you have a very special lady in your life at one time, Patrick?"

Patrick felt a bond of friendship for this young woman who was now to become mistress of Dunraven House. Many times since she'd married George O'Conor he had thought that if only Sally had not gone away they'd have married and in their family would be a beautiful daughter like Kathleen.

Before answering Patrick looked thoughtfully into his cup of strong dark tea. With a wistful look in his eyes he told Kathleen of his love for Sally and the day he lost her at Dublin's train station when she and her family left for New York. He told her of his effort to earn enough money to buy his own fare to follow her. How her letters stopped and he lost track of her. Then the tragedy of his mother's and father's deaths, the demise of family fortunes, his own three-and-a-half years in jail, and his gypsy existence until he found Dunraven House and James O'Conor. Kathleen saw a tear spill over and down the rugged face of the seventy-two-year-old man she respected so very much. Patrick made no attempt to wipe its path dry.

"Have you any idea of where she might be?"

"No, Kathleen. Next month it will be fifty-three years since she went away, and only for the first eighteen months did we correspond. I've never permitted myself to fall in love again." He looked into young understanding eyes.

"My dear Patrick, thank you for telling me. I know what it's like to love someone very much and then have to let them go. Perhaps someday when the time is right I'll tell you all about it.

"Now we have another trying day tomorrow, but I confide in you my friend that beside James O'Conor's coffin I spilled out my grief. Touching his cold remains I felt the warm presence of him coming from elsewhere and telling me to leave my grief right there. Go out, start anew with confidence because someone will protect you and your children. Patrick McGuinness I believe that someone is you."

At the funeral it appeared everyone in this part of County Donegal had come to pay their respects. The chapel pews had never before been occupied by such crowds. People jammed the side aisles and overflowed to the chapel grounds where special speakers carried Father Cullen's word to all. Many were crying, especially the employees of Dunraven House. Father Cullen himself faltered in his words when praising James O'Conor for his honesty and fairness, his love for two families, his daughter-in-law, whose children he adored. The loss to the O'Conor family was devastating, not only to them but also to many people whose livelihood depended on the generosity of those in authority at Dunraven House.

"This chapel of worship will miss a great stalwart of right and integrity in the quagmire of dishonesty and deceit so prevalent in today's world. It was only a short number of months ago that Cora O'Conor was laid to rest in our old cemetery. Who would have thought the great and honourable James O'Conor was so soon to follow his lady? This day is to be sure a sad one for all of us."

Father Cullen's mass for James O'Conor was almost another hour long. Then the oak casket bearing his remains was carried slowly down the centre aisle followed first by Kathleen dressed in black, a pathetic beautiful figure, with little Evelyn in white clutching tight to her mother's hand.

The pallbearers carrying the coffin were George, Sean O'Hara, Henry Moffat, Sean and Michael O'Neill, and Patrick McGuinness. As they emerged into the spring sunlight the crowd parted to make way for the tragic parade. Usually only men participated in the walk behind the deceased's coffin. This funeral procession was different. Mary Jane and the kitchen staff took their places immediately behind Kathleen, then a large number of Dunraven House outdoor workers joined the mourners (all those who wished to do so, according to Kathleen's instructions).

To them it was the end of an era like a country losing its king or leader. Dunraven House and its domain were their little country, and its king who had treated his subjects with care and respect was now dead. There would be no words of praise or rejoicing for the successor, only fear and foreboding when George David O'Conor took full control of his father's house and lands.

The procession moved slowly down the long pathway to the chapel gates where the hearse and cars waited to give mourners the final ride to where James' body was to rest beside his wife Cora.

The wake to honour James O'Conor's passing continued into early morning hours. It was late afternoon next day before the last of the mourners gave Patrick their farewell salute at the big front entrance gates.

The next morning Timothy's mother tearfully bid farewell to her second son Michael who was returning to the British Air Force.

George O'Conor as usual wasted no time. He summoned a meeting of all staff to be certain they understood he would now be in charge of every outdoor and indoor phase of Dunraven House's work operations. On this beautiful May morning in 1942 there was no joy in the hearts of those who now worked for James O'Conor's son.

On the 13th of September, 1942, the German 6th Army in Russia took over most of the big city of Stalingrad. As the hues of setting sunlight danced their way through the great windows of a bedroom in the north wing of Dunraven House, midwife Purvis slapped the bottom of another newborn. Robert George, Kathleen's third child, produced from his lungs the first cry of his life. Above the heather-covered hillsides, larks flew high in the sky singing their own happy songs and Kathleen O'Conor held her newborn son and feared for his future.

Although her own Republic of Ireland was still claiming neutrality, many of its young men and women had joined the Allied Forces to do their tiny bit to stop Hitler's juggernaut of aggression. Timothy had been one of the first to go. Her own tragic marriage seemed infinitesimal compared to what was happening in this home we call our world. Thousands of young soldiers dressed in the uniforms and battle gear of their country's fighting forces were dying in bitter conflicts. Kathleen feared for Timothy's safety in the prison camp. She remembered those questioning blue eyes and dark hair, his open honesty, healthy look and happy laughter. Now, after thirty months behind barbed wire far away in Eastern Germany, would his health be broken? Would those blue eyes have lost their sparkle? Would his happy laughter be gone? Would Timothy's bronze muscular body have been emaciated from hunger?

The prison-camp postcards of seven lines and the short one-page Stalag letters that came from Timothy were addressed to a Rachel Kernaghan in Letterkenny, Mary Jane's grandmother. Granny Kernaghan was happy to participate in the deceit, having learned from Mary Jane all about Kathleen's husband. When mailing to Timothy from Letterkenny, Mary Jane always visited Granny and checked for prison-camp mail. Timothy had been informed in Kathleen's first letter how to address return mail and he had followed instructions. Timothy did not think it was a strange request; he surmised George would be upset at Kathleen's receiving mail from someone in the British forces. In one of his prison-camp notes smuggled into Dunraven House by cook Mary Jane he had written: "Dearest Kathleen. I'm lying here on my bunk's allotted seven bed boards, having discarded my flea-infested straw mattress. Often I try to visualise you and my own dear green land. Now after all these months since my capture the enemy is still on the march overrunning other countries. I sometimes feel there will never be a day when I'll see your dear face again and the beautiful children you must now have."

Kathleen permitted herself the luxury of pretending she was holding Timothy's newborn son. Soon he would be coming in from working in the fields to rejoice and celebrate with her this new life they had produced. Those very precious thoughts were suddenly broken when George entered carrying a bottle and two glasses. "Come new mother, let's drink to another fine male O'Conor."

Knowing his tantrums if she refused Kathleen permitted him to fill her glass. He was drunk. She sipped only a few drops. "Drink!" he commanded. "I'm nursing the child George, and I hope you don't wish me to drink too much while I'm doing that." For once he did not force the issue but took the baby from her arms and held it high above his head repeating, "Another son! Another son! Another great O'Conor," then gave back the child to Kathleen and left.

She sat in the rocking chair that her Mom and Dad had bought for her as a wedding present. Her thoughts turned to Timothy and what it might have been with the man she still loved and had lost forever by her own decision, now that marriage had turned into a domestic tragedy and a nightmare of thoughts for the future. Kathleen knew with Timothy's considerate, understanding and loving ways he would have been at hand when necessary, to help with the children. She knew their home no matter how small or poor would often have echoed with happy laughter. As she thought of this impossible dream Kathleen realised Timothy may never return. Perhaps he would die in prison camp or survive to marry maybe an English girl, leave Ireland and she'd never see him again. Tears rolled slowly down her cheeks to splash softly on the upturned face of her child. She held him close and sobbed as if her heart would break.

It was hot for late September and on the green lawn outside Dunraven House the two beautiful sisters, Eileen and Kathleen, sat together under a large orange-coloured umbrella. Almost three years had passed since the breathless Eileen had delivered Kathleen's farewell gift to Timothy O'Neill at the village bus stop and made a promise, "I'll be fifteen next month, Timothy. I'll wait for you till the war is over if you want me to."

Both sisters were enraptured with the wonder and beauty of Kathleen's new baby boy. Eileen was holding little Robert and lovingly checking the tiny fingers and toes. "Aren't they perfect?" Kathleen said.

"They are wonderful," Eileen replied. Then the tears came and the shocking words tumbled out. "I'm pregnant."

Kathleen looked at her sister in astonishment. "You can't be! It's impossible, you wouldn't, you couldn't." Then the question came, "Who is the father?"

Eileen's voice trembled when she answered. "I don't know." Even with her sister's continued interrogation she maintained the father was unknown then cried out in despair, "What will I do Kathleen? What will I do?"

Kathleen was silent with deep, angry and disgusting thoughts about her husband. Could what she was thinking be true? She remembered when carrying this third child one thing had changed. Even before her late months of pregnancy George had refrained from sexually abusing her. Almost suddenly he had ignored sexual contact. To Kathleen this was a great relief, but often she had questions in her thoughts regarding his suspicious late-night absences and early-morning returns to their quarters. She knew from bad and bruised experiences not to question him.

Looking at her terrified and bewildered young sister, Kathleen put her arms around Eileen who was still holding the baby. "I will do something. Don't tell anyone. Remember, no one is to know, especially mother and father. Now don't do anything silly. I'll look after you and I will find out who did this to you. There must be strange circumstances you are not telling me, otherwise you'd never have permitted this to happen. Now let's go in for tea and see if Mary Jane has baked some goodies."

Eileen had kept her terrible secret for months, and before talking to her sister had contemplated suicide. It was after her brother had left home to join the British Navy and Kathleen's announcement of her third pregnancy that Eileen's ordeal began.

It had been a wild night, with gale-force winds screeching their way through the trees leaving a trail of debris and torn-off branches. The drenching rain hammered on rooftops and against window panes. Eileen thanked a good friend who had driven her home from a dance in the village, and he waited until she'd safely entered the house. Passing her Mom and Dad's bedroom she called, "You can go to sleep now, I'm home."

"Goodnight dear," her Mom replied.

Eileen closed the dividing door to her parent's residence. She ran through the breezeway to the cosy living quarters that she loved so much. Once inside she locked the door before realising she was not alone.

George O'Conor had always lusted after Kathleen's sister and had kept a spare key to her room. He had watched her blossom into the beautiful young lady, now in his power. Although driven with drink and lust he took his time knowing his prey would not get away. Eileen's struggles were useless in his powerful grip, and the gale blowing outside smothered her cries for help.

Afterwards he warned her: "If you tell anyone I was here, I'll put you and your family out of the house and off the estate. I am in sole charge now of Dunraven House and of all the workers attached to it.

118

Your old house was torn down a long time ago; there's little work out there and you have no money. I keep and feed you and your family. Outside of here you'll starve and I will not permit your sister to help or interfere. You are in my power. So I make a bargain with you. Kathleen is pregnant. You are going to take her place. I will come to your bed when I feel like it. It's a lousy night so you are going to have a drink with me and I'll stay a few more hours till the storm abates. Until then you will be my good and warm companion."

7

Lieutenant Robert Steele, September, 1942

For Sharon Marshall, days dragged by from weeks to months and then years. Time and loneliness were taking their toll. By May 1942, Sharon had received only a few prison-camp letters and seven-line cards from Tim but they were small consolation for lonely times. She had written to Tim's mother a number of times but there was no reply. The war news was bad. German armies moved further in the conquest of Eastern Europe and in North Africa.

Sharon had been going to the dances again but she always came home alone. Charlie and Peter were very good and made sure she didn't sit like a wallflower, but they never made any advances, just remained good friends. Then they were posted to another air base and she lost contact.

After work each day at Lloyd's Insurance Office she never missed checking for mail, but too often nothing from prison camp. Sharon was very lonely and despondent. Finally she volunteered to assist at the Officer's Club close to her home. She helped to serve refreshments to Army, Navy, and Air Force men from many Allied countries. It gave her morale a big lift and sometimes she would accept the invitation to dance with one of the officers, but still she made her walk home alone each night.

One September evening Sharon danced with a young American officer who introduced himself as Bob Steele. He was on leave from the 5th Air Corp. Bob was a pilot and spending two days in Lincoln before returning to his squadron. Sharon accepted his invitation to have coffee. She learned his home was in Orange County, California. He was single, five foot ten, and twenty-six years old. With his good looks, his slender build, fair wavy hair, blue eyes, and American Air Force Officer's uniform, Bob Steele made a very handsome picture.

Over three cups of coffee he talked about his "Golden State" California and with pride of his Mom and Dad, his young brother and his two sisters. Of course to prove how wonderful they looked, he produced pictures. Sharon was thrilled by his enthusiasm about everything, especially flying, and her thoughts were, "He's so much like my husband was. So many things in common, his conversation, interests, his openness about himself, his joys and fears." She felt attracted to this boyish American flyer, so much so that against her own self-made rules, she gave him her full name and address. Thanking him for an enjoyable conversation, she said good night and on her way home, thought, "What a foolish thing to do giving a strange American officer my address. I probably won't see or hear from him again. Anyway he is probably married and he probably lied to me."

Just the day before, Lucy, a girl in the office, had said "Americans, they are all single, at least all the men that come over here or so they say." Sharon smiled at the thought, knowing Lucy didn't care if they were married or single. She was always ready for a good time.

In Sharon's mail box one week later was a letter from Lieutenant Robert Steele. In four weeks he'd have one week off and would be honoured if she'd permit him to visit her in Lincoln. Sharon's lonesome days and nights, her waiting for news from prison camp, her faithful promise to wait for Tim, and thoughts of dark and dreary winter days just ahead were all in the mixture of her emotions. With misgivings regarding the decision, she replied and accepted his proposal but emphasising there was someone she cared for very much confined in enemy hands as a prisoner.

Bob Steele surprised her by arriving in a staff car. They had a wonderful week together. Each night he drove to his hotel and each morning early he would be at her apartment. Sometimes he'd drive her back to the hotel for breakfast and other times she would have fresh coffee with home baked scones ready for him. She felt alive again. They would dance at the club and talk for hours about many things including Tim and her dead husband, Frank. She used up her scarce grocery supplies for special home-cooked meals.

During the next two months Bob made a number of visits and brought supplies of wonderful American canned goods plus assorted chocolate bars, things so very scarce in Britain's strict food rationing program.

Sharon was falling for this wonderful American with whom she felt so comfortable. She wrote her parents trying to explain her thoughts and feelings and told them how much he was like Frank. "I still love Tim," she wrote, "but I'm living in the present. It's two-and-a-half years since Tim went to France. All that time I've almost closed myself in the apartment, refused invitations for evenings out, and stayed away for many months from other entertainment. I was resigned to a long wait that might never come to a joyful end."

Sharon told her parents Bob had asked her to move close to his air base. She was torn between her love for Tim, her promise to wait and now this decision she had to make. "It's tearing me apart. My friends at work endorse my companionship with Bob and say I should go." Then in a pleading request she finished her letter with, "What shall I do, Mom and Dad?"

Five days later at the end of her work day she emerged into a cold wet evening. There standing at the office's main entrance under his battered old black umbrella was her Dad. He had journeyed by bus and train. It had taken him most of the day.

"Let's go for something to eat. I'm starving," he exclaimed.

They talked about the war, her brother in the Army, about Mom, her Aunt and Uncle, and the neighbours in Coventry. When dinner was finished, he took both of his daughter's hands in his. Her Dad looked solemn and sad. Suddenly she realised that her father was getting old, he was fifty-six and showing it. With his eyes unwavering, he spoke his words softly.

"Your mother and I love you very much and we are concerned. You just can't become a recluse. You are a young and vibrant lady and already two men you have loved are gone out of your life. Frank is dead, and remember, Sharon, one has to think rationally. Tim may never return from prison camp and I'm sure he wouldn't wish you to sit at home waiting for the war to end. I endorse that sort of thinking.

"Go out my dear. Find what enjoyment you can. Bob seems a nice fellow and I hope to meet him soon but Lord knows the life of flying crews these days is a dangerous one and too often a short one. If your feelings are strong enough for this young American, go find what happiness you can. War isn't like peace time. It has no conscience and has a very cruel way of destroying love and happiness.

"If you've found companionship again, grasp it now because it may also be only for a short time. Remember all of us in this war are living close to the front line. The Luftwaffe bombing crews make it so as they rain death from the sky on helpless civilians. Each morning store in your heart every little grain of happiness you can find because you might need to draw on it at some future date."

Sharon sat still. She'd never heard her father speak with so much feeling and so much honesty and urgency. She knew there were tears in her eyes and already a few had overflowed.

Her father stood up. "Now," he said, "will you take me to your home and pour me a drink? They cost too much in this place."

Sharon kissed and hugged him. Then he paid for their dinner and walked out with his daughter while sailors at the bar looked questionably at the little grey-haired man walking away with a beautiful desirable young lady clinging to his arm.

Sharon wrote to Bob saying yes to his offer. At his request she kept her apartment. Against her wishes he paid six months rent in advance. "Just in case," he said. "I could end up in a similar situation as Tim or . . ." He didn't finish the sentence just shrugged his shoulders and Sharon recalled her Dad's words. The life of a flying crew these days is dangerous and often short.

In the small village of Ashport close to his air base Bob had rented a tiny cottage and Sharon moved in on a cold wintry late November day. They had a great time together. At her request he took her to see Bing Crosby in the film *White Christmas*. When Bob had a few days off he would drive her to London where they'd dine at ritzy restaurants and go to wonderful theatre plays and at times stand shocked at the terrible destruction caused by German Air raids that had already killed thousands of civilians.

Soon it was Christmas. Dancing at the air base's fabulous Christmas party Bob asked, "Why are you so quiet Sharon? You seem lost in thought."

Nestling closer to him as they danced she looked up. "Bob, you're the third man I've loved in my life. One is dead and my very first Christmas party on an air base was with Tim. I look around me here at all the wonderful food and fabulously dressed beautiful women and men. Then I think Tim is in some foul-smelling prison camp with little to eat and my feelings are that never again will I see him. I'm scared. You are here tonight but what about the tomorrows? I hate war."

Bob held her closer, looked down at the upturned green eyes shining with tears and whispered, "The war brought us together. It sent Tim to brighten the tragedy of your Frank's death and showed you how to love again. Your two wonderful men are gone and one may return. But the war is still here Sharon and if we don't challenge the unfairness of it and grab hold of the few opportunities this damned war gives us, we will regret our cowardice for the rest of our lives whether that be a very short time or many years. Now, it's getting late. Let's go to our cottage and light the fire. It's a freezing cold night."

They returned to the cottage to drink brandies by the fire. She felt very safe in his arms. The war seemed so very far away.

On New Year's Eve, Bob drove her up to Lincoln. She wished to send off a letter and parcel to Tim's prison camp and check her own postal box that might hold a Stalag letter or card from Tim. Of course this box was the only mailing address he knew. Sometimes Sharon thought Tim should be told about Bob. It was so hard for her to diagnose the effect it would have on Tim's morale. She refrained from doing that although she had a troubled conscience.

Her intuitions dictated her to leave things as they were. Sharon knew in her heart she loved two men.

The awful consequences that war leaves behind touches many lives but is often tempered by responses from people like Sharon's father.

"Go out my dear find what enjoyment you can."

"War isn't like peacetime. It has no conscience and has a cruel way of destroying love and happiness."

"Go find what happiness you can."

"Don't think those parcels or letters will ever get to the prisoners." Bob said breaking in on her thoughts.

Sharon looked at him with her mischievous smile. "Wouldn't it be cowardice Bob if I didn't take an opportunity this damned war has given me to send parcels and letters to Tim just to challenge the unfairness of it all? I'd regret it for the rest of my life if I didn't do it." She kissed the parcel and Bob placed his hand on it for a moment in a gesture of good luck that it would reach Tim.

"Thanks," was all Sharon said but there was a deeper message in her eyes when she said, "Let's go home."

Outside it was snowing and Sharon slipped on the steps. Bob stopped her fall then turned to her amidst millions of tumbling snowflakes falling like a great white wall of confetti. He took her in his arms, kissed her and exclaimed, "Happy New Year my beautiful Sharon. In a few hours it will be 1943. I will love you every minute of it and all the future years of our lives."

Part Two

8

Introduction To Stefan Jonsson

Now, dear reader, I would like to take you on another journey. We will leave Ireland for a while, but do not fret; in due course I will return you to the Emerald Isle with its beauty, wonderment and its tragedies.

Yes, Patrick McGuinness, George O'Conor, Kathleen, Eileen, and cook Mary Jane will all be there waiting for our return to pick up the threads and weave their journey to a conclusion.

Before that happens, I wish to introduce you to Stefan Jonsson, who will have a great impact on Timothy O'Neill's future. So let us push back time a few years to 1939.

For now we will also leave Sharon Marshal and Robert Steele in the little English village of Ashport close to his air base.

In the year 1939 many hundreds of frightened people were escaping the SS and Gestapo dragnet that reached far and wide in Germany and beyond its borders to the lands it had captured and now occupied. The doors of escape were closing for citizens who were anti-regime and especially for those of Jewish faith or origin.

Stefan Jonsson knew it was only the beginning of a terrible and horrific tragedy that would inevitably spread its terror across most of Europe. Hitler had unleashed his murderers and already concentration camps were being filled. Stefan had heard so very many horrible stories, but chose to disbelieve them until tragedy struck in his own life. Now he sat on the floor in the attic room of his mother's house in Stockholm, Sweden, making decisions that would change his life forever.

Stefan's decisions would mean the death of others. He was certain he would need a partner, maybe two, to carry out his catastrophic plans. Where could he find the person or persons in such a turmoil of vengeance that they would be willing to chance dying to obtain that vengeance?

On a Sunday morning two months after Stefan returned home from Germany to make for himself a secret hideout in his mother's home, something happened to hasten his quest for revenge. On this particular Sunday morning his mother attended her regular church worship. It was a special service with a young guest preacher rumoured to be very eloquent. The congregation was larger than usual, and after the service this good-looking dark curly-haired preacher was at the church doorway meeting members of the congregation and being congratulated by enthusiastic parishioners on his wonderful sermon. While shaking hands with members of the congregation as they left, he gave to each one a gospel pamphlet. He seemed so full of energy and glowed with enthusiastic chatter. Occasionally after short conversations with lady members and still holding the handshake he would give the gospel pamphlet, lean forward and kiss their cheeks. Stefan's mother stood in line and at first thought it was a little out of place, but he did it with such a carefree manner it didn't come across as being wrong. The young preacher smiled warmly when Mrs. Jonsson stepped forward and he clasped her hand in a strong grip. Up close she saw he was more good-looking than from a distance. His clear skin had no blemishes. There was just a slight scar under his left eye that showed white against his sun-tanned complexion. When he smiled he showed fine white teeth except for a front one that had a dark spot. Far from taking away from his looks, the dark spotted tooth and little white scar enhanced them and gave an air of mystery to him.

"Nice to see you. So good to be here." His handshake relaxed a little and she realised a small square of paper was being transferred to her hand. "Hope you enjoyed the service." Then very softly he said, "It's for Stefan. Don't lose it." Her shocked reply was almost inaudible, "But he's dead." Still holding the handshake and smiling he held out the gospel pamphlet and she received it with her left hand. Leaning forward he kissed her cheek and his whispered reply shocked her. "We know that and God knows the only way is the Gospel way. Remember Jesus died on the cross and rose from the dead. Give it to Stefan. Have a good day." With that he turned to the next person in line, a gentleman of the Church Council. Taking both of his hands he said for many to hear, "It's a great pleasure and an honour to preach in this house of worship to such a wonderful congregation. Hope you will invite me back. I have a few days free, perhaps I can be of use."

"Oh we will, we will," replied the Council member.

Home was a short distance away for Stefan's mother. Quickening her footsteps the small square of paper in her hand, she gripped it tightly, afraid to do otherwise. Soon, with heart pounding, she was tapping on the sliding partition to her son's attic domain the Morse code password for the day. The partition slid open. Breathlessly she told Stefan what had happened and gave him the small folded paper. Feverishly he unfolded the fine rice paper and his eyes glowed with interest. In small print was a message. "We know of you and from information received, you may have a desire to infiltrate the enemy camp. Someone will contact you." Stefan was silent, speechless and scared. Who could know of his whereabouts? Was the SS or Gestapo here in Sweden posing as ministers of the church? An incredible thought: Could this be fate giving him the chance for revenge? Who were the people who sent the message? Could this be a trap? Could the preacher be the messenger? Could he have written the note? It said, "We know of you."

Stefan began to sweat. "No one but no one outside this house should know I'm alive. I've got to move, Mother. I've got to get out of here. It must be an SS or Gestapo trap. No one could know I'm here, I'm sure of that. They must have found out I am alive, but how?"

His mother closed her eyes and shook her head. "Where would you go, son? There's no better hiding place and remember you're dead, buried in the plot beside your dear father. Oh my God! What if it is the SS or Gestapo here in our country?" Suddenly she pulled herself together. "I'm making lunch. I'll bring up some of that thick vegetable soup I made yesterday."

She needed time to think. If necessary, where could he go? He was presumed dead and buried so there was no place for him to go. His one safe haven was here and now someone knew. She was near panic but refused to show it. Stefan's mother was a good-looking lady, tall, good figure, a little overweight as happens to people who like good food and don't take enough exercise. In her late fifties Thora Jonsson's blonde hair showed only a slight trace of grey. She wore it fairly long and it framed a face that had at one time been very beautiful. That beauty still lingered. She had a wide mouth, high cheek bones, finely formed nose, and deep-set blue eyes that seemed to be forever asking questions. Usually it took some time for a person to realise it was her extra long eyelashes that drew attention to her dark blue eyes. Turning from the open sliding panel she said, "Sit down Stefan, and think about all of this. Don't make any rash decisions. I don't believe there's anywhere else to go. Now I'll go and get the soup ready." She moved quietly outside closing the sliding panel behind her.

Two mornings later Stefan's mother was making the morning coffee when she had a phone call. "Good morning, Mrs. Jonsson. This is the Reverend Lindstrom. I do hope you remember me."

Thora Jonsson almost dropped the phone. Taking a deep breath she answered, "Most certainly how could I forget?"

"Your preacher is having a week's vacation and I offered to continue with his visitation roster. He has marked your name for special visitation because of the loss in recent months of your dear husband, and of course the records also show the tragic loss of your only son, Stefan. It is a great sorrow to lose your life's partner and a son. I would like to chat with you and hope I can help lessen this burden of loneliness and fear you might have for the months ahead and the distant future. I hope to call this afternoon at approximately two o'clock. Will that fit in with your plans for today or should I make it tomorrow?"

Unable to think Thora Jonsson said, "Today would be fine." If she had to bluff about Stefan's being dead why not today? Why should she lie awake tonight worrying about tomorrow? Somehow she detected in the young pastor's voice an urgency and a little fear. Her gut feeling was that this person was not Gestapo or SS, but she must be very careful.

Taking a cup of coffee up to Stefan in his attic hiding place, she told him what had occurred. Stefan had his emergency haversack packed and it seemed he was prepared to kill if necessary to keep his freedom. Stefan's Luger was on the card table. The cup of coffee in her hand spilled a little into the saucer as she tried to control the shudder that rushed through her body. She handed Stefan the coffee then asked, "Will you see this man?"

"Yes." That was all.

"Where can you go, son? This is your one and only hiding place and remember the phone message was he would visit me." Stefan laid his cup and saucer on the table beside the Luger, turned to face his mother, then put both hands on her shoulders. "Mother you know that is not his motive for coming here. He's like a detective investigating a crime. It's me he wants to talk to whoever he is. He knows I'm alive and it's no use trying to bluff that I'm not. I believe they don't really know I'm in this house, but I give you permission to bring him up here and allow him to enter. Then I prefer you go back downstairs, understand? If he is either Gestapo or SS others will be waiting for a signal from him. They can't break down a door and barge into a home in this country like they do over there. Our own police and undercover agents keep an eye on suspicious persons who enter Sweden. If he is Gestapo or SS he won't leave alive, but I will. If by chance he is an underground agent working for the Allied cause then I'm with him."

"But Stefan," interrupted his mother, "this is Sweden. We are not in any conflict, we are neutral."

He looked into his mother's troubled blue eyes and smiled a somewhat bitter smile. "Mom, I'm not neutral and you know that very well. I never will be until I have claimed substantial retribution."

At two o'clock precisely the door bell rang. Thora Jonsson had washed, used a little lipstick, combed out her long hair and put on a light blue dress and her comfortable low-heeled shoes. She permitted the doorbell to ring again before opening it.

"Good afternoon, Mrs. Jonsson." His voice had an attractive lilt that made one want to listen more, and she thought that was why the congregation had been so attentive on Sunday. The voice was an important factor in his sermon.

Quickly she ushered him into the living room but he said, "Let's sit at the kitchen table. I think it's cosier and more personal." The word personal scared her but surely no harm could come from this pleasant young minister. She had coffee ready, with raisin scones and homemade strawberry jam. The Reverend Lindstrom sat across from her and devoured three scones and a cup of coffee in two minutes. His unwavering eyes seemed to be searching her face as if there he could read answers to questions in his mind. Thora refilled his coffee cup for the second time and sat down. Her deep blue eyes were half closed. Then without hesitation she said, "You are not of the church!"

He did not answer immediately and there was a long silence. "You have a sister in Hamburg, her name is Josephine."

Thora Jonsson bit her lip while questions raced through her thoughts. Josephine had come for Stefan's 'funeral' but he had been holed up in his attic hideaway. For two whole days she had stayed. She couldn't have seen anything or suspected that the body in the coffin was not Stefan's. She had used the downstairs guest bedroom and had never gone upstairs. Stefan had enough food in his room to make meals for five days, and his attic hiding place had been silent for the two days Josephine was a house guest. Did the Gestapo or SS have new suspicious evidence that Stefan was alive? Had they questioned Josephine? Thora knew her sister had no information to give them or had she?

Thora was in shock. "Mrs. Jonsson. Mrs. Jonsson!" The voice seemed to come from far away. "I asked you a simple question, Do you have a sister living in Hamburg?"

"Yes."

"Thank you," was the reply. "I do not have much time Mrs. Jonsson. May I call you Thora?"

"Yes if you wish, of course you can."

"Thank you, Thora. We have information that your son Stefan is alive and could be living incognito in this house. If so I'd like to talk to him."

"Who told you that preposterous story?" It was the only answer she could think of.

The young man smiled reached across the table and took her hand. "Thora, you know it's not a preposterous story, but the truth, and please call me Hans. Your sister Josephine is a very brave lady and is no longer in Hamburg. She is now working, shall we say, for a company of people who deal in espionage. Your sister moved to Stettin to feel a little safer, Hamburg had bad memories for her. Also she felt from Stettin it would be easier and more convenient to embark for Sweden if that necessity should arise. Those thoughts are questionable as scrutiny of all passengers leaving for a neutral country is becoming more strict each day. I have a message from her. She sends her love and this."

Hans gave Thora a sealed envelope. Her name was printed on the left-hand corner. With shaking hands she opened it. The letter enclosed was carefully written and certainly in her sister's handwriting: "Dear Thora: I am doing my little bit to avenge Nils' death. This young man is genuine, and you can trust him. The ring enclosed you will remember buying for my twenty-first birthday. If Stefan agrees to join us he may need it as a passport of sorts when he arrives in Stettin. Now you will have a big question to ask. How do we know Stefan is alive?" (Again, that word, WE, appeared. Thora shuddered at the thought of a number of people knowing Stefan was alive and in her house.) "It was before the funeral procession moving off just as I was getting into one of the cars. For some unknown reason I turned and looked up at the house. I saw Stefan at the attic window. He had the drapes pulled back just enough for me to have a glimpse and recognise him. It wasn't like him to do such a foolish thing, but I guess impulse on his part to see his own funeral procession. From then I knew that someday there would be an additional member to augment the brave people over here. Many have risked their lives each day to distribute vengeance on SS and Gestapo murderers."

Thora sat silently looking at the letter, her thoughts full of unanswered questions. Slowly she folded it and with the ring in her hand rushed up the stairs, gave the Morse Code signal, and before the sliding panel had opened properly she was relating the conversation that had taken place downstairs. She thrust her sister's letter, envelope and ring into Stefan's hand then in a trembling voice she said, "Read this, son. I believe it's all genuine."

"Let me decide that Mother." Stefan read slowly, his face grim as he digested the contents. "Send him up." Stefan's voice was harsh. "By himself," he added.

Thora descended slowly. The young man was pouring himself another coffee. "I will take you up now."

"I'll carry this coffee with me." Then calmly he asked, "Does Stefan have a coffee?"

"Yes." Thora had difficulty forming that one word and it ended in a whisper. Her thoughts were in shambles. What if things were not as in her sister's letter? What if the smiling pleasant young man in disguise as a church minister who preached that wonderful sermon last Sunday — surely he couldn't be a callous murderer or SS man or

Gestapo agent. Her trembling legs felt like jelly as she forced herself to climb the first two flights of stairs. She was followed by the young preacher who paused occasionally to sip his coffee. How could he be so calm? She felt anger that he showed no fear, and she was falling to pieces thinking of Stefan's Luger now probably in his hands and fully loaded. Did the minister have a similar weapon at easy access in his clothing? Her thoughts were in turmoil when they came to the bottom of the last twelve steps to Stefan's hiding place and stopped. Thora Jonsson stood motionless and hardly breathing. Who was this young taking those last twelve steps to Stefan's hideout and maybe his death? Or Stefan's? At that last thought she felt herself tremble.

The young man's name was Hans Schmitt and he was born in Hanover, Germany on the 18th of October, 1915. His father, a Lutheran minister for many years, had met Hans' mother (an English girl) while taking Bible study courses at a Lutheran college near London in 1912.

After their marriage they returned to Germany in the summer of 1914, shortly before World War 1. During those war years Georg Schmitt, Hans' father, served in the German army as a chaplain. When Hans finished high school in 1933 he was sent to live with his mother's sister close to Oxford in England. There he spent a whole summer before entering Oxford College to study English. When he returned home to Hanover in 1936, his father coerced him into spending a few more years at the Christian Theology Centre run by the Lutheran Church. Hans' mother was a dark-haired well-educated quiet and fragile little lady who did most of the secretarial work for her husband's church. She had a Jewish background on her father's side. His father's plans and dreams were that Hans would finish his theology training courses and someday take over his pulpit.

During the years Hans was at the Theology Centre his father, the Reverend Georg Schmitt, got to be known as one of the few ministers who were not afraid to preach numerous sermons against the tide of anti-Semitic propaganda that was flooding across Germany. One of Schmitt's favourite texts for his sermons was, "Those who are anti-Semites are the children of Satan."

One Sunday in 1939, Hans was away at the Theology Centre and his father was preaching on his favourite text to an almost empty church. People were now afraid to attend and listen. Reverend Schmitt had just begun his sermon when soldiers entered, accompanied by an SS officer. Hans' father, mother, and younger brother were forcibly taken away. He never saw them again. All he had left was a message delivered by an unknown person. It was from a concentration death camp named Auschwitz in Poland.

After Hans' family was taken to the death camp, Mr. Clementz, an Elder of Reverend Schmitt's church had volunteered to hide Hans. One Saturday morning Mr. Clementz returned home very upset. "I was secretly given this package by an old beggar in the marketplace. It is for you Hans. Someone knows you are here. It is not safe for you to hide in my house any more. I am afraid for my family. You will have to go."

Hans took the package from the very frightened man. It was small and there were just four words printed across the dirty wrapping paper. "Give to Hans Schmitt." Hans unwrapped the brown paper to disclose a small Bible and a written request, "Read Genesis first page."

He recognised the Bible as his father's, then found another small piece of paper attached to the first page of Genesis. With unsteady hands he very carefully peeled it off and read the words in his father's handwriting.

"My dear Hans, If you ever receive this Bible, please treasure and preserve it. I presume all you'll have to remember us by will be this little book of scriptures. Your mother and brother are dead. By the grace of God I've been able to thwart 'the children of Satan' who are exterminating all of those they fear. I know it will be only a short time before I will join your mother and brother. Take care of yourself son. Hide somewhere safe. Goodbye, Love, Dad."

Hans was frightened. He had few belongings, no money, and soon he would have no place to hide if Mr. Clementz forced him to leave.

Two days later an envelope was thrust into Mrs. Clementz's hand as she disembarked from a trolley car. "For Hans," were the only words a woman stranger said, and then she disappeared into the crowd. As though it were red hot, Mrs. Clementz dropped the letter into her shopping basket and hurried home.

"For you," was all she exclaimed when handing the envelope to Hans.

He sucked in his breath in surprise when he opened it and extracted one rail ticket to Stettin by express train leaving Hanover at

10:05 next morning. Also enclosed was a new identity card. His name was now Nicholas Meyer, 'Aero Engineer,' and that excused him for military service. There was paper money to the value of 1500 marks, a tidy sum for emergency. Of course no indication of who was the sender. On one other piece of paper this information was printed: A woman will meet you outside the main station exit on arrival at Stettin. Underneath were instructions: Destroy ALL incriminating documents, messages, old identity papers and notes, ALL.

Next morning the new aero engineer was on the express train that left Hanover at 10:12, seven minutes late, destination Stettin.

Hans Schmitt, alias Nicholas Meyer, alias Reverend Lindstrom, Church Minister, now was on a very important mission in Sweden to check on and bring back a full report on one Stefan Jonsson, who was supposed to be dead and buried, but who was very much alive according to his Aunt Josephine. She was now a courier with a variety of missions to accomplish for the Stettin branch of the independent underground movement. His instructions were to find out why this old aunt was certain that Stefan Jonsson had an axe to grind, the target being the SS or Gestapo. She said Stefan would be willing to sacrifice his life to satisfy this obsession to kill his enemies, especially the SS, who wore the skull and crossbones as their emblem.

From this man Hans needed a story, a sort of history to take back with him to Stettin's underground headquarters. A number of other volunteers would do a thorough follow-up investigation and verification of the information. This dangerous quest was now only four more steps on the staircase to what he could see was an open panel to an attic room. There was no welcome person at the entrance to greet him.

Hans changed the coffee cup to his left hand and felt in the front right pocket of his clerical garb. There he fingered the small automatic handgun equipped with a silencer.

Stefan listened to the slow careful footsteps getting closer as his visitor neared the top. He put the ring on his little finger and quickly read parts of the letter again. Stefan knew the old girl was a tough character, but he could not swallow that she had enough courage and will to accept the dangers and mental strain of an underground movement.

The letter appeared genuine, but he was suspicious of it being a trap, remembering his own ordeal in meeting with an unexpected SS death sentence. Many were the stories of torture to extract information. This very plausible letter could certainly have been written under duress. It seemed too good an opportunity for him to extract revenge. Why would this opportunity fall into his lap so easily? He was hiding in his mother's attic trying desperately to find a way to re-enter Germany to kill those who had destroyed his life.

It was all too clear, too clean. Yet he did remember his misguided impulse to look at his own funeral procession. For a few seconds he had pulled back just a little of the drapes to satisfy himself that it was happening.

He now held the Luger in a steady hand and pointed it at the open door.

Stefan was taken by surprise when a soft lilting voice said, "Stefan, I'm taking the next and last step to your hideout. Please be careful. If we do not trust each other and make a wrong movement it could be disastrous for both of us and also for others. I don't know if you still have coffee in your cup, mine is half full. Can we sit down and talk while finishing your mother's wonderful coffee? I'd like that. I know our organisation can fill your plan for retribution, whatever it is. We don't know what you wish to do, but I hope you will tell me the reason. I'm sure you have a story to tell and I believe you need help to attain your objective.

"My intuition is you have a gun in your hand. I will push my handgun across the floor into your room. If you put yours beside mine, I will enter on trust that you are not in possession of two guns."

There was silence from the room; then the minister again broke that silence with the scraping sound of sliding his handgun across the wood flooring. It stopped just inside the open entry space of Stefan's secret abode.

The Reverend waited. Seconds went by. His coffee was cold but he took a sip to quench the awful dryness in his throat. A few seconds passed. It seemed an eternity. Then a hand appeared holding a semi-automatic Luger pistol. The Luger was placed neatly beside the other weapon.

The first to speak was the Reverend Lindstrom. "Stefan," he called out," may I have permission to enter your private quarters?"

"Yes," Then there was a period of silence.

The Reverend moved slowly into the brightly lit room, coffee cup still in his left hand. The two men looked like adversaries before battle.

"Glad to meet you Stefan. My name is Hans Schmitt. For good reasons at the present time it is the Reverend Lindstrom, assistant at the Lutheran Church. Maybe we should have your mother bring us more coffee. Mine is cold. She is a wonderful lady, and it's not fair to keep her in anxiety. If she knows we are talking it will ease her fears."

Stefan looked in surprise at this person who had invaded his private and secret domain. He had not expected this outwardly calm easygoing and good-looking man in clerical attire. They both stood awkwardly meeting each other eye to eye.

Hans Schmitt again spoke first. "Stefan, don't you think it is foolish for us to stand here looking at each other like two prize fighters waiting for the first round bell to sound? Now that I'm here are you going to invite me to sit down?"

Stefan, thrown completely off guard, apologised. "Certainly, certainly sit here at the coffee table and I'll call mother to brew more coffee." He surprised himself by being so congenial, as it was not his intention to be friendly to this man. His suspicions were still very much alive. He knew how wily Gestapo and SS men could be until the information they sought was in their hands. When the unsuspecting realised they'd fallen into a trap, it was too late. They, like thousands of others became victims of the cruelty these people exacted with a relish unbelievable in human character.

Stefan sat quietly and listened as Hans Schmitt related the story of his family disaster. "A few Sunday mornings prior to my family being taken away to a death camp, a uniformed SS officer sat in one of the back pews. In his opening prayer that morning, father included the stranger in uniform. He tacked it on to his usual long and introductory prayer. 'Oh Lord, we welcome the uniformed stranger to this service. We pray for him. We ask your blessing on him as the protector of our freedom. We pray you will protect him and his family from all harm. In Jesus' name, Amen.'

"Not one of the congregation turned to see the man in uniform. They did not wish his scrutiny although many knew the stranger would be somewhere outside watching as they passed through the gates. My father may have planned to preach on another subject that morning, but I believe he purposely changed to his old text, 'Those who are anti-Semites are the children of Satan.' Father finished his sermon by saying, 'Man is not an island unto himself, steeped in his own religion. Especially at this time in our beloved country's history all religions must bond together whether they be Protestant, Catholic, Jewish, or otherwise. The freedom of speech and religion is a sacred thing worth sacrificing one's life to preserve. Now anti-Semitic literature and speech are prevalent to our ears and eyes. So when you go about your daily business, go out of your way to meet those of a different religion. Shake their hands and spread the trumpet call of friendship. Tell the outside world and perhaps we can help to stop the persecution of one of our fine religious groups.' He then announced the last hymn, 'Onward, Christian Soldiers.' As the small congregation filed out of church the SS officer was standing at the gate.

"I wanted to get a good look at this officer so that I would know him again. I was suspicious of him because of the way he entered, slipping quietly into the back church pew just as the service was to begin."

"Did you recognise him?"

"No, but I did perhaps better than that. The previous week a friend of mine was married at the church. My father officiated and I was one of the photographers. After I took pictures, the wedding party was whisked away to the reception. I stayed to help father lock up and later remembered I had left my camera on the back church pew. When entering the church that Sunday I picked up my camera from the seat where later the SS officer sat. It's a small camera and fits into my pocket.

"After services I was trying to be nonchalant, mingling with the parishioners leaving the church but with an eye on the officer close to the gates. He was looking intently at each parishioner that passed by. A warning bell rang in my head.

"I suddenly thought of my camera. Why not take a picture, close if possible, but how was this problem to be solved quickly? A hedge lined the driveway to the entrance gates. It was my job to keep it trimmed so I knew every thick part, every thin part and every hole. I knew there was a bird's nest and a hole very close to the gates and the officer would be directly facing me. A good subject, if I were on the opposite side of the hedge.

"I got my picture and it turned out clear and sharp like the wedding pictures. Now I could recognise this man anywhere."

"What did you do with the picture?" was Stefan's question.

"I keep it in the back section of my wallet."

"Oh, really?" Stefan was interested. "Can I see it, please?" He studied the now wrinkled snapshot and surprised young Hans by asking, "Can I keep this?"

"Why?" Hans asked with interest. "Do you recognise this SS officer?"

"Yes," was the only explanation Stefan was prepared to divulge.

"It seems important to you. You can have it. I have looked at it so many times I don't need it any more to help me recognise him."

"Thanks," was Stefan's terse reply as he put the snapshot in his pocket.

There was an awkward silence broken by footsteps on the stairs. It was Stefan's mother bearing fresh coffee, and the reheated remaining raisin scones. She studied the two men, so different in stature and looks. They were alert, the visitor appearing more relaxed than her son, but she detected the great tension between them.

Stefan was a much bigger man than Hans, tall with a heavyset muscular body like his father's. He had his mother's good looks, her mouth, high cheekbones, finely moulded nose, dark blue eyes and blond hair, which right now was tousled.

"Thank you, Mom, this looks great." It was his dismissal of her presence.

She couldn't resist a question, "Are you going to agree?"

"Mother that answer will be resolved one way or the other. Now be careful going down the stairs." It was Stefan's second dismissal, but again Thora Jonsson got in her last words before leaving, "If you want more coffee just shout." Reluctantly she left, side-stepping carefully around the two guns on the floor and closing the sliding panel door behind her. She was visibly shaken by this cloak-and-dagger meeting. She could find no plausible answers to her many questions and hoped her son would.

It was apparent Stefan had not come to any agreement with the soft-spoken young minister, whoever he really was, and she still wondered what mission he hoped to accomplish here.

Hans took a sip of coffee. "Stefan," he said, "your aunt joined us shortly after her husband was taken to a concentration camp. It so happened that a friend of hers was already in our organisation, and after interviews, investigations, double and triple checks, and an intensive interrogation by our recruiting committee, the door was opened for her to join this band of very dedicated people. She was shocked and saddened at your death. If she had not returned for your funeral I would not be here and you would be like a sailing ship becalmed in an ocean of opportunity for revenge but with no wind to help. I think we can help you to attain the commitment you have made to yourself. When your aunt returned from the funeral she immediately contacted headquarters and asked for a private interview. In these interviews the persons do not see each other and it's best that way.

Your Aunt Josephine told us that you have a personal quarrel with SS and Gestapo people. I know one of their many sins is breaking up and destroying families and killing those who resist them. She says you have a big axe to grind.

"Don't forget Stefan, it was a great shock when she saw your face at the attic window. Then she had to continue to the cemetery and stand beside the grave and listen to your mother's church minister read the burial service. 'I wanted to scream,' she told me. 'I wanted to shout, that Stefan Jonsson was alive and that I had just seen him!' Of course she wondered who was in the coffin. Many women would have broken down under the stress. Your mother stood beside her at the graveside. Aunt Josephine knew not to say anything until she returned to us.

"Now Stefan, it's your turn. I've unloaded my own sad story to you. Can you now tell me how and why you are here and in this prison you've made for yourself? You are dead and buried, Stefan. I can help you rise from the grave and start a new life. So, my friend, tell me all, every aspect, every detail of what happened to bring you to this full stop. Don't leave out anything. We want to know everything because small details not fully understood and checked could bring disaster to some segment of our operation."

Suddenly his facial expression relaxed. With a shrug of his shoulders he smiled and said, "By the way, I see your mother left the coffee pot. It's hot, let's have another coffee and then I will listen to you." Hans nonchalantly poured himself a coffee. He turned to Stefan, smiled his broad smile that showed his dark blemished tooth, and remarked, "You have the floor."

Stefan sat opposite, having already filled his own coffee cup. With a thoughtful expression he looked steadfastly at this young man. Before continuing with the request he stood up. From an inside pocket of his jacket he withdrew a small silver-coloured handgun. Stefan then took three steps to where the other two weapons lay side by side. He stopped and placed his handgun on the floor beside the others.

Hans waited until Stefan sat down then said, "Thanks, Stefan. I don't have a second gun. Trust me." Then he stood up took the three necessary steps to place a dangerous-looking switchblade knife next to the guns. Stefan had not seen any hand movement. The vicious-looking knife was just there in the young man's hand. From where? He didn't ask. "It's a handy weapon," was Hans only comment.

The two men looked at each other. Hans moved first. His hand stretched across the table and met Stefan's in a firm handshake that sealed the beginning of a friendship and a cause. This friendship would take them on numerous courageous journeys seeking revenge and repayment by many of those who had and were still committing atrocities. Their eyes met and Stefan thought that the scar below Hans' left eye would be a dangerous give-away to authorities who might be looking for someone who had escaped their murderous net. The scar and the blemished tooth would be instant points of recognition. His impulse was to mention this fact, but he felt this was not the right moment.

His thoughts were interrupted by that soft, lilting voice. "Stefan, I'm still waiting. Tell me, why are you here? Please start at the beginning."

Stefan took a deep breath, and began.

"I was born in Hamburg of Swedish parents. My father was vice-president of a large fish cannery operation. I completed my education at Stockholm University and majored in marine biology. In the fall of 1936 I obtained a good position in the research department of the cannery. When Hitler's troops occupied Sudetenland in 1938, I had already established myself in quite an important job. The military problems in Europe worsened, so my parents returned to Sweden and tried to persuade me to follow them. I declined. My job paid well and I had a beautiful girlfriend, her name was Ilsa. She was Jewish.

"Hitler's rise to power had changed many things. His anti-Jewish policies were not condoned by all but rumours persisted that he was persecuting anyone of Jewish origin. Stories of atrocities filtered through but most people didn't believe those tales. I worked hard and obtained promotions and had my own office. I felt quite important by the end of September, 1938. Things did not change much in the new year of 1939 but little groups of Swedish workers often sat at lunch and talked about what would happen to them if Hitler took Germany into a big war. In March, 1939, as you know, German troops crossed the Czech frontier and Monsignor Josef Tesco of Slovakia, a pro-German, declared that Slovakia was under German protection. We were scared.

"Again Mother asked me to give up my job and return to Sweden. I ignored her warning and set out to enjoy another beautiful summer. It was a shock when Hitler marched into Poland on September first, and then Britain and France declared war on Germany. Being fluent in three languages, English, Swedish, and German, I had made many friends among the buyers and in other areas of the business community. Many were wealthy Jewish people, but with Hitler's anti-Jewish policies there was a big exodus from the Jewish business community. Many people said I would regret my girlfriend being Jewish. We spent a holiday in Sweden, and Mother again tried to convince us to stay but again we ignored her advice. Each month Jewish buyers of the company's products became fewer until eventually they refrained from phoning in orders. To compensate for this lack of business, large orders for a variety of canned goods poured in from the German armed forces. Often when I tried to make phone contact with good Jewish friends there was no answer and the operator would inform me the number was out of order, so I presumed they had left Germany.

"The fifteenth of October, 1939, was my birthday. Polish resistance was no more. Radio and newspapers were making a great noise about a German U-boat that had penetrated the defences of Scapa Flow Naval Base in the Orkney Islands and sunk the British Battleship Royal Oak. Sailors were toasting each other at the bar in my favourite restaurant. Ilsa and I were shepherded to a secluded table in the dining room for the celebration of my twenty-third birthday. Ilsa was eight months younger than me. The first day of February was Ilsa's birthday.

"We talked about getting married and returning to Sweden because of the increasing anti-Jewish atmosphere. Ilsa's father was a dental surgeon who had his own practice and also worked at the hospital. He was a very outspoken critic of Hitler and his policies. Colleagues warned him many times about his anti-government outbursts. He was a stubborn man and felt that in his position he was protected from harm and that free speech should never be stilled.

"Ilsa had brought me a birthday card and a present wrapped in gold-coloured paper. Ilsa requested I open the gift first. It was a large gold pocket watch on a heavy chain, the glass protected by a gold cover. I pressed the release catch and the cover sprang back to reveal a shining surface beautifully engraved in Swedish: To Stefan, October 15, 1939. Time waits for no one, so fill your life with love, for time cannot erase that wonderful gift. Ilsa

"I ordered a bottle of good French white wine so we could drink a toast. Unfolding the card I saw two hearts on the front. One was labelled Ilsa, the other, Stefan. A chain joining them was drawn in ink. A poem was written on the back side in a bold, strong hand.

To Stefan, my friend, my love,
You're more beautiful than the heavens above.
Today we celebrate your birth.
May it be filled with joy and mirth.
For tomorrow we know not what will come.
Will we live by love,
or be killed by gun?
Whatever comes, be it good or ill,
My heart with love for you will fill.

Ilsa

"The waiter brought our wine and asked me to answer a very important telephone call. 'Don't open the wine until I return.' was my request to our waiter. The call was from Ilsa's father relaying a message from Sweden that my father had died from a heart attack and my presence was requested at home. Ilsa and I hurried from the restaurant. She was clutching the card and her gift to me. I glanced back to look at the cosy corner table. The full unopened bottle of French wine stood like a sentinel guarding two empty wine glasses that were never filled to toast our happy future together. Death had suddenly changed happiness to sorrow.

"I drove Ilsa home promising to call her next evening and said I planned to return as soon as possible. I kissed her goodbye. She thrust the watch and card into my hands, waved a farewell and hurried into the house.

"Things were happening in the streets of Hamburg that night. I was forced to make numerous detours. Roving gangs of uniformed men were breaking windows of certain stores and homes. People, young and old, were being dragged out and herded into black trucks that drove slowly behind the crowd. Many SS men were participating and giving orders. My impulse was to return to Ilsa's home and take her to safety. I knew the shops being wrecked were Jewish but I thought nothing would happen to Ilsa's home because her father held such a high position at the hospital. Convinced she would be safe, I drove to my bachelor room, grabbed a few clothes and caught the late boat to Ystad in Sweden.

"Next evening I phoned Ilsa's number. There was no answer, not even a ring. The Hamburg operator informed me the phone was out of order. I tried to reach my mother's older sister Aunt Josephine, who had married a Jewish man. They lived above their little jewellery store. Their number was also out of order. I was concerned, remembering the SS and the mobs breaking windows and throwing people into trucks. I phoned my work place and talked to people there asking them to check at Ilsa's home and to call back when they made contact. After agonising for hours I made frantic calls to four different people in my office who were under my jurisdiction. I was told they were not available.

"Two hours after father's funeral I was on the plane to Hamburg and I rushed to Ilsa's home. It had been ransacked and most of the windows broken. I ran to the house of the old neighbour, Frau Guggenberger. She opened the door only a fraction and would only say, 'It was the Storm troopers who took them away. They killed Ilsa's father. Please go away. I'm afraid to talk to you.' I rushed to my aunt and uncle's jewellery store to find it also ransacked and a banner across the front with the word JEW printed on it in large letters.

"Upstairs Aunt Josephine was sitting in her small living room. She was incoherent and staring into space. I had to shake her into semi-reasonable conversation. The SS and their henchmen had wrecked their store and looked on while the mob stole their stock of jewellery. Her husband was beaten up then dragged away to the crowd's cries of 'Kill the Jews!' My aunt was saved because she had her Swedish passport on the table ready for a trip to my father's funeral. Because she was not Jewish they left her alone. I made her coffee, stayed a short time, and left with thoughts of revenge.

"I learned that when the mob and the SS arrived at their house, Ilsa's father had opened the front door to them. He had no fear of the SS, at least he had never shown it. Many had been his patients when they needed dental surgery and only his expertise would do the perfect job. When a number of SS men entered and started to break up his home, Ilsa's father called them 'Hitler's bastards.' They beat him to death in front of his wife. Then they and the mob proceeded to wreck the home. Ilsa had locked herself in the small attic bedroom on the third floor, hoping that they would not come up. When they finished ransacking the two bottom floors, some SS men found the attic and her locked door, broke it down and after a time dragged her to the black-covered truck that waited outside.

"A few months after Ilsa's and her mother's disappearance, two messages were smuggled out of a concentration camp and delivered to Aunt Josephine. One said that Ilsa's mother had died in camp soon after arriving and that Ilsa had been sent almost immediately to a rest camp for German SS officers somewhere in the Black Forest.

"When I eventually came to terms with my grief and realised Ilsa would never return, I went back to work. Once I returned to her father's house, to discover a large printed sign was hanging over the door. It read 'Jews Lived Here.' The windows had been boarded up and nailed shut and the doors had been padlocked, but I found a kitchen window they'd missed. I climbed through then up to the attic where I sat for a long time amid the shambles of what was once a lovely girl's bedroom. I cried, thinking of how I'd refused to obey my intuitions that night. It was in Ilsa's bedroom that I made plans and swore that those who committed this crime would pay and pay dearly. I vowed to seek out men wearing the SS uniform to reap my revenge. So far I have accomplished nothing.

"Hours later I went down the broken stairway and retraced my steps to the kitchen window I'd entered earlier. Heavy boards had been placed against it. It took me several minutes to push them clear. I climbed through and was confronted by two Hitler Youth looking very proud of themselves. I recognised both of them. One was the son of an office worker in my department. His companion was the son of a lady who cleaned my office every weekend. Sometimes when there was extra work to do the boy helped his mother. He had always been polite. Now in his uniform with the swastika emblazoned on the arm he stood proudly and arrogantly beside the older boy. It was he who shouted loudest, 'Jew lover, Jew lover!'

"I stood trembling with rage, then before I realised what I was doing I grabbed hold of both by the front of their shirts and shook them until I thought their heads would spin from their necks. I threw them both to the ground and through clenched teeth warned them that if I found them near this house again I'd kill them both. Standing over the frightened pair I had the great urge to kill them right there, for in those few moments I could visualise in these two the nucleus of future trained SS murderers. Restraining myself I walked quickly to the front of the house and tore down the sign. By the time I got to my car I'd torn it into many pieces.

"The two boys had recovered from the scare and were talking to one of their Youth Leaders and pointing in my direction. Turning the ignition key, I raced the motor, slammed it into gear and sped away with at least a little satisfaction, but it was only the infinitesimal beginning of what I hope my future role is to be.

"Next morning when I returned to my office at the research department, the atmosphere was unfriendly. I'd been away only five days but the half dozen Swedish employees, although polite, made every possible effort to stay clear of me. It was lunch time in the cafeteria that same day, when my opposite number in charge of research in another department joined me and we sat alone. He was a pleasant young man about my age, a Swedish citizen and also a bachelor.

"Before sitting down he stood for a moment with his hand on his chair back looking at me. Suddenly for the first time I realised that this man by his looks could be my brother with his blond hair, blue eyes, clear sun-tanned square-cut features and six-foot husky frame. We had seldom been in each other's company although we talked by interoffice phone many times a week. Not often did he eat in the cafeteria.

"This was his last working day. He hoped to get a position with another company in Sweden. He sat down and moved his chair close then spoke in a low voice. 'During your absence my friend the district manager of this operation who as you know is German has been visited twice by high-ranking SS officers. With the spare key they entered your office, pulled down the shades and were there almost an hour on the first visit and much longer on their second. My advice is take immediate action and go home to Sweden.' It was clear I had offended the SS by associating with Jewish families, and he believed my life was in great danger.

"Finishing lunch, he stood up, put his hand on my shoulder and said, 'Please, Stefan do as I ask. Your mother has lost her life's companion a few short days ago. Do you want her to be grieving over your death, too? Believe me my friend, I know these SS people. They are ruthless thugs. It will be made to look like an accident. Make your decision quickly.'

"With that message of warning he left, and it was only then I took notice of faces at the adjacent tables. Our very confidential talk had been watched with interest by a number of employees, including the office worker whose Hitler Youth son had been shaken up the day before.

"Also coming through loud and clear was the fact that on my own desk was a large stack of correspondence to answer and a host of other jobs to attend to. My cleaning lady had called to complain that the office had been locked for more than four days. She requested I leave it open that night so she could catch up with her work. Without a second thought I told her I'd be using my office and working overtime trying to catch up with a backlog of paperwork.

"The busy afternoon passed quickly and employees went home. After two hours of hard work there was lots of correspondence remaining, so I decided to take a break at the small restaurant around the corner. It was a cool evening. I donned a warm sweater, left my jacket on the coat rack, and flicked off the switch leaving the office in darkness. Closing the door gently I proceeded along the corridor, down one flight of stairs, then stopped by my lunchtime partner's office situated directly below mine. I asked how he was making out. Although fourth generation Swedish, he had a German background and name, Max Wunderlich. On his desk there always stood the miniature flag of his beloved country, Sweden. 'I'm getting there but very slowly,' he answered. 'As it's my last evening I want to leave things just right. Think Stefan, early tomorrow morning, I'll be on the ship to Sweden. Make sure you follow me.'

'What about a break for something to eat?'

'No thanks. I prefer to finish this first but you can bring back a coffee. Here just a minute, I have my old thermos here on the shelf.'

"It was only a three- or four-minute walk to my favourite restaurant where I ordered a sandwich and coffee then took time to relax and read the evening news. Looking at my watch I was surprised to see it was 9:00 p.m. I'd been gone over an hour. Quickly I paid for Max's coffee and my own snack then hastened to our office building. Using my passkey to get in, I ran up the stairs two at a time. Coming close to Max's office I shouted, 'Coffee up! Ten minute break!'

"The sight I encountered was one that I tucked away beside the thoughts of Ilsa's father being beaten to death and what had happened to Ilsa and her mother. Max was slumped over his desk, his head resting on some unfinished paperwork. Grasped loosely in his right hand was a small calibre revolver. His head lay in a manner that made it clear the small hole in his right temple was self-inflicted. There was very little blood and the paperwork on his desk had soaked up most of the slow oozing red stream.

"Standing in shock for a moment, I moved closer and with disbelief picked up a picture that Max's left hand was touching. It was Ilsa. I realised this was not suicide but one more SS murder. This time someone had made a mistake. They had intended to kill me and make it look as though a grief-stricken lover had taken his own life.

"Working quickly during the hour that followed I changed clothing with the dead man, even to the yellow shoes that pinched my toes. Then I struggled upstairs with Max's limp body. As though setting some sort of stage play I deposited his body in my office chair, put my jacket on it and repositioned Max's head, hands and the picture of Ilsa in the exact pose I'd found them. A question hammered in my brain. Where did they get the picture? I'd never seen it before.

"I returned to Max's office to ensure there were no telltale bloodstains or other evidence to show that a mistake had been made. I carried the revolver and the blood saturated papers back to my office then carefully placed the revolver in Max's right hand. I spread his papers on top of those I'd been working on. Using Max's hair to lift the head I adjusted it to the right position so the trickle of blood would continue to ooze onto the paper. I'd checked Max's bloodied papers. They dealt with complaints regarding the slow delivery of a product, but the messages were so obliterated that no one would associate them with

Max's office. I knew that if this was an SS ordered killing there would be little or no investigation. From the inside of my jacket I took my wallet and removed a recent picture of Ilsa and me together with her birthday card and most of the money. I then replaced it in the pocket with my office passkey. The phone rang; it continued for at least half a minute. My first impulse was to pick it up, but I knew someone was checking to ensure I was dead.

"Taking a last look at what should have been my body, I left the brightly lit office. On my way out I checked Max's office again for any telltale signs of the murderer's mistake. Leaving his office in darkness I made my exit to the street. It was 10:55 p.m. when I closed the heavy main entrance door behind me. With Max's red-chequered thermos under my arm and carrying his briefcase with all the unmarked papers from his desk, I moved out of the shadows and down the seven steps to the sidewalk. There were a few pedestrians but no shadowy figures lurking in doorways. Traffic was light, a few motorists and one taxi picking up a fare on the curb. I strained my eyes but was unable to see the passenger. Then for a moment the taxi driver switched on his dome light and I saw him, the passenger was none other than the Hitler Youth leader.

"It was a short distance to where Max's car was parked. I had marked the ignition key before leaving the building in case I needed to get away in a hurry. For a moment or two I sat in the car planning the best route to Max's place. Fifteen minutes later I hurried inside and made certain the door was securely locked before stretching out on the single bed where I tried to relax and plan my next move.

"I congratulated myself on the good fortune of being alive and for a short time allowed myself to think over the horrors of the past week. Suddenly I sat up. Max's passport! Where was it? I would not get on the Sweden-bound ship without a passport. Springing off the bed I first searched Max's briefcase then his suitcase and his folded clothing but with no result. I did a complete search of that apartment, to no avail. I felt trapped with no escape to Sweden and for the first time in many days, felt panic. Could it be possible that Max had the passport in his desk drawer at the office? Now I had no passkey, so returning to the office was impossible and anyway the risk was too great this close to midnight. Looking at Max's tweed jacket I thought, 'That's where it is!' There was Max's bulky wallet but no passport in any of his pockets.

"Opening the wallet I discovered the bulkiness was caused by a large amount of money mostly in Swedish currency plus a fair amount of German marks. I decided to risk the passport check and maybe bluff my way through or with so much money maybe bribe my way aboard. One thing was sure, I had to get to Sweden.

"I spent a restless night and at 5:00 a.m. I was up washed and shaved. Not wishing to come in contact with the landlord, I hurriedly prepared my exit. The ferry did not leave from Stettin but from Swinemünde. I had often made the journey. Sailing time was eight o'clock in the morning, but I left the apartment at 5:20 a.m. without any definite plan of action regarding a passport. Driving for approximately ten minutes, I thought of one more possibility: the glove compartment. I pulled over and with clumsy shaking fingers turned the key and there was Max Wunderlich's passport.

"There was no problem at the loading dock. The authorities accepted Max's passport as mine and waved me onto the car ferry. I stayed in the car pretending to sleep, afraid someone on board might recognise me. The ferry crossing gave me time to think and relax. When I disembarked, I was composed going through Swedish customs; they were my countrymen. I gunned the car along the East Coast Road and sang a song, one that Ilsa used to sing to me. After passing through Karlsrona away eastward out to sea I could see the finger-like island of Öland. On vacation I had taken Ilsa over there to the small fishing town of Farjestaden where we had lunch in Kalma and camped overnight.

"I drove through Oshashamm and left the Island of Öland behind, but just before the road turned a little from the coast I saw a ferry ploughing its way towards the big Island of Gotland out there almost in the centre of the Baltic Sea. It was shrouded in sea mist and seemed so far away, just like my memories of those happy days on vacation when Ilsa and I drove this road and saw all those things together.

"Parking some distance from my mother's home I phoned to make sure she was alone. She listened as I told her what had happened. Then in a very calm voice, she promised to help. We have two separate garages. I requested she open the door of the one that could be locked. She needed five minutes to take her own car out of that side. I sat and waited those five long minutes, hoping none of the neighbours would pass by and recognise me then I drove home. My mother closed the door and locked it. In less than a half hour I was enjoying her home-baked scones and wonderful coffee.

"The house, of course, has this attic bedroom similar to Ilsa's, so I made a pact with mother. I would be the ghost in her house and this attic would be my domain. She was not to divulge anything about me. In the time since my father's death, mother had taken charge of things and was eager to help, both on my account and because she had been very fond of her sister's husband.

"In the late afternoon of the day I arrived home from Germany, one of the top management people from the company's Stockholm head office visited my mother. He was the bearer of sad news. I had suffered fatal head injuries when cleaning a small souvenir gun that had accidentally gone off. Apparently Mother put on a good act of grief at the loss of her son such a short time after her husband's death.

"So it was that 'Stefan Jonsson's body' was supposedly brought home to grieving relations and buried beside his father.

"At first I was concerned that when Max Wunderlich did not turn up in Sweden after leaving his job there would be inquiries that could result in SS or Gestapo opening up my assassination file again. Max was a bachelor, his parents were dead; so it could be a long time before he'd be missed.

"I wish to even the score many times for my friend Max and my own dead Ilsa." Stefan showed his feelings. Telling Hans about the tragedy of Ilsa's death had rekindled his strong desire for retribution, especially against all SS men. "I have often thought what sign I would leave to mock them as death strikes in widely separate areas on the first and fifteenth of each month when my vendetta of justice is continued and one more SS member is dead. They robbed me of my love and my future. The night Ilsa and I rushed from our birthday celebration dinner table when told of my father's death, we left a full, unopened bottle of good French white wine. I planned that wherever possible beside each SS victim, I will leave two empty glasses and an unopened bottle of good white French wine all devoid of fingerprints and incriminating evidence. The unopened bottle of wine will represent all the wonderful plans we had for a future full of happiness. It's all gone, destroyed by the men who use the skull and crossbones as their badge of honour. Ilsa's life is no more; she chose her own sad way out by committing suicide. Mine, like the glasses, remains empty, empty of hope that I will be able to attain my revenge."

Stefan turned to Hans and in a voice filled with emotion asked, "Can you help me, please? I need vengeance. I need repayment. I need retribution. My war will be continuous against these men. It will not diminish and I hope, God willing, it will continue for my lifetime. SS murderers will tremble and wonder which of them will be next when they see two empty glasses and the unopened bottle beside the dead body of one of their comrades."

Hans touched Stefan's shoulder. "I believe we can Stefan. I believe we can. Stay where you are. I will be in touch with you." Then he smiled a sad smile. "If per chance our enemies find me first someone will take my place, I promise, one of us will find you. Now I think you should call your mother and ease her fears. But first, let us return our weapons to their proper places."

When Hans picked up his switchblade Stefan asked, "Some day I'd like to learn how to use that. I notice you are fast."

Hans smiled. "It will be part of your training. Your Aunt Josephine learned fast. Like you, Stefan, she had her own axe to grind. I've already told you her home base is Stettin. Last month Aunt Josephine received a message.

"She was returning one day from the bakery and about to cross the street when a voice from behind said, 'Don't turn around. I have put a message in your basket.' Grasping the folded paper that nestled close to her meagre bread ration, she almost ran home.

"The smuggled message was from the concentration camp where your uncle was taken, and it bore sad news. He had been killed by a guard whose name and address were written on the paper. He was the son of a good friend of hers in Hamburg. She asked for a temporary move back to Hamburg in the hope that when her friend's son came home on leave, she might get the opportunity to kill him. 'Vengeance is mine,' she said, 'not the Lord's.'

"Through our own information network we heard this certain guard was at his mother's home on leave. Your aunt does not have to go there now because on my way here I made a side trip to Hamburg and the job is complete." With the switchblade still in his hand he said, "I told you it was a handy weapon."

"Thank you," was all Stefan could think of as a reply.

"I must go soon," said Hans glancing at his watch.

Stefan's look was serious. His words were clear and with much conviction he said, "I have information you should know before leaving. It is regarding your family. I have refrained from divulging it until certain I could trust you. You now know my experience with the two boys in Hitler Youth uniforms calling me 'Jew Lover' outside Ilsa's wrecked home. My impulse was to kill them but quickly they ran to their troop leader and pointed at me as I got into my car. You will also remember that on my way out of the office the night Max Wunderlich was murdered, a taxi stopped close by to pick up the Hitler Youth leader. I'm certain he murdered Max in mistake for me. I'm surprised he was still in the area over two hours later."

"Interesting," was Hans only comment.

"I believe you and I have a common interest in this man and may wish to join forces in tracking him down."

"Yes," Hans answered expectantly waiting for Stefan to explain.

"You gave me a picture."

"Yes."

Stefan took the picture from his pocket and placed it on the coffee table beside Hans.

"But I do not wish it returned."

"I know," replied Stefan. "It is a good clear picture of an SS officer who sat in one of the back pews in your father's church just prior to the Sunday your family was taken into custody and then to a death camp. I feel sure he would be the SS officer in charge of the soldiers who arrested your family. He must be a very industrious killer to be promoted so quickly."

"I don't understand," interrupted Hans.

Stefan was silent for a few moments then slowly and with hate in his eyes he said, "The SS officer in your picture was the Hitler Youth leader in Hamburg who believes he murdered me. It would seem he travels to different areas attending religious services where ministers speak truth and freedom for all. I think his job is to condemn those people to death camps. In my own mind I have condemned him to his own death. I hope you can help me accomplish that."

Hans showed no emotion in his reply. "If you are certain Stefan, I'd like to accompany you when that time comes and we will extract a confession before he dies." Then he added, "I'm sure we can help you decrease some of your hostility and anger, perhaps set you up in an area or city strange to you. Too many people might recognise you in Hamburg. How does Stettin appeal to you? I'm sure your Aunt Josephine would like that. Think about it, my friend. We will not keep you waiting for our judgement on my findings here. You will be contacted very soon. Now I have a ferry boat trip to make and hope everything will work out smoothly for my journey."

The two men shook hands, then instinctively embraced each other knowing the very dangerous plans that could evolve from their resolutions. Their decisions could direct them as saboteurs or one-man missions to various areas or as spies launched into the labyrinth of the SS and Gestapo's far-reaching tentacles. Where an error in judgement, or one mistaken word could end with a cruel torture and death.

Hans Schmitt, alias Nicholas Meyer aero engineer, alias the Reverend Lindstrom, retraced his steps down the stairs. He said his goodbye to Thora Jonsson. He thanked her profusely for the wonderful coffee and scones. At the door he held both her hands, kissed her cheek and said, "Thora, pray for both of us. To make sure you pray for the correct person, my real name is Hans Schmitt."

With a catch in her voice she replied, "I will. I will, Hans."

Hans Schmitt walked quietly down the garden path and disappeared in the gathering dusk, leaving Thora Jonsson with more unanswered questions. Standing at the door looking into the gathering darkness, she was thinking, "Does he have a car close by? Will he get a cab to the ferry? It's a long walk. He must have baggage. I'm sure he will get a cab. I should have offered him a ride to the ferry terminus."

With a sigh she closed the door and poured a cup of coffee. Sitting at the kitchen table she knew that in the future there would be fear in her heart for two men, and not only for her son.

Many hours after Thora Jonsson said goodbye to Hans Schmitt, a good-looking curly-haired young man with a small white scar under his left eye joked with the German official at Stettin. The official was checking passports of passengers arriving off the ferry from Sweden. One of the young man's white teeth had a blemish, a dark spot that didn't take away from his happy smile. After checking the young man's passport and identity papers, the official said, "Good luck, Mr. Meyer, being an aero engineer is a responsible position these days. We need people like you."

"I do my best," was Mr. Meyer's reply. Then he quickened his pace on the off-ramp because someone he knew should be waiting nearby with means of transport.

9

Timothy's Letter, Prison Camp, 1942

The third anniversary of Timothy's capture passed with no celebration except for the knowledge that spring had sprung in this dreary place named Stalag. He had learned to live with the frustration of captivity and the discouraging war news. The bright uplifting highlights of those years were the sudden arrivals of mail, sometimes after many months of disillusioned expectations.

Tim had received letters from both Kathleen and Sharon. Sharon had sent two parcels. She wrote loving letters and much news though some of the lines were blanked out by the censor. Never did her words indicate she was not waiting for him. Kathleen's letters were devoid of information concerning her marriage. Timothy decided she was happy with husband George, her children, and her security.

It was usual for prisoners to find another prisoner who would be compatible in sharing rations plus extras that came their way. Tim's partner (known as a 'mucker' in Stalag terminology) was a little Welsh-man named Ken Jones. During the years of captivity they'd shared food and the contents of parcels from home plus numerous ups and downs, but their upbeat personalities overcame the dreary months of depressing news and scary situations. It was a unique companionship laced with much understanding.

A mucker can be many things, a friend, a good cook, easy to talk to, good at sharing problems, reliable, honest, forgiving, strong in character, reasonable in his anger and frustrations. In that multitude of prison-camp muckers, there were many who did not attain the highest of marks for their honesty. This was especially so when it came to the rationing of the meagre food supplies. Tim and Ken's Stalag was no exception regarding those people who fell into the dishonest category.

One personality who became a close friend was a small, agile Scot with a great sense of humour. Ian McGregor hailed from Glasgow and before joining the Royal Air Force he worked with a travelling circus, where at each show he performed with his parents in a high-wire act.

Ian was soon known as Wee Jock McGregor, the Scot who bunked in the far corner close to the washroom. He boasted that he could walk a high wire without a net. Newcomers or visitors from other barracks were usually informed of this. So Ian was quite an important celebrity. For a while at least, until something better or more interesting turned up. His rich Scottish brogue made for easy listening.

He was given a few lessons on how to pick the locks on his handcuffs. Wee Jock boasted he could walk a high wire wearing Stalag handcuffs, and not fall off.

It was Tim who discovered that there was a young lady in the circus whom wee Jock hoped to marry someday. His desire now was to let her know he was alive.

"I'll give you my Stalag mail card," Tim volunteered. "We get one next week so then you can write to her. You can send it to your Mom and Dad." Wee Jock bowed his head before answering.

"My Mom and Dad were killed in an air raid many months ago. My girlfriend is all I have, Tim. A few months ago she was conscripted into the Women's Auxiliary Air Force. I have her mother's address in Glasgow. She will know where to redirect my mail. Thanks Tim, but you see I need only one card."

It was a surprise in mid-June when another batch of mail arrived in camp. Prisoners crowded around the barrack senior man distributing the fairly large bundle of letters. Expectation showed on their tense faces. They stood uneasily, hoping and perhaps praying in silence that their name would be called. Tim, having had recent letters from Sharon and Kathleen was surprised to hear his name and disillusioned to see unfamiliar handwriting on the envelope. Rushing to his bunk he read and reread the disturbing news. Cook Mary Jane Kernaghan had taken it upon herself to write Timothy telling him of the terrible tragedy of Kathleen's marriage. In detail she described the degrading situations Kathleen had been subjected to by George O'Conor.

Still clutching the letter, Tim walked the perimeter circuit of the prison camp for hours. Sometimes he stopped for many minutes and stared through the barbed wire to the open countryside. It was his Welsh mucker, Ken Jones, who fell into step beside him as Tim continued his marathon walk. Ken walked in silence indicating by his presence, I'm here pal, when you're ready to tell me your troubles.

It was Tim who spoke first. "I've got to get out of here, Ken."

"The letter?" was his friend's only reply.

"Yes, I'm going to escape from this place and get back to Ireland. Then I'll kill the bastard."

"It's that bad!" Ken did not push for clarification. He waited for Tim to explain. For sometime they continued walking in silence then returned to their barrack. Sitting beside his friend, Ken listened as Tim read the letter to him. He finished with a wistful look in his eyes, "And she was expecting her third child sometime in August. I must find a way out of here Ken. Will you come with me?" Ken knew that Tim was serious. "Let's go and talk to the escape committee. July or August would be a great time to go, harvest and all that. We wouldn't starve, there would be lots of harvest stuff Ken, fruits and vegetables. We could live on raw potatoes if necessary."

"An Irishman like you might live on raw potatoes but I'd like a bit of variety."

Ignoring the jest Tim looked earnestly at Ken. "If the escape committee accepts us, will you come with me? It'll take time to organise."

Ken wasn't sure it would be the right decision, especially if Tim's mission was to kill someone, but he knew if Tim was going out, he'd go with him. "OK, Tim, but I'm not looking forward to a diet of raw potatoes. You'll have to do better."

Tim hugged his mucker. "Ken, I will get you to Sweden and home. I must get home!"

First it was an interview with the escape people, the beginning of many, culminating eventually in early July when they exchanged identities with two army prisoners due to go out on farm work. Timothy O'Neill and Ken Jones took respective bunks in the army prison-camp barracks of two soldiers captured at Dunkirk in 1940.

Three Months Later

After brew time on a dark cold night in early October, 1943, a small group of prisoners gathered around Tim and Ken. Some sat together on Ken's bunk, holding Stalag-made tin mugs full of hot Red Cross cocoa. The two had promised to tell the gathering about their escape attempt. Ken decided the Irish were better story tellers than the Welsh, so he delegated Tim to tell of their exploits. The majority of those who listened would always remember Tim and Ken's story. Perhaps in years after liberation they'd recall that memory to tell their children.

The soldiers they swapped with took on the roles of Aircraftsman Timothy O'Neill and Sergeant Air Gunner Kenneth Jones. Before this changeover numerous meetings were arranged; they had to memorise much personal information about their counterparts. So at the gate check when leaving for the work camp there would be no hesitation in answering to their names and prisoner numbers plus other personal questions. No problems arose leaving camp. It was mid-July. With twenty other prisoners they were taken by truck to a large farm not many miles from their prison camp.

Tim and Ken felt strange in army khaki uniforms, and the corporal in charge, a prisoner himself, irked both of them by his aggressive behaviour. Tim didn't want to waste any time so after a few days of getting their bearings and investigating the best walk-away escape routes to the railroad station, he decided it was time to go. There was no barbed wire here, no machine gun posts, just a small party of twenty-plus prisoners working the harvest under guard. A big change from the soul-destroying curtailment of freedom they were accustomed to behind the high wire fencing in their Stalag enclosure.

Things were lax except for the British army corporal who took his job as senior rank very seriously. The two German guards delegated to keep the work party in line had no interest in a continuous check on manpower. It was their Allied comrade in the form of Corporal Atkins of the British Expeditionary Force who was their jailer. Tim said, "Atkins should be wearing a German uniform. When I get back to England I'll report him."

Tim planned a Saturday morning exit, when only one weekend guard and the BEF Corporal would be checking the count of prisoners at the usual time of 7:00 a.m. and 5:00 p.m. The guards took turns at weekends off.

Then came the weekend that Tim planned for their escape. Blue skies and warm sunshine were forecast. The wonderful smell of early harvest in the fields made Tim feel closer to his beloved Ireland. His family would also be at early harvest work, maybe working on Dunraven Estate for George O'Conor.

Tim heaved a bale of hay onto the old wagon, then turned to Ken and spoke quietly. "Immediately after morning check parade tomorrow. It's Saturday and we will have a ten-hour start before the five o'clock count."

"Sure Tim, sure!" was Ken's hesitant and not too enthusiastic reply.

Tim noticed the tone of the answer but ignored it. "We'll hide our civvy clothes and haversacks of rations in the hay storage shed tonight."

"Okay, Tim." Ken's voice faltered. Now it was crunch time. He didn't have the same revenge mission that was driving Tim to risk this escape attempt. Ken also had misgivings about taking off into unknown enemy territory as escaped prisoners. On this work party they were also impostors, not the Army prisoners they claimed to be. For Ken things were great working on this farm even with Corporal Atkin's behaviour. This was the first time in years he'd had an opportunity to join a work party, as Air Force prisoners were not permitted to take part in these labour excursions. Now Tim wanted him to go out into the unknown German countryside where both of them might be shot as escaping prisoners. He was scared, but had volunteered and promised to try this escape with Tim who had investigated the safest route to Stettin on the Baltic Sea and then over to neutral Sweden. Tim maintained there were many escapees from other prison camps who had already made the trip to Stettin. He had told Ken that another Welshman and a Canadian had got all the way to Stettin by train. They got to the docks but were apprehended and jailed for a while. Their prison-camp dog tags proved they were prisoners of war, so it was lucky to have and keep this proof.

When Ken asked how many got to Sweden, Tim's only answer was, "My Irish luck is enough for both of us. We will be among the first to make it."

Tim was adamant in his bid to reach the seaport of Stettin. He kept repeating, "It's the best route to freedom. Many others have taken it.

All we have to do is smuggle aboard a ship to neutral Sweden and hope for a quick return to Britain. Then to Ireland, where I have a score to settle at Dunraven House."

Saturday morning after check parade and breakfast, the other prisoners, including Atkins, had returned to their quarters for a relaxing day off. Tim and Ken made their way to the hay storage shed where they had stashed the getaway equipment. Quickly they changed into Stalag-made civilian clothing, buried the army uniforms deep in the hay and from another hiding place retrieved haversacks of "acquired" rations. After a few minutes watching to ensure the coast was clear, they made their bid for freedom. Walking nonchalantly, they headed towards the railroad station.

Tim was certain it was a good omen that the railroad station was close by. The journey was made with no problems. No one paid attention to them as they trudged along the road to the railroad station. They had previously obtained a train schedule. To their surprise the trains seemed to be on time. Making sure the platform contained no familiar military figures who might recognise them from the work party or from their compound back in the Stalag, they unhurriedly strolled to the ticket booth.

With well-practised German Tim asked for "*Zwei Fahrkarte nach Stettin*" (two tickets to Stettin). If questioned, it was their intention to say they were French workers transferred to a work camp close to Stettin. In their pockets were Tim and Ken's bogus work camp papers showing this to be the case. They were also armed with passports, compasses, German money and, of course, the civilian clothing they were wearing plus the two old tattered German haversacks, the type that most foreign labourers carried. The underground Stalag escape committee was very thorough when supplying would-be escapees.

Tim and Ken were surprised and elated when the old German station master, ticket seller and collector, flag man, janitor and any other position the small station required failed to ask any questions. He simply peered through his oversized wire-frame spectacles at the two figures facing him through the small dirty glass window.

Picking up the two tickets and ninety *Pfenning* (pennies) change from the currency, Tim turned quickly, excitement and relief showing on his face as this first big hurdle had been accomplished with ease.

Ken Jones had disappeared. Tim found him standing around the corner of the ticket office building looking very casual and unconcerned, pretending to read a day-old copy of the *Breslau Zeitung* as he leaned against the wall. He looked up as Tim approached holding out the tickets to make a V for victory sign. Ken nodded approval and then ignored Tim as two Luftwaffe officers from the nearby training base formed a single file on the narrow pathway to get past Ken. They were unconcerned with the surroundings and too deep in their own conversation to take any notice of two French workers who had almost blocked the exit to the platform.

Ten minutes later the steam engine clanked to a standstill. The rundown coaches were old and nearly empty, but the platform had suddenly become crowded as people rushed to get window seats while others hurriedly said their goodbyes. Where the hell did they all come from? Ken wondered.

Curiously enough there were very few uniformed figures boarding at this point, not more than a dozen, and they were all Luftwaffe except for one lonely looking sailor who was probably returning from leave; he was a long way from any ship.

"Maybe he is going to Stettin," mused Tim nodding towards the sailor.

"We'd better shut up," warned Ken. "Someone might hear us speaking English and understand it and you are talking too loud."

"Are you telling me to shut up?" grinned Tim.

Ken shook his head as an indication it was hopeless trying to keep Tim quiet.

"Are you mad at me, old buddy?"

"Get on the bloody train."

With haversacks slung on their shoulders they had waited until almost all passengers were aboard, and now they were looking quickly for a coach that contained no military passengers. Both were concerned that a sharp-eyed Luftwaffe type might recognise the British Air Force material used in making their suits.

There were no empty coaches and maybe that was lucky. Two passengers in a coach might stand out and cause suspicion. As the old station master and ticket collector came fussing down the platform towards them waving his arms to get them aboard, Ken let out a gasp of dismay and whispered, "Don't look Tim, Fritz, the school teacher is here. He is with the station master."

Fritz was a miserable middle-aged man, an ex-school teacher who was one of the guards at their Stalag prison camp and hated by all. His hobby was to sneak up quietly on prisoners who had picked the locks of their handcuffs and while screaming obscenities march them off at gunpoint. Even in midwinter's sub-zero weather he refused to give the poor offender time to don warm clothing to get through the shivering hours chained to the wire fencing, the penalty for daring to undo handcuffs. Ken had already been one of the victims of Fritz's obsession. Ken felt he would be recognised. Taking a chance they quickly picked a coach that had no occupants in uniform although that did not certify Gestapos were not on board.

Depositing themselves on the far side of the coach where there was sufficient space on the wooden bench seats, they sat together and held their breath when the old stationmaster and Fritz arrived at the door of the coach and opened it. They could visualise Fritz playing the big hero, his revolver pointed at them, recapturing two escaped and dangerous 'Luft Gangsters' from the enemy Air Force. A few seconds seemed like an eternity while Fritz peered over the old man's shoulder at the passengers and then decided it was too crowded. He quickly disappeared. They assumed he boarded the next coach. In the meantime the old station master slammed the door shut and was heard to exclaim angrily, "Was für eine Dummheit!" (What stupidity!). So Fritz lost his big chance to become a hero at least until they changed trains at the main junction.

Tim sat next to an old white-haired bearded man who had claimed the window position. Most of the passengers were country folk dressed in rough clothing, with the exception of two very large middle-aged ladies wearing black dresses, who sat across from the two fugitives. Sandwiched between them was a small skinny man with a bald head and a Hitler moustache. He looked bored and out of place attired in a pinstriped suit, white shirt and black tie. It was obvious they were going to some very special gathering, perhaps a funeral, judging by the black dresses and the black tie. They looked hot and uncomfortable this July day.

Tim and Ken made no conversation, just watched the passing countryside. It was a pleasant journey this beautiful morning and none of the passengers seemed concerned that the two young men sitting quietly together were not in uniform. There were many foreign workers in Germany. Two men of call-up age in civilian clothes would be a common sight in some areas. They could be volunteer French or Italian, or forced Polish labourers working for the Fatherland. They were both afraid to make eye contact with anyone close in case someone wished to start a conversation; that could be disastrous.

It was not a long journey to the main line, and a change of trains for passengers going north was necessary. Tim and Ken had one objective, keeping clear of Fritz until they were safely aboard the train bound for Breslau and Stettin. How this was to be accomplished was still in the hands of fate. They were concerned Fritz may have recognised them when he peered through the door and was now in the next coach preparing strategy for his greatest achievement to date in serving his Führer, the capture of those two escapees.

These miserable thoughts were interrupted by the shrill whistle of the old locomotive and the clanking noise as the train slowed and rattled its way to a stop. It was the crowded junction station where they must change trains. The two stout ladies moved to the platform in record time, leaving the little man to gather up the parcels and wicker baskets they had brought. He balanced the parcels precariously on top of the basket he clutched in his skinny hands. Then the poor fellow tried to make his exit. He almost made it and successfully manipulated his burden through the door to the platform. Then his luck ran out. Fritz alighted from his coach and before the little man had time to deposit his load, Fritz accidentally or deliberately swung the large haversack he was carrying from his right shoulder to his left. In so doing he hit the little man's burden and sent it crashing to the platform. From the wicker baskets spilled sandwiches, pies and cakes, sausage, liverwurst, and all sorts of other good things, a contribution to a funeral or wedding feast or just a party.

The two fat ladies sprung into lightning action moving so quickly that only Tim, Ken, and of course Fritz, saw the contents for those few seconds before they were crammed back into their receptacles. The little man stood white-faced and immobile, while Fritz lectured the two ladies about rationing and loudly expressed his displeasure that some people seemed to have an abundance of good things to eat while others starved.

Tim and Ken took advantage of this opportunity to disappear into the crowd. Without hesitation they boarded the more modern corridor-type train. They took the first available compartment close to an exit and a toilet. They obtained seats by the window and conversed in whispers. The only other occupants were a lady with a young girl of about six or seven. Then four young soldiers boarded and stowed their gear on the luggage racks.

Departure time came and there were no more passengers, so Tim and Ken settled down to feign sleep as the train puffed its way out of the station towards what they hoped would eventually be freedom in Sweden.

Tim's eyes appeared closed but they were open just a slit, enough for him to watch the young German soldiers who had already extricated a pack of playing cards from their equipment and were using the floor as a table. It was not a very comfortable way to play a game of cards.

The brakes were applied half an hour later and the big black locomotive slowed its coaches to a standstill. Their coach stopped directly in front of a big sign indicating it was Brieg Station. The train had been stationary for a few minutes before Tim opened his eyes and murmured in a low whisper, "We should eat some of our rations. It might distract people from talking to us." Ken agreed as he did not wish to start a discussion in English on how they were to divide the rations. Before that could develop there was one more addition to the complement of travellers in their compartment.

Tim's bladder had for some time been demanding relief. Now it had got to the point where drastic action had to be taken. Now it was a must. Taking a deep breath he whispered to Ken, "I'm going to the can." He stood up and in his best German excused himself as he interrupted the card game, moved to the sliding door, slid it open and stepped out into the deserted corridor. He had made a few steps towards the toilet situated close to the coach entrance when the big steam locomotive wheels did a crazy spin on the tracks and then gripped. Tim looked out the window. The large Brieg sign on the platform slowly slid from view. Running directly towards the coach was a young man. It seemed he had come from the direction of an old derelict waiting room near the end of the platform. The newcomer reached the coach and ran beside it for a few moments; then he wrenched open the coach door and threw in a beat-up old haversack very similar to Tim's and Ken's. With one great leap he seemed to catapult himself onto the coach floor from the platform at the very moment when another step would have taken him over the end of that structure. Tim helped the winded intruder to his feet then after two attempts was able to close the coach door. By this time the locomotive's wheels had twice more done their crazy spinning before eventually settling down to a normal clickety-clack as speed increased. Without a word Tim quickly made the move to his original objective. The young man seemed agitated, so Tim did not wait for any further developments.

When he returned, Tim was surprised to find the newcomer was settling into their compartment. He looked quite confident, having regained his composure. Picking up his haversack, he slung it up on the rack with a casual gesture as if to say, "I do this sort of thing every day." Seating himself next to the little girl, he nodded to Ken and Tim, then smiled at the girl and her mother, who was apparently undecided how she would accept his sudden intrusion.

Furtively he eyed the four soldiers whose game had been disturbed by his entrance. They were completely ignoring everyone, so engrossed were they in their card game. Many Deutsche Marks lay neatly stacked on the floor topped with a German army-issue water bottle to keep them from scattering as the train lurched from side to side.

The young man was clean shaven and good-looking. His bronzed complexion indicated he had spent much of the summer days outdoors. He wore dark civilian pants, a black pleated jacket, and a black peaked cap, similar to German Army Tank personnel. Underneath his black and white sweater he wore a brown shirt. Tim noticed a small white scar was discernible under his left eye. Could have been an accident or a knife wound that had healed leaving scar tissue that didn't tan in the sun.

The stranger nodded and gave them a broad smile, showing white even teeth except for one that had a dark blemish. He made no attempt at conversation.

Ken interrupted Tim's thoughts with the comment.

"He needs a dentist to fix that black tooth."

"I think it's just a defect," was Tim's whispered reply. "Your eyes are good Ken but it's not a black tooth, only a small blemish. You always enlarge on things and you missed the white scar under his left eye."

Ken didn't know how he had missed noticing the scar, but his reply to Tim was, "Certainly, it was the first thing I saw. I was waiting for you to mention it." Tim did not answer in many words just, "Sure! Sure!"

Taking off his peaked cap, the stranger turned it upside down on the seat beside him and casually reached for his haversack and took out a small neatly wrapped parcel. He placed the parcel in his cap, then threw the haversack up on the rack. Picking up his cap and contents, he made himself as comfortable as possible and undid the newspaper wrapping to reveal a thick sandwich of dark rye bread with some sort of meat filling.

As the stranger chewed slowly, Tim inspected him through narrowed eyes.

The new arrival finished his sandwich and delved into his sack again and produced another, neatly wrapped like the first. This triggered Tim to think that he was hungry, so nudging Ken who appeared to be in a very serious mood he asked, "Where the hell is our lunch? You're supposed to be looking after our nourishment."

"You're going to get us caught before we get anywhere." Ken's Welsh accent came through very strongly as it always did when he was disturbed. Being upset he forgot for a moment to control his own volume so his reply was very audible. The young newcomer raised his head, and with questioning eyes he looked steadfastly at both of them for some moments. It seemed he was about to say something but then changed his mind. A few minutes later Ken opened his old beat-up haversack and divided the cheese and rye bread scrounged from where they'd worked and the two large soda biscuits saved from a Red Cross food parcel. Wolfing down the sandwich, Tim picked up the biscuit and looked up to meet the eyes of the young man. As the newcomer nodded his head Tim realised that he recognised the source of the biscuit. He must be another escapee thought Tim, and by his appearance he has been on the run for a number of days. He looked very tired and Tim wondered just where he could have got the sandwiches so neatly wrapped. He decided that the starving young man had stolen some railway worker's lunch.

Without discussing his deductions, Tim whispered, this time for Ken's ears only, "Wonder what camp he's from?"

"I was asking myself the same question," replied Ken, "look at his socks and boots."

Tim lowered his eyes. Sure enough the boots and socks looked very like British issue. As both pairs of eyes inspected his feet the young man pulled them underneath the seat so that they would not be so conspicuous and at the same time he looked away. Perhaps he was having second thoughts about divulging he was an escapee in case his own intuitions about the two men in the opposite seat were wrong. So the journey continued in silence, and after eating their rations, Tim and Ken closed their eyes and snoozed for a while. When they awoke again, they pretended to read the previous day's issue of the *Breslau Zeitung*.

During one of their shut-eye times they were disturbed by a hustle-bustle as the young German soldiers picked up the cards and Deutsche Marks that were still on the floor, then donned their equipment in readiness for disembarking. The train slowed and stopped at a station where two lonely looking upright posts stood bereft of the sign bearing the station name.

"We must be close to Breslau," whispered Tim and Ken nodded in agreement.

The soldiers, who had been laughing and talking were now very quiet as they readied themselves. A number of military people were on the platform and when the young soldiers alighted, a burly Unteroffizier ordered them to line up. Then he marched them off in single file.

"Poor bastards," murmured Tim, "probably it's the Russian front for them."

A few civilians were on the platform but the majority were army personnel. They stood talking in congenial little groups. Their conversations were interrupted with occasional laughter.

A few minutes passed, then from the coaches at the rear, military orders could be heard. The station platform quickly began to look like a parade square as the coaches disgorged their complement of uniformed personnel. Immediately the casual conversationalists sprang into action turning into pompous-looking non-commissioned officers barking orders at their new flock. They worked with the tenacity of sheep dogs, dividing into small groups the crowd of recruits as they tried to form straight ranks. Tim and Ken looked on with interest until the locomotive groaned. Then with a hiss of steam and the noise of couplings taking up the strain they moved slowly out of the station.

Tim thought it all looked so familiar, just like the pompous corporals and sergeants at training centres back home shouting their commands and verbal abuse at new arrivals. They could fit in here perfectly just a change of uniform and language. Nudging Ken Tim whispered, "The last two or three coaches must have been jammed with recruits. Funny we didn't see them when we boarded the train."

"I think they were detached from another train. Remember we shunted backwards a little way before leaving and coupled up to something? I bet it was their coaches."

"Yeah! I remember that," Tim mused.

The lady and the little girl had moved along the seat to where the soldiers had been, so the other young escapee looked a lonely figure. There was no more conversation, all parties content to sit and meditate as the wheels did their clickety-clack song on the rails. Time passed, the outskirts of Breslau began flitting past the windows, and soon they were into built-up areas. The Allied bombers had left Breslau very much alone. It was too far away for one thing, and not as important at the moment as the Ruhr Valley industrial area known to aircrews as "Happy Valley." In time the bombing would probably come to Breslau. Russian and other Allied Air Forces would do the job of destruction and killing that goes with war.

For Tim and Ken, Breslau was a big hurdle full of checkpoints and Gestapo and other inquisitive prying eyes. They didn't have to change trains. This one was going all the way to Stettin with probably a change of locomotive and crew. Breslau was also the big city where German military personnel including prison-camp guards would find entertainment while on leave, so this could be a scary scene until they were under way again.

The five passengers sat silently for ten or fifteen minutes watching the activity two platforms over where a military train had stopped and German women in blue-striped uniforms were serving refreshments to the troops. A few minutes passed, then came a shrill sound from the locomotive, accompanied by shouting and running figures which disappeared into various coaches as the train prepared to move out of the station.

Preoccupied with this activity, Tim and Ken were taken completely by surprise when the corridor door slid open to permit the entry of an attractive well-dressed middle-aged lady accompanied by an elegant young woman in her twenties carrying a costly looking overnight case. A high-ranking Luftwaffe officer appeared at the doorway and casually surveyed the occupants, giving the three male passengers extra scrutiny. He was about to speak to them when the whistle blew. Instead, he hurriedly kissed the older lady and hugged the young lady. He turned at the doorway and stared for a moment at Tim and Ken and the other escapee. Something seemed to disturb him, and Tim was certain that he would have liked more time to investigate who they were. Time was on their side and the officer either had to get off the train immediately or stay aboard. Tim wiped small beads of sweat from his brow when the officer chose to get off. They could see his tall figure as he talked to a military police Unteroffizier. It seemed that he was pointing directly at Ken and Tim as the coach slid past. They could hardly believe their luck! There was no check, no Gestapo or even a railway official checking tickets. There must have been a few military trains through and railway personnel were overworked. Ken whispered to Tim, "Do you think we are in trouble?" and he gestured towards the platform they had left.

"Don't think like that! Remember number one in escape rules, never panic."

"Wish I had a drink," complained Ken.

"How about a cold beer?" suggested Tim with a grin.

Then Tim nudged Ken, "Look at our friend. Where does he think he's going?"

The other escapee seemed disturbed by the officer's pointing. He put on his cap covering his dark curly hair and retrieved his haversack from the rack. He was sitting on the edge of his seat as if waiting for the starter's gun in a hundred yard dash. Both Tim and Ken immediately thought of talking to him to try and calm him but this could prove fatal if he was not what they thought he was. They chose to ignore him. The two new ladies had been deep in conversation since leaving Breslau but now were making a fuss over the little girl, who was brushing her long fair hair.

The train had been travelling at a good speed for forty-five minutes when the brakes were applied and speed was reduced to a crawl.

Eventually it stopped at a small country station. It was getting late in the afternoon and the sun was low in the sky. Grass and foliage glinted in the sunlight as everything was wet after a shower. Tim opened the small air duct above the window. Soon the smell of freshly cut grass wafted in. A smell associated with freedom and his own Irish countryside.

On the station platform they saw the same military policeman who had talked to the Luftwaffe officer before leaving Breslau. There were two military personnel with them. They pointed to Tim and Ken's rail coach, then walked towards it.

Suddenly the new escapee rose from his seat and without looking at Tim or Ken moved swiftly past the ladies, slid open the door and disappeared down the corridor in the opposite direction from the nearest exit. It all happened quickly. One moment he was there and the next he was gone. The reason for his turning away from the nearest exit became apparent. Almost immediately standing at the compartment doorway was the military police officer and one of his men. Tim's heart did an Irish reel. Then to his amazement, while the officer spoke with the ladies, the other military person gave them a cardboard box and a thermos. With great heel clicking they bowed out without even a sideways look at Tim or Ken. So that's why the Luftwaffe officer had pointed at the coach leaving Breslau; it was to show where the ladies were. The military officer and his driver had driven fast to get ahead of the train.

"Must be a very important man," whispered Ken, "and we were lucky at Breslau station because they thought we had passed security before those ladies boarded."

"Guess so," replied Tim. "That was a stupid thing to do. Did he get off?"

"Don't know. Hope he gets through OK."

Again the wheels turned slowly. The locomotive spit out smoke and steam and the train moved forward.

"You look that side and I'll keep an eye on my side."

The station waiting room and the empty platform slid by when Tim dug into Ken's ribs with his elbow. They looked in consternation, for there on the other track was the escapee with a small shovel in his hand and his little haversack on his back. He was boldly walking along

174

the track. As their coach passed him, he stopped and pretended to check something at a rail joint then looked up and waved.

"Who the hell is he and where did he get the shovel? What a bloody nerve if he is an escaped kriegy."

"Strange, strange, strange." Ken shook his head in utter disbelief at the audacity of this man. They would not have been surprised to see him being hauled off by those Military Police or even shot while running across the train track and now here was foolhardiness paying off.

The two ladies took the lid off their box and uttered cries of delight like two hungry children at a picnic. Ken and Tim couldn't see all that was in the box, but the women shared cake, cookies, fragile-looking sandwiches and real coffee in china cups.

"I wonder what Fritz would say if he saw all these goodies?" whispered Ken. "Would he give another lecture like he did the other two women when their goodies spilled?"

The ladies finished their picnic, and at the next stop a railway official came aboard and took away the box and its contents of unfinished food and dirty cups. Watching the young women Ken said, "I'd like to have met the younger one in a more congenial atmosphere."

"Now what sort of atmosphere would that be?"

"Well," replied Ken, "just whatever your wild imagination conjures up."

It was dusk when the train stopped at a small country station and the ladies made their exit, having made no attempt at conversation. Leaving the compartment, they both turned and smiled a farewell. With darkness falling, the two men felt more secure. They ate another sandwich and Ken produced the water bottle. The water was warm but it helped to quench their thirst and wash down the bread and cheese. As the train rumbled through the night they talked about what to do when they reached Stettin. Tim took out the crude hand-drawn map of the route from the station to the dock area. It was another item in the escape committee's package. Now that they were the only occupants of the compartment, they conversed in English without whispering and that seemed strange. They kept their voices low in case someone was listening at the dividing compartment wall.

Tim looked at his watch. It was 10:00 p.m. and for a moment he thought, Why didn't I stay in prison camp? I'd be snuggled down in my straw palliasse, but maybe within the next few days we will be in Sweden. Then he thought of Sharon. It had been two years and four months since they'd kissed goodbye at the air base. Tim's last letter from her had been six months ago.

He was shaken out of those thoughts when the door of the compartment slid open. There stood the uniformed figures of a little chubby man and a soldier with a rifle slung casually at ease. Tim did not have to wake Ken. His eyes were already wide and questioning, but to their relief the men were checking tickets. Luckily Tim had a short time before made sure that Ken's ticket and his own were ready for inspection. He handed them to the railway employee in a casual manner as if he were conversant with the procedure like a regular traveller. In contrast to the outward calm his heart was doing flip-flops. Lady Luck was again on their side. With a "*Danke*," the little man returned the tickets and both men continued to the next compartment.

Tim could not believe that everything was going so easily. Must be all a big trap, he thought, and everyone knows exactly who we are. The Luftwaffe officer at Breslau spotted us as escapees and reported this to the Military Police. That's why he took it upon himself to present the ladies with the goodies at the next station and he brought an accomplice with him so they would both get a good look. Then the railway official when taking the empty box and thermos from the ladies told them who we were so the smiles they gave when leaving were cynical ones. Now the ticket collector with his armed escort was just another check to make sure we were still aboard. Tim was already picturing a line-up of military personnel at Stettin ready to pounce, and he knew the person giving the command would be that military police officer from the Breslau platform.

"What are you dreaming about?" Ken's voice brought Tim back to reality. "I spoke to you three times but you kept staring at the wall as if you were in a trance. Did those guys scare you that much? I asked you a question."

Tim shook his head as if to wake himself, apologised, and asked Ken to repeat his question.

"On second thought it wasn't a question. It was a statement of fact. This is the outskirts of Stettin. Look over there. That must be north. See the dark outline and the odd light? Then beyond that is an expanse of brightness. That's the moon's reflection on the waters of the Baltic

Sea. So we are here. Now all we have to do is get to the dock and find a Swedish sailor who will smuggle us on his ship. Do you remember how much the British government pays for each returned escaped prisoner of war?"

"I don't know and I don't care," replied Tim. "Anyone who asks we'll tell them the sky's the limit."

As the more densely populated areas of Stettin went by, Tim and Ken prepared for the big hurdle of passing checkpoints and then getting out of Stettin Station. They agreed to separate and go through different check gates then meet outside the main entrance. The corridor was already full of passengers ready to leave the train. Tim and Ken tried to appear busy with their haversacks, not wanting to get into the stream of those disembarking until the train had stopped. It took ten minutes before the big exodus began.

"See you outside," whispered Tim, "in the street by yourself. Don't bring anyone in uniform with you."

"Same goes for you," retorted Ken. In silence they joined the stream of passengers heading single file through the only gate open, everyone showing credentials to uniformed officials. Tim had stepped off the train first and was well ahead of Ken. When he neared the checkpoint close to him, there were six sailors. They'd had too much to drink and were laughing and jostling each other. The first three sailors joked with the officials as they passed through the checkpoint. It was taken in good humour. Apparently they were members of a U-boat crew and highly respected by all. Now the three waited beyond the checkpoint for their buddies. As Tim handed over his forged documents, one of the tipsy sailors immediately behind him threw a half-eaten apple at his waiting pals, but his aim was not true and the apple bounced off the official's hat without much momentum. It did however make the official angry enough to hand Tim his documents with very little scrutiny. Then he turned his attention to giving a tongue lashing to the culprit amidst the derisive laughter of his comrades. Tim covered the distance to the exit in a few quick steps. His impulse was to run, but he knew that would draw attention and he had noticed a tall blond civilian staring at him. Quelling the urge he marched smartly as if he had a definite rendezvous and knew where he was going. He would have very much liked to stand by and watch Ken's safe passage, but outside on the dimly lighted street he felt more secure. Once the train passengers dispersed there would be fewer people on the streets. It was getting late and night patrols would surely spot them and ask for papers. Tim was waiting in the shadows when the blond civilian appeared at the station entrance for the second time. Before again entering the station he walked close to Tim and hesitated a moment before proceeding.

Tim waited for five minutes, certain Ken had been caught. They had made a pact that in a situation like this they would wait for each other no longer than ten minutes, less if it was not safe. Checking the time Tim thought, What happens if I am left on my own? What will I do if I see Ken dragged out and beaten by military police? What can I do? The answer of course, was nothing. Just get as far away from him as possible, away from suspicion. Could that blond civilian be Gestapo? Tim's watch was ticking away the seconds to seven minutes when Ken appeared and quite calmly said, "Let's go and get a ship."

"What kept you? Did you see that blond civilian?"

"Nothing really," replied Ken, "just a dear old lady who had misplaced her identification papers, and they detained her while an official called for his superior. That took a few minutes. What blond?"

"Looked like Gestapo," Tim replied.

"Saw a blonde Fräulein that looked good and if she was Gestapo maybe I'd give myself up," Ken joked. "The old lady kept looking towards the entrance and telling the officials something in a loud voice. She let out a cry of relief when an officer came on the scene and the two officials jumped to attention. It looked like it was the naval officer's mother coming to visit her son before he went off to sea again. She was quickly processed and so was I. Look, there is the lady and the officer getting into that naval car. He's probably captain of a U-boat and will be out in the next few weeks somewhere in the Atlantic Ocean, sinking ships carrying our Red Cross food parcels. Wish I had one now. I'm hungry."

While Tim and Ken talked, the crowds dispersed and the protection of numerous people was lost. Quickly they made way towards the dock. It was getting too late to venture into areas that were defended and patrolled. They decided to change direction and look for a place where they could kip down for the rest of the night and wait until daylight to get their bearings.

10

Introduction to a Stranger

It was a warm night. Tim and Ken were thirsty, hungry and scared. Aside from the Red Cross Canadian chocolate bars for emergencies, they had two sandwiches remaining and a little water. When the odd person spoke as they passed, Tim and Ken returned the gesture with a nod and a half-raised hand in salute. After a time they were walking alone. This concerned them until Ken suddenly exclaimed, "Follow me!" He jumped over a low stone wall and Tim followed. Almost in unison they said. "It's a graveyard!" A small stone building in one corner looked like a chapel for funeral services.

"What better place to hide from prying eyes?" Ken said.

"Guess so," was Tim's not very enthusiastic reply. "I never liked graveyards. They are spooky."

"Let's find a sheltered spot. Maybe the building is open," suggested Ken. "You Irish are so superstitious. I suppose you believe in ghosts."

"Maybe," agreed Tim, "but ghosts or not, where is the caretaker? If there is one bet he sleeps in there."

"I doubt that," scoffed Ken. "It's a very small graveyard. Let's go see."

Moving quietly to the stone building, they tried the rear door. It was secure. Creeping close to the outside walls, they found the front entrance was locked, but little Ken was not giving up easily. Looking above the doorway he could see a window that might be unlocked. With Tim boosting him up, he was able to grasp the edge of the window

179

frame. With toeholds in the stonework he hoisted himself to the window and found that it opened inwards with only a few protesting creaks. Using one knee over the ledge he slid himself through and dropped quietly inside. His first thought was, If I can't open the door I'm trapped with no one to give me a boost up.

He stepped to the door and had difficulty with the old-fashioned lock. Ken very slowly guided the door open, hoping to deaden its creaky protests, and there was Tim like a guest waiting to be invited in. Ken bowed and chuckled. "The service won't commence for fifteen minutes but please come in and take a pew."

"Thank you Father," replied Tim in mock reverence. They closed and locked the door; then both froze as something falling to the floor made their heartbeats quicken. Flattened against the wall, almost afraid to breathe, they stood for a minute until there came the sound of purring, and a large cat rubbed itself against their ankles.

Ken exclaimed, "What do you know? A friendly enemy." He stooped to rub the cat's head and asked, "Are you the only one here?" In answer, the cat turned up the volume of purring and rubbed more vigorously.

For the first time in many hours they felt safe from prying eyes. Outside it was one of those summer nights when darkness seemed afraid to intrude and wished it could hesitate long enough to permit the morning sunrise to continue another day. The building was a memorial chapel with wooden pews, a small altar, and an old foot-pump organ. They tried to rest on the narrow pews but that didn't work — too narrow and hard. They moved to the front where a few feet of musty old carpet surrounded the altar. It was there they finally got to sleep.

At seven o'clock Tim sat up to listen. He nudged Ken, who was curled up on the floor with the cat sprawled next to him. "There is someone coming. Listen to the crunch of gravel. There must be a gravel path out there. We didn't see it last night."

Instantly Ken was alert and trying to shove the cat away with no results. It had found a friend and was staying close. Quickly picking up their haversacks, they moved to positions behind the old organ. The cat followed and continued its loving massage of Ken's legs. The footsteps stopped, and there was silence for a few seconds. Then a key rattled in the old-fashioned lock and the front door opened. Its hinges protested noisily until it banged against the inside wall and daylight streamed in. There was the sound of footsteps coming closer, and Tim dared to take a quick look, expecting to see the man who was about to expose them. Instead an old lady was shuffling her way down the aisle towards them. Approaching the organ, she called out something they did not understand, but the cat did, for it immediately scooted out and met the old woman at the altar. She reached behind the small podium and produced a dish. Then from a battered old can she poured liquid into the dish and set it down in the spot Ken had vacated. With the woman so close to their hiding place they crouched, afraid to breathe or move their protesting limbs.

The cat lapped greedily while the old lady talked to it. As the minutes ticked by, Tim's right leg, which was doubled under him, began to feel completely numb. To move and make the slightest sound could spell big problems. Five long minutes passed. The dish was licked clean and the old woman was still talking to the cat. Then, as if a timer had gone off she picked up the dish, wiped it clean using the hem of her black dress, and returned it to the podium shelf. The woman then moved to the opposite side of the altar where they could not see what she was doing. Completing her chores she shuffled towards the open door and out into the bright morning light, closing and locking the door behind her.

With relief they stretched full length on the floor.

"What do you think Tim?"

"Wish I had the milk instead of the damned cat," Tim replied as he nudged the cat away with his toe. "Go away, you Deutsche informer. It must be milk you got. I bet you told her we were here and she's gone for the police." Tim suggested they eat some of their emergency hardtack biscuits and chocolate.

"Okay but remember we were supposed to live off the land and keep the emergencies for just that, an emergency," Ken replied.

"There were no potatoes, apples, beans or tomatoes growing on the train, so how could we steal and live off the land?"

"Will you open your haversack, Scrooge? I was in charge of the rations in my haversack. Now you have the emergency one."

Tim grinned, "OK, I'll capitulate. Your request is granted but only because I'm damned hungry myself." With the altar as a table they divided the hardtack biscuits and a chocolate bar from one little emergency parcel, eating slowly to make it last.

"I think we should shave," suggested Tim. "Must be water somewhere."

"Let's look. Hope it's okay to drink."

"Should be water of some sort," Tim surveyed the area. "You look over there Ken," and he pointed to the corner where the old lady had spent a few minutes. "I'll check this other corner. And be careful!" Tim knew they were alone but he had an eerie feeling of being watched.

In the corner was a tap and small pail. The water was okay, so first they replenished their water bottle, then they filled the pail to half its capacity and used their Stalag razors and German soap to shave.

Taking a closer look, Ken discovered a sliding wooden panel to the left of the altar where the old lady had stopped for a couple of minutes. He would have missed it but for one small ray of sunlight. It was streaming through a tiny broken pane in a stained-glass window depicting Mary and Joseph with baby Jesus. The sunbeam shone like a searchlight directly on a spot where the panel was not flush with its neighbour, and the beam penetrated into the space behind the panel. Ken's eyes followed the slit opening all the way down and realised the panel was open ever so slightly. Looking at Tim he whispered, "Do you want to be the great explorer? I think there is some sort of storage room behind the panels."

"Let's share the honour," replied Tim. They inserted their fingers into the opening, pulled very gently, and discovered that the whole panel moved easily. With more pressure the panel opened and they found themselves looking at the business end of a revolver held in the steady hand of the tall blond man who had watched Tim leave the station. Without further adieu the stranger said in good English, "Come in, gentlemen. Come in and let's get acquainted."

Tim felt his knees tremble and he heard Ken take a deep breath. The revolver never wavered as its owner backed a little way into the room so they could enter.

"Close the panel," he commanded. Ken, who was following Tim, had an impulse to run but on second thought closed the panel gently, making sure it was tight against its neighbour. Beyond the man was a small table with remnants of a meal, half a loaf of brown bread, jam and cheese. A bottle of water or wine was next to a coffee pot that was giving out an enticing aroma. A one-burner electric hot plate rested on the table beside the pot. The element was still red — apparently the coffee pot had been taken off just before Tim and Ken intruded.

A small electric bulb shed a subdued but sufficient light. There was no window or apparent way out except for the sliding panel. There was a tiny storage area or clothes closet with a few rips in its protective curtain, and opposite this closet was a high shelf holding an assortment of kitchen utensils.

With steady blue eyes their captor looked them up and down. "Sorry I can't offer you a seat, but perhaps a coffee. Help yourselves. It's black, no sugar or cream. The cat got the cream. Oh, there's two mugs on the shelf." His tone of voice was friendly, his diction perfect, but the Luger pistol did not waver in his hand. A long slender finger was around the trigger, and Tim thought, This man has musician's fingers; what instrument would he be playing? Tim hoped that the black lethal instrument their captor now held was under complete control and that the owner did not have a nervous twitch in his finger.

They helped themselves to a welcome drink of coffee.

"Have some bread and jam or cheese." Their captor was becoming a host, so they both took advantage of his hospitality.

"Now let's find out who you are, where you are from, and where you are going. And a big question: why did you come here to this particular place? Did you expect to find someone here? Were you directed here and if so, by whom?"

There was one old chair in the corner of the narrow room. With the coffee mug in his left hand, their captor sat down. In his right hand the weapon still covered their movements. A full half minute of silence followed these questions. Tim and Ken looked at each other wondering who this person was. With tightly strung nerves they chewed on the bread and cheese. Tim knew he would never have got it down without the coffee. His throat was dry; the muscles refused to swallow. He had to sort of swill it down. His knees were a bit wobbly from the initial shock, and out of his shattered thoughts emerged one that asked, Is this person enjoying our fear and discomfort? Is this some sinister way of breaking bread and having coffee with prisoners prior to their execution?

Looking at the apparently calm, serene master of the situation with his steadily held revolver, Tim tried to say, "Who are you? What will you do with us?" That's what he wanted to say but found he could only emit an incoherent jumble of words. Ken broke the silence. "My friend described a blond man he saw at the station when we arrived. You must be that person. Were you waiting for someone? Did you know we were on the train?"

It seemed an eternity of silence before their captor spoke. With a smile on his face he replied, "Don't you think considering your present situation that it would be much better if you started off by answering my questions to you? Then perhaps I can tell you a little about myself. Now if I recall, I asked you who you were and where you were from." Addressing Ken he said, "If your friend is still tongue-tied perhaps you can answer these two simple questions and that will be a start."

Ken was tight-lipped and appeared deep in thought. Before he could answer, Tim spoke out with his strong Irish accent, "We are escaped prisoners of war from a Stalag in Obersilesia. My name is Tim O'Neill and my friend is Ken Jones. We are British Air Force personnel. If you want to see our military service numbers to prove who we are, this is my Stalag prisoner number." Tim pulled out the Stalag dog tag that was around his neck and Ken did likewise. Ken then volunteered the answer to question number two. "We had hoped to smuggle aboard a ship to Sweden."

"Very interesting," replied their captor and host. "You have come a long way and I'm surprised that at some point you were not arrested by security people. This is a very dangerous area for people like you. Security is tight. Did you come all the way by train?"

"We did," answered Tim.

"If I was in charge of security I'd start an inquiry immediately and someone would be in trouble. Two escaped prisoners travelling by train and not once coming under suspicion. But I'm not in the German security." Their captor rose from his chair and drained his coffee before he set the empty mug on the shelf behind him without taking his eyes off the two uncomfortable escapees. Revolver still in his hand, he took a couple of paces forward, put out his hand and asked for their dog tags.

Following instructions, they both tried to unbutton their shirts. "Never mind!" exclaimed the blond one as he stepped closer. Stretching out his hand he checked Tim's tag then Ken's. "Best you keep these safe and don't lose them." He then crossed the tiny room and sat down.

184

This time he lowered the revolver and set it on the table within reach. Tim and Ken looked at each other with relief in their eyes.

"Now that I know who you say you are, where you're from, and your hopes of transport to Sweden, I'd like very much for you to answer my other three questions, because your answers could very well make a big difference to how you will be treated."

"What were the questions?" Tim asked.

"Don't you have a short memory?" their captor said a little sarcastically. "Okay, then let's recap them for you. Why did you come to this particular place? Did you expect to find someone waiting for you here? Were you directed here by someone you met on your journey and if so, who was it?"

They both answered almost in unison, "We stumbled unexpectedly on this graveyard."

"All right, one at a time please. Tim O'Neill, you answer the question. Did you or did you not expect someone to be here, and were you directed here? You say you stumbled unexpectedly on the graveyard. Am I to believe this actually happened? That you had no previous communication or instruction from anyone regarding this place?"

"That is absolutely correct," Tim answered. "We were going towards the dock area. Then decided to wait until daylight when more people would be around, so we walked in the opposite direction this way and by sheer accident found your place."

Producing a slip of paper, their captor smiled before answering, "I'm inclined to believe you." Then quickly he asked Ken, "Who was your German compound commander?"

"Unteroffizier Kurt Manstein," Ken replied with hesitation.

Picking up the revolver again, their host asked Tim to step forward to the table, where he handed him a short stub of a pencil. "Write on this slip of paper your Stalag barrack number and the name of the prisoner who was the senior man in charge of that particular barrack."

Quickly Tim wrote Barrack 55A and Pat Whittle, Senior Man.

Turning to Ken the interrogator then asked, "Did you live in the same barrack as Tim?"

"No," replied Ken.

"Well then, please tell me in which barrack Tim lived and do not tell me the number of your barrack. Remember, not yours, only Tim's."

Without hesitation Ken replied, "Barrack 55A."

Moving to Ken, revolver still in hand, their captor held out the same slip of paper and stubby pencil. "Now Mr. Ken Jones, please write for me beside Mr. Tim O'Neill's, your barrack number." Ken quickly scribbled: 56B.

Returning to the table where Tim was waiting he asked Tim to write Ken's barrack number on another piece of paper. Tim wrote in bold print: No. 56B. Their captor nodded his head in an understanding manner before saying, "So you are escaped prisoners of war and have your prison-camp dog tags. Okay I believe your story. My friends, there are many Gestapo and other security people who would be hard to convince and some who when they find escaped prisoners do not wish to know the truth. They take great delight in treating those captives as spies or saboteurs. I think you were lucky to stumble onto this place. At the present time you will be safe here and I'll try to help you. Your chances of getting close to the dock area without being picked up by security would have been very slim indeed. I have a question to ask you, then I might tell you a little about myself.

"First my reason for being at the station when you arrived was to meet someone who failed to keep an appointment. Perhaps you can help me. Did you see anyone on the train who could be an escaped prisoner like yourselves? He would be wearing dark clothing, a short black coat with pleats in the pockets, a military-type peaked cap and, how do you say it in English, a chequered black-and-white sweater. Age would be twenty-five or twenty-six. He is good-looking and has a small white scar under his left eye. Sometimes when he smiles broadly you will notice a front tooth has a dark blemish. His hair is dark and curly. Did you see anyone of that description either on the train, on a station platform, or anywhere on your travels here?"

Tim and Ken, relieved to find this man a friend, were now happy to give information on where they had last seen the other escapee. He listened to their story of the unorthodox manner in which the young man boarded the train and his quick exit when military police appeared. From his pocket their host took a tiny map of the area printed on what looked like rice paper. With an x, he marked the station where this had happened, the time of day and date.

"Why would he jump off the train in such a hurry? The military police did not question us," Ken asked.

"He must have seen military personnel who would recognise him as a wanted man." Their captor picked up a small tin of tobacco from the shelf. Using the rice paper map with the information on it, he rolled a very neat cigarette. Before placing it in an almost full pack of a Turkish brand he rolled another layer of regular tobacco paper around it. The flimsy rice paper map was the exact size to make the perfect cigarette. It was complete with an edge of glue to secure the hidden message.

"I believe the young man who travelled on the train with you was not an escaped prisoner of war but one of our saboteurs returning from a mission. There is a warrant out for his arrest. They want to question him, and you have probably heard how the Gestapo question people."

Now that their captor appeared to have turned friendly, Ken and Tim could visualise Sweden and freedom as only a matter of time, but they still had no proof of who he was. He had not said he was underground and yet they had verified for him the description of the young man on the train. Maybe he was really a Gestapo agent leading them on. Could it be that they had played into his hands and that soon those looking for the young man, whoever he was, would know where to find him?

There was no way they could both converse and make some sort of plan. They were indeed trapped and this person was their only hope. No matter what their suspicions were, they were on a committed course and had reached the point of no return. With all these turbulent thoughts racing through their minds, Tim and Ken were brought back to the immediate situation by their captor, host and friend pouring himself another coffee and asking them if they'd like a refill.

He stopped, looked quizzically at them and asked, "Would you like to know something about me? What I mean is, why I'm here, and what my job is, and who I am?"

Ken answered, "We sure would like that."

Their captor was sitting on his chair, a mug of coffee in his hand. His pistol was within easy reach. Tim sat half-sitting on the table with one foot touching the ground. While little Ken leaned against the wall underneath the high shelf, they waited expectantly.

"I am Stefan Jonsson and you are lucky to have found me because Stettin has large security units of police, SS, and Gestapo. They are always vigilant and on the lookout for those trying to escape to a neutral country.

"In a few days, I will be moving on. I do not stay very long in one place. This mishap of one of our men being overdue on a mission has curtailed moving plans. We must be careful until I find out if he is safe or in their hands.

"For example if you were caught by SS or Gestapo after being here and meeting with me, or if you were persuaded by their methods of interrogation to divulge my description and current abode, it would be a sad day for the organisation. You understand that I must curtail your movements if you wish assistance in obtaining your freedom.

"I ask you one thing. Do not leave this place under any circumstances! I may have to go out for a short time in your interests and to inquire about my comrade's safety. Do you understand?

"When you saw me at Stettin railroad terminal I was hoping to meet my comrade. He is very important to me and the crusade. By your description I'm certain the person who travelled with you for a short time was my close friend and my partner in our war of retribution against the SS and Gestapo. Now I feel much concern for his safety." Stefan stopped talking and listened.

They heard similar noises to those that had disturbed them and the cat earlier, hinges protesting noisily as a door opened and then banged against a wall. Then the shuffle of feet coming closer. They knew the old lady had returned.

Stefan switched off the dim light and stood close to the sliding panel. Half a minute passed and the panel was slid partly open. A sunbeam like a tiny searchlight stabbed across the darkened room to be lost as it bored a lighted pathway through one of the rips in the protective curtain of the tiny clothes closet. Tim thought that it must be coming through the same broken stained-glass window that had permitted the other sunbeam to show up the misaligned panel. The panel that had caused them to come face to face with Stefan and his revolver.

Then Ken noticed something else that the new sunbeam had spotlighted; it disturbed him.

Stefan spoke a few words in German before handing a package of cigarettes to the old lady. Tim and Ken both felt that Stefan did not want to divulge their presence at least not yet. His concern was for the curly haired young man in black. The one who had boarded the train in such an unusual manner and alighted from it in a similar way. A few more hurried words, then Stefan closed the panel and pushed across three small locks before commanding the light to be switched on again.

Ken realised that the sliding panel had not been locked when they found it. So Stefan must have known they had been there all night and left it unlocked for some reason. Perhaps he was waiting for them to find it.

When the old lady shuffled her way to the door, Stefan waited until they heard it close. He knew she was outside when he heard the sound of the gravel under her feet as she shuffled away.

He continued. "My business here is underground work. I avenge the deaths of many good citizens. The older lady who came just now is my Aunt Josephine; she is one of our best couriers. It was through her courage and commitment for revenge that I was introduced to and became a member of this organisation. The SS killed her husband and they also caused the death of my girlfriend Ilsa, whom they took away because she was Jewish. That night long ago, SS men wrecked their family home, killed her father, and dragged my Ilsa and her mother to a waiting truck filled with many other innocent victims. Their crime was having their own religious beliefs. It took me six months to track down two of the three SS men who broke into Ilsa's locked bedroom. First I made them prisoners. I had to kill one of them before the other broke down and told me what they did to her, then he begged for mercy. I killed him slowly. I will find the other one and his death will be slow and horrible, as he was the first one to rape her. Ilsa committed suicide in the SS officers rest camp where they sent her.

"The last evening my girlfriend and I were together in a cosy little restaurant in Hamburg, we were celebrating my birthday. We had to leave in a hurry because of a phone call telling me of my father's sudden death. We left two empty glasses and an unopened bottle of French wine on the table.

"Now when I avenge Ilsa's death by killing an SS murderer I leave when possible, two empty glasses and an unopened bottle of good French wine beside the dead body.

"You may think this an odd thing to do but my reasoning is that the full bottle of wine represents the wonderful and happy life we had planned together. The glasses signify the terrible emptiness in my life since Ilsa's death. So as long as I breathe I hope a great number of the people who wear the same uniform as those who executed the terrible deed and are still committing dastardly acts will one by one suffer my retribution. Death."

Stefan looked at his two prisoners. "Don't you agree with me?"

Timothy answered in a strong affirmative, thinking of his own personal commitment to seek vengeance on George O'Conor for destroying Kathleen.

Ken's reaction was only a slight nod of his head and a noncommittal look.

Stefan looked at both of them, smiled and said, "I don't know why I told you all this. Maybe it is that you are the first Allied military men who have made contact with me. I am not in the business of processing escaped prisoners, although I do know quite a lot about that phase of our operation. Now it would seem to me that I have to get you two safely out of here and if possible on a ship to Sweden or a country friendly to the Allied cause."

With a chuckle he said, "I don't think you would like to go to Russia. I will be leaving you now for a short time. I have to make some contacts on the outside. Help yourself to bread and cheese. I will bring back extra rations. Again, I warn you, under no circumstances are you to leave this enclosure. If you meet me outside when I am with a certain stranger I may have to shoot you both, and that would grieve me. If you value your lives, please stay put. I have already confided too much in you. So please believe my warnings. Outside, if the Gestapo or SS were to get you and suspect you had any contact with me, I would have to make sure of your deaths before you were interrogated."

Leaving those warnings ringing in their ears, Stefan slipped out through the sliding panel and there was silence. They heard no footsteps going away, no door opening or closing, no crunch of gravel. Just a scary silence.

"Where did he go?" Ken asked.

"I think he is still there. Why?"

"Are you afraid? You look scared."

"You're damned right I am. Do you think all of that stuff he told us is true? Why would he tell us those confidential things? I think we are being sucked in. He'll be back with ten German soldiers."

"His story sounded genuine to me. I'm not convinced he's telling lies. Do you remember some of the working party prisoners from Stalag who were sent to Poland and returned with crazy stories about Jewish concentration camps where hundreds of people were forced to dig their own graves? They were made to line up at the edge of those graves before being shot so they would fall in. And those other places where bodies were being burned in some kind of furnace? It makes me think Stefan is telling us the truth and knows he can trust us. Well me anyway."

"Okay sure," retorted Ken, "trust you, the gullible Irish. I think we should get out of here before he comes back. He scares me and the bullshit about if you are outside I may have to shoot you. I'm telling you O'Neill, I don't like it. I think we have played into his hands listening to all that crap about tragedy in his life. I bet that poor bugger who jumped off the train will be caught very quickly because we pinpointed him. This Stefan guy has gone to check progress on the net they are closing around him because of our stupidity. Well they are not taking me in just yet. I'm getting out of here. Let's see what rations we can get together."

"You've sure convinced yourself Stefan is working for the Germans. Why are you so definite?" Tim was surprised at Ken's vehement reaction.

"Just a gut feeling I have," was Ken's only reply as he poked around getting together cheese, bread and jam. He stuffed them into the old haversack then turned to Tim and said, "Remember, we were to find our way to the docks in daylight. Now it's daylight. So let's go."

Tim was taken by surprise at Ken's attitude because he really believed, or maybe wanted to believe, that everything Stefan had said was true. Now his partner had suddenly upset the apple cart with a completely opposite decision.

"Are you coming with me?" Ken was ready for the road. "Come on, Tim. I'm getting claustrophobia in here."

Tim was upset, but he continued the tug-of-war conversation. "Come on Ken, do you think Stefan made up that story? Do you really believe that Ilsa is only a figment of his imagination? Do you think someone could come up with such a convincing story if it wasn't true? It all sounded logical to me. Don't you believe that Hitler and his henchmen are persecuting the Jews? Use your head, Ken. I can't understand why you have suddenly turned around and changed your attitude. I could see all along that you were very sympathetic and understanding. When Stefan told us about what happened to his girlfriend I thought that you were about to take on all the SS in Germany single-handed. I think you are up the creek in your diagnosis. I'm willing to take my chances at freedom with Stefan whether you think he is underground SS or not. Now, I need a cup of coffee. Hot or even cold, I still need a drink."

Tim picked up the coffee pot and poured himself a mug of the warm black liquid. Sitting down in Stefan's chair, Tim took a few sips and waited for Ken's reply.

Ken was standing in his favourite position with one shoulder leaning against the wall beneath the high shelf. On his face was the look of a card player holding all the aces. With a condescending air he asked, "Have you said your piece, O'Neill? Are you finished your spiel or is there more to come?"

"It's your turn," Tim replied.

"Well, thank you very much because I'm going to shoot down in flames your theory on our great and truthful benefactor, Stefan Jonsson."

With that, Ken took a few paces to the tiny closet, grabbed one side of the curtain and pulled it back with great ceremony as if he were unveiling a wonderful work of art. There to the consternation of both Tim and Ken were not one, but two full SS officer's uniforms complete with all the trappings. The highly polished boots were ready to wear, and there on the small top shelf were two sets of headgear with the hated skull and crossbones badge grinning at them.

Tim surveyed this find with consternation and then fear. "Why did Stefan feed us all this story? Why was he keeping us prisoner?"

"It was the sunbeam," Ken said.

"What are you talking about?"

"It was the sunbeam, just as I said." Ken was showing nervous anger because Tim did not understand what he was trying to say. "The sunbeam was shining right through the tear in the curtain and I saw a red armband with the swastika on the white circle. At first I thought someone was in there. Then I quickly put two and two together and realised it was Stefan's. He is an SS underground agent and we are only small fry. He is out to get the big one and I bet it is our friend who jumped off the train. We gave Stefan the lead on him and now he's on his track. Stefan must have lost the scent at the station when his man did not get off the train. We accidentally turned up in his web and gobbled up all that very touching story of his life. Something else that has just now rung a bell in this puny brain of mine. Stefan's revolver is a Luger P.08 issued to all uniformed Gestapo and SS. Now are you satisfied?

"Are you coming with me or are you going to stay behind? Then when Stefan returns with his prisoner, you can be executed after verifying he was the person in our coach. Can't you see it's a con job and that we are the pawns in this game? They know for sure that the person on the train is the one they are looking for, and they know what he is wearing. We are the ones who can identify him as being in our coach. They want to catch him before he gets a chance to change clothes."

"What about the old lady?"

"She's probably carrying messages from the SS headquarters to Stefan. This morning he sent her our donation to the program for the capture and death of some brave underground member."

"You're very dramatic," Tim replied. "Did you take drama classes at school? I believe Stefan is straight and can help us. There's a reason for all the mystery and that's going by my not-so-gullible good Irish intuition. So my little Welsh friend, I think you're wrong."

Ken ignored Tim's question. He was furious at Tim's sarcasm.

"Maybe the uniforms belonged to some SS that Stefan killed." Tim was getting stubborn.

"Look, O'Neill, if you want to stick around and eat your last meal of bread and cheese, that's okay with me, but I'll be gone to hell out of here in the next few minutes before that crazy man comes back. Did you notice his eyes? I'm sure he is insane. Probably the SS and Gestapo get all their recruits from insane asylums."

As Ken was finishing his latest speech, he was fumbling in the pockets of the SS uniforms. From the top right-hand breast pocket of the jacket he produced six photographs that shocked them both. They were of men and women mostly nude, some already dead and badly mutilated. Others with mouths open in desperate screams as their torturers continued. A couple of pictures showed smiling SS men in uniform watching. One picture was of five fully clothed prisoners. There were three men and two women with hands tied behind their backs. They were forced to a kneeling position with an SS man behind each one. The first two victims were already dead, strangled by a length of wire that cut into their necks. The third victim was in the process of being strangled while the other two SS men stood behind the last two. Each man had a length of wire in his hands waiting for the signal from his superior to go into action. Apparently the strangulation was being done slowly one at a time. The waiting victims would go through hell before their turn came. Each executioner would enjoy his moment of pleasure when his victim fought for life.

Ken pushed the picture close to Tim's face. "Look! Look! Do you believe me now? Do you recognise who that is?" He pointed his finger at a number of spectators in civilian attire. One of the spectators was none other than Stefan Jonsson. "Now do you believe me Mr. Timothy O'Neill from Ireland?" Ken looked at Tim and continued, "See, I don't have to draw you a picture, I can show you one."

With all this evidence Tim had to capitulate, although deep down he could not believe all that Stefan had confided in them was a lie. In the back of his mind something was telling him there had to be a reason for all this, even the photographs.

"Maybe he was there to kill an SS man."

"What do you want, O'Neill? A close-up picture of crazy Stefan cutting someone's head off?"

Tim was losing the battle. Ken apparently did not have the inner something that defied circumstantial evidence. Tim threw out his last card. "What happens if Stefan comes back with a Swedish sailor and arrangements made to guide us to a ship?"

"Do you believe in fairy tales?" Ken was adamant in his condemnation of Stefan, and Tim was beginning to doubt his own feelings. "Are you coming with me, or am I going to Sweden by myself?"

Tim picked up his haversack and put on his jacket. Hesitantly he followed Ken, who had quietly slid the panel open.

"The light. I'll put the light out." So back inside went Tim to switch off the light. He stepped out of the little room, making meticulously certain that the panel was closed, so that a casual inspection would not show a crack.

"Just in case you are all wrong, my Welsh friend. If we do not close this secret hideout and if Stefan is what he says he is, wouldn't you feel bad if he is discovered and killed because we failed to cover his tracks? This may be his one and only safe hiding place in all Stettin."

"Come on, softie. We know by the photograph that Stefan is just as bad as those men with the wire throttling out the lives of five innocent people. Try to explain why they did it. I shouldn't ask you that, because you'll try to come up with some plausible Irish fairy tale."

Now they stood where they had been at approximately seven o'clock that morning, when Ken discovered the sliding panel. "I gotta go for a pee," quipped Ken.

"I didn't see a washroom anywhere."

"We will have to go outside," Ken hastened towards the rear door and was about to unlock it when Tim said, "No, leave it. We'll both go through the window."

Ken shook his head. He couldn't understand Tim's obsession regarding the possibility of Stefan being straight. Turning to Tim he said, "You are big enough to get through without a boost. Now Tim, me boy, will you give this little friend a boost, so I can tumble out to fresh air if the coast is clear."

"It wasn't 'Tim me boy' a short time ago, when you were mad at me. Now you're kissing my ass to give you a boost up and telling me you're my friend."

Ken knew Tim wasn't really serious in his remarks, so taking a step towards the door, he indicated he would unlock it and said, "Well, there is an easier way out, so we will leave the door open."

Tim immediately grabbed him by the legs and hoisted him to open the window. He almost pushed Ken headfirst through the opening, and then followed. He had difficulty getting up and through. Once on the outside, he boosted Ken up again to close the window. On this first day of August, they looked around and the coast seemed clear. The air smelled fresh and clear.

11

Things looked different in the daylight. There was a gravel path that started at an entrance gate to their right and came close to the door of the building. Thinking about the crunch of gravel the footsteps made and then the silence before the door opened, Tim could now see the reason. Close to the entrance there was a well-trodden diagonal shortcut across a grassy patch. That's why the crunch of feet stopped before the key turned in the door.

"Let's go and pee before I burst," Ken broke into Tim's thoughts.

"Okay, but let's be very careful. It's going to be difficult getting out of here without being seen. There's a lot of traffic and people out there," Tim nodded towards the roadway.

Behind a large stone angel they got relief and then stealthily made their way toward the right side gate. They kept close to the hedge that formed a boundary along one side of the graveyard. Unobserved they left the graveyard, quickly mingling with the numerous pedestrians. It was not difficult to navigate towards the dock area, but soon the pedestrian cover became thinner. They began to feel conspicuous, too conspicuous for comfort.

After thirty minutes with Tim doing the navigation and Ken struggling to keep up with Tim's long stride he complained, "Who do you think you are, O'Neill? Do you think you're the leader or something? Slow up!"

Tim looked back at his little friend paddling along behind him. "You're calling me O'Neill again, you little Welsh runt. Sorry if you can't keep up the pace but we don't want to miss the boat." Tim was still convinced they should have stayed with Stefan, and felt that if things went wrong it would be Ken's fault.

They could see the dock area was close. Suddenly there was the blast of a ship's horn. "See, Ken, the ship's leaving; we'd better hustle."

"Probably for another German port," replied Ken, ignoring Tim. "I bet if we smuggle aboard a ship it will finish up in Hamburg or occupied France."

"Well, France would be better than here," retorted Tim.

Their chatter came to an abrupt end when they turned a corner and were suddenly within sight of the docks. Ken gasped, "Look at the bloody ships! Which one do you want?"

"The one painted grey flying the silly red flag with the swastika on it," retorted Tim.

"Aren't you a real joker, O'Neill." Ken could not see the funny side of it as he surveyed the line-up of six ships at dockside. "Why don't you try your Irish humour on those two guys with the guns?"

Tim turned as two dock patrol guards moved towards them with rifles at the ready. Before he could answer Ken, there was the command he had heard so many times since arriving in Germany, "*Halt! Wo gehen Sie?*"

Knowing that to obey the "Halt" order was imperative for their safety, they both stood rooted to the spot until the guards drew close.

"*Papiere bitte.*" It was the younger of the two who requested their papers while the older one stood back a few feet. Their accumulated ages would not have exceeded forty. Immediately Ken and Tim produced their Stalag-made identification and work papers. The young one passed them to his companion, who until then had been covering both of them with his rifle. Now the young guard took over while his mate checked the identification documents.

Tim started to explain in his best Stalag German. They were on the way to the work camp near Stettin. They had a couple of hours to wait before the camp truck came to pick them up. To pass time they'd taken a walk to look at the ships. Tim's stammering German seemed to be understood, and after a long spiel from the older one with the terminology "restricted area" coming through loud and clear, their credentials were handed back. With Tim's practised German "Thank you," the two guards went about their business of protecting the dock area from saboteurs or those who would like to escape from the Fatherland.

Ken and Tim left the area at a much slower pace.

"Did you see the activity? All those ships and sailors from the navy vessel? I bet U-boats are tied up there; we couldn't see them but there's two Swedish ships! How can we get aboard?" Ken was talking quickly, the words tumbling out.

Tim took over the conversation. "Yes, I saw all that but I also saw the barricades, the barbed wire, the patrols, the sandbagged machine-gun posts. I bet there's a lot of German naval craft we didn't see."

"It's the Swedish stuff we want," mused Ken as they trudged along retracing their steps.

Soon they were back amidst enough people to feel inconspicuous. Realising they were walking towards the graveyard they decided to try another direction but keeping close to the coastline.

"We don't want to be confronted with that SS Stefan and a man in uniform."

"You're passing judgement again on circumstantial evidence. Stefan may not be an SS as you maintain. He didn't say a 'man in uniform.' His words were 'someone in uniform,' could be a woman."

"Does it matter? Maybe you'd prefer to get shot with a woman present."

Tim was about to come back with a smart remark when he had to step quickly off the curb to prevent collision with two young German sailors and their girlfriends (well, maybe girlfriends for the day). He hopped back onto the footpath in time to hear Ken say, "The one on the outside looks lovely."

"A long time in Stalag and they all look gorgeous to me, even this one coming towards us." Tim chuckled his reply as the female in question passed them by. She was a very tall sour-looking young woman with a long face and wearing thick glasses. Her skinny frame was covered almost to her ankles by a green dress that hung on her as if draped over a clothesline to dry.

Ken looked serious when he replied, "You can sure pick them Timothy. Of course, if it was dark you could pretend she was Jean Harlow or Betty Grable." Ken hesitated and screwed up his face in mock thought before continuing. "In daylight on a cold day you could blow your breath on her glasses and fog them up. Then you might look good to her, even handsome. On a warm clear day like this Tim me boy, you'd be just out of luck. Guess you're stuck with me."

The good-natured banter went back and forth. They strode along, each one trying to hide his own fears from the other. They felt the tightness of their stomach muscles and the helplessness of being many hundreds of miles from anyone who could verify who they were. Ironically, prison camp was, in a way, more secure and for that matter, safer.

Images of drastic events flitted across Tim's mental vision. Perhaps they would be caught and tried as spies. Tim could visualise himself standing blindfolded in front of a firing squad waiting for the end when the officer in charge would shout the order to fire. Or, he imagined sitting in a small boat as they putted across the Baltic Sea with a brave Swedish seaman and being caught by a sea patrol. He could see all three being blown out of the water by German gunners. Then no one would ever know what had happened to them. He would never again wake up in Sharon's arms or be able to find out how bad things were for Kathleen. He'd never get the chance to even the score with George O'Conor.

Tim and Ken were scared stiff, but would not admit that to each other. Ribbing each other was a sort of escape valve to relieve tension.

"I'm hungry!" Tim exclaimed. "If we don't eat the chocolate ration now this heat will start it running out of the haversack. There's a public park across the street. Let's get a secure shady spot and eat some of this food. It'll feel better in my stomach than bouncing around in this haversack."

They entered the wide open iron gates, walked across the grass to a clump of trees and sat in a well-shaded hidden spot. Few people were in sight. In privacy they ate the bread and cheese, and divided a chocolate bar and washed it down with water from the bottle.

Tim suggested they look at the map. "I think there's another small dock towards the west end of this town and that's the way we are heading. It's where all the fish boats tie up. That may be what we want. A fishing boat lost at sea but finding itself in Swedish waters with you and me aboard. Doesn't that sound good to you, my little Welsh friend?" Ken was enthusiastic and agreed.

Tim took the map from his jacket pocket and spread it out on the ground. Poring over the Stalag-made map of the area, Tim and Ken could see that a short distance away was what looked like a small bay and the word "boats." Close by, three letters enclosed in a circle indicated a bar. Tim pointed out that it didn't say 'ships' just plain 'boats' and that indicated small vessels. His finger traced back to the area where they were accosted by the dock patrol. There the map stated the word 'ships'.

"I bet this is what we want, smaller boats, a mixture of fishermen. I bet there will be a few who take escapees like us to freedom and they will frequent the bar. Let's go and find a small boat with a Swedish flag flying or even painted on its side. If there's a bar close by that's where to find the fishermen." Tim stopped and thought for a second or two. "If that bar is close by do you think we could pass without blowing our identity? If so we might go in for a beer and hope to make contact. The best time would be later this evening, so why don't we lie low here for awhile? Seems a pretty safe spot."

They rested for a long time; in fact they snoozed. When Tim woke up he felt cold. The sun was on its way to bed and a cool breeze blew in from the sea. He nudged Ken awake and they ate more bread and cheese.

"Let's wait a little longer, then we'll make tracks for the pub. Doesn't that sound good?"

Ken wasn't overly impressed with the pub plan but said he was willing to take the chance. Looking at Tim he asked, "Do you know how to ask for two beers?"

"Oh ye of little faith," Tim quoted. "Didn't I ask for two tickets to Stettin? Sure I know what to say: *Zwei Bier, bitte.*"

"What happens if the bartender asks you what kind of beer?"

Tim hesitated for a moment, then with a thoughtful expression repeated, "What kind of beer?" He gave another moment's pause as if he was getting his brain in gear, "Let's look for some ads on the way," as if that would solve the problem.

"Don't be so dumb Tim. There will be blackout, no lights after dusk. Remember there is a war on. Or have you forgotten? Did you expect to see signs from here to the pub advertising a variety of beer? If you're asked what kind just point. Remember we are supposed to be French workers who can't speak German. And remember, the truth is you Irish don't speak English anyway but you are liable to say, 'It doesn't matter, just two cold beer.' I'll have to stand close beside you."

"Come on let's get mobile." Tim was not going to escalate the argument. Picking up his haversack, he brushed off some twigs and other clinging dirt from his clothes. "I got my good suit all dirty."

It was a forty-five-minute walk to the little bay. There were many small boats. By the moon's light they could see many were under naval jurisdiction. Certainly there were fishing boats and some of them had machine guns mounted on deck, but they saw no guards. They moved close as possible without being too obvious. On the narrow lane leading down to the marina they returned greetings from a couple of seamen who passed. At the end of the trail just above the concrete steps that led down to the boat area, they stopped. "Should we go down?" It was Tim who spoke. Then before Ken could answer, they both saw the uniform, the German helmet and the rifle slung casually on his shoulder as the guard sauntered slowly along the dock area.

Ken whispered, "He must have been standing in the shadows behind that abutment. Look, he was having a smoke."

The German soldier took a long drag, and although the night was not dark, the tiny red glow of the cigarette could be clearly seen. A last drag and he flicked the butt, sending it in a small red arc to extinguish itself in the water at the edge of the dock.

"What do you think we should do now?" Ken whispered. They were about to leave when they saw something interesting. The German guard had gone on his rounds but someone else was down there in the dark. Straining their eyes they both saw a shadow-like figure move aboard the third boat from the bottom of the steps.

"Did you see what I saw?"

"I did," replied Ken, "and he had only one leg but he could sure manipulate those crutches, and it wasn't Long John Silver's ghost. That was a real live person. Something secret is going on down there." They stayed another minute and watched but nothing happened, so they retraced their steps.

They found the bar. It was packed almost to capacity. A variety of uniforms filled the one big room. All twenty tables were in use, with chairs tightly wedged together. Around each one the German navy, army, and even the Luftwaffe were represented. Of course the biggest majority and easy to pick out were the fishermen and merchant seamen in civilian clothing. Without hesitation Tim pushed his way to the bar with German marks in his hand. He ordered two beers, paid for them, and returned to Ken who was standing against the wall close to the door. No seats were available, but they preferred to stand rather than be drawn into conversation at a table.

Sipping on the beer they surveyed the patrons. They wondered who in the crowd could be a Swedish sailor willing to take the risk of helping two escaped prisoners of war. How could one segregate the friendly Swedes from enemies?

The beer tasted good and quickly their glasses were empty. Both of them had forgotten to sip slowly to prevent frequent trips to the bar. They would be conspicuous if they remained that way and they needed to stay longer. Now one of them would have to run the gauntlet to the bar again.

"It's my turn." Ken was ready to take the chance. "What is it again you say? Zwei Bier bata?"

"No, no," said Tim quietly, "*zwei Bier bitte.*"

Ken repeated it a couple of times but with his Welsh accent it didn't sound right so Tim volunteered to take a second chance. He decided to wait until those at the bar looked less dangerous and less inclined to talk. How to really know this was of course a matter of guesswork. The line-up at the bar seemed to grow instead of shorten. After ten minutes of frustration holding their empty glasses, Tim decided he would chance it. If anyone spoke to him he would use the old prison-camp standby, "*Ich verstehe Sie nicht.*" (I don't understand you.) "Keep your fingers crossed, here goes."

Tim was a quarter way towards the bar when his path was barred by a short, pale-faced delicate-looking young civilian wearing horn-rimmed spectacles, who said while holding out two full glasses of beer, "*Zwei Bier, mein Freund.*" In an audible whisper he said, "Take them." Tim thanked him in German, and taking one full glass at a time in exchange for the empty ones, he returned to where Ken was standing spellbound after having watched the exchange.

"With my friend's compliments," Tim whispered as Ken took one of the mugs.

Their new acquaintance returned and joined them a full beer in his hand. He raised and clinked his glass against Tim's and then Ken's and in a low whisper said, "To your freedom."

The shock waves that ran through Tim culminated in his beer mug as his hand shook and his brain worked overtime trying to come up with the correct reply. Was this genuine or a trap? Was this innocent frail-looking person Gestapo? Did he really know they were escapees? If so, how? Was Stefan involved? Had he sent out a message to look for them? What would happen if he replied to his toast with the words, "To our freedom"? What would happen if he just said "Thank you"? That would mean the same thing. Tim wondered what Ken was thinking and if he would speak up first in English and blow it. So Tim decided it best to continue the masquerade as French workers.

Raising his glass he quickly said, "*Heil Hitler.*" In his best German he explained they were French workers about to return to their work camp with one of the German administrative staff. So they'd have to drink the beer quickly then go immediately or miss their ride.

The stranger continued, "It's okay, my friends, your Stalag-made jackets gave you away. These lights are too bright for your camouflage." Then addressing Tim he continued, "Your friend is wearing Royal Air Force issue boots and I bet if I were to empty your haversacks I'd find items from Red Cross food parcels." All of this conversation was carried on in an almost-inaudible voice.

Tim and Ken both looked at the speaker with blank faces of non-comprehension. Tim tried to evade committing himself to being an escaped prisoner of war. Again pulling on his German language resources that were getting ragged he tried to bluff his way with "*Ich verstehe Sie nicht!*" Then he pursued the theme in stuttering German, pretending he had no idea what was said. "We are French workers and not educated to speak other languages."

Suddenly and without change in his facial expression the young man continued the conversation in French, which completely blew their cover because neither Ken nor Tim could speak French. "Now gentlemen," continued the stranger reverting to English, "don't you think it would be expedient to talk in the language of your native land? It will save time and maybe our lives."

There was no further attempt at denying they were escaped prisoners, and Tim had not missed the words "our lives," which seemed to indicate this man's life was also in danger.

"I would like you to meet me outside immediately across the road from the front entrance two minutes after I leave you. When you are halfway across the road I will walk away down the hill towards the harbour and the boats. Where you were earlier this evening. Ah! I see it surprises you that I know you were there. You will follow me a short distance behind until I reach the steps that lead down to where the boats are moored. You've been there," he said with a smile. "I won't go down but will continue along the path away from you. Descend the steps to the dock area. At the bottom you will find a one-legged man on crutches waiting for you. He will take care of you. Obey his instructions and with luck by tomorrow at this time you will be in Sweden. I am going now. Good luck to you both and remember two minutes exactly and then follow me."

Consternation showed on their faces as they watched that small figure walk boldly out the door. Tim immediately checked his watch. "Jesus! Is that guy for real?" Because Ken's English was too audible it was Tim's turn to admonish him. "Shut up or you'll have us caught for sure. And please don't do it now that we are so close to getting on a boat. Just keep quiet for two more minutes and we will be crossing the road."

The second hand of Tim's watch struggled around the dial. They drained their beer mugs and set the empties on a low window ledge close by. They were outside when the second hand started on its last uphill journey of the two-minute mark. Seven other customers exited from the pub at the same time. Two were German naval officers, one was member of the Luftwaffe aircrew, and the other four were two regular soldiers, each with a female companion. Tim and Ken made up nine people crossing the road at the same time. They stayed close to the naval officers. They were in the centre of the little group and hoped their new-found friend would see them.

The group had gone only a few yards when suddenly a camouflaged military troop carrier swung around the corner. It stopped where their benefactor stood. Without waiting for soldiers to jump from the vehicle with shouts of "*Halt! Halt!*" their friend and hope of freedom took off, his small figure zigzagging its way in the opposite direction from where he'd told them to go. He ran towards the other side of the pub where there were a number of people, but he was too slow and too late. His luck had run out. At that particular moment there were no pedestrians close to him. From the floor of the carrier a spotlight pierced the evening darkness. It enveloped the fleeing young man in a bright circle of light, making him a target impossible to miss. Like a frightened rabbit, he changed course and made a swing to the left that would bring him back to the same sidewalk where he'd stood waiting for Ken and Tim.

There were two long bursts of automatic fire. Their would-be benefactor stumbled in his race for life and the momentum carried him a few more yards. It seemed that before falling he turned his head towards the spot where he knew they were, and Tim wondered if his dying brain was sending them a last message. Tim felt a sharp strange feeling of kinship with this brave young man and an overwhelming feeling that somewhere they had met before, perhaps in another lifetime.

To keep from being conspicuous, Tim and Ken stayed with the party of nine. They walked around the troop carrier and saw a soldier come up the hill from the dock area carrying a pair of crutches. He dumped them into the carrier and afterwards used a piece of rag to clean his hands. The group continued uphill on the sidewalk for a few yards to where the body was lying in the gutter. The head was resting on the curb. Two soldiers guided the party of nine around the body. As they passed, the officer in charge of the murder arrived, and purposely stomped on their friend's horn-rimmed glasses lying close to his head. Tim squeezed Ken's arm as a warning signal that meant let's go, don't hesitate too long. The officer's insignia showed he was SS.

Across the street another truckload of soldiers arrived. They formed a circle and cordoned off the pub. A big interrogation and identification check was about to begin. Tim and Ken had been saved by being with the military men. All those standing outside the building, and the odd person who had decided to get away from the scene, were being gathered in by a number of soldiers making a sweep of the grounds and the area around the pub.

At the corner, Tim and Ken casually broke away from the quiet group who had walked silently away from the body. Tim brushed a tear from his cheek as he said, "The park." Ken's melancholy answer was, "I suppose so."

It took them thirty minutes to walk the two-and-a-half miles. There were no incidents; they met no one and no vehicles passed by. They were two very scared escaped prisoners who walked that lonesome dark road. They climbed over the small side gate that they had found earlier in the evening. Quietly they walked among the dark shadows of the wooded area, and although they were very tired the events of the last few hours were too frightening and real to allow them the luxury of peaceful rest. They sat at the foot of a great oak tree, and for a few minutes neither spoke.

Tim opened his haversack and felt for a chunk of bread he knew was in the right-hand corner. During the morning, they had stopped in a quiet spot and equalised the stolen rations of bread and cheese in case they got separated. Finding what he wanted, Tim tried to hang the haversack on a small protruding branch, but the wood was dead and it broke, spilling the contents. Swearing, he searched around in the dark and retrieved his belongings.

They knew Lady Luck was still with them. A close check on their identification papers at the pub would probably have led to further interrogation. They felt good about that part of the evening but also frustrated because they'd been so close to escape and sad at how it had ended.

"Do you think Stefan had a hand in this?" mused Ken. "We've been watched by someone from the moment we arrived here. We were seen at the steps and followed to the pub. This scares me. It smells too much like Stefan watching us all the time. I'll bet he was the one who had that fellow killed so we would not get away."

Tim shook his head. "Ken, I'd hate you to be the prosecutor if I was in the dock. Why can't you give Stefan the benefit of the doubt? It must have been Stefan who sent that young man to meet us and made the arrangements for transport to Sweden. If so it wasn't his fault the SS decided to pounce. Someone must have split on the young underground agent. I don't believe it was Stefan and I still maintain you are wrong."

They sat for a long time in silence trying to absorb the tragedy just witnessed, thinking that in less than a minute they would have crossed the road to join their benefactor and probably on impulse run with him to their deaths.

Ken broke the silence. "Do you believe that we have souls and that they leave the body at death and come back into another life? If that is true what scares me is if I were to be killed and my soul returned to a new birth and that person should grow up to be like the SS. Maybe a secret police officer in another dictator-run country where secret police torture and murder people. Could that happen to my soul?"

Tim emptied his lungs in a long slow outflow before taking another breath. "I suppose you're thinking about all this because of what happened tonight. I don't know, Ken. Sometimes I believe when we go that's it. Curtains drawn. No more, just darkness. So live for today. Then at other times I believe that our souls do live on and come back. You scare me when you paint pictures like that. I don't think the higher power that directs all this would permit your soul to be involved in torture and murder and that's all the hope I can give."

Tim thought back to the quiet and beautiful county of Donegal in Ireland. How would Father Cullen have answered that question? Tim didn't think the old priest would have agreed with him, regarding curtains drawn, nothing more, just oblivion.

Ken stretched down to touch Tim's hand in a gesture of togetherness in a situation that both now knew could end in their deaths. He said, "Thanks Tim for that honest and sensible answer."

No matter if Father Cullen would have agreed. Tim felt sure that Ken and Father Cullen would agree that our souls do live on and return in a new birth.

Tim looked up to where Ken was sitting on a log. "Can't see you very well in the dark but my friend you look like a little Irish leprechaun sitting on that log with your legs crossed. Imagine a Welsh leprechaun." Tim laughed.

The night air became chilly and they moved closer together. "Damned cold for a summer night! Wonder where we can sleep? The park is locked up and there seems to be a stone wall all the way around, so I don't think there's anyone here except us. Let's look for a pavilion, bandstand, or even a rest room where we can get away from the wind." Tim was doing his leadership role. He picked up his haversack and looking at Ken sitting on the log he asked, "Can you get up or do you want to sleep where you are?"

"I'm coming, I'm coming," Ken struggled to his feet. They looked for more protection from the wind. Moving slowly through the trees they came to a clearing and could see the dim outline of a building.

"I knew I saw a bandstand when we were here earlier today," said Tim. They found the open bandstand had no protection from the wind. A roof, yes, but it wasn't raining. They went to investigate further. In five minutes they found a shed. It was locked, but the lee side of the structure was sheltered. They decided it would be quite comfortable if they had something to sleep on. They borrowed benches from the bandstand. Two benches together with the back rests on the outside made for a wide enough area. They lay down side by side as close together as possible for warmth, and used their half-filled haversacks as bulky pillows. The hard wooden bench reminded them of the Stalag bed boards before they were issued with straw palliasses.

"Don't you wish you were a little kid again and know what you know now? Why is it that the world has to be like this?"

"Yeah, wouldn't that be something?" was Ken's only reply.

"This haversack is sure hard on the face. Doesn't make a very good pillow," Tim was complaining. Then he suddenly remembered something. Sitting up he started to rummage through his haversack.

"What are you looking for?" Ken was also sitting up.

"I had a long brown thick woollen scarf I put in here before we left the camp. It would stretch over both haversacks and make more comfortable pillows for both of us, but Ken, it's not here now. Where could it be? I've lost it."

"Did we mix haversacks?"

"No, this is mine with the T on it. I must have left it on the ground when my haversack got dumped back there under the trees. Should I go back and look for it?"

"Let's try and get some sleep. We'll pick it up in the morning." Ken was in no mood to go looking for a scarf.

"Guess I know just about where to look. It would make a more comfortable pillow."

Ken did not answer and Tim realised that this was the end of the conversation He punched the haversack with his fist, laid his cheek in the indentation and went off to sleep.

They both slept the sleep of nervous exhaustion. It was somewhere around 4:00 a.m. when Tim thought he was dreaming that a bright light was shining on his face and he could hear voices, and dogs barking. Suddenly the dream became stark reality. A bright light was shining in his face and above him, paws on the back of the bench, saliva dripping from its jaws, was the biggest Doberman he had ever seen. Holding the brute back with a strong chain was a figure wearing the steel-grey uniform that Tim knew so well. He didn't have to look to see if Ken was awake for the words "Christ Almighty!" softly escaped the little Welshman's lips, sounding much more like a prayer than blasphemy.

"*Raus! Raus!*" The old familiar Stalag call was loud and clear. Tim and Ken obeyed, a little hesitant for fear the handlers might let the dogs loose. Three more German army personnel arrived with another dog handler with his snarling animal.

"*Papiere! Papiere, bitte!*" So often on these occasions of fear and stress Tim reached inward to somewhere in the makeup of his personality for strength which came in the form of a smart remark. Shading his eyes from the bright light he said in his best German, "Isn't it a bit early to wake us up? It's still dark. Our call was for eight o'clock, not four. Can you come back in a few hours? Make it seven because we've got to get on our way as early as possible."

In the dark and with the bright light shining in their eyes it was impossible to see the faces of the four soldiers, but there was a slight chuckle from one of them. Then came again the stern command, "*Raus! Raus!*" With a soldier at each end they quickly pushed down on the back of Tim's bench, catapulting him to the ground. He lay with the jaws of one of the dogs barely inches from his face. The bright light still focused on him.

Ken was sitting on the other bench, a second light blinding him from seeing what was happening to Tim. With the cold steel of a rifle barrel touching his chin, he fumbled in his pocket for identification papers. They both tried to bluff their way with the French workers' story. Ken said he understood only a few words of German (which was true). Tim prattled away in his Stalag German trying to say they had missed their ride to the work camp through some error in time and that they had waited until dark. As no one turned up they decided it would be best to find a place to sleep until daylight. Their intention was to seek help from the first policeman or military person that they met in the morning.

"*Du lügst das Blaue vom Himmel herunter!*" one of the grey-coated soldiers peered down at Tim and screamed at him. "You lie like mad!"

Tim could see in the light that this man was wearing the rank of Unteroffizier so he was apparently in charge of the party. Tim was afraid the officer was so upset that he might order the dog handler to release the dog's chain. Again the officer screamed at Tim in a high-pitched voice, "*Saboteurs! Saboteurs!*"

The handler had ordered his dog to heel, and as the dog backed away, Tim made the Unteroffizier lose his temper completely when he said in German, "Look, I think the dog believes me." Unbuttoning his holster the officer extracted his revolver and commanded Tim to stand up. Ken was sure that at any moment the Unteroffizier would cause Tim's soul to make that flight to wherever.

Looking at the second dog handler, Tim suddenly realised that wrapped around his wrist was the brown woollen scarf he had left on the ground — a costly oversight! The scent from his scarf had led the trained dogs to their makeshift resting place.

His thoughts were jolted by the officers' emptying the contents of their haversacks. The two bright lights revealed only bread and cheese. They had eaten the last of the Stalag Red Cross rations along with the chocolate bar. Tim and Ken stood almost side by side as their food was inspected.

"Where did you steal the bread and cheese?"

"We did not steal it." Tim was sure it was the correct answer because it was closest to the truth. "We brought it with us from the work camp in Obersilesia. We are escaped British prisoners of war."

"When did you escape?"

This question caused Tim to start a memory recap on the happenings since they'd boarded the train with two tickets to Stettin tucked away in his breast pocket. Was that a week ago or was it a month? So very much had happened in that time. Looking at the Unteroffizier Tim said in a clear voice, "This is the morning of the third day since our escape from a Stalag work party."

"You are spies. You are saboteurs. You escaped our net last night at the bar. We killed two of your companions but our files showed us there were two more accomplices. So you see? We have been recording your activities for many months and you made a slip by dropping this." He pulled Tim's scarf from the wrist of the dog handler. "It was a routine check of the park and the possibility of not catching you was weighted shall we say in your favour. But with this piece of material the dogs guided us right here."

Tim understood most of what the officer was saying. It disturbed and frightened him that they were being tied as accomplices to the two who had been killed at the dock the previous night. Again he emphasised, "We are escaped prisoners and request to see a higher-ranking officer." Tim's request was taken without comment and the two men were ordered at gunpoint to "March!" without their haversacks. The

Unteroffizier gave the haversacks to a soldier and said, "Evidence! Stolen food!"

Tim thought it curious that no attempt had been made to search their clothing. If they were saboteurs it stood to reason they would be armed. With four guns trained on them and the two dogs padding along at their heels, Tim could think of no way of escaping.

Outside the park gate was an armoured carrier. Tim and Ken were made to board this vehicle, and after a drive away from the waterfront area, it stopped at a foreboding grey stone building. There, with two soldiers on either side of them, they were escorted through two guard checks before being force-marched into the building and along a corridor to a fair-sized room. It was furnished with benches along the wall. A small table and chair were at each end. Behind one table was a German flag and behind the other on the opposite wall a large picture of Hitler. The floor covering was olive-green carpet. At the centre of the wall opposite the benches stood a large highly polished desk. Draped behind it on the wall was a banner with the SS insignia. The square centrepiece with its black swastika on a white circle background looked ominous. Outside that circle in each of the four corners were eagle emblems carrying swastikas in their talons. This was attached by embroidered chord to the name Adolf Hitler.

Tim was studying the eagle's wings when a new figure entered the room and the four army personnel came quickly to attention. Ken gasped in a whisper only Tim could hear, "It's him." Yes, it was the same SS officer who had stomped on their would-be liberator's horn-rimmed glasses.

Now in the lights of the room they could see his high cheek bones and fair sandy complexion. The officer was over six feet tall and looked in top physical condition. He laid his SS cap on the table and bared a close-cropped head of blond hair. Indeed this man was one of Hitler's and Himmler's chosen Aryan race.

He was standing only a few feet from the two captives. "You speak English?" His voice was raspy.

Tim rushed to answer. "Yes, we are escaped prisoners of war and are members of the Allied Air Force."

Ignoring Tim's answer the officer looked at both of them with disdain. "You are saboteurs and we don't waste time with your kind. In simple words you know the consequences of being caught." His English was perfect.

"We are escaped . . ." Tim got no further as the SS officer screamed, "SHUT UP! Impudent fool!"

Undaunted, Tim's rebellious Irish spirit came to the fore. He looked the officer straight in the eye and said, "I am telling you the truth. We are prisoners of war and we hope you will respect the Geneva conventions regarding war prisoners' rights."

Ken whispered, "Don't be stupid. Stop talking back," but the undaunted Tim again countered with, "We are Air Force personnel and prisoners of war. Don't you respect the Geneva Convention on the rights of prisoners?"

"You are saboteurs! You are spies!" The officer screamed and sat down in the plush chair, first taking his SS Luger P.08 from its holster. Drawing slowly on his cigarette he toyed with the Luger. He pointed it first at Tim and then at Ken. Addressing Tim he said, "You speak English like a native. You learned it well. Have you forgotten your own native Swedish?"

Ken spoke up in his Welsh English. "We are escaped prisoners from Stalag as my friend has already told you. We are not saboteurs or spies."

"Speak when you are spoken to. I will not warn you a second time. I see you learned English at different spy schools."

Tim and Ken were disturbed and afraid. This was not the usual German military. They were in the hands of the notorious SS murderers and in deep trouble.

Suddenly the officer's tactics changed. Smiling his friendliest smile he asked, "Where were you going when your plans went wrong? You were planning to take a boat out to sea? What were the names of your Swedish friends who directed you to the dock? Sad that your two accomplices at the dock had to die, especially the one who had a leg missing. Now tell me the names of those people you met at the dock. Tell me who you really are. Forget the story about being prisoners of war. Have you just completed sabotage in this area? Probably you have already sent back your message of success or failure to Sweden. It would be much better for both of you if you told me now because we will find out. I'm sure you have heard the SS and Gestapo have many ways of making people like you talk."

"We can prove we are prisoners of war." It was Tim again. He tried to pull out his Stalag dog tags. This proof around his neck on a length of Red Cross string would surely satisfy the officer that they were not saboteurs or spies. He reached in his shirt and immediately the officer was on his feet with the Luger pointing at Tim's heart.

"Keep your hands by your sides and don't ever do that again or I will shoot you."

The officer sat down and placed the Luger within reach. He looked up with dark anger on his face. It seemed something had triggered a new thought. He turned angrily on the Unteroffizier who got the brunt of a continuous verbal abuse. He had forgotten to order a thorough search of the two prisoners. Immediately this was done, and the Stalag dog tags given to the SS officer.

Now their only proof of identification had been confiscated and they were suspected of being Swedish nationals working for the Allies. Tim and Ken each knew that the other must be thinking the same thing. Gestapo and SS were looking for Stefan and their train companion but one thing was apparent. They had no idea what their suspects looked like and that didn't help Tim and Ken.

Ken was remembering Stefan's story and felt disturbed that he could have been very wrong in his condemnation of the man. It was probably genuine that he was waiting at the station for the man in dark clothing returning from a sabotage mission. Maybe they should have stayed and waited at the graveyard chapel. If Stefan had turned out to be SS it could not be any worse than their current predicament. The clothes closet and the SS uniforms still bugged him but maybe they were from SS who had been killed by Stefan and his friend.

Tim spoke up again. "You know we are prisoners of war. We are not Swedish. We are not spies. We are not saboteurs."

"Take them away." The command sounded like a death sentence. Tim and Ken both started to protest but were ignored by the SS officer, who had picked up his telephone and was already talking. It appeared to them that the case was closed.

With rifle butts prodding them they were forced to retrace their steps along the corridor and were almost pushed down three flights of concrete stairs, despite their protests. They were handed over to four brutal-looking individuals not in uniform, who virtually threw them into separate cells.

The situation seemed too absurd to be real, and as Tim sat in his tiny cell the events of the last twenty-four hours raced through his mind. How did they get into this dreadful situation? His first thought was to blame Ken because he had been the instigator of the decision to get away from Stefan. The circumstantial evidence against Stefan was perhaps enough if you had previously condemned him in your own mind. That's what Ken had done. Tim felt he should have stuck to his guns and allowed Ken to leave. Now the evidence favoured Stefan because the SS and Gestapo were looking for two Swedish nationals and did not know what they looked like. By a trick of fate, they believed Tim and Ken were the culprits. Tim felt certain Stefan had traced them and that it was he who had made arrangements for their escape. When things went wrong he knew Stefan would have melted away into oblivion to turn up again someplace sometime to again take revenge on the SS.

Tim looked around the cell. There was a wooden stool and the bench; no blankets, no toilet. The cell door was solid wood with a peephole. The walls were concrete. The cell was damp, cold, and very frightening. One tiny electric bulb was embedded in a fixture high up on the ten-foot wall. It shed only a tiny glow of light that did not reach the corners of that concrete hole in the ground. Tim was certain he must be at least thirty feet below ground level. Here there was no hope of getting a fair hearing. They were being railroaded through a process that lacked any sense of compassion or fair play. Tim had heard rumours about Gestapo methods of interrogation and he was afraid. If they could not convince their captors that they were escaped prisoners, the possibility of torture would be very close.

The one thing the Stalag escape committee had emphasised before they left camp was under no circumstances were they to lose their Stalag dog tags. They were the only identification to prove prisoner-of-war status. Any German official who wished to contact the Prison Camp Administration Department could confirm that their Kriegsgefangene (Prisoners of War) numbers corresponded with two escaped prisoners from one of the working parties. Now they did not have this very vital identification.

Tim sat sorrowfully looking at the grey walls, head in his hands, and his morale at its lowest ebb. There was no hope of contacting Ken. He was two or three cells away. The stark concrete floor had no covering and Tim was cold and hungry. He needed a wash and in the worst way to relieve his bladder. Twice he had tried to draw the attention of a guard by knocking on the heavy wooden door, but to no avail.

As twenty minutes passed, Tim sat still. His mind was trying to blot out the reality of his situation. He could hear noises coming from somewhere outside his cell. Tim got up and pressed his ear against the crack in the door. He distinctly heard crying and moaning from cells across the passageway. From somewhere else down the corridor a woman screamed. Suddenly footsteps stopped outside his door and a key rattled in the lock. Tim jumped back. He was seated on the bench when a jailer came in carrying a metal bowl of soup, which he placed beside Tim. There was no attempt at conversation. He was almost outside before Tim requested that he be permitted to use a bathroom. The guard turned slowly to meet Tim's eyes with a cold stare and made no attempt to answer the request. He then closed and locked the cell door. Tim picked up the battered and twisted spoon and the bowl of soup. It was cabbage, mostly water, not palatable, but he spooned the contents into his mouth taking care not to cut himself on the spoon's sharp edges. Placing the empty bowl and spoon on the concrete floor he sat on the hard bench, put his head in his hands and cried. His shoulders heaved in great sobs of despair. It was not fear just sheer frustration of the unknown future.

He thought of Sharon and the first night they made love. That seemed in another world. He wondered how his family was and his Kathleen O'Brien. If only he had made it to Sweden and then to England, he could have made plans for his own crusade. Similar to Stefan's crusade, Timothy's goal was to reach Ireland to reap his vengeance on George O'Conor for what he'd done and was still doing to Kathleen O'Brien. He thought of how he had told Kathleen such a very long time ago that he had joined the British Air Forces to fight for the freedom that would keep their families safe. Now here in this awful place he could be executed as a saboteur and his volunteering would have accomplished nothing.

Tim heard a sound outside the cell door. He was certain that on the other side of the peephole an eye was watching him. Instinctively Tim placed his hand over the peephole and held it there while the key was turned in the lock. Stepping back he waited. It was the same guard who had delivered the soup. He entered without a word and picked up the empty bowl and spoon from the floor. Then he retreated, again closing the door ignoring Tim's pleas, "*Wo ist die Toilette bitte!*"

The cell was dank and smelly with no ventilation. Another hour passed and Tim could not hold on any longer. He relieved himself in the corner farthest away from the wooden bench. His water trickled slowly across the uneven floor to finally accumulate in the corner underneath the wooden sleeping bunk. Finally he lay down and tried to adjust the wood rectangle at the head of the bench. It was on a ratchet and could be raised to certain degrees. It was used as a pillow or just something to lean against. He felt lost and bewildered at the events and was losing his ability to rise above the situation. The future looked bleak and frightening. At this point he believed his future would be very short and never would he see his friend Ken again. Their fate could be quick execution in the morning and the SS officer would report that he had caught and shot two saboteurs. Probably he would get a commendation for his brave action.

The hours crawled by. Tim tried to sleep but for many hours he lay on his bench looking up at the small light high up on the wall. Sometimes it appeared to be a watching eye. Other times he imagined it was the lens of a camera. It had probably recorded his every move since he was thrown into the stinking little cell. Later he fell asleep from sheer exhaustion only to wake suddenly after dreaming the SS Officer was sentencing him to death for urinating in his cell and that the evidence was on film. He looked at his watch that had fortunately been overlooked by the soldiers. It was 3:05 a.m. For the next few hours he lay and listened to faraway screams of both male and female inmates. Tim wondered what horrible brutality was taking place so early or had it gone on all night, and would his and Ken's turn come soon? Probably that's where they would next meet and be tortured to answer questions to which they knew no answers. "Oh, God," Tim prayed, "please get me out of here."

On the fourth day, at 6:15 a.m., the door creaked open and a new face appeared. It was a round fat red face and belonged to a middle-aged man. A civilian wearing dark clothing with a swastika pin in his lapel. Behind him was a regular German soldier. Without a word he walked in and laid a tray on the bench beside Tim. It was an enamel mug of ersatz coffee and two thin slices of rye bread skimmed with margarine. Then without a word he departed.

At midday Tim was permitted to use the bathroom under escort of another regular soldier. The toilet area was fairly clean. There were six wash basins, a number of them cracked, no stoppers, no mirrors. It was to do what you had to do in a hurry and "*Raus! Raus!*" Back to the cell.

At approximately 5:00 p.m. it was again the bowl of soup and a beat-up spoon. Tim was uncertain as to the origin of the soup but it was hot so he supped it quickly and it warmed his insides.

The days passed and once every twenty-four hours he was permitted to leave the cell and visit the bathroom. On this journey he saw no one and no matter how often he requested information regarding Ken all he got in return was a silent stare.

Tim was always hungry. The thin watery soup, the ersatz coffee and the slices of bread weren't sustenance for anyone. Each day he kept careful track of the passage of time. He wished to make sure he knew how many days had passed since their arrival. It had been day three of their escape when they ran up against the soldiers and dogs in the park. Now he was returning to his cell from the washroom, and repeating to himself. "This is day ten. This is day ten." It had been thirteen days since they started the escape venture and for ten days he had not seen Ken. Tim was afraid that something terrible had happened to his little Welsh friend.

Another seven days passed and Tim was very weak. He had seen no one except the guard who brought the miserable food ration that had now been augmented by a potato in the soup. On his daily visit to the ablutions, he washed his face. Every third day the guard permitted him to body wash in cold water and to dry with an old piece of torn cloth. His Stalag-made clothes were hanging on him and the stubble around his chin had mushroomed into the beginnings of a beard.

On the twenty-first day, when the guard came to pick up the empty soup dish, the civilian in dark clothing was with him. He carried a small stool, and on entering the cell he dismissed the guard. Settling himself on the stool in front of Tim, he said, "Shall we talk?" The round red face did not move a muscle. The voice came from lips that barely opened. "I see you have started growing a nice beard." This last sentence Tim thought, was supposed to be a joke.

"Had no choice," was Tim's retort.

"You still have a lot of spirit. I like that in a young man."

Tim felt he must be careful with this civilian. He was certain this was the real Gestapo and that he played a big part in causing the unearthly screams that echoed each night from somewhere down the passageway. Suddenly the visitor spoke quickly in a strange language that meant nothing to Tim.

"You don't speak Swedish? I told you just now that your friend had been shot when attempting escape. It was apparent that either you did not understand or you're a great actor."

"I don't believe you." Tim was not sure if this was the correct answer he should give, but it came out without thinking.

"Well my spunky young friend, we will find out through time if it is truth or not. Let's talk about you. What is your Air Force service number?"

Without hesitation Tim gave him the number 1006039, and followed up with his own prisoner-of-war number 27468.

Raising one eyebrow just a little the stranger said, "You knew that would be my next question. So good, you answered two in one. That will save time."

The questions continued. "When were you captured, and where? What squadron did you belong to? What was your barrack number in Stalag? Who was the German officer in charge of your compound?"

Tim answered all the questions, thinking his life depended on every word, and he was remembering that Stefan had asked similar questions.

And then suddenly, "Give me the name of the interrogation centre that you were taken to. When you were captured?"

Without hesitation Tim answered, "Dulag Luft."

"How long were you there?"

"Six days."

"Did you tell the interrogators any secrets?" He smiled a twisted sort of grin.

"I hope not," was Tim's reply.

"Who was the commanding officer of your squadron?"

Tim gave the name of his commanding officer.

The little man leafed through a few pages of documents on a clipboard, and Tim was surprised and shaken by his reply. "Squadron Leader Sharp was killed two months ago on a bombing mission to Cologne."

The civilian continued. "We have checked with your Stalag and also with records at Dulag Luft which verify you to be Aircraftsman Timothy O'Neill, ground staff air frame technician. Our information is that you are in Stalag language, 'a swapover.' Meaning of course that you changed places and identity with a working party soldier to make your escape. From your own prison-camp authorities, we have been told the soldier whose identity you took has admitted the swap.

"It is a very dangerous game you escapees play. You had another prisoner's dog tags and took his identity. If you were killed it is possible that his family would have been informed their son died trying to escape. Of course that would not have been true.

"You see we do want to make sure we pick up the people we are looking for. We believe the two men we are interested in are still at large. Captain Kersten who interviewed you and your companion is sometimes a little presumptuous and makes mistakes. However I would like to get my hands on the right people, not two escaped prisoners of war. So, young man, stay behind the wire when you get back to your Stalag." With that he produced two Stalag dog tags, and looking closely at the numbers, he repeated, "25545." Then with a fat stubby hand, he gave Tim the Stalag dog tags and said, "These dog tags are not yours. Keep them safe until you return to your prison camp and make sure your swapover receives them."

Tim could hardly contain his overwhelming relief and joy. The man said again, "When you get back to your Stalag stay behind the wire." It sounded like a commuted death sentence.

Suddenly Tim asked, "What about my Welsh friend, Ken Jones. Is he all right?"

"Yes he is alive and will be going back to prison camp with you."

With these welcome words ringing in his ears Tim watched the civilian leave the cell turn at the door and say, "Good luck. It will take a few days to arrange your transfer."

With mixed feelings, Tim sat staring at the wall and questioning his own interpretation of the conversation. Was he dreaming? Did all this happen just now? He fingered the Stalag dog tags and realised that he was not dreaming. They were real. Now he had to wait only a few more days. Tim's opinion of this civilian had suddenly changed. He could not be the one who would cause the screaming in the night; he would not be a member of the Gestapo; he must be an investigator for someone in a much higher position than this Captain Kersten and cared just a little about justice.

Next morning Tim was taken to a different washroom, permitted a hot shower, and given a fairly decent towel for drying. Washing his body under the hot water was wonderful, but he was upset at how skinny he had become. Later he was more shocked to see himself in a mirror. He looked dreadful with sunken cheeks beneath the scrubby beard and straggly hair, and his eyes appeared to have receded. Locked in his cell again he felt this must be the beginning of their release from the awful experience. The day crawled by but with a brighter outlook and hope at last.

Two more days passed and Tim was permitted another hot shower. There were no shaving supplies, so he washed his three-week growth with the gritty soap and rinsed thoroughly. On the way back to his cell he asked the guard, "Where is my friend? Did he also have a shower?" Again the stony-faced jailer gave no indication that he had heard the questions.

Tim stretched out on his bench, dreaming about how great it would be back in prison camp. "Yes," he told himself, "it would be wonderful in comparison to this solitary nightmare." At least he knew there were many others to share the miseries of prison camp, but here one could die alone. Tim reasoned that if he was going to die in this country it should be in Stalag along with his friends. He felt weak, but the shock of seeing himself in the washroom mirror had to a certain extent faded. Occasionally he felt his cheekbones and thought how sunken his face had become; even the whiskers could not hide that.

The long days in the cell had taken a toll on his congenial personality. For the first week he had tried to converse with the guards who brought the meagre daily ration. During his walk once a day to the bathroom they would not return his amiable gestures at conversation. Back in his cell, with the door locked, he often looked at it and said, "Okay. You won't talk to me so I'll converse with myself and hold a much more intelligent conversation." At times he would sing his favourite Irish song. Once after singing what he thought was a lusty rendition of Danny Boy, he was certain there were hands clapping in the next cell. Tim tried to make contact with whoever was in there but to no avail. He tried hammering on the concrete wall with his fists. Then taking off one boot, he used the heel to tap on the wall, but there was no answer.

Tim lay for hours and mentally retraced his life from the poor but cosy cottage of his Mom and Dad in Ireland. His childhood and happy early school days when they were very young, and enjoying all those wonderful days with Kathleen O'Brien. That summer of 1939 when he walked and danced with Kathleen. The dinner he had with her before leaving for England. Thinking of that he caressed with his fingers Kathleen's gift bracelet. For some strange reason it had not been taken from him. Tim felt this was a good omen.

He thought about Sharon, the wonderful girl who had taught him so much about love. What was she doing? Would they ever be in each other's arms again? It seemed that a massive wall separated him from everything he loved. The wall grew higher.

After so many days of keeping his mental outlook above the Plimsoll line of despair, his mental trips to the outside world and his memories did not help him much any more. Several times he dipped below the line and had to practically pull on his diminished resources to drag himself back. It was the little cell with the grey walls and light burning day and night, nothing to see but the colour grey. Even the wooden bench was painted the same colour. There was nothing to read, no one to talk to, and no hope of getting out, except maybe to be shot. His breakdown point had not been far away when hope in the form of the civilian had arrived, but how long would it be before that hope would be justified by his release?

It was the twenty-fifth day since he had bought those train tickets and Tim was sitting on the cell bench almost finished his daily soup ration. When the key turned in the cell door lock, he immediately swallowed the last two spoonfuls. He thought the guard was back to retrieve the empties. The cell door swung inwards and two new faces confronted him. They were not unfriendly, and one had an official-looking paper in his hand. They were both dressed in military uniforms, not Army, Navy, or SS, but Luftwaffe. To Tim, it was a welcome sight. German Air Force military police; it was almost like meeting old friends.

The one with the rank of Corporal spoke perfect English. "Aircraftsman Timothy O'Neill, we would like you to come with us and bring your gear. You are going back to your Stalag."

"I have no gear. Can I come with you now?" He was afraid they might say they would come back for him in five minutes and he could see that door closing again forever.

"Yes, you can come now. That's what we are here for. I see by the travel permits that our final stop is in Obersilesia."

Tim knew tears were dribbling through his growth of beard but they were tears of joy.

"Is my friend OK? I was told he had been shot."

"Your friend is alive. I spoke with him a short time ago. He looks in rough shape as you do but he is very happy to go back to prison camp. So if you please let's go and we will have both of you out of here quickly before some higher authority cancels this release order."

Walking unsteadily, Tim fell in between the two Military Police. Three cells away they stopped and opened the door. A little man stood there his thin face covered in fair stubby hair, his clothing looking six sizes too large and his eyes wet with tears.

"I thought you were not coming back. I thought I was having hallucinations and that you were only a myth and it didn't happen. But thank God it's true!" Ken's voice trembled with great emotion. Then putting his arms around Tim he sobbed, "They told me you were dead, shot when trying to escape."

The Luftwaffe guards gave them about ten seconds then the English-speaking one said, "You can rejoice when we get on the train." They felt secure walking between the two well-armed Luftwaffe personnel. As they moved up the three flights of concrete stairway to the entrance and exit area, the English-speaking guard who seemed to be in charge left his partner to cover Tim and Ken. He entered a glass-fronted office where half a dozen uniformed men sat at desks. The Luftwaffe military policeman approached the platform where an officer sat at a large desk. The MP saluted smartly, held out the papers and with a gesture towards Tim, Ken, and his partner, he pointed to the papers that needed the officer's signature. The officer very slowly turned over each page then picked up the telephone and for what seemed an eternity talked to someone. Occasionally he read from the papers and seemed to be asking the Luftwaffe policeman questions. Each time the policeman turned and pointed in their direction. Tim and Ken held their breath. What would they do if the officer refused to sign, or told him the release was cancelled?

Tim knew that he would be unable to bear up if he was returned to that stinking little cell. He could see Ken's lips were trembling with fear. Their thudding hearts beat faster as they watched the officer put down his telephone, pick up the papers, and speak to the Luftwaffe MP who appeared to be in an argument with the officer.

Something was wrong! Tim knew it and in a choking whisper Ken croaked, "I'm not going back. Let's both make a run for it then we can die quickly instead of slowly down there in the dark. Look Tim, the sun is shining and there is blue sky out there. At least in Stalag we could always look out and look up to see the blue sky, or clouds, or snow, or stars, or rainstorms. Hope to God we get out of here."

Now the military policeman was leaving the officer's desk. Stepping back one pace he saluted smartly, giving the Hitler salute, and within seconds was coming towards them. His stern expression gave no clue whether the documents had been signed or not. He reached the office door, opened it and stood at their sides. He did not speak for a moment but stood checking each page of the documents. Then satisfied that everything was correct and in order, he said in his perfect Oxford English, "Let's go boys, and catch a train."

Ken was heard to say in a low voice, "Thank you, Lord."

Turning to his partner, the policeman spoke to him in German. Tim understood by the conversation that apparently there was no love lost between the Luftwaffe and the Army, especially the SS. Their release must have been signed by someone who had much authority. They moved through the entrance doorway opened by an SS guard. After the documents had again been scrutinised they were out in the wonderful fresh air. Ken and Tim filled their lungs to capacity and then exhaled three or four times. Their Luftwaffe guard, the one who could not speak English, smiled and said, "*Gut, ja?*" Tim replied with enthusiasm, "*Sehr gut. Sehr gut.*" Yes indeed, he thought, it is very good, and hoped they would get away from this place immediately.

Suddenly as they neared the end of a concrete path leading to the driveway, a military vehicle drove up and blocked their exit.

Tim's heart missed a beat and there was a tug on his sleeve and then Ken's nervous whisper. There was a low wall on each side of the path and Ken whispered, "Let's jump the wall together and make a break for it." Their fear quickly turned to relief when one of the Luftwaffe guards quickly opened the wide side doors of the vehicle. Standing like an armed chauffeur he invited them to climb aboard. One guard stayed with them and the door was closed. Tim and Ken sat on a bench seat, their guard on the opposite one. The rear sliding windows were open, so fresh clean air wafted through the steel bars. Slowly they moved a short distance then stopped. The door opened and the English-speaking Luftwaffe policeman stood beside an SS guard who looked inside, checked the papers and was satisfied. Quickly the doors were closed. Within minutes they were through that last check and out onto the streets of Stettin. Tim asked their guard where next and was relieved to hear him say, "The railway station."

Fifteen minutes later, Tim and Ken jumped together to the sidewalk. As the empty vehicle was driven away, they breathed sighs of relief and willingly moved forward into the station with their guards.

In daylight, Stettin Railway Station looked different, but the memories of twenty-five nights earlier were clear. Even now Tim felt that somewhere in the crowd of sailors, soldiers, airmen, civilians, and railway workers, a pair of steel blue eyes was watching them. He was certain. He felt it. He knew it! Stefan was out there somewhere in that bustling crowd of humanity or standing quietly watching from a secure hidden corner and thinking how stupid they had been to leave his protection.

It took only ten more minutes, and they were through the checkpoint and on the train. The English-speaking guard sat facing them while the other was next to Ken. As the locomotive rattled its way out of the Stettin terminal Tim thought, "Now a new train journey play begins where the old one ended, this time with a cast of four."

The guards had put their snub-nosed automatics up on the rack but their sidearm holsters were undone and those guns could be drawn with ease. The English-speaking guard leaned over and spoke quietly. "Do you feel safe now?"

"We sure do!" They both answered almost in unison.

"I don't think you fully realise what sort of place you were in. It is the SS and Gestapo interrogation centre for the area and very few people who descend to those cells survive. I am at a loss to know who contacted a high-ranking authority to obtain your release. How did you get into such a nasty place?"

"We were caught sleeping in the park."

"You were involved with some civilians, I hear. Were they German or Swedish?"

With this remark Tim immediately started to build up the barriers that he had so quickly torn down. This line of questioning seemed to be running into a sort of interrogation.

"Did you know they would be meeting you on arrival in Stettin?"

Now Tim's and Ken's defences were on red alert. Was this seemingly kind military policeman in league with the SS? Had he been told to win their confidence, then interrogate them to find out if they had contacts in Stettin, before leaving prison camp? Tim was certain they were still looking for Stefan and the train escapee. The Luftwaffe MP had goofed by saying Swedish because that sent Tim and Ken the message to clam up. Well, they would not fall into the trap.

Tim explained, more for Ken's benefit, so he would know this was their story and with it they would stick: "We met no one and we had no intention of meeting anyone at Stettin Station. We had hopes of perhaps meeting up with Swedish sailors who might take us on board a ship for Sweden. We had a notion we might be able to smuggle aboard a Swedish ship. We came from a prison-camp work party to Stettin and slept in the park two nights. There was no chance of getting close to the docks, never mind aboard a ship. We made no contacts, so it turned out we got caught in the park on the second night. A long journey to Stettin for two nights in the park, only to fall into the hands of Gestapo and SS who tried to frame us as saboteurs. That's what happened and we are grateful to whoever secured our release. We have not the slightest idea of who that would be. When I saw you in Luftwaffe uniform I was certain that somehow an influential Luftwaffe officer must have discovered two Allied airmen were being held on trumped-up charges. I believed he could have used his powers to release us. What do you think?" It was Tim's way of turning the tables a little bit and indicating that they knew nothing.

"I have no idea," replied the guard. "I have only the information supplied to me by the senior command at Stettin. I just follow my superiors' orders and right now they are to return you two men to your Stalag in Obersilesia. Would you like something to eat and perhaps a coffee?"

Wide-eyed at the thought of food and coffee they immediately agreed. He took down a large box from the rack, opened it up, then passed meat sandwiches to everyone. Four mugs and a large thermos were produced from the second guard's haversack.

There were no more questions, and Tim presumed the guard believed he had done his duty by asking the questions. Shortly after, Tim and Ken fell asleep leaning against each other.

When nudged awake they were astonished to learn the next stop would be Breslau and a change of trains.

Ken said, "We couldn't have slept all that time."

Tim's reply, "We must have, because now we are edging through the outskirts of a large city."

Fifteen minutes later the train wended its way through a series of tracks to eventually slide alongside a busy platform. Breslau was the last big German city for those going east. It was a city of farewells and as always a dispersal area for military personnel going to the Eastern Front. That night was no exception. The locomotive hissed to a standstill beside a troop train that obscured their view across the tracks and platforms, but not for long. Almost immediately it slowly moved out with the usual shouts of farewell. Now they could see across to the other side where another packed troop train was waiting for the green light to move out.

Their English-speaking guard gave his instructions: "We have to get off here and move across the tracks to catch the southbound train. It will move into the slot when the troop train leaves. We must cross the bridge overpass so keep close." On the platform, with a guard on each side, they negotiated up the steel stairs to the overpass. Before they were to descend the other steps it was decided they would stay on the overpass until all army personnel were on the train. They leaned over the edge and watched.

Ken whispered to Tim, "It's an SS regiment."

Sure enough there was a big contingent of SS boarding the train. To the left of the ladies serving hot soup was a large SS banner being unfurled in salute to those brave men departing east to fight the Russians.

Tim spoke quietly to Ken. "Look down there at that SS officer, the big one screaming his head off at that poor little railway employee. I wonder why? That poor old man must be near eighty and shouldn't even be working." The SS officer was giving the man a dressing down and once he pushed him so hard that he almost fell, much to the laughter of other SS who were leaning out the coach windows.

The train whistle blew, coach doors banged closed, then the final goodbyes, and uniformed figures dashed to get aboard. The brass band that had been playing rousing marching music for the last ten minutes struck up the German national anthem. Of the few uniformed figures left on the platform, one was the SS officer who had been doing so much shouting. He was finding it difficult walking along the edge of the platform towards the rear coaches because jostling crowds of civilians were having last-minute conversations or shaking hands with men in the coaches. Tim and Ken and their guards started down the steps. They reached the platform as the locomotive shrieked its final farewell. The coaches slowly moved out and the large crowd of civilian well-wishers moved forward, turning in the direction the coaches were going as if they were all on pivots.

"Let's get close to the platform's edge so that we can get a good private compartment when our train arrives." The English-speaking guard skirted the crowd to direct them. The band was playing the anthem for the third time and the last coach was passing the crowd of well-wishers standing below the overpass. The hubbub of farewells was dying down when screams from a young lady standing at the platform's edge brought others hurrying to investigate. Their guards moved closer to see what had frightened the young lady. The sight that met their eyes was not for squeamish stomachs. The remains of the SS officer were on the track directly below the platform edge. He had been cut into pieces. He must have slipped or fallen between the coaches as he walked along the edge. Soon military men pushed the crowd back and brighter lights were switched on. This bathed the track and platform in light that had not been seen since pre-war days.

"Come. Let us find out where our train will be leaving from." Again the English-speaking guard was taking charge, sure that their train would not be leaving from this platform after all.

They were about to walk away and had made a right turn from the platform edge when Tim hissed, "Look to the end of the platform at eleven o'clock." Ken followed Tim's instructions and let his eyes travel to the end of the platform. There glistening in the extra light were two glasses, and standing like a sentinel guarding them was a bottle. Both Tim and Ken knew that the glasses would be empty and that the bottle was good French white wine and unopened. All would be devoid of fingerprints and incriminating evidence.

Their guards had not seen the glasses or the bottle and continued to hustle them across the platform to the stationmaster, who informed them the south train would now be departing from platform number four because of the tragic accident. They must cross the other overpass.

Now they headed towards those steps. When they were close to the overpass Tim and Ken simultaneously saw the two men standing in the shadows There could be no mistake about the identity of the tall blond figure. Even in the shadows there was sufficient light to see his face. It was Stefan. With him was none other than their train companion wearing dark clothing. Their foursome was a few feet from the first step when Stefan and his friend passed by so very close. For a fleeting moment Tim met Stefan's cold blue eyes as he passed and was sure a flicker of recognition was there. Tim never knew for sure whether Stefan really recognised the two bearded bedraggled prisoners as the same Air Force escapees who stumbled onto his hideout and who had later taken off with his rations.

When they reached the top of the steps and travelled across the overpass, Tim stole a long look towards the exit. At that moment the bright station lights showed two figures about to leave the station. He tried to send a mental message to make Stefan turn around before passing from view. He hoped Stefan would give some sign that he had recognised them. The tall blond unwavering figure and his short dark companion disappeared without hesitation out into the darkened streets of Breslau. That left Tim and Ken with the unanswered question. Had Stefan recognised them? Did he have contacts with some high authority who had the power to sign their release from the SS cells? Did his visit to Breslau have the twofold purpose of killing an SS man and checking on their safety for the last leg of their journey? Two questions were in Tim's thoughts: How long would it be before Stefan and his friend made a mistake and were caught? Would they survive the war?

As light from the roving searchlight beams filtered through the remaining glass in the barrack window, Tim surveyed the little group who had sat, stood, or lain on their bunks for such a long time listening to his story. The barrack lights had gone out way back during Tim's account of Stefan's escapades, but there had been a maintained circle of silence from surrounding bunks. An indication that a much wider audience had been listening.

Taking a deep breath Tim continued, "The rest of the journey from Breslau was uneventful and peaceful, and almost pleasant and all of you know what happened when Ken and I arrived back in camp. But I can assure you the fourteen days of solitary confinement in our Stalag cooler was a picnic in comparison to that SS cell in Stettin."

Then in the dim light Tim felt for the old tattered book he had placed on Ken's bunk. Finding it, he looked around in the darkened barrack room at the silhouettes of those who listened to his story. In an almost apologetic voice he said, "I don't think I'll be telling that story again. On behalf of Ken and myself our thanks to everyone for the great reception we got on our return from the escape excursion. Your gifts of food were certainly appreciated. Thanks fellas, someday I might have the opportunity to repay you. Perhaps when you visit me on the Emerald Isle or on a get-together for a brew at Ken's place in Wales.

"Before I go off to my bunk with it's palliasse of new straw I will answer a question that I know will come up sometime after I leave. It might be tomorrow or next week, or next month. The night that the SS man met such a horrible death under the wheels of the moving troop train was not the fifteenth but the first day of the month. It definitely was another instalment payment on the continuing debt the SS have to pay Stefan for destroying his life with a girl born under the sign of Aquarius on the first day of February 1916, and of course you know her name was Ilsa."

With that Tim made his way quietly between the bunks to his own domain and left a number of that audience in surrounding bunks unable to sleep as they tried to recap the story.

It was a disappointed Tim who lay on his new straw palliasse thinking of the failed escape attempt, but he and his mucker Ken were alive and with a strange feeling of safety behind the barbed wire in their Stalag. His mission of revenge on George O'Conor would have to wait until the cessation of hostilities or his liberation before that by Allied Forces. There had been no letters for almost four months. His thoughts strayed to Sharon and he knew there would be many servicemen asking for dances with the beautiful, dark-haired green-eyed wonderful lady. Tim fell asleep thinking of Sharon with someone else and the camp searchlight beams continued their sweep of the wired compounds just in case some brave prisoner attempted an escape with hope in his heart that he would reach home.

12

Wee Jock McGregor had been the first to meet Tim and Ken on their return to prison-camp barracks after their sentence of fourteen days in the cooler. He hugged both of them, then in his strong Scottish brogue said, "Thought I'd lost my two best buddies forever." Each day he joined them in their daily walks around the perimeter wire. At times he chattered away with stories about Scotland and his circus job. Where even with his father's own inspection of safety devices some tight-rope acts almost ended in tragedy.

October spelled out winter was coming, then November dragged its way to December's doorstep.

December turned very cold but as usual, Tim, Ken, and Wee Jock walked the wire with their collars turned up against the bitter wind. Those dark weary cold days slipped by with no mail from home. Tim's hope was for a Christmas letter.

One letter had come for Wee Jock. It contained a 'Dear John' from that sweet beautiful girl he had left behind in England. It wasn't to say she had another boyfriend. She had been married two weeks before writing the letter, and now she had returned from honeymooning at Blackpool Holiday Resort. The impact on Wee Jock was drastic. Tim and Ken had one hell of a time getting him to think rationally about it. Friends kept close to him for many days.

Then other important things in Stalag life took over, like trying to keep warm twenty-four hours a day. The scary existence was tearing apart the will to defeat this incarceration. Wee Jock was left to carry on with life. Just one more addition to the long list of those who had already received their 'Dear John' letters.

Preparations were already in progress for Christmas. Cigarette donations from the inmates had obtained extra black-market briquettes for the heater. The result was an atmosphere like London pea-soup fog in the barrack room. The old heater's oven was working overtime. Tin stoves were stoked to capacity with all sorts of combustible materials. The broken windows were repaired with cardboard and other materials. There were no outlets for the smoke or odours from a host of Christmas specials that were being cooked with much good humour and laughter.

Rumours were rife that the secret still would give up Christmas cheer. That thought was squashed when Pat Whittle announced all those who held receipts from donations of raisins and prunes from their Red Cross parcels were to hold them until New Year's Eve. Then the 'good brew' would definitely be ready for the most important and happy time of year. When all prisoners would toast in the year that would see them free. 1944! This announcement, like most of Pat's performances, was received with a mixture of boos and cheers.

Christmas day 1943 arrived and it too passed into history. The few days between Christmas and New Year's were quiet. Tim spent his time writing letters and cards to Sharon and Kathleen. He had received no mail, but writing gave him a sense of closeness though no certainty about any mail getting out of Stalag.

The last day of 1943 arrived and the New Year of hope was about to be born. Tim prayed that he would be toasting the Year of Freedom 1944 back in Ireland or England and, wherever it would be, with Sharon.

New Year's was just like Christmas, with relaxed guards and extra rations. The majority of prisoners were happy or pretending to be. The camp Kommandant permitted the inner compound gates to remain open until after midnight. Prisoners from other compounds mixed and visited with each other. It was a welcome suspension of rules and it seemed everyone took advantage of this New Year's gift.

The brew that had been fermenting in some secret place for many months was distributed to those who held receipts. Prison-camp life and food had lowered resistance to many things and alcoholic drink was certainly one of those. It resulted in dozens of inebriated prisoners and many expected hangovers for New Year's Day.

A few minutes after midnight prisoners were shaking hands slapping backs and wishing each other a Happy New Year when someone shouted, "Wee Jock is climbing the wire!" Jock had donated many raisins and prunes and received too many receipts for his own good. No one had been checking on his drinks. Tim had talked to him around ten o'clock. He had been feeling no pain and had said, "I'm getting out of here soon."

"Sure Jock," Tim had replied. "That's what we all hope for in 1944."

"I'll be home afore anyone," was Jock's reply. Then he excused himself saying, "Got to spend a few receipts."

No one had seen him leave the barrack and now there was a big exodus as almost everyone grabbed outdoor clothing and made a mad rush for the door. The night had turned rotten with a cold wind and blowing snow. Ken and Tim reached the doorway together then made their way quickly to the trip wire at the extreme north corner of the camp. They were shocked to see Jock's small figure perched on top of the outer post. All around him lines of barbed wire fanned outwards. How he'd been able to climb the barbed wire in his drunken state or how he'd got to the outer post across that entanglement of wire between the inner and outer fences no one knew. Tim felt that it had to do with his high-wire circus experience.

The sentries in the two closest machine gun lookout boxes each had a searchlight trained on Jock. He was like an actor playing his part on stage and spotlighted from both wings. A number of prisoners were shouting and asking him to come back if he could or just stay there. Others were calling up at the sentries asking them not to shoot and asking that some guard bring a ladder.

Jock started to make his way up the strands of wire that were strung outwards at forty-five to fifty degrees along the top of the perimeter fence. He was using each strand like a rung on a ladder. There was a warning burst of machine gun fire from the sentry box to the left.

"Don't do it! Don't do it!" shouted Jock's mucker, hoping his voice would somehow ride with the piercing cold wind to his friend's ears. The unconcerned wind was singing its way through the wire, oblivious to the tragedy that was being enacted. Its companion the gritty snow swirled like silver sand in the searchlights' glare that had engulfed Wee

Jock as he clung to the wire. Somehow he swung himself to the underside of the wire and like a fly on the ceiling used the same wires as rungs climbing down with his back to the ground below. He worked his way down to the perimeter wire. This time he was on the outside and must surely have been bleeding profusely from so many contacts with barbs on the wire.

There was much confusion now as Wee Jock was halfway down the outside wire. German-speaking prisoners were cupping their hands and screaming up into the wild night, "The man's drunk, please don't shoot him." They were hoping the sentries on duty would understand. One of them did wave his hand as if he realised the situation and used his intercom to speak to the guard in the other box. Hundreds of prisoners' voices blasted their way through the night telling Wee Jock to put up his hands when he reached the ground. The gritty pellet-like snow swirled in continuous eddying currents around the compound. When Wee Jock reached terra firma he was held in the searchlight's glare. He looked like a scared rabbit that some pit lampers had cornered. Hesitating for a moment he turned towards the astonished crowd inside the wire and raised his hand in salute. With drunken staggering steps he turned and proceeded to walk away from prison camp.

"He'll bloody well freeze to death," someone said.

"He won't get away with it, they'll shoot him," volunteered another.

In one last effort, and almost in unison, a host of voices screamed after him, "Jock, stop! Come back, put your hands above your head." He heard the roar of voices above the storm and his only reaction was to half turn and give us the finger.

"Christ! Is he stupid! He has no rations with him, no warm clothes and probably no idea where he's going. How the hell did he get out there?" It was a newcomer voicing aloud his opinion.

The sentries in their boxes had now understood the message and were waiting for outside guards to accost the stumbling prisoner and bring him back. It was strange they had not already done so. They were continuously walking their allotted beats outside the wire and should have been waiting for Wee Jock to descend. Wee Jock had gone only a few yards when one of those exterior guards, who apparently had not been at his post, was seen running along the outside perimeter track. He looked very young and had his rifle at ready while he yelled,

"*Halt! Halt!*" Perhaps he had been celebrating New Year's while on duty and had missed one of his rounds. Another guard was seen hurrying from the opposite direction. The young one stopped a few yards from the corner post, levelled his rifle in Wee Jock's direction then continued his command, "*Halt! Halt!*"

Wee Jock had already stumbled around in a wide circle and was going nowhere. Without any more warnings or consultation with the other guards the young soldier fired two bursts from his automatic rifle. Wee Jock spun around as if he were completing some special finishing steps to a dance then crumpled in a small, tragic heap. Everyone looked on in horror as the swirling snow immediately began to cover his body.

The roar of protest at this wilful execution of a prisoner who had no chance of getting away continued for many minutes. "Don't come inside the Air Force compound! You'd better ask for a transfer!" All kinds of threatening remarks were hurled in German and English across the wire. The other guard was gesticulating at the younger one and everyone surmised he was asking the same question. "Why did you have to kill him? He wasn't going anywhere." A number of guards arrived to disperse the angry crowd. As Tim was being herded towards his barrack he took a last look across the perimeter wire. Through the driving snow he could see that silent white mound and the two guards standing beside it. The camp loudspeakers crackled to life, drowning out the hubbub of voices, but were unable to silence the screaming wind that distorted the announcement. "Attention! Attention! All prisoners must return to their own barracks. Compound gates will be closed in ten minutes and lights out in twenty!" The birth of the new year had seen its first tragedy, at least in this prison camp.

Tim lay in his bunk that night and thought, "Why? Why? Why did this happen, especially to Wee Jock?" Ken came and they talked, trying to understand their own recent escape from probable execution and Wee Jock's unnecessary murder.

Wee Jock was buried two days later and a few men were picked to attend his funeral. Later an enquiry began into who had started the fermentation process. What barrack was it in? Did the barrack commander know? Where had all the ingredients come from? Were there any guards involved?

The British medical officer who had been captured in Crete toured each barrack and lectured on the stupidity of the incident. The outcome of the investigation was not revealed to the inmates. After that no one ever again suggested collecting dried fruit to make a fermented brew.

So the New Year of 1944 began with sad thoughts of one more prisoner. Wee Jock would not be going home, and chances were his girlfriend who had sent him the 'Dear John' letter would never know the true story of his death. Maybe that was how it should be.

With anger and frustration surging through his troubled thoughts, Tim sat at the table close to the heater. The black-market briquettes had all been used so the heater was now dead cold like Wee Jock's small cold body in that frozen ground.

Part Three

13

Hi! Dear reader, it's me again, your author. Remember I promised to return you to the Emerald Isle with its beauty, wonderment and tragedies, but first I wished to introduce you to Stefan Jonsson and part two of the story.

I'll certainly keep my promise and will return you to Ireland and Dunraven House. But first, let's make a side trip to England.

You will certainly remember the American flyer Lieutenant Bob Steele and Sharon Marshal, who with each other shared so much happiness in that cosy cottage in the village of Ashport. Sharon oft-times thought that Timothy O'Neill should be told about Bob, but it was hard for her to diagnose the effect it would have on Tim's morale while in prison camp. She refrained from telling him and it troubled her conscience, but her intuitions told her to leave things as they were.

Sharon knew in her heart that she loved two men. Let's find out how the villagers received these unmarried lovers after they moved to the cottage on that cold and wintry day in late November, 1942.

Ashport Village, England, 1944

The small village of Ashport, close to the airfield where Bob Steele was based, had one street, one store, two places of worship and the Brass Bell Pub, the villagers' main gathering place for six days a week (closed Sundays).

Village folks were very proud when in late November 1942 an American Air Force Officer and his beautiful lady come to live in their midst, so they treated Bob and Sharon like royalty. They were invited to all important functions of village life and proudly introduced to visitors. After living in the village for a short time Bob and Sharon were surprised to hear themselves being introduced as Mr. and Mrs. Robert Steele by very straight-laced and religious villagers. Perhaps being close to the air base, they knew the short life expectancy for aircrews and had closed the door for a time on what they believed to be very improper — a young man and young woman unmarried yet living together as man and wife.

When Bob was on flying duties Sharon would often be invited to dine with some village family. It seemed everyone wished to share her fears until Bob returned safely.

Other members of Bob's squadron spent time at the Brass Bell. It was there that these young Americans far from home would spend time out from the awful terror of slaughter in the air. In this quaint English pub they'd enjoy a few hours of youthful conversation and laughter with comrades who flew with them.

On a few occasions Bob invited his own crew to have dinner at their little cottage. He was so proud of Sharon. He often said, "When I finish my tour of operational flights I'm taking this beautiful lady to Orange County California in the good old USA." When there was a stand down from duty for a few days, they sometimes drove to Coventry. They spent Coventry time with Sharon's Mom and Dad, who were so happy she had found this wonderful young American.

It was after D-Day, the sixth of June, 1944, and Allied armies were making good footholds in France. Robert had been flying day after day, and Sharon had not seen him for two weeks. When he did get a few hours off, she noticed the strain of those deadly hours in the air. He had lost that boyish look. The mischievous sparkle in his eyes was gone, replaced by dark lines underneath. His wonderful smile and his laughter seemed to be forced and for moments he would occasionally withdraw in silence. Perhaps he was reliving some terrible tragedy in the air. His squadron had lost nine aircraft in the space of forty-eight hours and had received no word of survivors.

Sharon was delighted when Bob came home one evening to say, "I have five days off and we are going to London just you and me. We will block out this crazy war, then we'll dance, sing and have the most wonderful time of our lives doing whatever we wish to do. Do you agree, Sharon Marshal?"

"I agree! I agree!" she exclaimed and rushed off to fill her travel bag with feminine finery. Then she packed Bob's necessary clothing in his brown leather travel bag. Sharon felt so very happy and relieved that he was free for a few days, and it was rumoured that the war would end soon.

They stayed two nights at the American Officers' Club, but it was too crowded and they wanted privacy. Bob contacted a friend in London who was able to produce an apartment to rent in the St. John's Wood area of this great capital city. Robert had the staff car so they were thrilled and happy to have this bonus of their own private apartment.

It was during dinner at an American Officers' Club on the last night of Bob's off-duty time that he told Sharon a big secret. "I have only three more operational missions and my tour of duty will be finished." He looked at her with a happy enthusiastic smile she had not seen for some time. "My commanding officer has recommended me for a promotion and soon I'll have a desk job back in the good old USA." Then Bob looked steadfastly into the depths of those soft jade-like green eyes. "My dear Sharon, after I'm freed from operational duties and that will be in a few days, will you marry me? I'll take you back to California. Every man in my crew has already volunteered to be best man."

Sharon reached across the table with both hands and grasped his in her trembling fingers. "Oh! Bob I will! I will! I love you so much. Yes! Yes! I will marry you right now if you wish."

Then on a sombre note and holding tight to his hands, she said, "Bob, if Tim O'Neill is alive I'd like to be here and talk to him when he comes home, otherwise my conscience will always trouble me. It would feel like I was running away without an explanation. I do love you very much and I know our lives will be filled with much happiness."

They drove back to their apartment and over a glass of brandy drew a plan of the house they would build in Orange County, California. They changed the kitchen plan three times and the bedroom twice then in block letters at the top they printed OUR NEW HOUSE IN

THE GOOD OLD USA, then signed their names and the date, June 17, 1944, London, England.

Bob folded the paper and put it in the top left pocket of his uniform and said, "Now it's almost as close to my heart as you Sharon. We will get an architect to copy this and I'm certain you will have many changes to make."

He took her in his arms and kissed her, and she looked up at him with wonderment in her eyes.

"My own dear Robert, I love you and I am the happiest girl in the world. This is a wonderful evening and a new beginning for our future. Let's drink a toast to years of peace and happiness and to the wonderful children we are going to have."

Bob looked serious for a moment then pulled her close and said, "Sharon Louise Marshal, what a courageous and fabulous wife and mother you are going to be and I will love you forever."

It had been a glorious summer day, and as dusk dropped its curtain on the houses of Harrow Avenue in St. John's Wood, Bob and Sharon welcomed the privacy it gave. Holding hands they sat close on the third floor's little outside patio, immune to the traffic below. Just two young people caught up in the reality and horror of war who for this short time were blocking out that reality by reaching further into their future with plans and dreams.

It was almost midnight when the air raid sirens sounded and Sharon snuggled into Bob's arms for safety.

Late next evening, the eighteenth of June, search crews had been working all day sifting through the rubble of #12 Harrow Avenue in the St. John's Wood area of London. The large three-storey apartment house had been demolished the previous night just before midnight. It had been a direct hit by one of Hitler's new pilot-less V 1 flying bombs (known to Britain's population as the Doodle Bug). A number of permanent residents in the house had been killed; others were trapped, but miraculously with non-life-threatening injuries.

A little before darkness the search crews found two bodies in each other's arms, an American Air Force Lieutenant and also, they surmised, his girlfriend. In the top pocket of the Lieutenant's uniform a police sergeant found and then unfolded a sheet of paper. On it was the drawing of a house plan; at the top, printed in block letters were the words: OUR NEW HOUSE IN THE GOOD OLD USA, and two signatures. The date was June 17, 1944, LONDON, ENGLAND.

Ashport Village, England, Anytime

Dear Reader: 1944 was many decades ago, but if one day you should find yourself passing through the little village of Ashport in England, stop for a while.

Call in at the Brass Bell Pub for a refreshing drink or maybe tea and a sandwich. Remember they close Sunday but the cemetery will be open. Ask about Bob Steele and Sharon Marshal. Even today there will be someone willing to tell how the village folk way back in 1942 adopted a young American airman and his girlfriend and mourned their loss when both were killed.

That person will probably show you a beautifully framed black-and-white picture hanging in a prominent position on the East inside wall of the pub. It is of two young people, an American Air Force flyer with a very beautiful girl. Inscribed underneath are two names, "Lieutenant Bob Steele and Sharon Marshal, May, 1944."

Whoever you talk to will direct you, I'm sure, to the village cemetery, that is, if you would like to see the stone placed there in memory of Bob and Sharon.

You can't miss the cemetery. It's only a hundred yards down the lane behind the pub. Open the gate, then close it gently. If you don't, it will close itself slowly at first then with a rush and a loud clang and you'll feel that you have desecrated this hallowed place. In spring or summer you would be amidst a wonderland of flowers surrounded by age-old oak and birch trees.

Take the first turn to the left, walk for two minutes, and on the way check the old tombstones on either side. The dates go back to the sixteen hundreds.

This narrow path will widen into a circle and from there the paths branch off in four directions. The attraction will be a large granite cairn that stands alone, its place being the centre of the circle and the cemetery. Look a little closer and read the inscription on the polished stone plaque dated 17th of June, 1945.

The residents of Ashport Village dedicate this stone in memory of Robert Steele and Sharon Marshal, killed by enemy action on June 17, 1944. We deeply regret their tragic deaths. Once strangers in our village, now and for always mourned as we would our own loved ones. May their souls stay united.

In small print you will read:

Unveiled at an interdenominational memorial service on June 17, 1945, the first anniversary of their deaths.

You might wish to stay for a while in that beautiful and unique cemetery before closing the gate very quietly to continue on your journey with mixed emotions.

Stalag, Germany

For Tim O'Neill and Ken Jones, 1944 was turning out like any other prison-camp year. The same daily routine behind barbed wire where life was always in the hands of the enemy.

June sixth, D-Day, brought new light into Tim's dark foreboding thoughts of never seeing Sharon, Kathleen nor his dear Irish countryside again.

Now a great armada of ships had landed Allied Armies at Normandy beach in France. Tanks and infantry were moving inland.

Tim and Ken knew two things. Time and survival would be dominant in their thoughts and actions. They felt liberation was certain.

When? It was an unanswered question.

Blue skies and warm temperatures of the June summer were appreciated by prisoners who basked in the sunshine. Conversations remained 'plugged in' to news about the Second Front battlefields in France and how long before liberation?

The Western allied armies were pushing east, the Russians west and at some future date the German fighting forces plus civilians and prisoners of war would all be caught in the squeeze.

Tim had a strange thought. Could it be that through some twist of fate, or an impulsive move like Wee Jock's, he too would lose his life in the turmoil and destruction to come? Their Stalag would probably form the front line battleground of their liberators and their enemies who kept them prisoners. Many combatants and non-combatants would die. Sharon might never know where, or how he died. Her long wait for him would have been in vain.

There were rumours that when Russian front-line troops liberated prison camps, especially those with inmates of many thousands, instead of sending them back for repatriation gave all physically fit prisoners rifles and ammunition then told them to kill Germans, any Germans. Through the years Stalag rumours were heard on an almost daily basis. This latest one scared everyone. It was impossible to believe that liberation troops would issue arms to thousands of prisoners and say, go to it. Ken declared, "What a ragtime army it would be!"

On the seventeenth day of June, 1944, there was a letter for Timothy O'Neill in the Stalag mail bag. Fate had decided on his receiving one more letter from Sharon. The letter had taken exactly two months from its mailing date to delivery. In her letter, Sharon had written that by chance she met Charlie Ward and that he was now a Corporal attached to a squadron in Yorkshire. Her Mom and Dad were fine and sent their best wishes and their prayers for his safe return. Sharon said the geraniums she planted in her new window boxes were coming along fine. She called them her little children who were tended to with loving care.

Tim's plans were that one day Sharon and he would have their own home with a garden where she could plant a variety of flowers with her geraniums.

For Timothy O'Neill from county Donegal in the Republic of Ireland the knowledge of Sharon Marshal's death on the 17th of June, 1944, was still many months away. Those months were to contain other physical and mental pain, degradation, tragedy, and terrible conditions that forced him into decisions he never expected to make. One of those decisions concerned his prison-camp mucker, Ken. It would haunt him for many years.

The excitement of the Allied armies landing in France had passed and so had summer. There was no quick liberation, and Ken had been very ill. He had the flu and couldn't shake it off. Prison-camp existence, the escape, and time spent in SS cells had all taken their toll. Ken never fully recovered his health after those ordeals. There came a new fall, another winter and a Christmas with starvation rations. Then another New Year numbered 1945. It brought no thoughts of celebration. Red Cross food parcels were not getting through. Prisoners had to exist on the daily issue of one serving of a watery soup, three slices of the horrible tasting rye bread plus four small potatoes. It was not much sustenance or cause for laughter and rejoicing. Only fear, hunger and weariness at the uncertainty of their future in the hands of those armed guards watching their every movement.

The roving searchlights at night were still seeking out would-be escapees. Blizzard conditions and the freezing cold of thirty degrees Fahrenheit below zero made it not the time to escape, especially now when the liberating Russian armies were not far away.

Thoughts of liberation were sabotaged when their German captors issued evacuation orders. Prisoners were to march west in the sub-zero weather and so away from those Russian liberation armies. Tim had concerns for Ken and the many hundreds who were in poor physical condition. They didn't have much hope of surviving a long march in East Germany's winter.

They were given no choice, and the evacuation of over forty thousand inmates from their overcrowded Stalag began. Prisoners were herded like cattle out onto frozen roads and winter snow. "March westward!" was the order.

Tim stuck close to Ken for many terrible days. With starvation food rations and awful road conditions, they trudged westwards across the frozen countryside. Guards prodded them with rifle butts, even the sick and those who faltered or lagged behind.

As each terrible day passed, Tim stuck with his mucker Ken. Each day he encouraged him to keep going and often helped him along ice-covered roads, over the hills, and through snowdrifts. They had been through so many scary times together, their escape, the train journey to Stettin, Stefan, their discovery in the park, then the SS cells and their unbelievable release. The soul-destroying years of confinement took an unbelievable toll on one's power to rise above the onslaught or to remain sane. Now, as they bowed their heads into the driving snowflakes, this nightmare march continued. Conditions were atrocious, the guards brutal, and Ken's strength was failing fast.

Weeks passed, awful days and worse nights spent shivering in draughty barns and storage sheds, crammed together in darkness where thousands of men fought for their own survival, as they waited out the freezing nights. In some cases trying to protect their footwear and winter clothing from those who in summers past had sold theirs for food and who now in desperation preyed on weaker prisoners and the sick.

During the frigid nights of January and February 1945, in these stinking barns with no amenities, Tim knew Ken's will to continue this awful march was at zero. His own strength was failing and he felt sure that soon he would be unable to assist Ken. Maybe it would be today or tomorrow, but he would have to make the big decision. Leave Ken to fend for himself or die with him. Right now he had to wait for the pre-dawn door opening to another day of struggling along frozen roads. Their only hope was the advancing allied army. Rumours filtered down the weary bedraggled column of stumbling humanity that they had become pawns in a war game of surrender. If terms were not met, all prisoners would be shot. The question was, would they still be on their feet when liberation troops broke through, or would their frozen bodies be lying somewhere by the roadside on enemy soil?

For many days Tim continued to virtually drag Ken along. It was decision time. Not a case of how much longer he could continue on the frightening trail but where could he leave his exhausted mucker. A few days into the month of March, Ken gave up completely as he had no physical resources left. Tim pulled on his own nearly exhausted resources to keep Ken on his feet until they could reach a rest barn. Tim knew this was the day he would have to leave his prison-camp comrade with the many others whose physical strength was exhausted. They were to be sheltered from the elements in a barn, praying relief would come quickly from Western or Russian forces.

Tim had considered staying but another prisoner, a medical corps orderly, volunteered to look after the exhausted men until help came.

The crunch time had come, now it was every man for himself. Tim stole straw from a shed and made a fairly comfortable bed for Ken before a guard came and tried to push him outside. Tim promised Ken he would note the name of the next village, and give the information to someone in authority. He would ask them to tell their medical corps where to find the group of prisoners who needed immediate help.

The guard was still prodding Tim with his rifle as he knelt beside his best friend. Tim took off his frozen gloves, unbuttoned his jacket, and unwrapped his own big woollen scarf. Gently, he opened Ken's frayed old greatcoat, wrapped the scarf around his neck and crossed it over his chest. Then tucking it under Ken's arms, he buttoned the coat up to his neck. "It will keep your chest and your Welsh heart warm," he joked. A weak smile was the only return and then Ken lay back in the straw.

The guard shouted *"Raus! Raus!"* and gave Tim a brutal thud with his rifle butt between the shoulder blades that sent him sprawling on the dirty floor. He struggled to his feet and looked steadfastly at his enemy. Then in his Stalag-taught German he said, "Now I will remember your face. The Allied armies are not far away. You will very soon be my prisoner!" His bit of satisfaction was rewarded by another blow from the rifle butt, this time to his ribs. Tim controlled his anger. This confrontation had gained him nothing but abuse and pain, so he decided to be more careful, because there was an overdue appointment with a certain George O'Conor, master of Dunraven House in County Donegal, Ireland. Tim had no wish to miss that.

After seven more days of horrific conditions, each new day saw the ranks of stumbling humanity depleted by scores. They fell down with a crash like dead men or trees in a storm or sank slowly to their knees in the slush, pleading for help from the unsympathetic guards. Others stumbled off to the roadside where they sat dejectedly in little rivulets of water as the melting snow joined with other rivulets to form small frigid rivers that would freeze again when night came.

Tim and other survivors of the terrible ordeal were liberated by the Allied Forces. The night before they had been billeted as usual in a dark, dirty farm building.

Next morning there were no hostile guards hassling them to start another gruelling day. The guards had fled and in their place were American forces, tanks and infantry in a continuous flow of armour. Massive six-wheeled trucks arrived, then moved off in convoys filled with grateful survivors of the march. They wheeled away from the front line to safer positions. Before leaving, Tim found a US medical officer and gave him the position of the village named Krossen near where Ken and the others needed immediate help.

Tim's group was flown to England on March seventh, and after a warm welcome at the air base close to London, they were taken to an Air Force Medical Centre for ex-prisoners. Under protest, he was made to stay in hospital three weeks for observation and recovery from his ordeal. On the second day after arrival, each patient received letter cards that were already printed with the answers to questions their loved ones would be likely to ask. The easiest action was to score out the answers that didn't apply. Tim had his ready to return minutes after receiving them. One went to his mother in Ireland, another to Sharon's address in Lincoln. After two weeks he had received two letters from his mother but nothing from Sharon.

It had now been more than a year since Sharon's letters had stopped. At first he had blamed the Stalag mail, but now his thoughts reverted to the multitude of service personnel who had passed through Britain in the five years since he had been taken prisoner. Lincoln City would have seen Sharon in the midst of hundreds of Air Force men; how could a beautiful lady wait five years without at some time meeting a man she could care for?

Tim asked to be discharged from the hospital, but his request was denied. However he was given a forty-eight-hour pass to "visit a dear friend" in Lincoln.

When Tim turned the corner to Sharon's Lincoln flat, he had butterflies in his stomach. With foreboding thoughts he knocked. The door opened but not to Sharon. Just an old gentleman who stared for a moment at the speechless young airman before asking, "Yes, young man, what do you want?"

"Do you know what happened to Sharon Marshal who used to live here?" Tim stammered.

"Don't know. The place was empty when I got it to rent eight months ago."

Tim heard himself say, "Thank you, sir." He ran to Lloyd's Insurance where Sharon had worked. Surely someone there could tell him where she was living. He knew the office closed at 4:00 p.m. and already it was 4:10, but he reckoned someone would be working late. The door was locked. He rang the buzzer then peered through the window and saw no movement.

"Coventry. I must get to Coventry. Sharon's parents live there." Tim didn't have the number but he knew the address was on Birch

Street. If he tried to get there now it would be dark and probably midnight by the time he arrived. He paid for a bed at the Salvation Army's Hostel for Service Men, then hurried to the dance hall where he and Sharon had met. Tim found only one face he recognised: the coat check lady and sometime bar maid. She remembered him and Sharon when he showed her an old picture of the two of them together with Charlie and Peter at the bar.

"That was away back in forty or forty-one, and you're Irish. Yes, now I remember. You three drank Guinness and the lady brandy. I remember because I brought the wrong beer once and your friend refused it. I got in trouble with Art the bartender who said once they are poured and to the table, no returns. Your friend asked Art to the back alley to decide the issue. Art chickened out and you got your Guinness."

Tim remembered all of that, but did not wish for her to expound any more on the subject. "Have you seen the lady or do you know anything about her?"

"No, not for a long time. I know for a while she was serving coffee at the service club down the street, but that was a long time ago."

Tim tried the service club but to no avail. "It's five years son," the old doorman reminded Tim. "There's been many volunteers come and go since you were taken prisoner."

Early next morning Tim travelled by train to Coventry. At the station taxi stand he asked, "How much to Birch Street?" The taxi driver had to check his map before answering, "About three quid."

Tim had only ten quid left but reckoned he could get back to the Medical Centre on that. They arrived at the corner of Birch and Oak Streets. "What's the number?" asked the driver who had made no conversation since leaving the railroad station.

"I don't know," replied Tim. "All I have is a name, a Mr. and Mrs. Marshal."

"Best that I drop you off here and you can start knocking at the first door. You won't be popular young fellow. It's Sunday morning and most of them will be in bed. Anyway if you look, half the houses are gone. The German Air Force did a job on this street. Sure glad they got their just deserts. I say we should wipe out all their cities. They started it."

Tim looked at the long rows of semi-detached homes and saw the great gaps on both sides of the streets. He could visualise a great giant striding this way and at each step crushing the little homes and their inhabitants. He remembered the German's prison-camp propaganda about Hitler's new secret weapon. The pilotless V1 and V2 flying bombs gauged to run out of fuel over English cities then fall indiscriminately on populated areas. This was old destruction by the Luftwaffe bomb crews and Coventry had been one of the most bombed cities in England.

Tim broke into a cold sweat. Could it be that Sharon, visiting her parents, had been killed with them in one of those raids? In a trance he moved from door to door asking, "Do you know of a Mr. and Mrs. Marshal and their daughter Sharon?" He was an hour into his quest when he was directed across the street to a yellow house with a cat sitting in the sun on the doorstep.

Tim's hand shook as he knocked on the stained-oak door. It opened almost immediately, and Sharon's father stood in shock for a moment before exclaiming, "Good Lord, Tim O'Neill! Never thought we'd see you again! Come in son, come in. We heard some prisoners were home. Sure glad you made it!"

Janet Marshal hugged Tim and cried, "Oh how I wish Sharon was here, but thanks for coming, Tim!"

"Where is Sharon?" After his question silent seconds passed, then Sharon's mother turned to her husband and cried out in despair. "He doesn't know, Peter! He doesn't know!"

"Sit down Tim."

"I'll make some tea," and Janet Marshal disappeared into her kitchen.

Her husband spoke in a steady voice. "It's been five years since we spent Christmas with you and Sharon at her place in Lincoln. We always thought of you as family, but now you're the last one to be told. We have lived with this tragedy for more than a year now and it never gets any easier; Sharon is dead."

Tim's tears were flowing before Peter Marshal had finished his last words.

"How? Where?"

"It was one of Hitler's self-propelled rocket bombs. Sharon had gone to London to visit a friend of ours. The rocket hit around midnight on June 17th, last year. Both were killed."

Tim felt this could not be happening; it had to be a bad dream, too devastating to be true. He would wake up and then go to find Sharon. No! No! This could not be. He had lost Kathleen to George O'Conor five years ago and Sharon had filled that void with her love and understanding.

Fate could not be so cruel as to extinguish that wonderful light after all the years of waiting for their miracle meeting. To be told Sharon was dead just didn't make sense to Tim.

He was stunned and thought, Will it be that all I have of this beautiful lady is the little bundle of letters still tied together with string from a prison-camp Red Cross food parcel? Those letters that held the wonderful words she wrote to me in prison camp? For the rest of my life is this all I will have of my fabulous and loving Sharon Marshal who was waiting for me?

Then he remembered and asked, "Did you say she was killed on June seventeenth last year?"

"Yes Tim why, does it make any difference?"

"Yes, her last letter was delivered to me in prison camp on June seventeenth, last year. I have it with me. I've always carried her last letter in the top left-hand pocket of my uniform and I replace it when the next one arrives. Then I put the older one away with the others all tied together with Red Cross parcel string."

With trembling fingers, Tim produced the letter.

"See," he cried, "I've written on it. Received 2:10 p.m. June 17, 1944."

Then Tim's grief came in a great wave of uncontrollable sobbing that he felt would never stop. A long time later it was Sharon's father who eventually said. "I'll take you to the cemetery."

Janet Marshal stood beside her husband and instinctively she held out her arms to Tim. When they both had dried their tears, Tim said, "I'm ready now to go to Sharon."

On the way they stopped at a florist's where Tim bought a single red rose. At the small polished granite headstone the two bareheaded men stood in silence. The inscription was simple: *Sharon Louise Marshal, age 26. Killed June 17th, 1944. War took from us our beautiful daughter.*

Still clutching the rose, Tim moved forward and knelt at the head of the grave. He placed the rose there and whispered, "Sharon, I love you." After a time he replaced his cap and walked away to catch up with Sharon's father, who had left him to be alone with his memories.

On their return to the Marshal home, Tim accepted the tea and cookies Sharon's mother had made for them. An hour later Peter Marshal drove him to the train station.

With a hand on Tim's shoulder and a strong handshake, Sharon's father said with great emotion, "Tim, all of us have to continue with our lives. You have weathered the brutal storms of war, now be thankful that for a time we had Sharon with us." Hesitant to cut his last link to his Sharon, Tim watched in despair as her father drove away and the car disappeared along Carter Street.

The announcement that his train would be leaving in five minutes brought him back to the reality of this day. He must return to the medical centre.

Peter Marshal was sitting in his chair reading the Sunday paper when his wife, from behind his chair, put her arms around him and said, "Thanks for being kind and not telling Tim that Sharon was with Robert when they were killed. I was afraid he was going to ask who the other person was." Holding onto his paper and without turning around, Sharon's father reached up and put his free hand over one of his wife's and said softly, "I was afraid he might just do that. I don't know, Janet, how I'd have answered the boy if he'd asked the question." Janet Marshal smiled, leaned over and kissed the bald spot on her husband's head. She picked up his cup and said. "I'll make you a pot of fresh tea, you haven't supped a drop of this."

On the train journey back to the medical centre, Tim's thoughts were in shambles. Sharon was dead. Ken, his prison-camp pal was missing. Ireland, his family, George O'Conor, and Kathleen were only a day's journey by train and ferry boat.

It was late when Tim arrived at the air base where the medical centre was housed. He was standing at the check-in line with others who were returning from weekend leave. His thoughts were of all the nights when Sharon had driven him to similar check-ins and had kissed him goodnight with only a minute to spare before the 11:59 deadline. Now amidst this jostling crowd of happy ex-prisoners Tim felt very lonely. The only thing that helped a little was that he met an old Stalag friend, Archie Duggan, one more survivor of that terrible march.

Next morning early Tim showered and shaved, then turned to leave for the dining room. At the far end of the long washroom the door opened and two hospital orderlies entered. Between them they were holding up someone dressed only in his underpants. His skinny stick-like legs were nothing but bones with skin stretched over them. His body was the same. The man's bare feet made hesitating motions like those of a youngster searching for stability to take that first step into the future. Tim watched as the trio approached and overheard one medic say, "You'll have a sit-down shower first, then to bed. We'll get some nourishment for you. The doc has ordered special care and that is what we will give you."

Shower stalls were through the doorway close to Tim. The trio hesitated as one of the medics picked up a wooden stool, then the shaved skull-like head raised itself with great effort so that the sunken eyes met Tim's. Then the recognition and tears tumbled down the crevices of that pitiful face. The feeble hesitant voice stumbled out words that scorched Tim's conscience and almost broke his heart. "Tim, you left me to fend for myself, and I couldn't do it." It was Ken Jones, his prison-camp mucker and escape partner.

Tim dropped his towel and the medics stood back as he put his arms around Ken and hugged his emaciated body. Ken kept repeating his words of condemnation, "You left me. You left me."

Tim said gently, "Ken, you are alive. You are alive. We will talk later when you are stronger." The medics took over and gathered Ken in their arms while Tim carried the stool and placed it in the shower stall. "Where did they find him?" he asked.

"We're not sure. This batch were flown here direct from Germany because they were in such bad shape. From papers with them I think this one was found starving to death in a hay storage shed near a small German village named Krossen. That's what it said on the transfer slip. He should have been taken care of by army medics in the area but somehow he was shipped back with a group of others through Frankfurt. People at that receiving centre got on the ball and flew them all here pronto. This guy's in rough shape and keeps saying you left him somewhere."

It was no use trying to explain what had happened. Tim knew the medics wouldn't understand. With a lump in his throat he walked towards the door and saw Archie Duggan standing there and realised he had witnessed the reunion. Without a word they both walked down the corridor with Archie's hand on Tim's shoulder. Before they reached the exit Archie broke the silence. "I heard what your mucker said. Tim you have already told me the story, so don't blame yourself for his condition. Any one of us could have lost partners in similar circumstances. Remember you almost died too but, you stubborn Irish leprechaun, you made it. Your mucker is Welsh and as stubborn as you Irish, and sometimes the Welsh also refuse to die."

Tim thought how helpless his mucker had been when he had tucked the woollen scarf around his chest and under his arms and buttoned his threadbare greatcoat up to his neck to keep him and his Welsh heart warm. Leaving Archie, Timothy went for a quiet walk on the hospital grounds, trying to resolve the struggle with his conscience. If he had stayed, could things have turned out better for Ken? Eventually he decided that if he had stayed to look after Ken he might have used up the last tiny spark of energy needed to light the fires of his own recuperation. If that had happened there might never have been a card written home to say, "I hope to be with you in a few days." Instead his family would have received an Air Ministry letter saying, "Regret to inform you, your son has been buried," and it would go on to say where. "Any further information you require, do not hesitate to write and quote this file number." It would have ended with, "I am, dear sir, your obedient servant," and been signed by some desk clerk for Air Commodore, c/o Records, Royal Air Force.

Later Archie and Tim went for a long walk. The spring flowers and neatly trimmed grass, the cleanliness of the beautiful grounds, and the bright day all spelled out that spring was here and glorious summer would follow regardless of the tragedies that had happened.

They visited Ken that evening. He was in a room with three others, his bed to the right of the window. There were screens around it but the orderly had not drawn the one that would have blocked the view of the garden. Ken was propped up so he could see the flowers, green grass, and blue sky.

"Only a few minutes," The orderly was stern, but he nodded his head in an understanding way.

"How is he?" Tim asked.

The orderly looked up. "You were his mate in prison camp?"

There was silence and it appeared there was something the orderly wished to discuss. Then he seemed to change his mind. "We think your mate will pull through, but remember, not more than five minutes."

Archie and Tim tried to make conversation with the pitiful figure lost in the hospital bed. The sad sunken eyes were not looking at them. They seemed to stare past them, perhaps seeing the beauty of the spring day. Tim put out his hand and touched Ken's as it lay helplessly on the bed covers. The long pale fingers closed for a moment around his. The eyes sent a message that Tim couldn't decipher. It seemed the mood changed, his fingers relaxed their puny grip and the hand was withdrawn a little. Instinctively Tim followed and tried to place his hand over Ken's again. Tim was hoping Ken would understand the deep hurt at seeing him in this condition. Ken withdrew his hand again. In his eyes Tim read the accusation.

The orderly raised his arm and pointed at his watch. So with a last look at that tragic face they left. Archie did not discuss what they had just experienced; he shared only one thought. "Never blame yourself for your mucker's condition. Don't permit that germ of remorse to grow till it has you believing something that is not true. You barely made it yourself. You did what you had to do."

Tim went to bed early and dreamed of watching Ken step out in front of him on the march. He had great difficulty keeping pace with him and was losing ground. Ken was taking big strides away from him. The distance between them was becoming so great that Tim knew he could never catch up. Then he noticed a strange thing. Ken was marching far away down the road showing no sign of fatigue. There was something different, something that Tim hadn't noticed before. The road was smooth and dry. There was no ice, no ruts, no snow, no hills to climb, and the straight flat road seemed to merge with a white cloud away in the distance. All the way it was lined with the same spring flowers that were growing outside Ken's room.

Tim was up very early the next morning. He had lain awake since four-thirty unable to get back to sleep. He shaved and washed quickly. Breakfast consisted of porridge with a lot of cream, two boiled eggs, and toast. He waited impatiently until ten-thirty. It was the earliest time permitted to visit the sick ward. He hoped Ken would be more responsive this morning so he could tell him about his dream. Tim hoped it indicated a straight smooth sailing down the road of life when he got back to health again. Walking through the recreation area, Tim crossed the short path with its manicured lawn on each side. He climbed the seven steps to the sick ward entrance. He ignored the girls at the reception and information desks although one called after him, "Can I help you, sir?" He knew where he was going.

Tim thought if Ken had not sent a card home he would fill in the extra one he had acquired. Four more paces and he looked up at the number to make sure it was correct. He turned into the room looking to see if the curtains were still drawn around Ken. The other occupants were asleep. The curtains were not around his mucker's bed. They were neatly pulled back and the bed was bare. No pitiful figure propped up on pillows. Tim stood a few feet inside the doorway and did not know how long he had been standing there when a quiet voice from behind him said, "He died at four-thirty this morning. I'm sorry, we did all we could."

Tim turned quickly. Two people were standing there. One was the orderly and the other, the owner of the soft voice. It was the medical officer who had processed Tim on his arrival. They talked together for a few minutes in the corridor, and the officer was very sympathetic about Ken's death. Tim told him about the years they'd spent together in prison camp and their escape together. They talked about the circumstances of Tim's leaving Ken. "I would have done the same thing," said the medical officer, "and I'm not saying that just to make you feel better. Sometimes circumstances leave us no alternative but to look after ourselves."

Tim didn't have to tell Archie Duggan and the others about Ken's death. They had already been informed. He spent most of the afternoon by himself and made little conversation with anyone. It was late, just before sunset, that he went for a walk. The weather forecast was for change and already dark clouds were hurrying to ensure the forecast would be correct. Tim strolled along the pathways bordered by flowers. The brightly coloured blossoms were in keeping with the spectacular sunset that gave the dark clouds their tinge of gold. It forced their glittering edges to send millions of tinted beams down to earth before the sun settled low in the western sky. It seemed unwilling to say goodbye to the day that had contained so much grief and anger. Suddenly it was gone, disappearing beyond the unseen Ireland. It reminded him of sitting on a rock, high up on the heather-covered slopes above Lough Swilly an eternity before. He had watched similar hues of red and gold blend with low clouds into one great carpet of breathtaking beauty. It was there he had decided to join the British Air Force.

Now the war was still going on with no quarter given. Tim thought of the tragedies that men were this very moment still inflicting upon their fellow men in Germany. He tried to remember the last verses of a poem that he had copied into his prison-camp logbook. It was way back probably around the end of 1943. They were not his words and the poem had many verses. He felt that if his mucker were listening and looking down on this frightened world, he would agree with the words in the few verses Tim remembered.

He stood in a secluded part of the beautiful flower garden and looked up at some tiny shadows of light that were somehow left in the darkening sky. He felt sure his mucker was listening and waiting for him to begin. Taking a deep breath he began, and a new brisk wind seemed to carry his words upwards and away west to catch up with something or someone.

> Perhaps you gaze from where you are
> On a world that should be fair
> And in which nothing 'ere need mar
> The joy that should be there.
> A world that's big enough for man
> To live a life that's free
> Where every nation, creed, and clan
> Could live in harmony.
> But instead you see as you look down
> A scene of hatred, greed, and strife
> Where the reaper reaps a field that's sown
> With a seed that man calls life.
> Throughout the world death's horse steps high
> All this and more you see,
> And perhaps you murmur with a sigh,
> "Lord, what fools ye mortals be!"

Tim spent some time in that lonely part of the hospital garden, long enough to remember the hardships and fears he and Ken had gone through together. He hoped Ken was now at peace.

With troubled thoughts he retraced his footsteps. Sharon was dead and now so was his long-time prison-camp comrade. What new tragedies would he find at home in Ireland?

Tim's thoughts were not peaceful. A few more days and he would be home in his mother's cottage. There was still a score to settle with George O'Conor, and Tim had suffered many hardships and grief to make the journey possible.

14

Retribution

Victory Day in Europe was a week old when Timothy knocked at the door of his Aunt Molly's house in Derry. It was May 15th. He had lived through many tragic experiences since he had first asked her to keep his uniform. The reception was much warmer this time. "Sure glad you're alive, Timothy O'Neill. It would have broken your mother's heart if she'd lost both sons."

"Michael's dead?" His question startled Aunt Molly.

"Oh my God! Didn't you know? But how could you? Nobody told you. Michael's plane was shot down early March 1944, and they were all killed. I'm sorry, Timothy." She put an arm around him. Timothy did not feel grief-stricken at learning of this one more tragedy, only numb. He was becoming immune to tragic news and wondered what other terrible things awaited him at home.

"Thanks for telling me, Aunt Molly. Is everyone at home OK?"

"Yes, yes." She rushed to reassure him.

Next morning, Timothy in new civilian clothes set off on the last leg of his long journey home. Five-and-a-half years is a long time. Looking out the bus window at well-known landmarks he sometimes had the feeling that he had never left. The past was only a bad dream. No, it was all too real and too tragic to ever forget. Now he had other questions in his thoughts. Would there be an opportunity to have conversation with Kathleen? Would he be permitted to see her children? Eileen would be twenty now or close to it, and probably married.

Perhaps George O'Conor would bar him from visiting either of them at Dunraven House.

Timothy was close to home and had no real plans for his confrontation with George. He would talk to Mary Jane Kernaghan and make some arrangements to meet Kathleen when George was away on business.

His reception at home was the best his mother could afford. She had invited friends who had not snubbed him when he joined the Air Force also other young men who had joined the British military and were home on leave. It was a happy time and there were a number of mothers whose sons or daughters were still away in England or European war areas. Some brought their own baked goods to add to the celebration. Timothy danced with young ladies he had known in another lifetime but didn't recognise. Of course young girls ten or twelve years of age have a habit of growing up in five years. Timothy had been away longer than that.

Now his father was proud that Timothy had served in the cause to defeat Hitler's domination. Later the two men sat by the peat fire while Timothy related stories of prison life and his own escape with Ken Jones. Kevin, curled up in a blanket at Timothy's feet, was enraptured with his brother's tales of escape and SS dungeon-like cells. He asked so many questions that his father finally warned, "Only one question every ten minutes, Kevin." It was long past Kevin's bedtime. Two more ten-minute periods passed and Kevin fell asleep.

Next morning Timothy walked to the village to visit Bruce McAlister, whose father owned the mechanic's shop and gasoline station. Bruce invited Timothy to the pub for a pint of Guinness and was interested in his friend's stories. Timothy was cautious asking questions about Dunraven House, but Bruce was full of information about the O'Conors. Without having to ask, Timothy learned the village gossip. Mary Jane Kernaghan had been fired more than a year ago. George O'Conor, while on a business trip across the border to Strabane, had caught her in a post office secretly mailing letters for Kathleen. O'Conor demanded that Mary Jane show him the letters. She refused and when he tried to grab them she hit him with her umbrella. O'Conor punched her so hard she fell unconscious to the floor. On the way down she hit an information notice board that had a glass front; it broke all over her. They had to take her to the hospital. He grabbed the letters and ran.

Bruce gulped down the remains of his Guinness and called for two more pints. Then he continued with his gossip regarding George O'Conor.

"It was bad weather when O'Conor arrived home and he threw all of Mary Jane's possessions outside during a heavy rainstorm. Apparently Old Patrick McGuinness the handyman filled his wheelbarrow with Mary Jane's sodden clothing and took them to his place. When he returned to save more of her possessions, O'Conor was there with a gun and told him that if he didn't leave that pile of garbage in ten seconds the next shot will be aimed at his heart. Old Patrick didn't want to die, so he left, and we heard that O'Conor went inside and beat his wife so much the doctor was sent for and told to hurry. No one has seen her outside the property since. He has an old woman there who looks after the children. When he goes away on his binges with other women, her mother sneaks in and helps.

Remember the beautiful girl his wife was when we were at school? O'Conor was always a proper bastard but could be very pleasant to the ladies. I heard he's away right now on what we call one of his 'excursions.' He's got a flashy sports car and every time I've seen him he has a different young woman with him. Got lots of money now that both his mother and father are dead."

"What happened to his father?" Timothy asked.

"Fox hunting and the horse threw him. He broke his neck."

Timothy wondered how many more shocks there were. One thing was certain. It was time to visit Dunraven House. He was in fair shape physically but prison camp and the march had taken their toll. Any confrontation with a six-foot-tall strongman like George O'Conor could be a one-sided affair, but Timothy didn't have time to wait. His anger and hatred of the things O'Conor had done and was still doing to Kathleen seethed like a volcano in every fibre of his body. Timothy wished to speak with old Patrick McGuinness.

It was late evening when Timothy found Patrick finishing some chores in the cow barn. His shirt hung on a nail close to a lantern that illuminated the end of the barn. Timothy was surprised to see this man in his mid-seventies and in such superb physical condition. He was carrying fodder to the cows and throwing heavy bales as if they were featherweight. Patrick stopped his work. "Well young fellow, what brings you here?"

Timothy looked at this man who for twenty-five years had been working on the O'Conors outdoor staff. "I have my own plans for an appointment with George O'Conor. I've been waiting for many years to even the score with the man who enticed the girl I loved away from me by false promises, then took pleasure in destroying her."

Patrick looked at Timothy. "Son, I don't think you're ready for that match. Why don't you leave it for a month or two and work on your muscle building?"

Timothy was surprised Patrick had not opposed his desire for revenge. It seemed as if Patrick had also been waiting all the years for Timothy's return. "I'm ready now, Patrick. What I lack in muscle strength, I'll make up in hatred. When is George coming home?"

There was no answer. Then Timothy realised Patrick was looking not at him but over his shoulder at something or someone. "Hello, George." It was Patrick's warning. Timothy swivelled just in time to dodge George O'Conor's fist.

"How dare you come on this property without my permission, you O'Neill scum and traitor?" George had been drinking just enough to be dangerous. Timothy had forgotten how big and broad-chested he was. He side-stepped the next blow and straightened George up with a heavy punch to his mouth. "You destroyed Kathleen, you O'Conor bastard."

"I'm going to kill you!" was George's reply. The two men fought for twenty minutes. The outdoor staff had all gone off duty. Patrick was the only spectator, but the full moon frequently snatched a look from behind swift moving dark clouds. It seemed as if the moon was not permitted to watch this altercation but was defying an all-powerful master by peeping through breaks in this evening's cloud cover. The fight moved from the barn to outside the storage sheds. From there they punched and bloodied each other across the cobblestone yard and close to the horse's water trough. Patrick was surprised at the power and energy of Timothy who was no match for the stronger man. It seemed hatred plus vengeance gave Timothy that extra edge for the moment. Both men were bleeding and badly bruised but neither gave any quarter.

Timothy knew Patrick had been right in suggesting he wait a few months before taking on this battle. Prison-camp life, the long march and poor nutrition were telling on him. But for Kathleen's sake he had to keep going. Timothy rallied, wading in with energy derived from despair at the thought of O'Conor winning the contest. George came at him with both fists flailing. He deluged him with hammer blows. Timothy heard him say "Now I'm going to kill you, O'Neill." George drove his fist into his antagonist's middle and as Timothy doubled up, George uppercut him with a two-fisted punch that sent him sprawling backwards on the cobblestone square.

Timothy was on his knees trying to get up. Above him George held a steel fence post raised above his head with intent to crush Timothy's skull. Timothy knew that blow would mean his exit, but he couldn't move. He seemed paralysed to save himself.

The crushing blow never came.

From behind George two hands snatched the fence post from his grip. Turning to see who had dared to interfere, he met Patrick's gnarled ham-like fist. The blow sent him teetering and was followed by another. George fell in a crumpled heap beside the water trough. Patrick picked up the senseless form of the master of Dunraven House, then propped him over the edge of the trough and buried his head in the water. George came to and struggled to free himself. Patrick relaxed his grip and permitted him a few gulps of air and time to look at the face of the man who had been his boyhood friend. George heard Patrick say before pushing him under the water again, "George, pretend you are a kitten."

Patrick let George catch his breath for a moment but still held him in a vice-like grip. Each time before dunking him under he made sure George understood his words: "This is for destroying a beautiful lady. This is for Eileen and you damned well know why. This is for my friend, your father, because I believe you were hiding at the gate and somehow caused his horse to throw him against the stone wall."

When Patrick permitted George his last gulp of evening air he held the struggling man inches from the water. "This is your last breath, George O'Conor. Now you go to meet your God. I don't think He will be pleased with you. This is for all the people you have destroyed on this estate also for those I don't know about. Now as you drown think about what I have said."

George used some of that last breath to mumble a plea for mercy, but Patrick showed none. He submerged George's head under water and held the struggling man in his grip until the body was lifeless.

Timothy, bloodied and still dazed, had stood watching Patrick drown George, with no inclination to stop him. It was like watching an execution. The accused had already been tried by judge and jury. Timothy could visualise his choice of twelve good citizens of the jury. It was Sean O'Brien, Kathleen O'Conor, Eileen O'Brien, Patrick McGuinness, Mary Jane Kernaghan, his own father, plus six members of the outdoor work staff. The jury's verdict was "Guilty on all counts, without a reasonable doubt." The judge was of course Father Cullen who read the sentence, "Death by drowning. Sentence to be carried out by Patrick McGuinness, Dunraven House handyman."

Timothy's daydream was interrupted by Patrick's steady voice. "Do you want to help?" George's body was sprawled in Patrick's big wheelbarrow, arms hanging over the sides, legs dangling in front. Timothy swallowed saliva and blood, but forced out the words, "Yes I do." He then walked with Patrick and his gruesome load to the Dunraven House sawmill. The giant waterwheel turned slowly from the continuous flow of the river. Patrick stopped where the cobblestones ended at the soft riverbank soil. It was at this spot many years before that Patrick had warned little George to be careful. "If you fall in close to the big wheel, it could push or suck you under and you'd drown."

"No I wouldn't. I could swim away from it!" was young George's reply.

Patrick took off his boots, tied them together with the laces, and slung them around his neck. Then he put George's boots on. In the dark among surrounding trees Patrick found a large broken tree limb about eight feet in length. With one long stride from the cobblestones he was able to place the tree limb askew on the river bank to look as if it had fallen there in a storm. Without turning around he took a step backwards again. From the cobblestone yard he picked up two sturdy wood planks. Without stepping off the cobblestones, and using the tree limb to support the planks, he placed each one on the limb just a few feet apart. They were long enough to make a bridge to the cobblestones that would leave no indentation on the grass or soft river bank soil. Still wearing George's boots, Patrick walked the few steps in the soil to the river bank and the tree limb where he stepped onto one of the planks. On the tree limb were new branch shoots with their young leaves. Patrick stooped and crushed them to indicate someone could have sat or fallen over the tree limb. He returned by the plank to the cobblestones where he changed to his own boots then replaced and tied George's.

Moving to the wheelbarrow and its gruesome load, Patrick lifted George's body under the armpits while Timothy lifted the legs. Carefully they negotiated the two planks carrying the body between them. At the water's edge, on Patrick's command after the third swing, they let go. George's body arched out over the bank and bounced off the giant wheel before plunging into the water. Calmly they crossed back on the planks to hard ground and Timothy helped Patrick return the lumber. They inspected the wheelbarrow for telltale signs then took it back to the storage shed.

Just then the dark evening was bathed in brilliant light. From behind the receding cloud cover the moon had decided to reappear. Perhaps it wished to take part in the last act of this earthly play before curtain time.

When Patrick and Timothy walked to the great iron gates at the main entrance to Dunraven House, the moon pulled a cloud around itself to darken its light. So two men moved like shadows to the exit.

Patrick spoke, "Go home, Timothy. Your mother and father will ask what happened to your bloodied face. Tell them it was a few young men in the village who felt you should not have gone to fight for the English."

"Thanks Patrick," was all Timothy said but the embrace and handshake between the two sealed a friendship and a secret. It overshadowed the capitulation of German forces that ended six years of bloody war in Europe. To Patrick and Timothy it was the end of an evil dictator in their lives who had destroyed people they both loved and had left a long trail of sorrow in many homes.

Three days later George's body was found downriver. At the inquiry it was believed he had returned in late evening from a business trip. The committee's finding presumed he must have crossed the cobblestone yard from his garage after parking his car perhaps a little intoxicated, as was his habit. No servants had seen him in the house. For some reason he made his way to the river close to the sawmill, not far from the O'Brien house and close to the path. Then the committee concluded that Mr. O'Conor had stumbled over a tree limb probably torn off in some previous storm. His footprints were discernible in the soft river bank soil. Their imprint went to the felled tree limb and stopped there.

Because of the inquiry the funeral had been postponed for a number of days after the body was found. By that time Timothy had healed quite a lot. His father and mother were still upset that he refused to say who had beaten him up. Timothy's only answer was, "I fight my own battles in the village."

A note written in a hand that Timothy recognised was delivered to Timothy's home by a Dunraven House employee. The same hand had written on an October day in 1939 the words, "Dearest Timothy, of me this is all I can give. Please remember us as we were in each other's arms last night. Wear the bracelet for luck and may the good Lord bring you safely home. My love and prayers go with you. Kathleen."

Timothy's memory raced back to that October day when Kathleen's out of breath fifteen-year-old sister Eileen had stopped him from boarding the bus saying, "I almost missed you, Timothy," and had pushed a small package into his hand. "This is for you. It's from Kathleen. She loves you, Timothy, but is marrying George to help all of us. I'll be fifteen next month, Timothy O'Neill, and if you want me to, I'll wait for you till the war is over."

On his wrist Timothy still wore the silver bracelet that had been in the package with the note. He read again the inscription, "I love you," and Kathleen's initials. He believed it had saved his and Ken's lives more than the Stalag dog tags they wore in the SS cells. The inscription, written in English, dated the 12th of October, 1939, could have been a big factor in their identification and release.

This newly delivered note read:

> To Mr. Timothy O'Neill:
> I heard you were home and join with your parents, family and friends in rejoicing at the wonderful news. I know you will feel great sorrow at the untimely death of my dear husband, the father of my children. As you were part of the group who years ago enjoyed dances and fun with George in the village, I'd appreciate it very much Timothy if you would be a pallbearer at the funeral. I'm sure George would have liked that.
> Sincerely, Kathleen O'Conor.

What a twist of justice! Would Patrick also be invited to help carry the coffin?

Timothy's thoughts were racing to justify George O'Conor's drowning. Timothy decided George O'Conor was in the same category as the evil murderers and torturers he had heard in action when he was in the terrible cells of the SS interrogation headquarters in Stettin.

Timothy would always remember the screams that echoed those corridors. He could visualise George in the uniform of an SS officer, so Timothy felt no compunction or troubled conscience by George O'Conor's death.

Timothy wanted to see the beautiful girl who had agreed five years ago to have dinner with him at the hotel on his last evening before going to England. The girl who said, "I do love you very much. I think I always have since we were children playing together."

He tried to recapture his last mental picture of her slim silhouette in the lantern light at the door of her home as she turned, waved goodbye and went inside. Now, five-and-a-half years later a new page had been turned in their tragic history.

The seating arrangement at the chapel service had Timothy and the five other pallbearers to the left of the altar and George's coffin. Timothy was on the outside. He waited with heart pounding for Kathleen to arrive and take her place in the velvet-cushioned O'Conor pew, second row from the front right in line with where Timothy was sitting. To enter the O'Conor pew they would have to stop right beside him.

There was a murmur of conversation among the congregation. Timothy turned as Kathleen approached with two of her children. She wore an elegant black suit, a white blouse, and a wide-brimmed black hat. Little Evelyn was in white. Sean was dressed in a black suit, white shirt and small black bow tie; his footwear, patent leather shoes with silver buckles. Kathleen, only twenty-four, was a beautiful young mother. Almost beside him now, she ushered the children into their seats. He saw her white face, the quivering lips and the tragic look. For seconds she hesitated and the sad blue eyes that met his seemed to say, "I'm sorry, Timothy." Then she quickly sat between her children. The two women behind Kathleen were also dressed in black and white. One was Kathleen's sister Eileen, a gorgeous-looking young woman with a stunning figure. Her words were but a whisper, "Hello, Timothy. Thank God you made it home." Then she slid into the seat beside little Sean. The second lady was a surprise, Mary Jane Kernaghan. She smiled at Timothy. He wondered if this was her victory smile.

George was laid to rest in a new grave beside his father and mother. Father Cullen's chapel service would always be remembered for its brevity. There were no words of praise or great sorrow. Patrick, Timothy, Kathleen's father, plus three of the Dunraven House inside staff carried the coffin to the hearse and from the cemetery gates to the graveside. The irony was not lost on the three men who had hated George O'Conor the most. They were George's pallbearers at the request of his widow. She was sole owner of Dunraven House with her children as heirs. She was now mistress of all this vast estate with all its farmland acreage, sawmill, cattle, and many other resources, and of the employees.

Afterwards funeral guests gathered at Dunraven House. Many of James O'Conor's old friends and their wives arrived in their grandeur to find a different class of people mixing with them. Cora O'Conor would not have approved.

Kathleen had invited all of Dunraven House's indoor and outdoor staff who wished to attend George's wake. Only a third of the sixty employees accepted. Kathleen knew why and it was not because of her. One of those employees delivered a large card, no black edges, no written condolences. On its face was a picture of a beautiful lady sitting in a garden surrounded by flowers. Written inside were the words, "We respect you, we love you, and we gladly accept you as our employer. We will not shirk from our duties to ensure that you and also our families can go forward with faith in the future security of Dunraven House. A dark cloud has moved from our lives and may we say with all respect also from yours. We hope the future brings for you and your children all the rewards you deserve."

It was signed "Dunraven House Staffs," the plural indicating that both the indoor and outdoor staffs endorsed what was written. All other available space was covered with signatures.

At dinner Kathleen placed her five-year-old daughter Evelyn immediately on her left, then Eileen and Timothy. To her right was the male heir to Dunraven House, four-year-old Sean, then her mother. Next, where James O'Conor would probably have sat if he had been alive, she placed her faithful employee and friend Patrick McGuinness. Next to Patrick were her father and, of course, Father Cullen.

To all present the arrangement indicated that a new queen was in charge of Dunraven House, one who believed all people, rich or poor, employer or employee should be treated with respect.

Before dinner Kathleen moved among her guests shaking hands and thanking people for coming. She avoided Timothy. Kathleen had changed into a black silk dress with white lace collar and cuffs. Her hair was tied back with a broad black silk band. The new mistress of Dunraven House looked beautiful. Timothy realised the dress showed how thin and frail she was. No longer was she the robust, healthy, well-curved girl who had accepted a ride to the village so many years ago, the girl who had jumped from the jaunting cart unassisted and sprinted across the road with her auburn hair flying in the wind.

That day was so very long ago. Old Kate had trotted all the way to her stable while he sang, "I'll take you home again, Kathleen." He was unaware that before his dinner date with this beautiful girl ended, his rose-coloured world would be shattered when he looked into unwavering blue eyes and heard her say, "For the family's security, I've accepted the marriage proposal of George O'Conor."

Now she looked so very frail and tragic. The blue eyes had lost their sparkle; it had been replaced by a sadness that was breaking his heart. During the chapel service he had only quick glances at Kathleen. Here he watched her every moment as she mixed with guests. He'd tried to get close but she avoided him. Twice he was close enough that when she looked up he met her eyes with a message that he wanted to talk. Each time she had turned away, then quickly moved among the other guests.

Timothy's memories and thoughts were interrupted by a hand on his arm. He turned and met Eileen's deep blue eyes. "Penny for your thoughts, Timothy O'Neill. Where are you? Thinking of some pretty girl you left in England? Or is it Kathleen?"

Timothy had to drop his own eyes from the demanding look in Eileen's.

"Let Kathleen be, Timothy. Please let her be. She is walking a very narrow path between sanity and a complete breakdown. She has always loved you and now her prayers have been answered. You are home safe and she has been delivered from the beast she married, but fate has not yet showed all its cards. My dear sister is a very sick lady. Now don't ask me, Timothy. In her own time and very soon she will tell you. Kathleen wants to see and talk with you just as much as you do her, but not in this crowd. You haven't touched your drink."

Timothy looked in disbelief at the beautiful woman beside him. His memory of five-and-a-half years ago was of Kathleen's fifteen-year-old tomboy sister, not this lovely creature sitting next to him. She raised her glass, clinked it with his, and said, "To whatever the future brings."

Mary Jane Kernaghan was back in her kitchen and her staff served up a delicious meal. There were no loud empty speeches, just Father Cullen saying grace and later speaking for all the guests present at this sad farewell to yet a third O'Conor. "As God takes away he also gives and his gift to this family is Kathleen O'Conor's three wonderful children." He surveyed the mixture of rich and poor then with a slight shrug of his shoulders decided not to continue with his oratory. Instead he read a short passage from his prayer book and with a loud "Amen!" picked up his glass of Navy rum and plopped into his chair.

Father Cullen was one of the last guests to leave. Kathleen walked with him to the foyer and stopped at the grand entrance. He was in a talking mood.

"You have in your young life Kathleen tasted too many tragedies. The loss of your father and mother-in-law and now your husband. You're a brave young woman who now must face great decisions for yourself and those three beautiful children. If at any time you feel the necessity to have a talk with me other than in the confession booth do not hesitate."

At the great doorway Father Cullen hesitated and turned to her. When he took her hand in his, she looked up and met his stern eyes. "Bless you my child. Sometimes God works in a mysterious way." Then he was gone, still steady on his feet. She was certain there were tears in his eyes.

She looked after him in surprise. Did the old honourable Father remember when she had confessed her sinful wish that her husband would have a fatal accident?

She felt sure Father Cullen was telling her in his own way that all kinds of prayers are sometimes answered.

A few days later Eileen visited Timothy at his mother and father's cottage. She carried a message from Kathleen, an invitation for Timothy to dine with her at Dunraven House.

In his new civilian clothes he arrived fifteen minutes early at the north side entrance of Dunraven House. Kathleen's invitation had requested he use that entrance. The door was wide open so there was no need to knock. Kathleen had been watching for his arrival. Timothy stood in the foyer. From down the long hallway he saw this still very beautiful lady walk towards him. She wore a light blue dress, royal blue jacket, and white high-heeled shoes. Her long hair was let down. She strode towards him and it seemed as if a million diamonds glittered and danced in its auburn beauty. Wonder-struck he stood watching her approach, then put out his arms and she ran the last few yards.

"Oh, Timothy, Timothy," she cried as he held her close. "I love you and you know I always have. Please hold me tight. I need you to do that so I know you are really here."

He looked down at the upturned face and kissed each tear-filled eye. He covered her quivering lips with his own. She returned his kiss with an urgency that needed no explaining, then with her hand in his as they had done when children, she guided him to her luxurious living room. They sat together on a love seat with a view of the gardens; and beyond, the Lough Swilly waters were calm and its golden sandy beach sparkled in the sun's light. When she turned to him he noticed that around her neck was the silver chain and locket he'd bought her at Rathmelton Fair when they were so very young. He reached out and gently took it in his fingers, kissed it and said, "Light blue dress, royal blue jacket, white high-heeled shoes and this locket?"

"Yes Timothy, I put them all away the day after you left to fight for the English. My mother kept them for me. I promised never to wear them again until you came home alive. Yesterday I retrieved them and you are too good and too kind to tell me that now the dress is three or four sizes too large."

He took both of her hands in his. "You've had a tough time Kathleen, and Eileen tells me you are sick."

She placed a finger over his lips. "Later Timothy I will explain. Now come with me. Mary Jane has our dinner prepared and ready to serve and George O'Conor is no more."

There was no grand table set up with silver candelabra, no elegant Sheffield silverware, or crystal goblets full of red and white wines. Just a simple table setting in a room with a huge window that extended almost from floor to ceiling. She had asked Mary Jane to place the table for two at an angle to the window so that the evening setting sun's brilliant colours would not disturb their dinner. It would send a rainbow of searchlights dancing across the Italian marble floor in a display of beauty to celebrate their reunion.

Mary Jane stood by the small table. "Welcome home, Timothy," was her only comment but the bear hug to her huge bosom conveyed much more.

The roast-beef dinner was delicious and time spun out while Kathleen asked question after question about prison-camp life, how many of her letters he had received and what his plans were when he returned to civilian life.

"I always hoped to travel and visit many countries. I had thought of staying in the forces as my career. There's not much work in these parts."

Kathleen made no comment regarding Timothy's thoughts of staying in the services. She talked about her children and the characteristics of each, then asked, "Would you like to come tomorrow and meet them? The two older ones know about you. Robert is too young. I've told Evelyn and Sean their mother had a very good friend away fighting in the war. That he was helping to protect all of us and that I loved him very much and that they would meet him tomorrow because he is home safe. Will you come tomorrow Timothy and meet my children?"

"Yes Kathleen. For many years I tried to visualise your children but I've already seen that they are more beautiful than I imagined."

Mary Jane produced a dessert of two small glasses of thick custard with a spoonful of strawberry jam in the middle and fresh cream poured over it. Into china cups with their matching saucers she poured tea.

It was the dessert and tea in china cups that triggered Timothy's memory to his last dinner with Kathleen. It was at the hotel on that cold early October evening in 1939.

How could he forget the awful feeling he'd had when Kathleen told him of her intentions to marry George?

The table setting was identical, even to the white Irish linen table-cloth and napkins. It was the same menu and the same two people but what a period of tragedies and triumphs the previous years had produced!

The sun's rainbow had celebrated this reunion with encore after encore of changing brilliancy. Its beams had danced their way across the marble floor before the final curtain of darkness. Mary Jane lit two red candles, refilled their cups with fresh tea and then gently closed the door as she left.

Timothy looked up and started to say, "Now I remember all this." Before he could continue, Kathleen interrupted, "Yes Timothy, I tried to make it as close as possible to remind us of our last dinner together so very long ago." She replaced the china cup on its saucer and her eyes met his. She stretched out both her hands and he clasped her fingers with his own and held tight.

"Kathleen, I love you. How can I help?"

For seconds there was silence, then from trembling lips came her answer. "Timothy, I have an illness and other complications which the doctors don't know how to cure. I feel that I have only months to live. Timothy, will you marry me now? I don't want anyone else but you to be a father to my children and you will be master of Dunraven House."

"Maybe before I die you will fall in love with Eileen because she loves you so very much, as I do, and has waited for you. I would be happy if I knew you and Eileen were to adopt my children. To love them and each other and have Dunraven House as your home to bring up your children with mine. Oh Timothy if only I could turn back the years. I have always loved only you. I did marry George to give my family security. You must believe that I never expected it to be so awful. I prayed that I would not die before you came home and now my prayers have been answered."

Timothy let go of Kathleen's hands and moved to her side. She stood up and he took her in his arms and kissed her.

"Kathleen, I love you and of course I'll marry you. We'll fight this sickness together and I won't let you die." In the living room they sat close on the love seat, and talked for a very long time. Then Mary Jane brought them brandies. He told Kathleen of Ken's death and how his own conscience troubled him. Then he told her all about Sharon Marshal.

"You loved her, Timothy."

"Yes," he answered, "very much, but you were my first love."

It was close to midnight when Mary Jane knocked gently on the door. Kathleen was asleep in his arms. He carried her like a little child to the big bedroom and laid her gently on top of the covers. He kissed her forehead and walked home.

Under the moon's bright light, it was the first time in many years Timothy felt he was entering the gateway to a new life and his destiny.

The next day, he returned and spent a wonderful time playing with the children, and stayed for dinner. Sean asked that Timothy put him to bed. Kathleen said, "See, Timothy O'Neill you have already made one big hit."

The next day, he brought Kevin to visit Kathleen and her children. Later Kevin told his mother, "It was like visiting a queen in her castle."

Three more days and Timothy had to return to England but not for long. Then he was given many weeks leave of absence from the Air Force before demobilisation.

Father Cullen married Kathleen and Timothy on the eighteenth of July, 1945. After the ceremony, they drove to Dublin, and in a Grafton Street store, Kathleen bought new clothes for the children, and under pressure from Timothy they went to shows. They bought tickets to a banquet hall dinner and dance. They visited Trinity College. They took in a day at the horse races. Timothy bought large ice cream cones and when Kathleen's ice cream fell off as she turned to leave, the vendor called, "Hi beautiful lady, come back and I'll give you another." They bought chocolates and laughed at things that weren't even comical. He took her on the ferry to England and then by train to London where she was aghast at the terrible destruction wrought by German bombings. Thousands were still in uniform but London was a happy place. Six years of war had ended. At Buckingham Palace, Kathleen watched the changing of the guard three times. They spent one glorious week doing everything possible. Occasionally Kathleen had to take a few hours' rest, but she seemed to have gained much more energy than usual. "It's the excitement," she would say, "of being Mrs. Timothy O'Neill."

At night in each other's arms they would talk for hours trying to recapture all the happy memories they could think of until one of them fell asleep. Back in Dublin they picked up their car again and toured Ireland. Many times during those weeks Kathleen repeated, "Timothy, I never dreamed lovemaking could be so wonderful."

They arrived home on the thirty-first of August after a very happy honeymoon.

Four months later the clock in the grand entrance hall of Dunraven House was striking the last midnight chimes of 1945 when Kathleen died as Timothy held her frail body in his arms. It was Kathleen's request that in the little cemetery close to Dunraven House a new grave be opened as far away as possible from George O'Conor's.

There was no wake for her, just a few sad family members and friends gathering to mourn the loss of the young mother, dear friend and loving wife of Timothy O'Neill. It was Mary Jane who said that during Kathleen's last five months of life, she had been able to cram into it more joy and happy times than in five years with George O'Conor. Best of all she had learned what real love was all about.

For Timothy the poor young man, whose only hope at one time had been to earn a few shillings by digging peat and doing menial tasks, now came a big adjustment. He was owner of this great mansion, its lands and all of its widespread resources. Timothy extended Patrick's supervision area to bring other staff under his fair and honest jurisdiction. He moved Patrick into one of the estate houses close to Eileen's mother and father. Timothy also gave him an increase in salary, which Patrick said was too much. Timothy's answer was, "It is in keeping with your experience and years of service."

Patrick and Timothy had never talked about the night George O'Conor drowned. Between these two men it was a secret they'd take to their graves. They became good friends and soon Patrick was like another Grandpapa to Kathleen's children.

The great north-wing bedroom had not been used since Timothy married Kathleen. They had taken over the rooms that had been James O'Conor's. Now Timothy moved again to a small bedroom above the luxurious living room where Kathleen and he had sat on his first visit and looked out on the flower gardens and beyond to Lough Swilly, the strand and its golden sand.

Eileen continued to live in her own little private quarters semi-attached to her mother and father's home. Every day she helped Mary Jane with the children's needs. Mary Jane had acquired two jobs, her own plus that of a part-time baby-sitter for the three children. She herself had volunteered. She loved the children as though they were her own.

Months passed, and Kathleen's family was often invited to join Timothy and the children for dinner. Eileen and her mother assisted the Dunraven House cook in her kitchen and always there was a place set for Mary Jane at the big table. When household supplies were needed Timothy would volunteer to drive Eileen. They gradually began taking trips by themselves, with no excuses of purchasing supplies for Dunraven House.

It was Christmas Eve 1946, seven days before the anniversary of Kathleen's death. Two people stood by her grave. Together they placed on it a large Christmas wreath. Then, holding hands, they stood in silence for two minutes.

Timothy spoke first. "Eileen, I loved your sister. I loved another lady named Sharon who was killed in a bombing raid on London. Could you love me enough to marry me?" Without moving and still holding Timothy's hand, Kathleen's beautiful sister watched snowflakes trying to cover the wreath.

"When I was fifteen Timothy O'Neill, and Kathleen was to marry George, I promised to wait for you until the war was over if you wanted me to. Do you remember your answer?" Before Timothy could speak, Eileen continued, "I do. You thanked me and said, I appreciate your wonderful offer but please don't wait for me because I have the world to see when the war is over. Then you kissed my cheek and boarded the bus with Kathleen's gift in your hand. I stood dejectedly waving farewell. You sat in the back seat and never once looked my way. Now, Timothy O'Neill, will you please let go of my hand?" There was a silence for a moment then Eileen turned to him her blue eyes shining with tears of joy and said, "Timothy O'Neill, I've always loved you and this time I'm not letting you go. I would marry you tomorrow, if I could, and if you are going to see the world then I'm going with you. Please take me in your arms and kiss me and not on my cheek."

Timothy took a deep breath. "Thought you were going to say no!" Beside Kathleen's grave he took Eileen in his arms. He kissed her and held her for a long time, while falling snowflakes laid out their white carpet covering Kathleen's grave and the wreath.

Shaking snow off themselves, Timothy and Eileen picked up the wreath and placed it upright against the new black marble headstone with gold lettering and the simple words: Kathleen O'Neill July 17, 1920–December 31, 1945. Sadly missed by her children, and loving husband, Timothy, Her Mother and Father, Her Sister Eileen and Brother Brian.

At Dunraven House it was a children's Christmas. Patrick cut down a silver spruce tree that everyone had a hand in decorating. Timothy held the wooden stepladder while little Robert climbed up to place an angel on the tree's top. He came down and stood looking up at it for a long time. Timothy asked, "What is it, Robert?" The little boy pointed to the tree top. "That's my Mummy up there." With moist eyes Eileen picked him up and said, "Yes, Robert. Isn't she a beautiful angel?" It was a wonderful and happy Christmas dinner within the walls of Dunraven House with happy people who loved each other. During a moment of silence at the dinner table it was tough old cook Mary Jane Kernaghan, with a tear finding its way down her cheek who spoke quietly, "I know Kathleen is here, and she is happy that we are together."

On New Year's Eve Eileen and Timothy sat in front of a big log fire on a white polar-bear rug that James O'Conor had brought back years ago from a trip to Canada. They had an Irish coffee made by Mary Jane.

Timothy looked at his watch. "In thirty minutes it will be 1947. In springtime Timothy O'Neill and Eileen O'Brien will be married."

Eileen took a sip of her drink and smoothed a part of the rug that wasn't ruffled. With her face turned from him and eyes fixed on a burning log that looked as though it might soon fall onto the hearth she said, "Timothy, beside my sister's grave you asked me to marry you and I accepted. Now before this old year is gone, I must tell you something. I'll understand if you decide to retract your offer. I love you, that is true and I know you love me so I don't want anything to come up in the future to destroy our happiness."

Timothy put down his coffee. "Eileen, whatever it is nothing can change my love or my decision."

"During Kathleen's last pregnancy I was raped by George O'Conor in my own bedroom. It being separated from Mother and Father's home, no one heard my cries for help the first time. He had let himself in using a duplicate key and waited for me to lock the door before I knew someone was in my room." She told Timothy of George's demands and his threats to throw them all off the estate with no jobs, no house and no money. He said he would prevent Kathleen from helping us in any way unless I made a deal with him that he could come to my bed when he pleased. His father had been killed in the accident, so he was in full control of the estate. I got pregnant and was considering suicide when I told Kathleen, but I wouldn't tell her who the father was. She confronted George. She suggested to him that since her pregnancy had begun, he hadn't demanded any sexual favours and that it was different from past times. She questioned him on where he was on the many nights he came home very late and when no car had been used. George absolutely denied having anything to do with my condition, then promised he would help to obtain a secret abortion 'out of the goodness of his heart and his generous disposition.' He said it was to protect the good name of Dunraven House. He informed Kathleen that too often these days young girls were led astray. In a show of anger George promised to find who was responsible for my problem and personally mete out suitable punishment. Then he got drunk and beat Kathleen for accusing him.

"I had my abortion in Belfast. Kathleen took me for what was supposed to be a few days' vacation. Now Timothy O'Neill, that is my confession to you and never to Father Cullen or anyone else."

Timothy tried to quell his fury at George O'Conor.

He cupped the beautiful face in his hands. "My dearest Eileen, what an awful burden for you to carry. Thank you for telling me. I still love you and I will care for you and help to erase this awful memory from your life. George O'Conor is dead; fate sometimes is slow but reaps it own revenge in its own time. You are still Kathleen's pure and wonderful young sister. Now let's you and I bury this memory with no headstone or marker to remind us. We love each other and the double brightness from our love will light the way and guide us through any dark roads in the years ahead. I will be honoured to walk out of the chapel on our wedding day with you as my wife." Timothy put another log on the fire and lay down on the rug beside her.

"Oh Timothy," she cried. "Wouldn't it have been awful if I had married someone else while you were away? I could never have loved anyone as I love you."

They refurbished the master bedroom, a complete change. Eileen's wish was to keep the north wing as their living quarters because it was more compact. The new extra bedrooms that Kathleen had put in for the children were close to what would be Eileen and Timothy's bedroom.

One day Timothy and Patrick were having lunch from a basket of delicious sandwiches and other goodies Mary Jane had packed for taking out to what they called "the far field," where a number of fence posts had to be replaced. Timothy had volunteered to take the lunch to Patrick who was supervising and working with two of the outdoor staff. They sat away from the others. Timothy was pouring tea from a thermos into Patrick's big enamel mug.

"Patrick, what do you know about George's visits to Eileen's bedroom?"

He still remembered hearing what Patrick had said to George before pushing his head under water. "This is for Eileen, and you damned well know why." Patrick supped his tea and took a bite from a chunk of home-made soda bread covered in fresh country butter. He chewed for a while and washed it down with a gulp of tea, then he uttered only three words.

"She told you?"

"Yes," replied Timothy, and waited for Patrick to continue.

"I knew what the bastard was doing, Timothy but I felt powerless to stop it. If I'd accosted him, he would have thrown me off the estate. Then the girls would have had no one to look out for them. I saw him use his key to get into Eileen's room one night and then I watched him visit on a regular basis. Telling Kathleen wouldn't have helped. I thought of catching him coming out of Eileen's place and somehow knocking him unconscious and throwing him in the river. After Kathleen's baby was born, he stopped his visits. Things settled down until you came along. It was my great pleasure to help rid Dunraven House of the most unconscionable bastard I have ever known. Does that answer your question?"

"Sure does, Patrick. Now, don't eat all of that soda bread. I'd like some."

Never again were words spoken about George O'Conor nor of his misdeeds and the circumstances of his death.

280

Eileen and Timothy's wedding date was set for the middle of May. Her mother produced her own old wedding dress. She had hoped Kathleen would wear it but Cora O'Conor had stopped that. Now she asked Eileen if she would like to wear it. "Yes, Mother if you'll permit me to change a few things."

"Certainly dear any changes you want. It's just that I always dreamed one of my girls would wear this dress on her wedding day. It's just like new," she said with pride. Eileen knew the material was well preserved. She had been expecting the offer and had already engaged a good seamstress in the village to do the alterations.

Timothy and Eileen made numerous trips to other towns with long lists of wedding requirements. It was an exciting time for Eileen, who had never been further away from home than Letterkenny until Kathleen took her to Belfast for the abortion. Timothy promised that on their honeymoon they would visit Dublin, and that he'd take her across the Irish Sea to England, Wales and Scotland.

In London he'd find the best hotels and restaurants. "Pick anything anywhere in the travel brochures you would like to see and we will go there because I love you Eileen O'Brien."

Part Four

15

A Stranger in the Village

It was early April when the village gossip was all about the lady staying at the local hotel. She wore grand clothes and left big tips.

One day in the butcher's shop, Cassie McGreevy met Molly Todd and said, "Maggie Black looked in the guest register book when the desk clerk was on her tea break. The lady signed her name as S.E. McDermott, and Maggie says there's no Miss or Mrs. before her name and no man with her. Maggie thinks she's fairly old, maybe seventyish, but looks about sixty. She has a nice face, could be a rich widow on a tour of Ireland and the rest of the world."

"Maybe she's odd and that's why she's on her own," volunteered Molly.

"Aye but she might be one of those retired film star people from Hollywood," suggested Cassie. "Maybe she got her face lifted up. I heard they do that over there. Makes them look ten or fifteen years younger. They don't marry you know, just live together in those Beverly Hills places and keep their own names. It they don't like it then they move out and find some other guy to live with."

"Shameful!" said Molly.

"Oh, I don't know about that Molly. I'd love to change my old man. He drinks too much and goes to sleep every night soon as his head hits the pillow. I think it's a good idea. These film star people are way ahead of us."

"I'm shocked at you Cassie McGreevy. You'd better go to Father Cullen's confession booth soon."

"Och Molly, you know yourself I've seen you looking at that wee new bus driver with more than a casual glance. He's on every third day and as soon as his bus stops you're always here at Willie McQuire's for chops or sausages or something. You know he takes his fifteen-minute tea break next door at Sadie's Tea Shop, and you always find some excuse to go in there. Maybe she'd give you a part-time job serving tea on the days it's his shift to drive. Just look, you're wearing your Sunday dress. I think you've shortened it again, quite a bit this time. You're blushing, Molly, Och! Sure maybe both of us should go one day to see Father Cullen and confess our thoughts.

"What are you buying today Molly, sausages or pork chops? Oh, talking about meat, I almost forgot. When Thomas came back from his tea break that day he told Maggie the lady likes a good steak and doesn't mind paying the price. He told our butcher friend here. Now Willie McQuire toddles off almost every day with special cuts of meat and all sorts of things for this lady. Delivers them to her himself. How do you like that? Now that Willie's wife is dead nearly six months he's maybe on the lookout again. Think I'll ask him for two steaks same as he delivered to the hotel. Did you hear old Todd Bailey has been extra busy in the post office? Milly said there's been a pile of mail and parcels come from overseas all addressed to the hotel, so she must have known where she'd be staying and do you know it all came by aeroplane? Takes money to do that. Bet she's a very rich film star." So the village gossip continued.

The very next night, when old Don Macauley was having his first pint, he told his drinking partner Peter Connolly that his wife Bridget had heard the lady was looking for a family member dead or alive and that there was a reward for good information.

Peter took a sip, then looked into his beer for a few seconds before replying. "I knows that, Don, many peoples from across the 'lantic have been through this way looking for dead or alive relatives. They want to put the names of dead or alive people on what they call a family tree. Sounds foolish to me, but these people from over there are all a bit strange anyway, don't you think, Don?" and he nudged his buddy. Don Macauley's only reply was, "Maybe you're right, Peter, maybe you're right."

One day Patrick was brushing a young stallion, son of the beautiful chestnut who had thrown James O'Conor to his death, when two police officers arrived in a black car. "You are Patrick McGuinness?" It was the senior officer who asked.

"That I am and have been for seventy-six years."

"You live here?"

"Yes."

"How long, sir?"

"Since October, 1920. Why do you ask?"

"We have been doing some investigating of old records, in regard to missing persons. You understand?"

"I guess so, but what's that got to do with me?"

"You have a prison record, Patrick McGuinness?"

"Yes I was given three years and six months because of a crooked judge who was indebted to the bank for a large amount of money. He was, so to speak, in the pocket of bank manager Walter Mulligan. After my father's death, Mulligan wanted me out of the way so he could steal our family business and home for his bank to sell at a profit to Harper's, our opposition. The day after my father's funeral he came to our home and showed me official-looking papers which said father owed a considerable amount of money. All legal necessities were in process to take over the business and our home. He gave me an ultimatum to be out of the house in a few hours and to take nothing but my personal effects. I threw him out and he laid charges. Now, is there anything else I can tell you, gentlemen? If not I've a lot of work to do."

"Mr. McGuinness," the senior officer smiled and said, "we know everything you have told us is true. The bank Mr. Mulligan was manager of had, over the years, taken into receivership quite a number of small farms and businesses, all under suspicious circumstances. The owners apparently were jailed for many months on trumped-up charges, although their offences were very minor. Being in confinement, they were unable to make loan payments to Mr. Mulligan's bank, so of course the bank foreclosed. Always the court judge who handed down the jail sentences was a Mr. Harry Murphy. He is dead and so is Mulligan." Patrick thought it best not to say that he knew Mulligan had been gored to death by a bull.

"In your absence, Mr. McGuinness, the high court has given you and the others complete pardon and an apology." The officer handed

Patrick a large envelope. "Your certificate Mr. McGuinness, and verification of these facts. We would like you to meet with us at the village hotel at approximately six o'clock this evening. No need to ask at the desk. Just go up to the second floor and knock on the door of room twelve. There are some papers we would like you to sign. Can you make it for six?"

"Oh yes!" Patrick was still in shock at this unexpected happening.

"Very good sir, and by the way you are invited for dinner. Please dress accordingly."

Patrick dressed himself carefully in his navy blue double-breasted suit. The one he wore on all important occasions. He was a handsome man and looked smart in his suit, white shirt and dark blue tie. From a shelf in his bedroom closet he took his black boots. When he finished, the spit and polish shine could not have been outdone by a palace guard.

The old stairs creaked as he climbed slowly to the second floor. Number twelve was the corner room, very large with a connecting door to an adjoining bedroom. It had a great bay window where one could look out at the harbour and away up the Lough. He had been there once helping to move heavy furniture. Patrick hesitated for a moment, then knocked on the panelled door. Half a minute passed and he was about to knock again when the door was opened by an attractive elderly dark-haired lady. She was dressed elegantly in a black two-piece suit with a white flower in her left lapel. She wore a white blouse and two sparkling gold necklaces, with matching bracelets around her wrists. The black high-heeled shoes made her a few inches taller than her actual height. Patrick looked into hazel eyes and apologised, "Hope I haven't disturbed you Madam. I'm very sorry, I must have been given the wrong number."

In a soft voice with an American accent that had a certain Irish lilt to it she replied, "No, Patrick McGuinness you have the correct number. It has taken me three years and this is the end of my search. You are staying right here!" and she held out her arms.

For Patrick, fifty-seven years scattered to the four winds. It was the sixteenth of June, 1890 again. He was at the train station in Dublin holding hands with Sally O'Hagan. They were promising to love one another forever when her father interrupted and guided her to the waiting boat train. Sally's father was taking his family to New York on the SS Cumberland. Now Patrick looked at this beautiful lady, her eyes brimming with tears of joy. "Sally O'Hagan? No, it couldn't be. But it is." He choked out the words. For a long time like young lovers they held each other and cried.

They stood at the bay window looking at the little boats in the harbour. With his arm around Sally's waist Patrick was still murmuring, "I don't believe this. How did you find me and why?"

"I'll tell you the whole story. Now, sit down Patrick." She took one of his huge worn hands in both of hers then looking into his questioning grey eyes began her story. "My father got his wish and opened a grocery store in New York. It mushroomed into a chain-store operation and we became very wealthy. Remember Patrick how very hard you worked at two jobs? In one of your letters after that first year you wrote to say you were unable to save enough money for a ticket to New York, but hoped it would be soon.

"I kept all your letters Patrick. Eighteen months later, your letters stopped and I couldn't understand why. My only answer was that you had changed your thoughts regarding our plans. I waited eight years hoping one day that you would find me. Father died of a heart attack at fifty-eight. Before mother passed away four years later, she confessed that after the first eighteen months in America my father started to pay the postmaster at our corner post office to intercept outgoing and incoming letters between you and me and mother helped. She often said, 'I'll mail it for you honey, I'm going that way,' but she destroyed my letters to you. The postmaster seemed such an honest man, and I often took my letters to him personally. He was always so kind. 'Sorry no mail for Sally from The Old Sod.' Often he'd put special stamps and stickers on my envelopes saying that would hasten their arrival to you and all the time he was being paid to turn them over to my father.

"When I was twenty-seven, I married Ken McDermott, one of Father's store managers. I have four children, two sons and two daughters. And Patrick, I am the grandmother of nine grandchildren. You will meet every one, I hope, very soon.

"My eldest son is chief executive officer of the company. His name is Patrick Kenneth McDermott. I don't think my husband ever realised the significance, just Sally wanting an Irish name for her son.

Father shrugged and said, 'You made your point girl,' but he knew he had won the battle to keep us apart.

"Ken died seven years ago. Three years ago I decided to try and find answers to the question of what had happened to Patrick McGuinness. My long investigation led me to this village and you. Someday I'll tell you how I traced you. Now why did such a handsome man as you never marry? What a lost treasure all these years that some good woman could have had."

Patrick hesitated for a few moments before answering. "When I lost you Sally, I vowed never to love again and I've been so stubborn Irish I kept that vow. I didn't know if you were still alive but I've always loved you." His steel grey eyes were very sad. "There have been many lonely years Sally, but at Dunraven House I found a family where tragedy always sat on the fringe waiting its chance to interfere, and all too often it did just that.

"I felt it was my destiny to try in some way to shield innocent people who were at the mercy of a cruel and greedy master. My belief is that I've been able, after twenty-five years, to help erase forever an evil influence from the lives of those living at Dunraven House and on its estate. May that legacy bring to them the love and the happiness they so deserve."

"Patrick all of us have our own destiny to find, and I'm glad that you were part of another family. You must have a multitude of stories to tell, and in the years ahead I hope to hear them all." Sally stood up. "I'm proud of you, Patrick. Now would you join me and the police officers for dinner?"

Patrick turned her to him and took both of her hands in his. She looked up at him with questions in her eyes.

"Sally it will be an honour to descend the stairway with you. Before we do, I have a question to ask. Do you remember when we were young and often on our walks home we stopped on O'Connell Bridge to look down at the Liffey's flowing waters? Remember on dark evenings it reflected light from the gas street lamps?

"We played at deciphering imaginary messages from the many reflections and pieces of flotsam. You always found our initials, but there was one dark night you saw the replica of the house we'd dreamed of buying some day in Kingstown. It was floating towards us and you cried out that you could see the lighted windows and the big double doors. Your dream Sally was to fill that house with happy children. Fate decided I was not to be part of that dream.

"For you it came to fruition in New York with a beautiful home and your children. Many decades have gone by since those precious O'Connell Bridge dreams. Sally we don't have decades to look forward to. Whatever time God grants us in our future I would like to spend with you. Will you marry me?"

Sally already had tears in her eyes at the mention of O'Connell Bridge. "Patrick McGuinness that was my intention if I ever found you. I will marry you because I love you and I hoped that I would not have to ask you. Now can I take your arm, my wonderful gentleman. We will go meet the officers who are patiently waiting."

The handsome man with the elegant lady on his arm descended the stairway. At the dining room entrance they hesitated for a moment. Two waitresses opened the double French doors to reveal an archway of spring flowers and a banner that read, "Happy Reunion, Sally & Patrick!"

Sally squeezed Patrick's arm as they walked under the archway and whispered, "For us." He was too emotional to answer but for a moment sought her hand returning an unspoken message of unbelievable happiness.

To a standing ovation from not only the two police officers but also the Dunraven House families and staff, they took their special place at the great table set for a very important dinner. Of course Father Cullen was there to share in this wonderful evening of celebration.

Still dazed by the transformation in his life Patrick whispered, "Sally you knew about all this and the police knew when they sent me to room number twelve."

"Yes dear Patrick. Remember I said that someday I'd tell you how I found you? What I didn't say was I met two people, Eileen O'Brien and Timothy O'Neill, who love and respect you very much."

"Where did you meet them?"

"I promised to tell you everything about my long trail to you and all the people I met on the way. That will take time, but you and I will have the rest of our lives to fill in and recapture the past fifty-seven years. Now let's enjoy these fabulous people and thank them for helping to launch us into our future of happy days."

The amazing celebration for Patrick and Sally's reunion continued into the late hours. This day was surely a golden milestone in their lives. Of course there were speakers, and Father Cullen was in great oratory form. After twenty minutes holding the guests at his mercy his final words were for Patrick and Sally:

"We have," he said, "celebrated here tonight a reunion of two people who were torn apart fifty-seven years ago by forces beyond their control. They were separated by thousands of miles by the mighty Atlantic Ocean and by so many decades of silence. This reunion was their destiny. Now the love they shared in youth will renew their lives and bring years of happiness." Father Cullen picked up his half full glass of rum. "Let's stand and drink a toast to Patrick and Sally's happy future." Father Cullen sat down.

Patrick slowly moved his chair and stood up. He was nervous. The sad look that often had showed in his eyes was gone, replaced by a new light.

There was silence, everyone waiting to hear what Patrick had to say.

"Friends when I walked into this room a few hours ago it was the second unexpected surprise this evening. You will excuse me if I say the first surprise was a more joyful one. Nothing can surpass that moment when the door of room number twelve was opened to my knock. I'm still in shock, and I keep asking myself how and why all these wonderful things are happening to Patrick McGuinness."

Looking down at the smiling Sally, he half turned, pushed his chair out of the way and held out his hand. She took it and stood beside him. Releasing Sally's hand, Patrick put his arm around her and continued:

"I lost my beautiful Sally on June 16th, 1890, when her family moved to New York. As yet I don't know how, but as everyone can see I'm not dreaming, I do have beside me on this 1947 spring evening my still beautiful Sally. I have asked her to marry me and she has accepted."

After the standing applause at Patrick's disclosure, he thanked Father Cullen for his words of wisdom. To the police officers he said, "I presume you just followed Sally's instructions."

"It was a great pleasure," replied Sergeant O'Hara.

Patrick drew Sally closer and surveyed the gathering of friends and guests.

"All of you wonderful people have helped to make this the happiest day for me in fifty-seven years. I know Sally must have played a part in organising this gathering, but it is our sincere thanks to all of you for just being here and giving us this everlasting memory."

It was getting late when Patrick and Sally sat down. A number of people presumed it was nearing the end of this memorable evening. Another guest decided she had something to add to the evening's oratory. It was Eileen O'Brien. Everyone was interested to hear what the late Kathleen O'Conor's younger sister had to say.

Eileen stood poised and beautiful, then with clear diction and her soft Irish accent she began:

"My good friend Sally gave me permission to divulge a chance meeting. It took place a few days ago in Letterkenny. Timothy had taken me across the border to Strabane to buy special material I needed for my wedding. I think everyone knows we will be getting married on the fourteenth of May.

"On the way home we stopped in Letterkenny at the hotel for dinner. I had a conversation with the lady sitting by herself at the next table. It was her third summer in Ireland. During the first summer this lady had spent most of the time in Dublin. From there she made numerous trips to many parts of south and midwest Ireland. I invited her to our table and she accepted. She explained that her journey was to experience the beauty of this land. She also hoped that it might be possible to locate an old friend who had once lived in Dublin. From the information she had gleaned, he'd been gone from there for many years.

"In her travels she decided to see the northwestern parts of Ireland and a few weeks ago had stayed overnight in the little town of Ballyshea, a long way south east of here. She had a meal at the village pub named The Iron Plough and had a conversation with a woman named Irene, who turned out to be the owner. When Irene discovered Sally was looking for a Patrick McGuinness, she immediately informed her that if it was the same Patrick McGuinness she knew, he had lived and worked on a farm close by, but he had left there after harvest time in 1915. The woman said she had heard from an old delivery man that this person was working on farms and always on the move. It seemed he was heading northwest. Last news of him was around 1920."

Hearing this, Patrick stood up and took Sally in his arms, then he kissed her and repeated several times, "You are a wonderful lady."

Taking her hand they crossed the floor to where Eileen stood smiling at this wonderful couple. Patrick and Sally hugged Eileen.

Then Eileen exclaimed, "I'm not finished yet. I have a very important question to ask Patrick and Sally. "Timothy and I have a wedding date with Father Cullen at the chapel, May 14th, at 11:00 a.m. Would you Patrick and Sally like to make it a double wedding?"

Sally looked at Patrick and 'yes' was the answer in her eyes.

Father Cullen downed the last of his rum, stood up, and above the noise of the hand-clapping and good wishes, was heard to say. "Sure and 'tis a happy day."

There had never been a more exciting time in the village than the event planned for the chapel on May fourteenth. The hotel was booked solid, and so were all the rented rooms in the village. Cassie McGreevy, Molly Todd and Maggie Black sent their men to the pub every night and gave them extra beer money to listen for rumours, ask questions and find out all they could about the rich American lady and Patrick McGuinness. The men were warned not to get drunk and forget what they'd heard.

There had never been a double wedding at the chapel and it caused a big commotion in the village. Cassie, Molly and Maggie were unable to sleep nights wondering why someone would come from America looking to marry Patrick McGuinness, especially when New York must be full of eligible men.

Each morning they met at Sadie's Tea Shop, swapping information their men had gleaned from the previous night's pub listening and questioning sessions. In her rush to hear the latest from Cassie and Maggie, Molly Todd even forgot to wear the shortened dress and it was the wee new bus driver's day on duty. Cassie wanted to know, did rich American men come on their own to Ireland looking for new wives and suggested, "If we pool our resources we could put an ad in New York newspapers."

"Now what in the name of the world put that in your head Cassie?" asked Molly. "Your man's alive. You're not thinking of sending your soul to purgatory forever by leaving old Harry?"

Cassie thought for a moment. "Well Molly, if the American was rich enough, think I'd chance it. Maybe he could give me a whole lot of heaven on earth before I die."

"Och, go on Cassie, why don't you go in to Willie McQuire's and buy that wee roast of beef you just talked about before he takes all the best stuff up to the American bride-to-be. There goes my wee bus driver. Talking to you I never had a chance to catch his eye. Now I've three more days to wait. Think I'll shorten my hem another couple of inches and remember to wear it next time he's on duty."

16

The Double Wedding, 1947

The spring morning of May fourteenth seemed to endorse the happiness of this day. It spread sunshine over sea, sand, hills, fields and glens. Two brides prepared themselves for new lives that a short time before had seemed to them an impossibility.

Eileen O'Brien was at her parents' small home, where in fearful days of the past she had endured such terrible times at the hands of the previous owner of Dunraven Estate. Now she would soon be the wife of the man she had loved for many years, Timothy O'Neill, the new owner and master.

Fate had turned over another card to make this impossible dream come true. To Eileen's mother, who was never told of those fearful times past, this was the happiest day of her life. Her youngest daughter wearing the dress she had worn on her own wedding day and marrying Timothy O'Neill, even if he had fought for England.

From the estate's staff Eileen had asked a good friend to be her bridesmaid. They were having a joyous time preparing for the big day.

When Sally had asked Patrick what friend was chosen to be his best man, he looked at her with questioning eyes. "Sally, I hadn't thought of that! Now that you've asked I guess my good friend Shawn O'Brien would be my choice. Of course the problem would be Shawn's obligation to walk his daughter down the aisle to the altar."

Sally's reply solved Patrick's problem. "I think it is quite good etiquette for him to accomplish those two things. After Shawn answers

Father Cullen's question 'Who gives this woman in marriage?' He can then move to your side as best man."

"I'm sure that will be all right with Father Cullen."

At the village hotel, Mary Jane Kernaghan and Sally O'Hagan McDermott had gone out on the balcony that extended from room number twelve. It was too warm to wait in a stuffy hot room. They had poured two crystal glasses full of red wine and moved to the balcony to enjoy the view. Sally turned to Mary Jane and raised her glass. "To my volunteer bridesmaid and now my friend."

"I'll drink to that," said Mary Jane as they clinked glasses.

For a few solemn moments Mary Jane looked down at the oak-stained deck. Then she said, "Sally, it's an honour for me to be bridesmaid to you and to know your story. Patrick was always a question mark in my mind. I'm so happy you found him. I raise my glass to toast you, a courageous wonderful and yes, still beautiful lady. I wish you and Patrick many years of happiness to catch up on the time you both have lost."

"Thank you Mary Jane. We will do just that." Sally spoke and as their glasses touched, Sean O'Hara, James O'Conor's lawyer friend stood in the open doorway. Mary Jane's thoughts raced back to the time exactly five years to that day when the same Sean O'Hara, distraught and mud-stained, had brought the news of James O'Conor's tragic death in the riding accident. Her hand shook and she spilled a little wine, but this time O'Hara was smiling.

"Ladies don't spill wine on your beautiful clothes. I wish that there was time and that I could join you, but people are waiting. It's going to be a very happy day."

Sally's light blue suit and shoes complemented her cream-coloured blouse and soft wide-brimmed hat. Mary Jane, thrilled at being Sally's bridesmaid, was the happy wearer of a crepe dress in pale cream that matched her shoes.

Patrick, of course, wanted to wear his old suit but Sally had persuaded him to go with her to Letterkenny where they had a tailor make him a new blue serge suit. Patrick had won when it came to boots. His own, as we know, had a shine better or equal to any palace guard. Sally and Patrick each wore a sprig of white heather.

Eileen looked breathtaking in the white wedding gown. It had emerged from the one her mother wore. The village seamstress who worked on it had accomplished a superb job.

Her bridesmaid wore a long dress of pastel pink. Sally and Eileen carried bouquets of fresh spring flowers.

For Kathleen's daughter Evelyn, now almost seven years old, the double wedding was an exciting experience, especially being flower girl for two brides.

The boys, Sean and Robert, ages six and five, were not thrilled. This was another big family occasion when they had to dress up and keep clean.

On this glorious Irish day Father Cullen's chapel overflowed with villagers and country folk of all denominations. The old priest was officiating at the happiest wedding service in his memory. He showed his great joy all through the service. One could almost feel that the marriages now taking place under his guidance were the culmination of his own plans.

The old priest's face was alight with pleasure when he pronounced Eileen and Timothy and then Sally and Patrick to be man and wife. The organist slipped into her seat, and to the strains of Mendelssohn's Wedding March the radiant couples walked together into the sunshine to start their new lives.

Immediately they were surrounded by a hand-clapping crowd showing their happiness and showering good wishes on the newlyweds. Molly and Cassie had planned to be in front of the crowd to have a good look at the two brides. With so many people, they were unable to find a position to see much.

Patrick felt sure he'd wake up and find it was only a wonderful dream. There was the squeeze of a soft small hand in his; he looked down at dancing mischievous hazel eyes, then listened to Sally's soft American Irish accent as she whispered, "I love you, Patrick McGuinness. If I let go of your hand, and run away along the bank of the little stream that's over there, and if I turn around with outstretched arms, would you run to me and pick me up? Give me a bear hug, and whisper, 'Sally O'Hagan McGuinness, I love you'?"

To the delight of everyone that's just what they did.

Patrick also added, "Sally O'Hagan McGuinness, I know I love you and now I'm married to you."

The great dining room at Dunraven House resounded with the sounds of laughter.

At the head table the two new brides and grooms were surrounded by happy people. It was a wonderful climax for those who had so often lost hope in finding happiness in this beautiful house.

Father Cullen covered all the bases in his best wedding reception speech. For him it was a great day. After a few drinks of his favourite rum, he hugged each of the newlyweds, and with tears in his eyes said, "I prayed for something like this."

Late in the evening, only a few guests were still partying when Mary Jane Kernaghan approached Patrick, Sally, Timothy, and Eileen. Very carefully she set her drink on a small table. Then putting her arms around Eileen, Mary Jane broke down. With tears streaming down her rosy cheeks, her words silenced everyone within hearing distance.

"She's here, Eileen. She's here. Your sister Kathleen was here all evening. I saw her, Eileen. She wore a white dress and her auburn hair was long and beautiful. She glided without a sound through the house. Always she was smiling. Eileen she is happy. It was so wonderful."

Father Cullen standing close by, overheard Mary Jane's words. It was his "Amen" that made the group turn and see him nod his head and repeat, "Amen."

"It happens, Mary Jane. It happens."

Then he hesitated for a moment and said to the newlyweds. "I'm so glad everything has turned out this way."

To Eileen he said, "Your sister Kathleen, came back to give you her blessing. She must be thrilled at how all the turmoil in your lives has this day turned into much happiness." Before speaking again he looked steadfastly at the two couples he had so recently joined in marriage.

"I will be leaving now, but before I do, I'd like to add my blessing. Patrick, you and Sally are in the autumn of your lives. Timothy and Eileen are in the springtime, but you have one wonderful thing in common. Love, and that is ageless. May the brightness from each of your own new marriages light up for you all the signposts that point to continued love understanding and happiness."

Then with a shy almost embarrassed look that was foreign to his character, he stood in silence. There was a feeling he was about to confide some personal secret of his own lonely private life. Instead he took a deep breath and made a request that included those guests who were standing close by: "It's been a wonderful day for me and I think for all of you. I will remember it for the rest of my life. Now I would ask you to repeat the Lord's Prayer with me." A very solemn group complied with his request. Father Cullen added his own "Amen."

The little man who knew so many confidential confessions and had been involved as the healer in so many Dunraven House tragedies said, "Good night."

As he walked away Eileen thought, He is getting old and tonight he looked very old. It will be one more tragedy to come when Father Cullen passes on. From her childhood memories to this very day he was always to some degree a part of everyone's life.

Next morning, Mary Jane and her staff served a scrumptious Irish breakfast to the newlyweds and to those guests who had stayed overnight.

Then it was time to say farewell. Eileen and Timothy were off to Dublin. From there they'd go across the Irish Sea to England, Wales and Scotland as he had promised. They said goodbyes to overnight guests, their parents, and the children, Evelyn, Sean and Robert. Mary Jane promised to take good care of the children with the help from many friends who had volunteered.

An emotional foursome stood beside Timothy and Eileen's limousine, which still displayed a few remaining decorations.

Starting out on new adventures were "Autumn" and "Spring" lovers. They stood for moments of silence holding hands to complete the circle. Within that circle, among these four people were so many flashbacks and memories. Now it was a new time, their time, and time to forget the tragedies of the past years. Each person knew their wonderful yesterday was the real beginning of the healing process. One could say that fate had taken them on a journey that had its ending and its wonderful new beginning right here. After Eileen and Timothy promised that next year they with the children would visit Patrick and Sally in New York, they hugged each other and said their tearful goodbyes.

Eileen was like a small child who had been presented with the most sought-after prize she had ever wished for: the same man her sister had loved and married. She was thinking how by the strange twist of fate her sister Kathleen had died after giving her blessing for Eileen to take her place as Timothy's wife.

The windshield wipers were working furiously to keep up with an Irish summer squall that had swept in from the sea. The heavy downpour sprayed the limousine and countryside. She looked at her new husband and smiled. Along the roadside were little groups of pedestrians huddled under raincoats and umbrellas. Others in ones and twos plodded along through the deluge and occasionally looked skywards trying to guess when the rain would cease.

Timothy looked very serious as he concentrated on driving the large limousine along the narrow winding roads. Eileen moved closer, then put her hand on his shoulder. He took his right hand from the steering wheel and placed it over hers.

Timothy spoke quietly, "Happy, Eileen?"

"Absolutely," was her response.

They had a wonderful time touring Ireland, then it was off to England as he had promised.

London was alive again and many people were still in uniform. Everyone seemed to have a definite purpose or plan and were accomplishing their tasks with happy and relieved expressions. The legacy of six years of war was still very evident, with gutted buildings and vast areas of rubble but no more V1s or V2s raining death from the skies.

After two more weeks of happy times their plans were to make the train journey to Edinburgh, Scotland, to visit Edinburgh Castle, walk slowly along Princes Street, investigate every interesting-looking shop and then all the wonders of the Scottish Highlands.

Their last night in London was at the Ritz Hotel. Expensive, but this was their honeymoon. Even so they never forgot their upbringing in their poor but happy little cottages in Ireland. For both of them being together and here was like a fairy tale, and they intended to make it be happy ever after.

At dinner in the hotel dining room on this, their last night in England's capital, Timothy felt so proud of this beautiful lady who was his wife. The dining room was crowded when they were ushered to their reserved table. Eileen looked elegant.

A number of military people were seated at dinner. Timothy conjectured that a big percentage were members of the occupation forces in Germany who were on leave before returning. Some were in deep and serious conversation while the laughter from other tables sent his thoughts in another direction. He surmised the happy laughter was outpouring from lucky men and women who had survived the onslaught of war, and now were on their way to demobilisation. This was their reward, being alive and returning to civilian life.

Timothy and Eileen enjoyed a scrumptious meal. They drank a toast to each other and talked a lot about their coming trip to Scotland. Eileen was excited. She had never been on a train and tomorrow they would take the express from Euston Station and first class to Bonnie Scotland. Timothy signed the dinner tab to be charged to their room. With envious glances from numerous males, he guided his lady towards the exit.

There were two tables, one to the right of the exit that was occupied by four Air Force officers. Sitting at the table to the left were three men. Two were high-ranking British Army officers, the other a civilian. As Timothy came close to the table he saw that almost hidden on the floor was a pair of crutches beside the civilian. Poor guy he thought, must be a wounded officer having some sort of reunion with two fellow comrades.

The two in uniform sat side by side. The civilian was opposite them.

Eileen held tight to Timothy's arm as she felt self-conscience among all the uniformed personnel. They were passing close to the last table. Timothy smiled at the officers sitting together and said, "Good evening," to which they returned the greeting. The civilian had his back to Timothy and Eileen so he half turned to see who spoke the greeting. Eileen felt a tremor of shock flow through Timothy and she was afraid.

He stopped and his face showed consternation. Eileen felt him tremble. She moved close against him and tightened the pressure on his arm. For Timothy it was a face from the past; he looked into steady blue eyes and saw the square-cut features and blond hair, the muscular body sitting upright in his chair. Timothy knew if this person stood up, he would be six feet tall.

Timothy knew Eileen was holding so very tightly to his arm that it hurt, but he was in another time zone; it was July, 1943. On enemy territory he waited in the shadows outside the city's main railroad station for his comrade Ken. Tim was praying that Ken would get through the checkpoint with his forged identity papers. As he waited, it was for the second time that a tall blond civilian appeared to be interested in him. On this second occasion he walked close to Tim and hesitated before entering the railroad station as Ken emerged.

It was in Germany's big city of Stettin on the Baltic Sea, that later Timothy and Ken, escaped prisoners of war, took refuge in a cemetery's small chapel. There they discovered a loose door-like panel that slid open with little effort to their fingers, and they were shocked to find themselves looking down the barrel of a Luger pistol held by the same tall blond civilian Timothy had seen at the railroad station.

The same blond civilian now sat at this hotel dining room table with two British Army Officers.

"Is there something wrong young man?" It was the officer with red hair who spoke.

Timothy was still frozen in silence, and like the rush of a mighty waterfall the memories flooded past. The little harbour with many boats and the one-legged sailor on crutches beside his craft. The beer parlour and the young man who was to guide them to the boat that would take them to Sweden, and the tragic ending to that contact.

He and Ken had disobeyed this blond civilian's request and warning to stay hidden until he returned to the room behind the panel. There was important business to attend to and part of it was the possibility of getting them on a boat bound for Sweden. On leaving they also stole some of their benefactor's food supplies. The consequences of departing from that secret shelter had been horrific.

Timothy stared at the blond civilian while these thoughts and pictures played in his mind. Eileen's voice broke through: "Timothy! Please! The officer is asking you if anything's wrong. Please Timothy answer him!"

It was Stefan who spoke and brought Timothy back to the present.

"You are, I believe Tim O'Neill, an ex-prisoner of war, and we have met before under circumstances that were extremely difficult. Now, are you going to introduce me to your beautiful lady?"

Stefan with both hands on the table pushed himself to a standing position.

Timothy apologised for his lapse and said. "Stefan Jonsson, it would have been impossible to have even the most insignificant thought that our paths would ever cross again. Especially in the circumstances I see here, and you remembered me! This is my wife, Eileen, and we are on our honeymoon. Tomorrow morning we are off to Edinburgh, Scotland."

Stefan steadied himself on his one leg, leaned forward and shook Eileen's hand. "I wish both of you many wonderful years together. It makes me happy to see Tim safely home." He then introduced Lieutenant John Forbes and the red-headed Lieutenant Robert Morris, ex-members of the Allied Underground Resistance Movement in Europe during the long hostilities. With a grim smile, he said, "We are lucky to be here enjoying freedom."

Instinctively Timothy's eyes travelled to other tables nearby. Somewhere close there must be another civilian, a good-looking younger man with dark curly hair and a slight scar under his left eye. When he smiled one would see fine white teeth except for a front one that had a dark spot.

Timothy and Eileen were invited to join the three men, and over a bottle of champagne they swapped their stories.

Hans Schmitt was turned in to the Gestapo by an informer and suffered through many days of torture. He died without divulging secrets. Stefan volunteered the information that he eventually found the informer. Timothy knew not to ask how the informer died.

Timothy then told Stefan of Ken's death and asked the unanswered question. "In Breslau Station when the SS Officer's mangled body was found on the rail tracks, Ken and I, plus our two Luftwaffe guards, were close enough to see. As we proceeded to another platform, you passed close by with your partner but made no sign of recognition. Did you recognise the two bearded and bedraggled prisoners who had ignored your order to stay safe in your secret room, and who also stole part of your food supply?"

Stefan's answer was clear. "Yes, I knew who you were. When possible we keep track of people we are interested in, and although difficult, it was gratifying to see both of you out of SS hands and on your way back to prison camp."

So without saying so openly, Stefan let Timothy know it had been Stefan and his contacts who had managed their release from certain death in the SS dungeon cells. Timothy wished Ken were alive to know this information. In some way Stefan was connected to those SS uniforms behind the torn curtain. Was it possible that Stefan had infiltrated the ranks of the SS?

Nothing was said about the young man wearing glasses who had accosted Tim and Ken in the pub, or the Swedish sailor with one leg, or the tragic end to their attempt at freedom. Timothy asked how Stefan lost his leg and the explanation was short.

"When Hans was taken by the Gestapo I tried to interfere and this is the result, but as you can see I escaped with my life. My thanks for that is to another brave comrade. I had received a serious leg wound and some months later my leg had to be amputated. Isn't it better Tim, to be alive with one leg than dead with two?"

Then John Forbes, Robert Morris, Stefan Jonsson, Timothy and Eileen O'Neill spent a couple of fascinating hours talking together about anything but the recent war.

John, Robert and Stefan drank champagne toasts to the new bride and groom and to each other. Apparently they had met for the very first time in person just two weeks previous. Before that, their connection was a multitude of secret contacts throughout the war years. Never did they know the real person, as contacts were by code only.

Timothy made a solemn toast to Stefan and departed friends that included Hans Schmitt and his own prison-camp comrade Ken Jones. When it came time to say goodbye to this amazing gathering, Eileen stood up with a glass of champagne in her hand.

"I do not wish to leave this memorable and exciting meeting of Stefan and Timothy without saying what's in my heart."

It wasn't just the beautiful young woman standing with a half glass of champagne in her hand. It was the sound of her soft Irish brogue and eloquence of speech that silenced people within hearing and caused some to rise from their tables and to move closer.

"I wish to thank a man who risked his life helping two prisoners of war escape from certain death. For me this happy day would have been only a sad dream if he had not taken those risks. It has been an honour and a great pleasure to meet you, Stefan Jonsson. I have certainly heard much about you from Timothy and learned so very much more this evening. I'm certain that fate, as an extra bonus in our lives, planned this almost impossible and unexpected meeting."

Eileen looked at those who had moved closer. It was a gathering of colourful uniforms. She was surprised to see almost everyone was ready to drink a toast. She raised her glass and in clear tones that echoed throughout the dining room Eileen continued, "My toast is to a brave and wonderful human being, Stefan Jonsson. May you find peace in your life and a happiness that will erase much of the pain and tragedy you have endured for such a long time. You will be remembered, Stefan, and forever there will be a place in our hearts for you and an invitation to our home in Ireland."

She gestured with her glass to John, Robert and Timothy sitting at the table across from their one-legged friend. They moved and stood on each side of the seated Stefan. By now there were many uniform-clad listeners.

Eileen raised her glass high. "To a wonderful man, Stefan Jonsson." This was echoed throughout the dining room by the many voices.

Stefan stood up on his one leg and asked for his crutches then he moved forward a few paces to Eileen. He held out his hand but instead of a handshake she looked up, saw a tear in his eye, and on impulse she kissed him.

When the applause subdued most returned to their tables and a few officers remained. Although Stefan's real story was unknown to them, they wanted to shake his hand.

Now it was time to be on their way and bid farewell to this unbelievable gathering and wonder. Would there be a day when Stefan Jonsson accepted their invitation, and knocked on the doors of Dunraven House in County Donegal, Ireland?

In the hotel bedroom that night Eileen snuggled close to Timothy who was almost asleep and whispered, "Timothy, it was fate and Kathleen's spirit together, that arranged tonight's impossible meeting. You must believe it because I do!" They went to sleep in each other's arms.

Patrick and Sally

When Timothy and Eileen's honeymoon limousine crossed over Rye Bridge and sped off to disappear on the winding ribbon of road that lead to the village, Patrick and Sally had the sad feeling that part of their own lives had gone with them. The wonderful yesterday may never have happened but for Sally's chance meeting with Timothy and Eileen at the hotel in Letterkenny. Would fate permit a future meeting in New York or at Dunraven House?

That question was overshadowed by an immediate and wonderful itinerary they wished to unfold and follow. They planned to leave most of Sally's luggage and Patrick's personal belongings at Dunraven House. Then travel light and make a circular tour of Ireland before returning to say their final farewells.

Driving to the west coast, they took the narrow road south. Sally was thrilled to see the little cottages scattered here and there beside the narrow and twisting road. In fascination she viewed the stark naked beauty of it all. They stopped and she stood in a field where stone replaced hedges. The stones and rocks that had been sweated out of non-arable land by poor farmers in an attempt to improve the soil after their own good crop-bearing land had been taken from them. Sally planned to tour old English mansions that had been built not far from those stone hedge fields with their tragic history.

When Sally and Patrick arrived in Dublin it was Patrick's first time since July 1904, when he had taken to the road after his release from jail. With Sally at his side he stood by the double entrance gates with a brass name plate that read 'Erindale'. Looking beyond to the still well-kept lawns and gardens of his old family home he said, "Sally, there's nothing here for me, that house is empty of all the good people and good times I knew. I have those good people and happy times with me in my memory and always I will carry them with me." He turned to Sally, "Would you like to see your father's old grocery store?"

She smiled, "Patrick, you've forgotten it took me three years to find you and many months of those years were spent in Dublin area. I have been to what is now McQuire's Grocery Store. Peter McQuire and his wife are both dead, and the grocery store is managed by one of the McQuire daughters and her husband. I visited there for a very short time, and have no desire to return."

Patrick and Sally spent a month exploring many parts of their Irish homeland; then it was time for their return journey. For Patrick a new discovery was before him. In his thoughts was a big question. How would he be received by Sally's family? She had assured him everyone was looking forward to meeting this Patrick McGuinness, the first love of Sally O'Hagan.

At Dunraven House they arrived to a happy reception. Mary Jane had been on the lookout and had recognised their car crossing Rye Bridge. She knew it would be a few minutes before it reached the big entrance gates. Those gates had previously been opened in welcome. When Patrick and Sally's car passed through, they were delighted to see the little group waiting for them. Like a mother hen, Mary Jane had gathered her three chicks, Evelyn, Sean and little Robert, who was jumping up and down with excitement. That evening, Eileen's mother and father were invited for dinner. It was a small farewell gathering and again so different from the large crowds and lavish spreads of food and wines that had been the rule under Cora O'Conor's jurisdiction.

Seated at the massive mahogany table were the only O'Conors alive: Kathleen's three children. The senior O'Briens, Shawn and Maureen, sat next to Sally and Patrick. Of course the owner of Dunraven House, Timothy O'Neill, with his bride were away on their honeymoon

Mary Jane had organised this farewell meal for Patrick and Sally. It was served by two volunteer kitchen staff and Mary Jane was coerced into sitting at what for many years had been Cora O'Conor's special place at the table. The ties that bound all of these people together in strong friendship, reached far into past years and although family names were different, they were a family that had emerged victorious from many tribulations.

Early morning on the second day of their return to Dunraven House; Sally and Patrick were to start on their long journey to New York. They had gone for a walk to capture again the beauty and tranquillity of getting to the beach by using a familiar river-bank path where they could listen to the music of clear crystal waters tumbling languidly over timeworn rocks. Rocks that had their very own history of being sought out by bare feet looking for a secure crossing of the little sea-bound river. At the beach, Sally could not resist walking barefoot on the golden sands.

They returned hand in hand to the grand entrance of Dunraven House where Patrick stopped. "Sally, I would like to take a few minutes just to walk around. I want to have a last look and say goodbye to the outdoors staff." Patrick's first stop was the milk house where twenty-seven years before James O'Conor had given him a corner to sleep in, plus a job. The Dunraven House open carriage, Cora O'Conor's pride and joy, stood rotting with decay in the shed next door. He made a stop at the stables where the son of James O'Conor's beautiful chestnut horse was standing peacefully munching from his manger that had been recently filled with oats.

Patrick stroked the horse's neck and said, "Your father carried a real gentleman on many fox hunts." From there he walked along the river bank to the saw mill and close to the big water wheel, where he stood for two minutes. After skirting the horse trough Patrick left the path and walked across the lower field where separated from others, the estate's Hereford cattle were grazing. On the way he picked some yellow primroses for Sally.

Sally looked out the bedroom window at the beautiful scene beneath her. The well-trimmed hedges, lawns and flower gardens, and beyond in the deep green pasture, sheep and cattle were grazing peacefully. Farther away she could see the little houses in the village and the spire of Father Cullen's chapel, the narrow twisting road to there was like a silver ribbon. Soon she and Patrick would take it on their journey, away from this beautiful part of Ireland.

Sally's daydreaming of the upcoming tour with Patrick was interrupted. Her expression changed and Sally's smile expressed her thoughts. Audibly the words came out. "What a wonderful man."

The big bronzed man in his seventies was crossing the lawn towards the house. He was holding in his hand a bunch of small yellow flowers. As Sally looked, he dropped a few. Quickly he stooped and picked them up, then made sure the bunch was again tidy and neat. The big shy man put the primroses to his lips and kissed them.

Her thoughts raced back to when they were very young. To one beautiful spring day in April when they had boarded the Lucan steam tram and alighted at Dublin city limits. Hand in hand they had walked into the Irish countryside with its lush green grasslands.

There to greet them were multitudes of yellow primroses that fought for space on each side, making the country road appear as a lighted pathway.

Sally busied herself on the pretence of packing a few last-minute necessities until Patrick opened the door.

"Sally," he said, "there's thousands of these primroses out there and I picked you the best ones." They laughed together. She thanked and then kissed him.

"Now my dear Patrick, are we ready to start this wonderful journey together?"

"I've been ready Sally ever since you opened the door of room number twelve at the hotel."

"Come on then. Let's go," was her happy reply.

They bid farewell to Mary Jane and to Eileen's and Timothy's parents.

The chauffeur stood by the limousine with the door open as Patrick and Sally approached. All their luggage had now been stowed away. Sally looked astounding in a plain grey suit and white silk blouse with matching white gloves and shoes. Wisps of sleek black hair with just a few streaks of grey peeped out from under the wide brim of her white rattan bonnet. The burgundy ribbon that trimmed it drew attention to her soft hazel eyes alight with new life. Sally made herself comfortable in the limousine and waited for Patrick who stood outside taking a last look at what had been his very existence for the best part of twenty-seven years. He quickly moved in beside Sally and taking her hand in his, quietly said, "I love you."

They left six people waving a sad farewell.

Sally spoke quietly, "I have asked the chauffeur to stop at the hotel. I would like to say goodbye to the staff. They were so kind to me and showed great co-operation when we planned your surprise dinner. We are also stopping at the post office. I have all these letters I wrote to my family in New York. Patrick, I must air mail them before we go."

Cassie McGreevy and Molly Todd were sitting in Sadie's Tea Shop waiting for the bus to arrive. It was Molly's wee bus driver's day on shift.

Willie McQuire, the butcher, came in for a cup of tea. He sat at the table with Cassie and Molly. After pouring a spoonful of sugar into his cup, he stirred it slowly and said quietly, "Molly, I know you're in here waiting for Wee Sammy O'Donal. Do you two know Patrick McGuinness and his American bride are back from their honeymoon and have been in the post office for the past ten or fifteen minutes? When I came in here, they were leaving."

It was like being in an earthquake; big Cassie and Molly were in such a rush to get out they spilled Willie's cup of tea and upset the sugar bowl. They ran to the post office and Molly had her skirt so tight that even with inches off it, she had to take small steps. When they reached the post office, the limousine had gone.

"It's Willie McQuire's fault," complained Molly. "He purposely didn't tell us until too late to see them."

Old Todd Bailey came to the door of his post office.

"If you two want to stand there and cry, it's okay with me. On the other hand if you want to see Patrick McGuinness and his American bride, I can tell you where. The limousine has stopped at the hotel and both the bride and groom have gone inside."

The news that Patrick McGuinness and his bride were in the hotel spread like a fire out of control. The pubs emptied, stores closed, and in a short time it looked as if the whole village population had surrounded the limousine. When Patrick and Sally emerged from the hotel Sally quipped, "Patrick, what a wonderful send off."

The village folk made way for them. Many called out compliments to Sally. Now they were able to have a close look at the unbelievable person who had come from America to marry the old handyman who worked at Dunraven House.

Molly Todd and Cassie McGreevy were front row spectators and parked themselves at the limousine's door. In silence they gawked at Patrick's bride.

"Wish I'd married an American!"

Cassie was startled at Molly's loud remark.

As she nudged her friend Cassie said, "Ssh! Molly. Ssh! I'm sure she heard you."

Ignoring Cassie, Molly continued, "'Tis grand film star clothes she's wearing and look at her face. She looks too young to be in her seventies. Bet I was right Cassie. She must have got her face lifted up."

Sally about to enter the limousine overheard the remark. She hesitated, and with a smile turned to Molly.

"Thank you my dear for the compliment. It is the only face I've got. It never was as you say, 'lifted up.' I wash every day with ordinary soap and water. Like your own wonderful face and skin, I too was blessed with an Irish complexion. I was born and spent my youth in this wonderful green land. I wish you much happiness and a long life."

Molly was left speechless. As the limousine started to move, she timidly raised her hand when Sally waved goodbye.

Epilogue

Sally and Patrick arrived in New York on the liner *Queen Mary*. They disembarked to a wonderful welcome from all of Sally's family, her sons, daughters, their wives and husbands, plus nine grandchildren. A large green, white and gold banner, Ireland's colours, was unfurled. The edges were trimmed with painted shamrocks and in large bold letters it said WELCOME HOME, SALLY AND PATRICK!

For Patrick it was an emotional moment. Here in this welcome were the missing pieces of his life. Sally had produced these sons and daughters much like the ones he had dreamed they would have had together if her father had not destroyed those dreams. Now Sally's wonderful families were ready and willing to fill those very empty spaces in his life.

Patrick was received with joy and gladness. They already knew from their mother's correspondence that she had found her first love and would be bringing him home as her husband.

In the summer of 1948, Timothy and Eileen with Kathleen's three children made the journey to New York. They had a wonderful time.

Patrick and Sally promised that very soon a return visit to Dunraven House would be in their plans. They were an inseparable senior couple with so much energy and good health that each day they continued to enjoy their very own happy togetherness.

Dunraven House, Ireland, Spring, 1949

A year after Timothy and Eileen's New York visit, Patrick and Sally made good their promise and returned to Dunraven House for a late spring three-week vacation. They were delighted to find cook Mary Jane helping Eileen with her new baby girl soon to be christened Kathleen Eileen O'Neill.

This was another happy reunion but with one dark cloud of sadness. Father Cullen had died two weeks prior to their arrival.

It was unknown until after the good Father's death that his burial plot was next to Kathleen's. Was it by choice or by fate? Had her old friend the priest reserved his burial plot before or after Kathleen's death?

Once more their time dissipated and was lost in the wonderment of this beautiful part of Ireland. For Patrick it was another whirlwind of mental pictures, a rewind of such a large part of his life with its tragedies, its love, and also the accomplishments he had participated in as a senior staff member of Dunraven House.

The morning prior to their departure for New York, Sally and Patrick placed two identical wreaths of spring flowers, one on Kathleen's grave and the other on the newly turned soil of Father Cullen's. For a few moments they stood in silent remembrance.

When they closed the graveyard's white gate behind them, Sally stopped to look back at the polished granite headstones reflecting the rays of mid-morning sunshine.

The O'Conor graves of James, Cora and George were close to the white gate. Kathleen O'Neill's and now Father Cullen's were much farther away.

It was right there beside the white gate that Sally made a big decision.

Their happy three weeks ended with hugs, tears and sad faces as Patrick and Sally bade farewell to the new Dunraven House generation of O'Conors, where now reigned so much love and understanding.

New York, February, 1952

Patrick and Sally had almost five years together. Into those years they had infused so much happiness that it made up for a big percentage of the years they had lost. It was on the twenty-third of February in the winter of fifty-two that Patrick McGuinness died, three weeks after celebrating his eighty-first birthday.

He had had a bad cold that developed into pneumonia and his very unexpected death. When Patrick passed to the other side of life, Sally was at his bedside holding in both of hers one of Patrick's work-worn hands. She stayed only a short time then leaned over, kissed his forehead and said, "Patrick, it's been a wonderful five years. Somewhere out there in the great beyond wait for me. I don't want to lose you again."

Dunraven House, Ireland, May, 1952

In the late spring of the same year Patrick died, Sally decided to make what in all probability would be her last visit to Ireland.

So it was that a family group stood quietly in the small graveyard near Dunraven House. They stood close together at the foot of Kathleen O'Conor's grave. Holding hands, they waited in silence, each with their own thoughts on the tangled web of tragedies and love that fate had played out in this small part of the world.

Sally's arrival the previous day at Dunraven House brought much joy to everyone. They had been wrong when with news of Patrick's death they assumed she would never visit Dunraven House again.

Embracing a silver urn, Sally, now eighty years of age and still an attractive lady, stood a little distance from the group. When she moved to the side of Kathleen's grave and opened the urn, a soft Irish wind rustled the leaves of three nearby oak trees; then there followed an eerie silence. It felt as if unseen spirits not earthly had come to join this group so they could listen. Sally spoke quietly, her words clear and her diction perfect.

"My dear Kathleen: Springtime three years ago, Patrick stood right here with me beside your grave and we visited with you for awhile. When leaving this quiet and beautiful resting place, we closed the white gate and there I turned to have a farewell look. From that morning's sunshine the polished headstones reflected a myriad of coloured rays and we were certain that from yours, Kathleen, the beautiful reflections were much stronger. To Patrick and myself we felt it was a message

314

telling us of your love and appreciation that we had made the journey from New York.

"It was there, Kathleen, at the white gate, I made the decision that if my Patrick were to leave this world before me I would bring his ashes home to Ireland and this peaceful graveyard."

There followed a minute or two of silent meditation before Sally continued, her voice trembling with emotion. "Now, Kathleen, I sprinkle these ashes to circle your earthly remains. They are a symbol of Patrick's love for you and your children. As he did in life, may this circle of Patrick's ashes represent the protective wall he tried to maintain around you and yours during his years of service at Dunraven House.

"All who know its history and will visit this hallowed place, will always feel the presence of Patrick McGuinness, James O'Conor, Father Cullen and you my dear Kathleen." Sally hesitated before she emptied the urn's remaining ashes and a tear found its way to soft Irish soil. Then, clasping the empty urn close to her bosom, she continued, "Now my dear Patrick, in this beautiful corner of Ireland is where you belong, so I am leaving you here to rest in peace with those you love until our souls unite in the great beyond."

The little group of mourners stood heads bowed for a few moments then in silence walked to the white gate. Leading the way were Timothy and Eileen with Kathleen's three children, then Eileen's mother and father.

For a short time cook Mary Jane stayed with Sally at Kathleen's grave, then slowly they walked to the white gate. Sally was last to walk through. She turned, closed the gate very quietly, then raised her hand in a farewell gesture.

With an emotion-filled voice she cried out, "Oh! What a wonderful man! What wonderful memories I once thought could never be mine." Then like a little child she took cook Mary Jane's hand and held it tightly all the way as they walked in silence to the great entrance hall of Dunraven House.

In that beautiful northwest part of Ireland, in the county of Donegal at a place called Dunraven House, close to Rathmullan on the banks of Lough Swilly, a family will always remember with great respect and love the man called Patrick McGuinness. The man who seemed to come from nowhere but behind the scenes of their everyday life became in shadow a solid corner of strength and good. Unknown but to only one of those involved, Patrick McGuinness had erased from their lives a great burden of fear and so had opened a door to love, freedom and happiness. Was he wrong?

If you wish to have John McMahon's best seller
Almost a Lifetime
a true story now in its fourth printing

request it from your favorite book store
(Published by Shamrock Publications
ISBN 96844-540-3)

or contact the author at
PO Box 615
Saltspring Island B.C. Canada V8K 2W2
shamrock@saltspring.com